## ABOUT THE AUTHOR

Martin Baker is a novelist, scriptwriter and editor. He has worked as a broadcaster at LBC, a city reporter for *The Times*, money correspondent for the *Independent*, investment editor at the *International Herald Tribune*, associate editor of *Sunday Business* and been a columnist for *The Sunday Telegraph*, among other newspapers. Now a fellow of the Royal Society of Arts, he read law at Oxford and qualified as a lawyer before pursuing his career as a writer. As well as the planned series of Samuel Spendlove books, he is also the author of a bitingly satirical critique of the market capitalism, *A Fool and His Money*.

**VERSION THIRTEEN**

*London 2016*

# VERSION THIRTEEN

**MARTIN BAKER**

*Tim —*

*Best wishes,*

*Martin*

unbound

This edition first published in 2013

Unbound
4–7 Manchester Street, Marylebone, London, W1U 2AE
www.unbound.co.uk

Typeset by Palindrome
Art direction by Mecob
Cover design by Dan Mogford

A CIP record for this book is available from the British Library

ISBN 978-1-78352-002-2 (special)
ISBN 978-1-78352-001-5 (trade)
ISBN 978-1-78352-000-8 (ebook)

Printed in England by Clays Ltd, Bungay, Suffolk

For Nicola

# PART ONE

*THERE HE WAS, a young man, yet already a creature of habit. Let him flirt with the girls by the side door of the nightclub. What a pretty boy – lithe-limbed, curly black hair, dark, lustrous eyes. How cute and youthful he was. And how infinitely, timelessly old – because soon he was going to die.*

*He was heading down the street, arms swinging – a relaxed, confident fellow in a black leather blouson and Versace jeans, all perfectly complemented by a swagger and a smile designed for the female eye. He was just yards away from the next hotel lobby bar and another set of admiring glances. But then he fell, tripped by some drunk's discarded bottle. There were plenty of drunks in that part of town, plenty of empty bottles. Syringes, too.*

*The young man cursed in a strange language – definitely not Russian. He began to pick himself up, slowly. Maybe he was a little drunk.*

*The perfect opportunity.*

*'Here. Let me help you.'*

*A gun handle cracked down on the back of his head. An acute observer might have noticed an older man in a suit dragging the young man down one of the many pitch-black little side alleys off the Kultura Prospekt. Most people would have seen nothing, just another drunk being helped by a business colleague. It happened all the time in clubland.*

*The older man dragged the youth into a tiny yard. Now he had time and space.*

*'Wake up. Wake up.'*

*He should have brought water with him. Maybe he'd cracked the bastard's head too hard. He slapped him in the face. Once, twice.*

*'Wake up, you shit,' he breathed heavily.*

*Eventually the young man opened bleary eyes.*

*'Who are you? What happened?' he slurred.*

*'What's your name?'*

*'Um . . . um . . . Shamil.'*

*'Look at me, Shamil. Do you remember a girl, blonde, pretty, young, Shamil?'*

*'Uh . . .'*

*A hard slap across the side of the face brought a trickle of blood from Shamil's mouth.*

*'Sure about that? Don't remember the nice Western girl? The secret parties? The illegal whisky? The drugs?'*

*'Oh, mister . . .'*

*'Cute girl, snub-nosed.'*

*A light of recognition in Shamil's eyes, then the darkness of fear, pure fear.*

*'Oh mister, oh mister. Sorry, sorry, sorry. Please, mister . . .'*

*'She's dead. And you're not as sorry as I am. Not as sorry as you're going to be.'*

*The release of the safety catch made enough of a click to be audible over the din of the night traffic.*

*They were some twenty metres from the street. Three giant wheelie bins containing foul-smelling detritus screened them from the dingy back doors of the nearby clubs and cafes. They were alone, apart from the occasional scuffle of rats and feral, urban wildlife in the furthest shadowy recesses.*

*Shamil was trying to create distance between himself and the gun. The path to the bins had been frequently trudged; the snow was a churned brown mess of dirt, grease, offal and the nameless excrescences that the paying customers never saw. Shamil was slithering backwards through this filth.*

*'Listen, don't hurt me.' He'd gathered himself a little. Enough to speak English. Shamil held up a hand, palm out. 'My father is very rich, very powerful. He's a warlord. He can help you in ways you cannot imagine . . .'*

*The gun's aim did not waiver. Shamil groaned, trembled. A dark flowering at the groin, the sharp odour of his piss.*

*Then he threw back his head and began to scream. That was a mistake.*

*The first shot went straight through the sternum. The dull, plosive sound of the silenced bullet followed by the surprisingly sharp crack of metal on bone. The second shot went into the stomach with a short, violent squelch.*

*But that wasn't enough for the man with the gun. The boy would die now, certainly. In a sense, the job was done. But it wasn't a dum-dum bullet. He hadn't had the time to procure anything fancy that would flatten on impact and pulverise the internal organs.*

*He marched up to the sprawled figure and lifted the head back. There was still a tiny scrap of light in the eyes, a vestige of life. He pushed the gun up into the young man's mouth, making sure the barrel of the weapon was tilted upwards. Then he pulled the trigger.*

*Damn. There was something on his jacket. He took out his handkerchief and began to wipe away at it. It was a splat of greasy yellow brain tissue, a heart-shaped stain an inch or so in length, right there, on his lapel. Small, but noticeable.*

*A dab of the finger, and his mobile offered an orb of milky-grey light.*

*'Buy order – executed.'*

*He snapped the phone off and looked back towards the street.*

5

*All was as it should be – the surging flotsam and jetsam of Moscow life cruised by in an unstoppable tidal wave of trivial appetites and desires. That was all other people's lives amounted to. And his own? Maybe not even that. He walked back down the alley and merged back into the endless, teeming flow.*

# CHAPTER ONE

SAMUEL PULLED BACK the curtains and whistled softly. Moscow – there was no place like it.

From his eyrie at the top of the Hotel Ukraina, he felt as though he could almost reach out and touch the grey city laced with softly drifting snow. Below him was the fat arc of the Moscow River. The water moved slowly and persistently, transformed, on the surface at least, into huge immobile slabs of ice. It was not so much a waterway; more a traffic jam of frozen rhomboids, the discards of Arctic geometry. On the far bank, some three hundred metres away, stood the shiny white wedding cake of the White House, executive seat of the Russian government.

He closed his eyes for a half-second, and summoned up the city map he'd studied in the back of last night's taxi. A spidery configuration of concentric circles flicked up into his inner vision – the little icon by Platforma Savelovskaya didn't do justice to the architectural solidity of the White House. Nor, it seemed, the political reality. Samuel smiled at the thought of the journey in from Domodedovo airport, the taxi driver and his tobacco-stained teeth. *White House? Home to a bunch of criminals!* The driver had wound down the window and spat messily into the darkness.

Now morning had come with a watery, funeral-parlour light. A couple of giant factory chimneys belched out pale smoke that turned solid in the freezing air. It looked good enough to eat –

carcinogenic candyfloss. To his right, he could see a vast, squat shape with huge, inverted ice cream cones stuck on it. The foreign ministry was the perfect counterpoint to the Ukraina. Another neo-Gothic Stalinist monument, it was one of the Seven Sisters, part of the same architectural bloodline as Samuel's hotel. All seven had been built in a style designed to demonstrate the power, permanence and immensity of the state, and the insignificance of the individual. Now the Seven Sisters were just monuments to past paranoia, but, like all paranoiacs, they lacked true consistency and confidence. The feathery detail in the mini-turrets and spires, elaborate finishing touches, were garish make-up hastily applied to the features of a brute.

Samuel stood in the large drawing room of his suite. It was typical of Kingston P. Blandford to book him into one of the best rooms in the hotel. Blandford was very generous with money, especially when it was someone else's. Samuel wasn't quite sure who'd be paying the bill, but Blandford might just solve that problem with a flourish of his gravity-defying corporate credit card and a stroke of the Mont Blanc.

The piano centrally positioned at the foot of the high-ceilinged salon wall was beautiful, but elderly – and slightly out of tune. A perfect fit for its surroundings. The dark, thickly varnished oak slats on the floor of the drawing room were warped by decades of excessive artificial heat in Moscow's winter and the oppressive humidity of the summers. Samuel could easily imagine an era when the room had been filled with people. A 1930s regional Party boss would have come to town and stayed in regal splendour for a Communist Party Congress. Drawing-room soirées – fuelled by vodka, embellished by Chopin, some fearful girl from the Moscow Conservatory at the keyboard, the evening ending with a short trip across the exquisitely laid parquet floor and the boss's bedroom romp with that year's research student.

Samuel went back into the bedroom and hunted for his ear-warmers and the essential black leather gloves. Earlier, the snow had been falling like icy arrows fired at an acute angle. Milder but persistent huge flakes now drifted down in slow spirals through the thickening white kaleidoscope of the sky. The tumult of billions of snowflakes, each individual, unique, presented itself as a solid, comforting, wall of white. He could use some of that solidity – or even the appearance of it – himself.

Samuel glided over to the large, uneven bed and pulled on a pair of thermal socks. The mattress was lumpy in the manner of a school dorm, or maybe one of those chilly, damp rooms he used to have back in Oxford. That was a while ago, yes, several years. It seemed like decades.

Samuel pulled a hand through a lock of rough blond hair and pondered. The Ukraina's vast Stalinist exterior was daunting. It was supposed to be. But the interior made him feel almost comfortable. It was somehow familiar, offering an indefinable but palpable sense of ease. Something appealed to the ascetic, the part within him that had cherished the long, solitary days in his Radcliffe Camera carrel. He'd actively sought a state of mild discomfort. It helped him escape from the physical world. Only with his metaphysical hair shirt could he think his 'best' thoughts, make the connections that produced advances in knowledge, good insights. But that was back in the day – when the only problems he'd had to solve were academic.

Samuel reached into his pocket. The scrap of paper was velvet-soft from frequent perusal; an obituary from *The Times*. Peter Kempis, his mentor and tutor at Oxford, pictured in the prime of life, stared cheerfully up at him – thick, dark, carefully parted quiff; heavy, bottle-end spectacles, oatmeal tweeds – a sherry glass in hand. The deceased always seemed to be shown at their best in obituary photographs – a courtesy the press did not always extend to the living.

But praise from the press was irrelevant. Samuel had now come to bury Kempis – in Moscow, of all places. Was it the country he'd been working for? Mother Russia? Surely not. Whatever Kempis had been – thinker, drinker, a louche intellectual – he was a citizen of the life of the mind. He wouldn't have been working for something as vulgar as national glory – Britain's or Russia's – and certainly not money. No, Kempis, servant of two spy networks, would have had just the one true mistress – the grand, romantic notion that all men were equal in opportunity, rights and dignity, more recognisable to others as international socialism.

What would he have made of the Ukraina's aircraft hangar of a lobby, throbbing with the citizens of the not-so-new, and not-at-all socialist Russia? Earnest young women and men in uncomfortable hotel tunics strove to offer service levels that could only be audited – and they could be audited at any time – as first class. The young men were happy to be tiny cogs in this new capitalist economy. Their fathers and grandfathers had faced conscription into the Red Army. Being patronised by Western tourists was a big improvement. The women seemed happy enough, too. These Western men were rich. Many were even available.

Ill-assorted leather chesterfields and dainty velvet-covered chairs dodged each other behind marbled columns. Some of the seats were occupied by locals, whose origins, if not betrayed by fine Slavic cheekbones or dark Tartar eyes, were conclusively revealed by a sustained enthusiasm for indoor smoking – a national sport, set for abolition.

Whatever the language, the locals and the visiting businessmen all offered the same thing: mobile phone, low-grade, shouty business-speak, a humourless avidity for money.

Fewer in number, but still a discernible group, were the fat men with gimlet eyes and shiny suits. They spoke little, if at all – just watched his progress through the crowded, smoky atrium with neutral gazes. Samuel detected no real curiosity, merely the habit of surveillance. He supposed they were gangsters of some sort. The bulges in their jackets would be rolls of cash, maybe even guns. How else could these walruses command the attentions of their pretty, skimpily dressed female companions with their cigarettes shaped like white needles?

Samuel smiled once more and shook his head. Being inconspicuous was as outdated and incongruous in modern Russia as a fat girl at a fashion show. Russia was a land of ostentation and instant gratification. In the short trip from the airport last night, he'd seen well-stocked shops full of expensive, imported goods. Some Russians even preferred foreign vodka, the French-distilled Grey Goose being the tipple of the moment. The city was covered with bright advertising hoardings and neon signs. Materialist displays of wealth had engulfed the city.

This was business. This was good, according to the mercurial Kingston P. Blandford. Samuel had got to know Blandford – or rather, Blandford had got to know him, it was difficult to say – at one of Kempis's drinks parties. The Canadian was pleasant enough, but as enigmatic as he was persistent. He seemed to be some sort of professional networker, a man who'd lived on the borderline of the military and industrial worlds. Now a freelance facilitator, a cocktail-hour attaché, Blandford's life appeared to be a permanent business meeting. But the one thing he could be certain of was that appearances, first impressions, especially in Kempis's circle, were inevitably a deception, a trick of the light.

Nothing in Blandford's world was to be taken quite seriously. That included Blandford himself. He'd once hinted at some sort of connection to the aristocratic Blandford family, with its huge estates in the south of England. He fought shy of claiming acquaintance with his Lordship himself. But the possibility of a being a distant relative was just the kind of ambiguity Blandford liked to have about him, something he would smilingly neither confirm nor deny.

When Samuel had said he was coming to Moscow, Blandford

had pounced. How would he like 'an interview with a billion dollars'? There were huge opportunities out there for a man with Samuel's connections and skills. There would be any number of useful introductions he could make. And – a half-smile from the older man – there were the sybaritic pleasures of the New Russia.

Samuel was intrigued by Russia for his own reasons, though.

The outer door of the hotel was solid oak and fully eighteen feet tall, built for the giants and heroes of the Soviet Union. Three security guards watched his efforts to get out with tight-lipped disdain. Tourists and Western businessmen were of no interest, unless they checked in with a suitcase full of cash.

Samuel's appearance did not speak of money. The dark suit hung well enough on his tall frame, but it wasn't a Valentino. The white shirt was well laundered, but there were no Gucci collars, no ostentatious diamond cuff-links. With his slightly overlong blond hair, broad forehead and wide-set blue eyes, Samuel looked like a dressed-down rock star, or an extra from a Tarantino movie.

A small grunt, beery even though it was only just past breakfast time, issued from one of the beefy men. They shifted slightly to let Samuel pass.

Before the door swung shut behind him, the cold gripped Samuel like an iron clamp. The traffic thundered by on Kutuzovsky Prospekt. The road was impossibly wide, designed to prevent human beings from crossing it. The cars and lorries that hurtled back and forth across the river had turned the virgin snow into thick brown slush. The White House and the Novy Arbat waited for him on the far bank. The Arbat district used to house intellectuals and artists, and had consequently suffered terribly after the 1917 Revolution. Nowadays it was a brilliantly lit strip of consumer excess, complete with sushi bars, Uzbek restaurants and an ever-growing community of casinos.

Samuel looked at his watch. 'Be outside the hotel at 10.30 sharp,' Blandford had commanded. But he was already five minutes late.

Samuel uttered a quiet oath. The hotel was about as big as St James's Palace in London, and had several entrances. Blandford, the Svengali of the international rendezvous, had probably gone to the wrong one.

Samuel began to walk up and down in the little quadrant of space enclosed within the Taras Schevchenko embankment and the huge avenue before the bridge. Grizzled Russians in fur hats and huge overcoats called out to him from their cars, more in hope than expectation. Their only English was 'Taxi?' They could tell even from Samuel's '*Niet*' – not badly accented, merely too polite – that he was not a Russian.

Samuel had already seen a couple of private vehicles pull to the kerb for pedestrians holding out their hands to stop them. Even in oil-rich Russia, car-sharing in the form of roadside bargaining for taxi fares was encouraged. Not, Samuel suspected, because it was a hangover from Communist rule, nor a last vestige of the collective spirit, and certainly not because it was ecologically sound. This was a cheap form of travel, and the Russians were an intensely practical people.

Samuel stamped his feet. Lack of punctuality was no joke at minus seven degrees centigrade. He looked at his mobile. An unfamiliar network name, MTS, blinked up from the centre of the screen. 10.43. Perhaps Samuel should go in and call.

He heard it before he saw it: a thick, heavy, wet churning. Samuel turned expecting to see a vast sled, a snow plough the size of a double-decker bus. He was not entirely disappointed. A stretch Hummer limousine stopped in the snow with a wet sigh. These things were, he reflected, still basically the armoured cars they had evolved from, even if this one did have chrome plating, bull bars, mirror windows, and enough in the way of aerials and strange-looking electronic gadgetry to make it a passable imitation of a mobile military command-and-control centre.

It had five passenger windows down its side. The middle panel opened silently to reveal an interior of impenetrable darkness.

'Get in,' commanded a voice in heavily Russian-accented English.

Samuel hesitated. Where was Blandford?

'Samuel Spendlove? Get in.' The Russian voice did not like to be disobeyed.

Samuel did not move.

'Aw, come on, Samuel. Get in, for Chrissakes, before we all freeze!'

Blandford's cheeky grin, floppy hair and faintly ruddy complexion appeared from the rearmost window. He had to be close to sixty, yet somehow retained the air of an errant schoolboy – slightly naughty, but eager to please. The wind whipped up another thick flurry of snow.

'Since you put it like that . . .'

Samuel shook the snow from his coat and climbed in.

JUST ANOTHER HOTEL, just another committee room, just another meeting. Or maybe not.

William Barton sat quietly at the far end of the compact conference space, away from the raised dais and its cluster of illustrious speakers, one of whom was currently being questioned from the floor.

Barton used his vantage point and the temporary hiatus in proceedings to do a quick survey and a little basic maths. He counted sixty-nine people in the room, including the stenographer. The man at the keyboard was one of a few who wasn't worth several hundred million dollars. He wasn't the chief executive of a major corporation, a prominent politician, a senior banker or a media mogul. The others were – and they were members or invited guests of the Bilderberg Group.

Barton shifted his slim, besuited frame in his padded chair, and played with the soft folds of his jowls and chin. The hangdog look sat uncomfortably with a body his doctors told him was that of a man twenty years younger.

He looked at the pale, bespectacled stenographer sitting just outside the soft orb of electric light that bathed the speakers. His hands glided deftly over the small computer on his lap – the only person in the room permitted to take notes. All mobile phones and electronic equipment had been checked in before the delegates had entered the auditorium. There would only be one record of the proceedings, but there would be no note of the names of the speakers, supposedly to promote ease of expression, freedom of speech. When it was all over, the electronic material would be deleted and a paper copy archived. That way, the proceedings of the semi-secret annual gathering of the Bilderberg Group would be distilled down to a few flimsy, old-fashioned sheets of paper. It could all be destroyed at the flare of a match.

The flare of a match. Barton craved a cigarette – that clean, hot, delicious procession of smoke down the back of his throat. At least here in Bergen, in the middle of nowhere, he could smoke as much as he wanted. Reiko, his fourth and definitely his last wife, hated cigarettes. She was probably the only person in the world who could tell Barton what to do – and she did, often. But she could be safely disobeyed while she remained in their New York apartment. He would be in the open air and inhaling mightily in less than half an hour. Barton chewed his bitter orange-flavour nicotine gum and grimaced quietly.

A journalist was coming to the end of a long, unnecessarily complicated question. The Bilderberg Group invited journalists to attend on the same terms as everyone else – no discussion of what was said, no word of the location of the meetings (unusually, given the mediocrity of its restaurants, Bergen had been chosen this year). And no details of who had attended. This last was the most closely guarded secret of them all. Inviting a couple of senior journalists

15

was a gesture towards openness, and it flattered their egos.

Above all, it was an opportunity for some of the most successful people on the planet to engage in intelligent discussion about key issues. The message was clear: despite the secrecy, there really wasn't anything sinister about it. Somebody in the Group definitely understood PR.

Barton reckoned that the total wealth of the people in the room exceeded $600 billion dollars. If you calculated power in terms of military might, there were seven representatives from nuclear sovereign states. The Bilderberg Group had first met in 1954, with the original purpose of cementing relations between Western Europe and America. Now politics was a global game, and the idea was simply to keep everyone onside with the US, the world's policeman. At the far side of the room Barton recognised Remco Kuqi, a dark, thickset billionaire businessman from an Iranian Jewish family that had fled to Baghdad after the fall of the Shah in 1979. Now based in the West, he still had close contact with his home country. By brokering the subtlest of contact between Iran and the West, Kuqi had built an impregnable business empire.

One of the journalists, a sleek, self-important type who wrote lengthy love notes to the establishment in the *Financial Times*, was batting a conversational ball back and forth with a former president of the World Bank. The notional topic was something arcane, to do with settlements in the international credit system. But all that really mattered was that the room saw them talking to each other.

'I'll be watching, Mr President. We'll all be watching,' said the journalist as he sat down, a sycophantic grin painted on his face. Barton winced inwardly at the mock-oppositional nature of the exchange. The journalist's agenda, like that of the overrated rag he wrote for, was utterly supine. All he wanted to do was keep his place at table with the good and the great. He'd never break a story or tell a truth – that might upset someone in a position of power.

*He'd be watching?* Well, maybe. But he wouldn't write or do anything meaningful, Barton would bet his own hairy arse on that.

Bob Zeffman was up next. The US Senator shuffled the papers for his presentation and hummed and hawed into the microphone. Zeffman was worth about $2 billion. Probably much more, come to think of it. He was a frequent visitor to Bermuda, the Cayman Islands and Liechtenstein, a trait common among offshore hoarders. Barton suspected that part of Zeffman's wealth had been accumulated illicitly. He might even be hiding income from the US tax authorities.

Zeffman was a stupid bastard in that case. If Barton used his media machine to expose him, Zeffman's political career would be over and he would probably end up in jail. What use would all that money be then? Knowledge wasn't just power in a case like this. It was control, pure and simple. And Barton, like quite a few others in the room, loved control. Zeffman had allowed greed to get the better of him. True, Barton was addicted to tobacco, but he had his cravings contained. You couldn't say the same of Zeffman's power-tic. So he might be one of the richest men in the world, but he was weak.

Barton expected that Zeffman had got one of his bag-carriers to write the speech. He was waiting for the break, the quick nicotine hit, and proper conversation – the realpolitik of the corridor. But Zeffman surprised him. Barton found himself engaged, interested: the senator had some smart ideas, themes he articulated well. Zeffman said he'd made plenty of money from high oil prices, but he conceded that this was nothing to be proud of. Inflation, worldwide price increases fuelled by high commodity and fuel costs, was creating anxiety. Western Europe, which had had it so good for so long, was being de-stabilised. The unions, which Zeffman referred to as 'the dark forces of organised labour', were demanding high wage increases and were whipping up unrest. There was popular support for their wage demands. People were

17

taking to the streets in the big, important European countries: France, Britain, even Germany had all witnessed mass protest. Government was being systematically weakened by worker power, and the higher wage awards were themselves an extra inflationary pressure that further strengthened the unions' political position. Inflation had to be controlled, said Zeffman, and commodity prices needed to come down.

Barton scanned the room. A well-known executive from a US defence company, which had done extremely well from successive US wars, was nodding in agreement. The 'dark forces' reference would once have been seen as a challenge to states such as Russia, which was bound to have its informants in the room. But fewer governments were keener on controlling the masses than modern Russia's. Barton couldn't detect any reaction, positive or negative. The early morning session was drawing to a close.

He examined the programme. The speaker after the coffee break was not to be missed. Wendy Collins was the wife of the legendary Hugh Collins, and co-trustee of the $200 billion charitable trust the couple had established with some of the money they had made from the technology industry. Barton would be back promptly, listen carefully, and then talk to Wendy Collins. Charming the spouse was the best way to get to the husband. He loved all this access. Access, as George W. Bush had said (and proved, because he had so little else to recommend him to the world), was power.

Barton stepped out into a Bergen wind that whipped into the alcove by the hotel side-entrance. He drew hungrily on a cigarette. Just the three minutes, and then back to the thrill of the contact machine.

'There you are, William. I was kind of wondering where you'd disappeared to.'

'Bob! Fascinating presentation. Profound.'

Barton's pale eyes narrowed very slightly. He hardly knew Bob Zeffman – he knew all about him, of course. Knowledge was

Barton's business. But they'd only actually met a couple times in the past five years.

'Thanks, yeah, thanks,' said Zeffman. He looked out at the passing traffic on the road.

'Cigarette?' asked Barton.

'No. No, I'm not a smoker. I came to find you.'

Barton nodded and said nothing.

'William, we have a problem. It's one that may need your active help, maybe even your direct intervention.'

An inhalation, a raised eyebrow.

'We, um, my friends, would be very grateful. Let me explain.'

Barton threw the cigarette to the floor and crushed it firmly beneath his shoe.

'Please do, Bob. Please do.'

THE HUMMER SMELLED of chemical air freshener. Samuel couldn't quite place the scent in the natural world, but he recognised something favoured by minicab drivers from Khartoum to Kansas. Underlying the sharp chemical smell was the dull odour of cigarette smoke.

As Samuel's eyes became accustomed to the gloom, he was able to make out the figure next to the diminutive Canadian. The two of them were sitting opposite Samuel on a leather bench seat. For all the outward appearance of girth and enormity, the interior of the Hummer was surprisingly cramped. Samuel's knees were almost touching those of his companions. The other man was smartly dressed and had a full head of dark hair. Mozart's Clarinet Concerto in A was playing on the surround-sound speakers, competing with the thrum of the tyres over the cobbled streets. The modern suspension of the vehicle couldn't quite smooth away the vibrations. They were travelling at considerable speed, probably twice the legal limit. Samuel guessed they must be just about the biggest, heaviest and deadliest thing on the streets of Moscow.

They were hurtling up the Arbat, a brilliantly lit sports cafe on their right, an Irish bar on their left, next to the latest set of luxury flats under construction. The shops were packed with people, all decked out in fur coats and hats. The clothes store Abercrombie & Fitch made its usual marketing statement: a large, mildly pornographic poster of a male model hung over the awning of a soon-to-be opened outlet. No one had spoken for some moments. This was unusual for Blandford, who made a living out of inane prattle.

'Drink, Mr Spendlove?'

A well-modulated, thickish Russian accent. The 'r' in drink was melting into a 'v'.

'Yes, please.'

Almost before he had spoken, Samuel heard the fizz of a bottle opening. To his relief it wasn't the bouncers' breakfast of beer. A tumbler of ice and sparkling water was set on a tiny serving table next to him.

'Do you mind if I smoke?'

The most perfunctory of courtesies. His host produced a cigarette and a lighter before he could answer. The process of lighting and inhaling allowed Samuel a first proper look at him. Mr Billion Dollars was dark-skinned, perhaps from one of the 'stans'? Maybe the oil capital of Baku? The hair was luxuriant and glossy, flecked with grey at the temples. The eyebrows were strong and thick, almost meeting in the middle, and there was a hint of sullenness to the mouth, but maybe that was just the pucker as he drew on his cigarette.

He shot his cuffs. A fleck of blue winked at Samuel – a tattoo, the hammer and sickle of the military, crossed carbines and the number 40. *40th Division? 40th Army?*

Samuel looked away, but the large brown eyes had registered his interest. The man smoked on for a while in watchful silence.

'You notice the tattoo,' he said at length. 'Done years ago, in a

20

far-away land. I was young, and foolish.'

Samuel nodded, and let another silence settle.

'Medulev. Marat Medulev.' He leaned forward and held out his hand. A cool, firm grip. Samuel shook, feeling as though he'd passed some sort of test.

'How do you do? Samuel Spendlove – as you know.'

'Indeed. Kingston here talks favourably of you.'

'Ah, he speaks highly of everyone.'

'That's not the case, Samuel. I'm ... picky,' interjected Blandford, smiling. Blandford had been away from home for years, and spoke in a strange mid-Atlantic patois, half-Toronto, half-Henley Regatta. Beneath this, Samuel detected a slight release of tension.

'You're a fellow with exceptional qualities, Samuel, not least of which is modesty.' Blandford was pleased with himself. He had brokered the introduction. It was unclear to Samuel exactly what Blandford would get out of all this, but there would a hidden agenda of some sort, no doubt.

'Kingston here is not the only one with a high estimation of you, Mr Spendlove.' Medulev drew on his cigarette, wound down the window, and tossed the glowing butt onto the pavement, paying no regard to the passers-by. The Hummer had slowed to a crawl now on the busy Gogolevsky Boulevard.

'What's that?'

A constellation of blue and red lights was flashing crazily at the top of the street. A restaurant and bar had been cordoned off with red-and-white tape, keeping passers-by clear. The traffic was oozing through the bottleneck at an excruciatingly slow pace. Ahead of them a posse of bike-mounted policemen blew whistles and gesticulated aggressively, to no discernible effect.

Medulev glanced out of the window.

'They are – how to say this best? – cleaning the streets.'

'A fire, perhaps?' said Blandford. Several ambulances formed part of the flashing throng. They were edging closer and closer.

'I doubt it,' said Medulev. 'Look. The windows of the restaurant are all destroyed. Someone has been playing with dangerous toys.'

'So what is it, do you think?' asked Samuel.

They were almost level with the centre of the action now. A body, covered head-to-toe by a blanket, was hastily pushed into the back of one of the ambulances. Crowds of pedestrians looked on fearfully from the far side of the tape. Sand had been scattered over several large pools of blood. Medical teams were removing two other bodies; screens were being drawn round two more.

'A shoot-out, most likely,' said Medulev. 'A gangster incident, judging from the number of bodies. They are almost a thing of the past now that we have strong government. But events like this still sometimes occur. Single killings are more common these days. Journalists and researchers are often the victims.'

Samuel knew that local journalists were regular prey for hit men in the bad old days of gangster-capitalist Russia in the 1990s. Russia's 'business interests', or whoever paid the muscle men, had even wiped out Paul Klebnikov, an American who edited Forbes Russia and published books on post-Communist society. But the political fall-out from even that assassination had been minimal. So journalists and researchers – Samuel's business card described him as a researcher – were fair game if they inconvenienced the wrong interests.

Medulev closed the window. He shook his head with slow, theatrical sadness.

'Messy, so very messy. Such a waste.'

The deep brown eyes turned towards Samuel.

'But in here, all is order. All is well.' Medulev waved his hand as expansively as the interior permitted. 'I thank you for coming. May I call you Samuel?'

Samuel looked Medulev steadily in the eye: 'I'm not sure what the protocol is for conversation in bomb-proof limousines. Would calling me Samuel stop you killing me if you felt you had to?'

Blandford spilled fizzy water over himself and almost fell off his seat.

A moment's silence. Then Medulev burst into laughter, loud and long.

'You, Samuel, you would make a good Russian. Very direct. No bullshit.'

'I don't do bullshit, Marat. I know that business is done differently here.'

'We are new to the game, Samuel. A new country at the capitalist Monopoly board. The rules, the laws, are random sometimes. They have rough edges. As a former lawyer, you will understand this.'

'I was told the only lawyer in Russia was the Kalashnikov. I don't know what you want of me, but if it brings us anywhere near that kind of thing, I don't want to be involved. Excuse my plainness.'

'It's a great virtue, tovarish,' said Medulev. He was smiling broadly now. 'We will drink vodka together later. Make toasts. Will you forgive me? Excuse my country's business methods? We can be crude.'

'Forgiveness? I'm not a priest, Marat.'

'Good, good. You live a life uncontaminated by religion.'

'And unpolluted by God.'

'An agnostic with a sense of humour. That can only help.' Medulev monitored Samuel for a reaction. 'OK. Now, we have people to meet.'

THE CAR GLIDED to a halt with surprising smoothness. Medulev opened the door, and stepped out. Samuel and Blandford followed.

'See what has been designed for your amusement?'

A helicopter emblazoned with the insignia of corporate empire was landing in a roadside park.

23

'Isn't that illegal?' asked Blandford.

Medulev began to walk. 'We have already discussed what is legal. Come. It will be quicker this way. And you will be able to see Ostankino.'

Medulev patted Samuel on the arm, a signal to follow. There was something strained in his manner; the casual attitude felt forced. It seemed odd, but not dangerous. Not yet, anyway.

Samuel glanced up at a huge advertising hoarding. Kalashnikov. Not the rifle, but a new brand of vodka, fronted by Marshal Kalashnikov himself. The doddery, rubicund old man was pointing at a bottle and smiling down at them from the poster.

The pilot of the helicopter, a dark, curly-haired youth, waved them in impatiently. Blandford stopped. He stood beneath the chopper blades, staring at the craft and its pilot as if he was searching for something. Or had just found it. Medulev clapped his hands and beckoned impatiently.

Blandford woke from his reverie, and scrambled up into the craft – suddenly all business and bonhomie again. He pointed at the hoarding. 'That's the markets in action for you, Samuel. The warrior and inventor of global terrorism's favourite weapon, the AK47, is leveraging the brand value of his own name to hawk booze to the masses. You gotta love it.'

'I suppose you do,' said Samuel. 'And when we go for drinks later, who'll be hosting the cocktail party? Comrade Molotov?'

Blandford laughed uproariously. Medulev didn't.

# CHAPTER TWO

THE HELICOPTER LANDED in a snow-covered field. Its blades whipped up their own miniature, flake-flecked vortex. Samuel stared down into it, momentarily mesmerised – in Moscow, but lost. Medulev jumped out of the craft, turned and extended a hand. They jumped down, and within seconds the helicopter was gone. Blandford stared after it.

The snowfall was less urgent now. The flakes were softer and larger than before, covering the oaks, limes and birches of the cemetery. They formed a thick white coverlet that baffled all sound. Samuel watched his breath thicken into cold clouds, then slowly disappear.

Medulev led the way through the gates of the cemetery towards a small church topped by a trio of golden onion domes. Blandford was quiet now, almost sombre. Samuel followed, the last of the three. The quiet was punctuated only by the measured tread of their feet on the fresh snow.

An oak door opened, and a Russian wearing a heavy coat and a fur hat waved them in. The church was cold, and empty save for the coffin. It sat on a metal stand, surrounded by wreaths of white and yellow flowers and scores of candles.

There he was – Kempis – Samuel's mentor, a man who played God. Now just a collection of matter, a husk who resembled the kind, solicitous – and quietly dangerous – man who'd been a friend to him and his father. Kempis hadn't been religious, so far as Samuel knew. But then, what *did* he know? He'd sort of suspected that Kempis might have been a spook. But was he really a double agent, a Russian spy, now being buried with the state baubles for services rendered? This wasn't the affable Kempis he'd discussed legal philosophy and played chess with. Whatever he'd been, the man in the box had been the closest thing he'd had to a father for the previous decade.

And whatever he'd been, he was gone.

'How did you know him, Marat?' enquired Samuel, his voice low.

'He worked with my organisation,' said Medulev. 'I hardly knew him myself.'

'What organisation would that be? The KGB? Or is it called the FSB nowadays?'

Medulev glanced away, then back. Eventually he smiled.

'Cheka, NKVD, KGB, FSB. It's all intelligence-gathering. It was and remains a vast business in this country. Our role is to keep people informed. The people who really matter. You will see when you come to Ostankino.'

'It's a commercial complex,' said Blandford. 'The operation is a kind of media village. And it incorporates a dealing floor. Everyone seems to have some involvement in the financial markets these days.'

Samuel looked through the open door of the church. Dark-coated figures were beginning to gather outside. 'Not everyone in business is a spook in the New Russia, Samuel,' said Blandford with authority. 'Making money is at the top of the agenda now.'

'Maybe so. But just about everyone at this funeral is a spook. Talking of which, who do you work for, Kingston?' asked Samuel.

'Who'd want to employ a cocktail-bar warrior like me, Samuel?'

He had a point.

They sat on the wooden benches, waiting for the other mourners to settle themselves.

'Kempis was a friend of your family?' asked Medulev.

'To three generations of us,' said Samuel. 'As much as he could be.'

Mourners were shuffling into place now, shaking snow from their coats, snuffling wetly.

'To us, Dr Kempis was a hero of Russian citizenry, one who helped in the battles that pitted us against Western Europe.' Medulev's voice had dropped to a whisper. 'But to you, he was a dear friend. So perhaps the loss is greater. As Stalin said, "A single death is a tragedy, a million deaths is a statistic."'

The church was soon almost full. Samuel looked around him. He could only see one woman. The rest were grey, dark, anonymous men. A Russian Orthodox priest appeared and stood behind the coffin, facing the congregation. The service was conducted entirely in Russian, except for one reading in English. The elderly Brit at the lectern looked like another Oxford academic attracted by the excitement of a double life, but Samuel did not recognise him.

Now they were walking through the cemetery, past grave-stones of ancient Communist Party stalwarts, broad-featured, lightly idealised faces emerged with dark determination from monumental slabs of marble and granite. The great and the good of a long-defunct Soviet society were gathered there: scientists, composers, heroes of the Revolution, writers – Samuel assumed only those who produced politically acceptable tracts of Socialist Realism were allocated a place in the heroes' burial ground. If this were the city of the dead, they'd ended up in one of the better-heeled parts of town. Many of the graves were surrounded by low wire fencing; cages for captives who had no capacity to escape. The fast-settling snow was swiftly converting the tombstones with no tree cover into monumental lollipops.

Medulev walked on for a while and then halted. He nodded into the middle distance, and turned to his companions.

'Samuel, I leave you now.'

Medulev gave a short formal bow. His overcoat was open, and Samuel caught a glimpse of metal beneath his jacket. Gangster capitalism might be yesterday's news, but guns were still a popular accessory in Russia.

Medulev waved, turned his back and joined three others – the woman Samuel had noticed in the church, and two men. Both men wore shapkas of mink on their heads – traditional in the Arctic, increasingly fashionable in Moscow.

'Interesting,' murmured Samuel.

'Medulev? He's a piece of work. What do you think he's got in mind for you?' asked Blandford.

'He had a weapon, Kingston. Did you notice, or don't you care?'

'People wear guns here. It's the gun-crime capital of the world. These are business tools.'

'Doubtless. But seriously, how many billionaires carry guns?'

'Medulev isn't a billionaire!'

'But I thought he was Mr Billion Dollars?'

'Not at all.'

'If not Medulev, then who?'

'You'll find out later,' said Blandford. His smile widened.

They were almost at the graveside now. Some things changed, but death and its rituals varied little. Samuel thought of his father's early death, and the obsequies. The priest – hatless, bald, all glistening scalp and sweat beneath black vestments on a hot summer day. Today everything was veiled in snow, but it somehow felt the same.

He looked about him. There were forty or so of them, gathered around in clusters of four or five.

Samuel looked at the dark wooden coffin with its top-half open. The old man's face was sunken, the mouth drawn in by the escape of the soul. Samuel remembered the endless glasses of pale luncheon sherry he'd sipped with Kempis back in All Souls, back in Oxford. He remembered how the don had harboured him, fed him, hidden him when he was a desperate fugitive, accepted that he wasn't the man the world believed him to be. Kempis had hidden him from the French and British police, from half the world, it seemed at the time. Samuel hadn't known back then just how good Kempis was at hiding things. He looked again at the stretched, cold features – was Kempis hiding something even now?

The priest was well into the burial ritual, and the mourners were murmuring responses. Kempis's posthumous decoration, his Order of Supreme Citizenship which acknowledged him as a Hero of the Russian Federation, hung by a silk ribbon from the lapel of his dead man's suit. The moment had come to close the coffin.

'*Podozhdite!*' cried Samuel. His accent was not good, but the pallbearers understood. They stopped. Samuel stepped forward and kissed Kempis on the forehead. The skin was icy cold. Snow had gathered on the face. He allowed his lips to linger in a last gesture of farewell, then withdrew to stand beside Blandford once more. The other mourners watched impassively. The snowflakes from Kempis's brow began to melt on Samuel's lips. He let them be. The taste was strangely sweet.

Kempis's coffin was closed and lowered into the ground.

The service was soon over and the mourners began to shuffle towards the cemetery gates. A few metres away blue-jeaned punks and Goths with black eye make-up and dark-purple hair were standing by a grave. Many of them held bottles of vodka or beer. A party seemed to be in full swing.

'Vladimir Vysotsky,' murmured Blandford in response to Samuel's look of enquiry. 'Poet, singer, drunk. Died in the Brezhnev era. Kind of a Russian Jim Morrison.'

Samuel nodded. A girl punk with spiky black dreadlocks and a Pussy Riot T-shirt drank from a bottle, cigarette in hand. The dark hair, the rebellious demeanour summoned up Lauren and their time together in his Paris. She'd taken him to visit Morrison's grave in the huge Père Lachaise cemetery. They had consumed the best part of a bottle of bourbon. Then, escaping the joss-stick wavers and hippies, they'd made love near the grave. He closed his eyes. Thinking of that moment intensified his feelings of loss now. He would never see her again.

'Mr Spendlove?'

He felt a touch on his shoulder and wheeled round.

'I'm sorry if I startled you. I wanted to meet you. This occasion, while of course a moment of loss and grief for us all, presented too good an opportunity.'

A dainty, leather-gloved hand: 'Anna Barinova.'

The woman was petite and dressed in black from head to toe, with the exception of a small white ruffle of lace at the throat. She wore a pillbox hat with a veil. The partly concealed face was heart-shaped, the eyes a startling cornflower blue. If Samuel hadn't known better he would have taken her for an Irish colleen – but no. This woman was another of the exotic mixtures that Russia offered. Tartar and Cossack? Slavic and Uzbek? She was nearer forty than thirty, but had a trim, almost bird-like figure and a nimbleness of movement. Though her hands were small, the grip of the leather glove was firm and businesslike.

'I was going to reiterate the offer to visit our organisation in Ostankino.'

'You're a colleague of Medulev?'

'In a manner of speaking, yes,' she replied. 'But I can see you're in no mood to discuss business now. You were obviously close to Dr Kempis. Perhaps, if you are feeling better later, we could have dinner – in his honour?'

Blandford bowed and smiled.

She pressed a business card into Samuel's hand. 'I would like to entertain you at the Pushkin Café. I'll send a car to your hotel at 7.30. We'll see if we can bring Dr Kempis back, at least in spirit?'

'Why not, Madame Barinova? Why not?' said Samuel.

Blandford beamed at his side.

'Very good,' she said. 'Marat will join us.'

Medulev was approaching, his hat covered in snow.

'Would you care for a ride home?' She gestured towards a fleet of Hummers.

'No, thank you. Maybe I'll look around the cemetery for a while.'

'Very well, Mr Spendlove. Till tonight.'

Barinova motioned to Medulev, who glanced at Samuel and Blandford, and hurried after her, towards the cemetery gate. She wore black fishnet stockings and black, patent leather shoes with extremely high heels. Yet when she walked she seemed to glide across the snow.

Just before she passed through the gate, Anna Barinova turned back to Samuel, as though she knew he was watching her. She paused, raised her right hand, smiled.

'Well, well, well,' said Blandford.

'Well what?'

'You seem to be very popular. That's a dinner date to die for.'

'How so?'

'Anna Barinova's how so! She's Russia's first and only self-made female oligarch. *Mrs* Billion Dollars. I've been pestering Medulev to get me in front of her for months. If she wants to talk to you, it'll be something worth hearing.'

'Anna Barinova . . . ? So she's married to some guy called Barinov?'

'Was. Her husband's dead. He was a promising student, a university sports star who took to drink once the support system fell away. A classic case. A winner in the old order, a loser in the new. The fall of Communism swept away the good, the bad, but above all, the weak. She's had a succession of boyfriends since – or should I say married men in positions of industrial or political power? Sleeping with the right people has helped her build a business empire which spans banking, the media and retail.'

'Sounds impressive. Also sounds like the kind of thing men say about successful women.'

'Maybe, Samuel. But the funny thing is that all of her lovers came to messy ends – a senior politician, a government intelligence operative of very high rank, a security services entrepreneur . . . all dead.'

'Were they all ex-KGB?'

'Nearly all the most powerful people in the post-Communist regime are ex-KGB. Anyway, the boyfriends all died – the ones we know of, at least.'

'But I'm not a Russian politician. Nor a secret-service operative.'

'But Kempis was.'

'What's the connection, Blandford? Not sex – Peter wasn't interested in women. Nor money.'

'Who knows? Let's find out tonight.'

Samuel took one last look in the direction of Kempis's grave, turned up the collar of his coat, and began to walk in what he hoped was the right direction.

SAMUEL AND BLANDFORD were out on the street again. They had taken a long, not particularly alcoholic, lunch at a wittily named little cafe, The Discreet Charm of the Bourgeoisie, on Lubyanka Prospekt. Darkness was already drawing in, and the snow, which had seemed so benign in the steely-grey light of day, had turned into a hostile night-blue sleet.

'Citizen cab time?' suggested Blandford. He liked what he called his creature comforts, and had argued long and hard – and unsuccessfully – that they should call a car. But Samuel wanted to try holding out his thumb, confident that their Russian was sufficient to get them back to the hotel.

After a few minutes a young man in a clapped-out rust bucket stopped. They told him the address and got in. The driver looked at them, opened his mouth to say something, thought better of it, and shot off in the direction Red Square. They skirted round the Kremlin and Alexander Gardens and then headed westwards, back towards the Ukraina. There would be plenty of time for them both to bathe and shave ahead of their dinner date.

They were stuck in a traffic jam now. Their driver had tried to take a short cut down a side street and uttered his first words of the journey – a string of violent expletives – when he found a car abandoned in the middle of the road. Vehicles were backing up behind them. The noise of drivers leaning on their horns was painful. Gone were the days when Muscovites simply put up with things. Samuel and Blandford paid the driver and jumped out.

Blandford was staying at the Kempinski, just over the river from Red Square, with superb views of the candy-striped and golden onion domes of St Basil's Cathedral.

'Can you find your way back to the Ukraina from here, Samuel?'

'Sure. There's time for a rest before dinner.'

'Don't nod off. Remember, the car's coming for you at 7.30.'

'Kingston, you're so eager. I'll be ready and waiting.'

It was quite dark now. Within a few minutes Samuel was walking on the north side of the embankment beneath the Alexander Gardens. Cars swept by, their headlights yellow and cold in the looming indigo of the early evening. Mercedes, Volvos, Bentleys – Blandford said that the Moscow Bentley concession sold more cars than any other city in the world. Samuel could believe it. He must have seen two dozen or more already that day.

The Ukraina was in sight at last. He was walking along a narrow street, which looked as though it would take him to the front door of the hotel. Behind him a vehicle was approaching at speed. There was something about the revving of the engine, the coarse, fierce sound it was giving out, that made Samuel turn. He saw the dark, boxy shape of an ancient Russian Zhiguli mounting the pavement. Sparks were showering down from its undercarriage. The car was intent on something, hunting something – him.

The pavement was narrow. He began to run, desperately looking for an escape route. The Zhiguli was gaining on him. He put his head down and ran hard, his lungs now screaming for oxygen. A shot of pain from his right shin – badly barked by the handle of a casually abandoned trash can. But adrenalin, the urge to flight, pushed him on. The car was closer now, the sparks from its groaning undercarriage plainly visible. At last, a narrow alleyway – a way out. He turned sharply away from the road and kept running.

But his black shoes were made for funerals, not running on ice. He fell hard, sprawling on the snow. His trousers were ripped at the knee. He could feel the warmth of his own blood turn instantly cold as it mingled with the snow and ice.

He was back on his feet now, legs pumping hard. Someone was running after him – a snatched look back. His pursuer was a fat bear of a man with a white beard. Why this? What had he done? He had attended the funeral of a family friend who he had never realised was a Russian spy, talked to a rich woman and her sidekick. Or had he? Was anyone who they seemed to be?

He was coming to the end of the alleyway. There was an even narrower ginnel leading to the main street. He vaulted a couple of overturned trash cans, attempted a third, and fell. His hands broke his fall, but the skin was grazed badly. He was soaked in sweat, covered in snow and street ordure. But he picked himself up and ran on. In a few seconds he would be safe.

Just as he stepped out into the broader street, he banged hard into an old woman with tightly coiffed white hair – and bounced right off her. She looked as though she should have been selling jam at a country fair, but she'd braced perfectly for the impact, sending Samuel sprawling with the skill of a martial artist.

'Stop, Mr Spendlove.' She seemed completely calm. 'I have something for you.'

Samuel panted hard, exhausted. His male pursuer now caught up. The man wasn't in good shape. He was gasping big lungfuls of freezing air.

'Who are you?' asked Samuel, looking from one to the other. The old woman was wearing a Lenin lapel badge. She could have been some sort of ex-Spetsnaz trooper. She was, literally, old guard.

'We were friends of Dr Kempis.'

'I . . .' Samuel tried hard to regain composure. The pain of the knocks and bruises of the chase was beginning to make itself felt. He focused and thought back to the funeral, panning across the mourners in his mind's eye. 'If you were his friends, why weren't you at the funeral? I didn't see you.'

'We honour his memory in different ways. He asked us to give this to you.'

The woman handed him a plain white envelope. 'Samuel Spendlove – by hand' was written on it in purple ink. It was Kempis's unmistakable, spidery script – the same fragile lettering he'd found hundreds of times in his pigeonhole at Oxford. But something told him this wasn't an invitation to drinks and dinner. The man and woman began to walk away.

'Stop! Who sent you?' called out Samuel.

'Ha! And we were told you were clever,' said the woman, not breaking stride. 'Kempis – he said you would come.'

'Wait!'

'Our job is done. Goodbye,' called the man.

Samuel followed them back down the alley and watched them get into their car. A speeding Saab estate careered round the corner, its horn blaring. A collision seemed certain, but the Zhiguli suddenly jumped forward, engine protesting furiously, and disappeared into the Moscow night.

Samuel looked again at the envelope and stuffed it into the inside pocket of his coat. He was soaking wet, freezing cold – and angry. It was just typical of Kempis to do this. His method of delivering a message, and a posthumous one at that, was to put Samuel in fear of his life.

Samuel fumed quietly as he marched the final few hundred metres to his hotel. Kempis's obsession with the flamboyant lived on, at everyone else's expense. From the grave, the old man was producing rabbits from hats, pulling strings, manipulating. He'd come to the funeral to say a final goodbye, and lay his demons to rest. Now this. The fact that he couldn't confront him with all this games-playing sharpened his anger and his sense of loss. But perhaps that was the intention.

It was absolutely infuriating – and yet . . . By the time Samuel strode into the lobby of the Ukraina, tugging at his gloves and un-buttoning his coat, he was smiling. Kempis. Would he ever give up?

Samuel's sodden, bedraggled appearance attracted a couple of looks, nothing more. The indoor heat burned his ears and nose quite painfully. He stabbed at the lift button for his suite, and came to a conclusion. He was done devilling for Kempis. He would throw the envelope in the bin, have a bath, and then go to dinner. Tomorrow, he would return to London and put all of this behind him.

He did indeed throw the letter in the bin as soon as he got back to his room. Let them take Kempis and his silly games out with the garbage. The bath was run, and Samuel was steeping in scented water when he heard the chambermaid enter. The bin would be emptied and the letter gone.

Goodbye, Peter Kempis, goodbye.

*The pale, waxy skin – that cold kiss, the snow melting on his lips – the tiny protest from the frozen hinge of the closing coffin lid.*

'Hold on! Hold on!' He sprang out of the bath and wrapped a towel about him.

The young chambermaid was a pallid blonde girl, maybe a country maid. She started at Samuel's appearance in the doorway.

'You've got something I want,' he said in faltering Russian.

The girl looked at Samuel's dripping torso and blushed.

'No, no, not that.'

He made his way to her and delicately picked Kempis's envelope out of the refuse sack on her trolley.

After the maid skipped out, Samuel set the envelope on his desk, and climbed back into the bath. Kempis had won that little game of cat and mouse. He couldn't throw the letter away, damn it. But he'd have his bath before opening it. If Kempis was watching from beyond the grave, he would have to drum his fingers.

# CHAPTER THREE

SAMUEL FOUND BLANDFORD strangely silent in the Barinova car. After a few minutes of watching the streets of Moscow slide by through tinted windows, they emerged from the pale-cream leather interior of the chauffeur-driven Bentley and stepped out onto the Tverskoi Boulevard off Tverskaya Street, just opposite Pushkin Square. The Pushkin Café stood before them, impregnable in its antique, half-timbered beauty.

'I'm surprised the Soviets didn't pull this place down. Surely it was a symbol of capitalist decadence?' said Samuel. Then, a challenging postscript: 'What say you, Blandford?'

'I ... Well, it's here now. Let's get in, shall we?'

Blandford hurried on ahead, as though he had some clock to punch, some deadline to make. Samuel watched him nod at the doorman and scurry into the building. There was a simple word for Blandford's behaviour: *jumpy*. But why? Suddenly he seemed to be seeking cover, running from something – this from the man who was supposed to be running *towards* things – certainly towards dinner with a Russian billionaire.

Samuel laid an absent-minded hand on his breast pocket. Kempis's envelope, still unopened, nestled inside. He'd been intending to tell Blandford about the old man's posthumous theatricality, but the Canadian's dark mood held him back.

Walking into the restaurant was to travel back in time. The waiters wore pea-green tailcoats; a trio of musicians in black penguin suits played Schubert in a corner; ancient bottles of medicine glowed dully behind a long, copper-covered bar in front of them. Orbs of soft ochre light reflected a warm, cheering glow atop the mini neo-Corinthian pillars that sprouted out of the bar. The place was an apothecary's shop from the pages of *War and Peace* crossed with a high-tech pastiche of Maxim's in Paris – a pricey playing field for supermodels and the self-consciously smart.

Blandford murmured something to the front-of-house manager, who led them to an ancient metal cage. The lift's Victorian dark-brown metal doors yawed slowly open, then swallowed them. After an interminable wait, the lift settled, and slowly, slowly, they ascended.

In the corner of the low-ceilinged mezzanine floor of the restaurant sat Anna Barinova and Medulev. Both were smoking cigarettes. Anna had a green-and-gold Sobranie between her dainty fingers. She smiled broadly in greeting. Medulev stood up, features creased into a thin smile.

The corner table, as all others on the mezzanine level, looked out over the pharmacy bar, but it was sandwiched between two sumptuous walls of books. It had an intimacy to it, the only part of the restaurant that was a place to see rather than to be seen. A niche for the super-rich – the kind of table a top-level security guard would advise taking.

They exchanged pleasantries as the waiters draped napkins across their laps. Champagne was ordered. Samuel quite liked the idea of sampling Georgian wine, perhaps Kindzmarauli, Stalin's favourite. It was now possible to obtain Georgian wine again, but trade relations were still difficult after the border disputes and mini-wars. So apolitical, conspicuously expensive French champagne it had to be – preferably Dom Pérignon or Krug, and vintage too. Nothing else would do in the New Russia – even if no one was watching.

Anna Barinova ordered the most expensive bottle of Krug on the menu. She was wearing a tight-fitting, dark-navy dress – entirely backless, cut to the waist in a daring V-shape. A billionairess with the body of a gymnast. The lighting – perhaps the reason she had chosen the table? – made her look almost girlish. With her dark hair piled high, and the pretty, faintly vulpine cast of her features, she had a hint of Audrey Hepburn about her. Why the change of look? Wasn't this a business meeting?

A drink arrived, saviour of the hour. A clink of glasses. 'This is quite a place, Madame Barinova,' said Samuel. 'I'm very impressed. Do you mind if I . . . ?'

'Oh, you mean the books? Please do, Mr Spendlove, please do.'

Samuel got up. Maybe that would push Blandford into playing the ringmaster again. It was his damned circus, after all.

Samuel wandered over and removed a couple of volumes from the nearby shelf. They would have made an antiquarian drool. Leather-bound and soft to the touch, most were in German; their gothic script dated from the mid-nineteenth century. He selected some early editions of Goethe and Nietzsche, turning the pages with care.

A gaggle of young diners from nearby tables looked at Samuel with some distaste. At first, he couldn't understand why he was getting such disapproval from the Gucci gulag. As a former academic, he loved books. It was a pleasure to handle and touch and look at them, even if his German was weak. But then he realised: this was unacceptable behaviour in the Pushkin Café, temple of post-Communist consumerism. The censorious looks were for Samuel's failure to understand: the things in his hands weren't books, but accessories. The beautiful leather spines were there to create an atmosphere, nothing else. They were miniature pieces of furniture, and Samuel had no right to rearrange them.

A line from Goethe sprang up at him. His German was just about good enough to distil the sense: 'Whatever you can do, or dream you can, begin it. Boldness has genius, power, and magic in it.'

Maybe. But boldness could wait a while. He snapped the book shut, and rejoined the table.

Blandford was a passive spectator still, while Medulev was talking earnestly in Russian to Anna Barinova. Her searing blue eyes rested on Samuel for a moment; her smile deepened.

She waved a bejewelled hand. A waiter refilled their glasses. Another stood at her shoulder, pen hovering over pad.

'Mr Spendlove? Have you read the menu?' She regarded him over the edge of her own large, leather-bound folder. 'And the wine list?'

'Yes, but it would be presumptuous of me to order the wine, Madame Barinova. Or may I . . . ? Anna?'

'Of course.'

'And, please – call me Samuel.'

Medulev looked away momentarily – distraction, disapproval, disappointment?

Anna Barinova ordered with the quiet authority of a Russian aristocrat distributing gold to the poor. Blandford and Samuel opted for the blinis and the caviar, the borscht and the steak in halting Russian. Medulev, speaking in English, ordered a bear steak. His words tumbled over each other in a long, aggressive snarl.

'Rare, sir?' asked the waiter. Both were Russian, but protocol demanded he use the language in which the order had been given.

'Rare? I don't care if it's *extinct* after I've eaten it. I just want my fucking steak,' snapped Medulev. The waiter blinked. His English wasn't strong enough to cope with puns.

'Marat, Marat,' cooed Anna. She placed a delicate hand on top of his.

Medulev grabbed a carafe of chilled vodka, a shot glass, and muttered '*za druzhbu*' – 'for friendship' – and downed it in one.

Samuel knew a little toasting etiquette. This perfunctory

greeting was something Russians despised. Toasting was an art to be enthusiastically embraced. It was an opportunity to make clever little speeches about the occasion, the company, and, as the evening wore on, life in general. This, though, was the obvious fakery that US nationals and Soviets perpetrated on each other over Cold War dinner tables.

'Come now, Marat,' coaxed Anna. 'We have a long night ahead of us.'

'My apologies, my friends,' said Medulev. He grabbed a biscuit canapé with some *shproti*, smoked sprats in olive oil, and a slice of salted and pickled cucumber on top. The oil and salt were well-recognised antidotes to the potentially devastating effects of vodka. 'Toasts later.'

Their hostess spoke into the silence that had settled on the table. 'So, Samuel, is it true, what my friend William Barton tells me?'

Barton? Samuel reached for his glass with deliberate slowness, and raised it carefully to his lips.

'That depends what he's been saying, Anna,' said Samuel at length. 'I work for a Barton foundation. But the man? I've never actually met him.'

'Come, come, Samuel. Don't tease.' She had a musical laugh. 'What you did for Barton shot you to world fame.'

'Infamy, I'd say. Thankfully, everyone's forgotten about that now.'

'But here you are. I wouldn't say you were forgotten.'

'Maybe that's why I still have a research bursary. The terms aren't exactly onerous – no publication deadline, and I can research anything I want – the history of meteorology, the effect of derivatives trading on long-bond yields with specific attention to the reverse yield curve, the semiotics of topiary.'

'The semiotics of topiary?'

The waiter placed a plate of grilled bear meat in front of Medulev.

'I suppose that boils down to why people have hedges shaped like chickens. See how I can make a difference to the world?'

She laughed. The din of other table talk and the valiant efforts of the string trio swirled round them.

'So . . .' A diamond flash as the billionairess sipped her champagne. 'Barton tells me you have a perfect memory.'

*Too perfect: an innocent woman on a slab, fished from the Seine after days in the water, a madman with a knife, a killer with a crossbow, an endless series of bogus trade codes, none of them his – a romance that failed.*

Samuel gulped from his glass. 'Perfect? There's no such thing. What I do have is an eidetic facility that offers near-perfect recall. It's just a quirk, an eccentricity.'

'I may have a proposition for you, as Marat has indicated. This quirk, as you put it, may be helpful. That word – "eidetic"– it means you have a photographic memory?'

'Providing I've given something such as a picture or a piece of text what you might call "proper attention", then I can recall an image or the information in my mind and retrieve it at will. It's like storing canvases in an attic – or photos in the memory of a digital camera. You can forget about the images completely, but they're there. You can retrieve and look at them at any moment.'

'Samuel,' she looked into his eyes. The pressure on his arm was quite discernible now. 'Would you show us? Could you take out a mental picture of the menu and let us choose dessert, please? You did read the menu, didn't you?'

'I have an aversion to games and publicity stunts these days.'

'Please . . .'

'Really . . .' He looked at her, expectant – pleading, demanding. 'Anything for an easy life – but just this once, mind.'

He bowed his head for a moment, then looked up from the tablecloth: '*Strawberry, blackberry and redcurrant Pavlova. Named for the queen of Russian ballet, Anna Pavlova, doyenne of*

*the Bolshoi, this piquant confection of the finest fruits, picked in
the woodlands of Peredelkino, is served in a heavenly combination
of meringue and imported cream from prize cows fed on luscious
grass on the British island of Jersey.*

*'White Russian Brandy Snaps. Exquisitely hand-crafted cones
of the finest white-sugar syrup, subtly impregnated with seeds from
specially selected Honduran vanilla pods . . .'*

Samuel recited the entire dessert menu, word for word, without
a moment's hesitation. He finished to a round of polite applause – a
familiar, always annoying sound.

'Excellent,' smiled Anna. 'Now, tell me. What wine do you
think we should have? Did you give the wine list some proper
attention too?'

'Only the French and Californian reds, the champagnes and
the sweet wines,' said Samuel. He looked about him. They were
rapt, listening to every word as though it had divine significance.
Suddenly he felt very tired.

He cleared his throat. 'You could go for the Brown Brothers
Australian Orange Muscat . . . *a rich, honey-flavoured wine with
undertones of custard but a clean, sustained finish of buttery lemon
with a hint of lavender.'*

Anna was gazing him like an adoring child. Medulev's attention
was elsewhere. He was muttering into his phone. Was that Farsi?
Now the Russian stood abruptly.

'Would you excuse me? There's a small errand I must run. I
shall return.'

'Please, Marat. Go. Do what you must,' said Anna, teasing a
point of light from her cigarette. 'But remember, we have guests.
We must show them true Russian hospitality. Don't be long.'

Medulev nodded, and was gone.

Blandford peered down into his lap, then clicked his tongue
impatiently.

'Could I borrow your phone, please, Samuel? Mine's died.'

'Really?'

'Sorry. Urgent business.'

Samuel reached slowly for his breast pocket and felt for the Samsung he'd acquired at the airport. What the hell was this, if not business?

He produced the phone. The Canadian grabbed it, and rose from the table with an apologetic wave of his hand.

So now they were two. OK . . .

'What do you make of our friend Marat?'

'It's difficult to say,' said Samuel. 'You know him. I don't. I can see he's a complicated and intelligent man.'

Stick to the positive, and wait. He sipped his water.

'Correct, Samuel. As well as English, and Russian of course, he speaks French, Farsi and Pashtu, including a couple of sub-dialects. Marat has lived through difficult times to become a rising star in our organisation. He may be difficult, Samuel, but he has his reasons.'

'It seems like we're the only ones not finding life difficult tonight.'

'Well, let's make things easier. Have a little something, and I'll tell you more.'

She motioned for coffee and waved a manicured finger at a trolley laden with liqueurs.

'Marat . . .' She sipped delicately from her glass. 'I've known for a long time. He was an ideologue, one of the few who didn't mind conscription under the Communists. He fought in Afghanistan as a boy.'

'The 40th Army. I saw the tattoo.'

'Of course you did. Well, like many he was traumatised by the experience. I got to know him years ago when he came to Moscow State University to study Persian, then worked in Teheran as an interpreter. He's able, loyal too . . .'

Samuel watched her talk, her precise gestures, her flickered smile, her sharp blue eyes. So the proposition, if it came, when it

45

came, would involve working with Medulev.

Samuel nodded: 'Teheran? That would be where he picked up his French.'

'Yes, and his English! You may find his accent curious. His teachers were Persian.'

'Marat saw a lot of troubling things in Afghanistan.' She spoke quietly. 'The system he believed in did not serve him well out there. Nor the poor boys who were shot, of course. Others – boy soldiers – were held captive in a pit for days on end. The Afghans would cut their ears, then their noses off. They'd pull out their tongues. Death was a blessing to these boys, but not to Marat, or the other the comrades who recovered the bodies. When Marat came back to Moscow he was a changed man; he spent seven years teaching in the Dzerzhinsky training academy at Pskov.'

'Is that a KGB school? He more or less said he'd been an operative this afternoon.'

'Yes, Samuel. An elite school. So secret that few in the KGB itself knew of its existence.' She paused, monitoring his reaction. Samuel remained impassive. 'Information is the tool of the developed economies, and of the developing ones like ours, Samuel. We had a knowledge economy under Communism, just as you do in the West.'

'Only your knowledge was nationalised.'

'Precisely. Instead of delegating control, the Soviets used the KGB.'

'But to what end, Anna?'

Now there was a different tenor, the rigour of business, in her words.

'Yes, there was military and political purpose in the Soviet era. Now the common motive in the New Russia is profit. So Marat moved to serve business after the end of Communism. He became a broadcaster at the Persian service of MosGov State Radio, and then a producer.'

'Propaganda – the means of production of the knowledge economy?'

'No. Propaganda used to be demagoguery, now it's marketing. Profit is our master now, Samuel. It treats us all with equal contempt. Though Marat would tell you that he works for me, not for profit.'

'So . . . now Marat's . . . head of programming for one of your television channels?'

'Yes, my financial channel, ABTV. You know they say that knowledge is power? Well, knowledge is money too.'

'He's got a great job. A great boss too, if I may say so . . .'

'I am a good boss, too good, I think.'

Samuel cocked his head slightly.

'Oh, Samuel, can't you tell? Marat's in love with me. At least he thinks he is. His heart is still buried somewhere between Teheran and Afghanistan. I'd like you to come and see our operation out in Ostankino – and meet someone else, someone special. We have something I'm sure will interest you. Dr Kempis thought so too. Will you come? Please?'

The living and the dead were ganging up on him to probe his natural weakness, his curiosity, the very same curiosity that had got him into such a mess in Paris. Anna was leaning in to him, waiting for his answer.

Suddenly, she sat straight up in her chair.

'Marat!' said Anna brightly. If she was annoyed, she showed no sign – what an operator. 'Your business is done?'

Medulev sat down, took the vodka carafe from its ice bucket, and poured them all a shot.

'It is. And now, a toast,' he said, solemnly. 'To a long and prosperous life, filled with happiness and meaning.'

What was there in those brown eyes? Real sadness? Quiet fury? Boiling resentment?

They nodded solemnly at one another, Russian-style, and drank.

'So you haven't seen Kingston at all?' asked Samuel. 'He marched out of here a quarter of an hour ago – with my phone.'

'Kingston lives for business nowadays,' said Medulev. 'The next meeting is his life, and his life is the next meeting.'

'OK. I have a toast now,' said Samuel. 'To a long and prosperous life, filled with happiness and meetings! To Kingston, our temporarily absent friend!'

They drank and ate a little *shproti*.

'How well do you know Kingston?' asked Medulev.

'Not so well. A friend of mine from Oxford was with him at Princeton. I studied there briefly a few years ago. I think he wanted to get to know me after my Paris adventures. Some people like notoriety.'

'Life is about the simple pleasures, Samuel.'

'There was a tutor at Oxford, a novelist, who said that life should be a series of simple pleasures.'

'An interesting idea. Did that make him happy?' asked Anna.

'*She* was called Iris Murdoch, and no, I don't think she was very happy. Lots of mediocre sex with men and women, and plenty of drink and depression.'

'It doesn't sound such a bad way to live.'

'Blandford, from what I've seen of him, seems to adore his little pleasures and distractions. He's always on the move, meeting for the next deal. His world is composed of light sessions in hotel gyms, business card exchanges. And for company? Chocolates on the pillow at night.'

'There's more than that, Samuel,' said Medulev. 'I've known him for longer than you, and maybe a little better. Kingston is a remarkable man. Strong, resilient. He has suffered.'

'Tell, Marat,' said Anna. 'How fascinating. I love to hear about suffering.'

'Do you really, Anna?' asked Samuel.

'Samuel, how do I say this?' He was locked into those deep blue eyes, 'I am not a cruel woman, but suffering is passion. Suffering is . . . voluptuous.'

'Really? In my little world, avoidance of suffering is a working definition of happiness, Anna.'

'Blandford . . . he had family problems,' said Medulev. 'This is all I will say. Business is now his life. He has been asking to meet Anna for months. So here we are. Except . . .' He looked round the restaurant. 'I find his absence strange.'

'I didn't know Blandford had family,' said Samuel.

'This is my point. He is a strong man in a surprising way.'

'What family problems?'

'A terrible accident. Terrible. But – no more for now,' said Medulev. 'He's here.'

Sure enough, Blandford was bouncing along towards them. He seemed somehow restored; the game-show-host smile was back home and receiving guests. He sat down.

'Sorry, sorry, sorry, folks. It was California. Conference call – not even lunchtime there. Had to take care of business. Just went on and on. I see the toasting has begun.'

Anna Barinova began to pour them all a shot. 'Yes, the toasting has begun. I have one to make, to Samuel – and to our proposition.'

'He's accepted? Anna, you are a very persuasive woman. Congratulations,' said Blandford.

'I am told I have my moments, Kingston, but you're premature. I may have helped Samuel understand a little about us – and I think I've persuaded him to come out to Ostankino.'

'Thank you for organising this meeting, Kingston. And Marat. Well done.'

'My pleasure, Anna, my pleasure,' said Blandford.

He was beaming now. The Californian call must have gone well.

'Samuel, your phone.'

'Keep it, Kingston. It's a pay-as-you go I got at the airport, and the credit's just about used up. I'll go the expensive route and use my old one for the rest of this trip.'

'No, I insist, Samuel. Really, I do.'

Blandford pushed the phone into Samuel's hands, then grabbed a glass.

'To friends and family!'

Samuel downed the shot and forced down some more *shproti*. They'd almost finished the carafe now. Blandford held it up.

'Shall we have another? I'm getting into party mode.'

'No, Kingston,' said Anna. 'I think not. Samuel and I have matters to discuss in private, and we both need clear heads.'

'Gentlemen,' she looked at Medulev and Blandford in turn. 'You may leave us. Thank you.'

To Samuel, she seemed perfectly sober. Had she been playing Stalin's trick? The old control freak would get his staff to serve him water from a vodka carafe, and watch as everyone else at the supper table got so wasted Stalin could see behind their paranoia.

Medulev got up, with obvious reluctance.

'Marat, please,' said Anna. 'This is business.'

Out of instinct, Samuel checked the phone in his lap. The call register showed no incoming calls. But there was an outgoing transaction – a few seconds, to a Moscow number. He looked up sharply at Blandford, but he was busy kissing Anna Barinova's hand.

'Very well,' said Medulev. 'Come, Kingston. We have the rest of the night to kill.'

Blandford gave a short bark of a laugh. 'Indeed we do, Marat, indeed we do. Let's go.'

The two men peeled off their jackets to reveal matching dark circles round their armpits. Samuel wondered where Medulev's gun holster had got to. They walked off, arms linked round each other's shoulders in the transient brotherhood of vodka. What a jolly, mildly inebriated mess they presented – unable even to eat or drink like grown-ups. One of the jackets was even stained, evidence of the night's debauchery. Samuel managed a wry smile as they weaved their way through the restaurant: Blandford's ability to blend into society – any society at all – never ceased to amaze him.

# CHAPTER FOUR

MEDULEV WAS AT the bar getting drinks. Blandford looked around at the bewildering display of high cheekbones, pert breasts, dark, almond-shaped eyes. The women were gorgeous, dripping the cheap glitter of the New Russia.

The Electric Circus was the latest hot place to be in town – the place to be seen. A blonde woman, squeezed into a tight black dress, approached him. The material clung to the contours of her lithe body in a way that spoke eloquently to any heterosexual man. Beneath what was essentially a large silk handkerchief, she was naked. And clearly available – for a price.

'You are American, yes?'

'Canadian, but what's the difference?'

Even by the standards of the Electric Circus, she was beautiful. Her rich, thick hair fell onto her shoulders like an iridescent lion mane. Her eyes were golden-green and impossibly huge. The Electric Circus was subjected to some of the strictest 'face control' in Moscow. Only goddesses with sweet, sexy faces, tiny waists and full breasts were allowed in.

The crowd was composed largely of goddesses, and men like Blandford. He was sweaty, smelly, business-suited, and pushing sixty. It was the men's role to bring money into the nightclub, and the goddesses' to take it off them.

Medulev fought his way through the throng carrying a bottle of vodka and two glasses. He stood behind the girl. Blandford invited her to sit with them, and Medulev went to get another glass.

Blandford poured two shots of vodka, and drank his straight down. He held his head in his hands for a few moments, thinking back to the moment the call had come, a few days before . . .

*'I've got one.'*

*'What?'*

*'You heard. Do you want it?'*

*'I suppose I do. Can't do business without it.'*

*And with a little waiting around in the cold – and a lot of cash – a few hours later there'd been a dully dangerous Vektor SP1 pistol and silencer lying on his freshly turned-down hotel bed. The bribes to find the gun dealer had cost more than the gun itself. But that was business. Wasn't it?*

Blandford shook his head, looked up, smiled. The girl leaned towards him and spoke into his ear.

'You feel good?'

'Never better. What's your name?'

'Maria. You want to feel even better? You want to stay with me tonight?'

Medulev settled the bottle of vodka into an ice bucket, and stared into the middle distance.

This woman was meltingly desirable – just like Deirdre had been at that age. But Deirdre, his wife, was long dead. No, this girl was more like his daughter. Since she'd been nine, he'd brought her up on his own – ever since Deirdre's lymphoma had kicked in. Suddenly he'd been Daddy, Mummy, teacher, mentor, keeper of dreams – all rolled into one. His girl, his little blonde angel . . .

He shook his head slowly, trying to clear the memory, shake off the pain.

'Is this how you make your money?' Blandford smiled weakly. 'You seem, I don't know . . . there's something about you that tells me you're a smart girl. You don't have to do this.'

Maria breathed in deeply, sending a tiny, exquisite tremor through the ripe curve of her breasts.

'Please, Mister. No small talk. You want me? Is $300. You like blow job? I am best in all club. $200. This very good deal for you.'

She drew back again, defying him to challenge her status as the queen of fellatio.

'I'm sure you're right. But, no. Thanks. Not for me.'

The girl turned away, a sour twist to her lips. She made a sign to a group of girls standing at the dimly lit bar, holding her first finger and thumb a centimetre apart. *Small dick, small wallet, girls. No trade.*

Medulev snapped back into action.

'*Za vas, za nas, i za gaz!*' he bellowed. He was sweaty, vodka-happy. The drink had done its job.

'To you, to us, and to gas!'

Blandford laughed. 'Gas? Shouldn't that really be "to you, to us and to oil"?'

'Yes, Kingston, my friend, but oil doesn't rhyme.' Medulev was looking over at another coterie of girls. They sat along the far corner of a bar that stretched across the back of the main salon – expensive ornaments on a mantelpiece.

'Here's to our buddy, Samuel, anyway. He's buying the drinks.'

'What?'

'Elementary security procedure. Pick a name, anyone except your own, but someone in your circle of associates. Then use it. If something bad happens elsewhere in this wicked, wicked world, you can prove you were here with your friend.' A tiny smile. 'If something bad happens here, our friend Samuel was at the scene. He paid in cash, and his name was on the tab. Good for bars, whorehouses, hotels.'

Medulev grunted appreciatively. 'Prudent. The tradecraft of capitalist Moscow. Little things help cover the tracks. But will

Spendlove do it? He's not going to worry about his name being on some bullshit bar tab.'

'Well,' said Blandford. 'If Anna is as persuasive as she seems, I'm sure he will.'

Medulev stood up. 'Come on. It's time for another race. We have little time to lay our bets.'

Blandford rose and followed Medulev unsteadily through a corridor, up a set of stairs and into a dark room. The chill and a heightened sense of echo told him it was a large space. The gloom was an almost impenetrable pitch-black, until you noticed the tiny luminous studs set in the ceiling. It was as though they were outdoors, under a giant, velvet-dark sky with thousands of dimly twinkling stars.

'How long have we got?' asked Blandford, fingering a thick wedge of dollars and roubles in his trouser pocket.

'Just long enough. Which one do you fancy?'

Written up on a board behind them, a list of names.

'Do they change the animals for each race, or just the names?' asked Blandford.

Medulev laughed. 'Just the names, my friend. Unless the rats get so hungry they eat one another.'

It was easier to see through the gloom now. Medulev and Blandford were standing on a bridge raised above what looked like a figure-of-eight sculpture. After a while, Blandford detected a kind of racetrack, with individual lanes divided by partitions a few centimetres high. It looked like a very large toy-car racing game.

There were thirty or forty people dotted around. Some were just indistinct shapes, corners of the room that suddenly moved. Nearby stood yet more scantily clad girls and groups of muscular men, their wrists bound with gold watch bracelets that sucked in what little light there was. Despite the dark, one man was still wearing wrap-around sunglasses with gems set in the bridge and the arms of the frame. The strong smell of masculine sweat wrestled with

55

aftershave and deodorant, chemical parodies of alpine flowers and bales of musk.

An upward scale of four musical notes saw a large black rectangle on the wall opposite spring into digital life. The pixels on the screen glowed ruby and sapphire.

'Come on,' said Medulev.

The screen displayed a list of six names in English and in Russian. Against each was a set of odds, a betting price – 2/1, 15/8, 4/1. Three young women sat at a long desk just in front of the screen. They wore the skimpy uniform of the Electric Circus – a short, dark-blue toga-style tunic with a stripe of white lightning running diagonally down from the shoulder. The uniforms were cut to reveal a dramatic wedge of flesh, including the gentle settling of bosom on chest, when viewed from the side.

'Boris's Breakfast. Fifty dollars,' said Medulev tossing a note on the table. An electronic whirring produced a slip, which Medulev duly pocketed. 'And you, Kingston? Where does fortune tell you to wager?'

Blandford looked up at the names: 'Copacabana Collective, Red Under Bed, Sexual Metric, Low Hanging Fruit . . . They all sound the same.'

'I like the names, don't you?' said Medulev. 'The mixing and matching of Marxism and capitalism.'

'I guess so,' said Blandford.

A din rose from the corner of the room. Punters slammed money down on tables, poured drinks down their throats, sweated, cursed, grabbed the girls' arses, laughed harshly at the squealing, called for more drink. The things people did – and all this in the name of entertainment. What they were capable of in business made him shudder.

'OK. Lenin's Urinal. Twenty bucks. That's the one with the gold colours, right?'

'Of course. Gold urinals were promised to the workers in the fantasy world of revolution, a century ago – a world where material wealth was despised. Well, we've got Lenin's Urinal now – it's a rat with a diamanté collar and your money on its back. But twenty bucks? Is that all?'

'I'm not really a gambling man.'

'I suppose not. I never thought you were a party animal either. Maybe you are learning to love Russia, eh, tovarish?'

'I'm just a good-time guy, out for a few laughs.'

They went over to join the crowd on the bridge. The race began, and the crowd whooped and hollered, threw bits of cheese to encourage their own rodents and distract the opposition. The food often landed in the wrong lane entirely, but this merely added to the audience's hilarity. It was this reaction that Blandford found oddly consoling. People could enjoy, yes really enjoy these inane pleasures.

Low Hanging Fruit romped home, a 3/1 winner, and they finished their vodka.

'Staying for the next race?' enquired Medulev.

'No. I think I'll head for the hotel. I've had quite a night,' said Blandford.

'Are you sure? The next race is the Baby-Face Bearded Marxist Tycoon Chase. It's fun. They pin live cockroaches to the rats' backs. It makes them go crazy. Real fun to watch, but maybe too cruel for your tastes.'

'Don't worry about that. It sounds great, but I gotta go,' said Blandford. 'I'm pooped.'

'OK, my friend,' said Medulev. 'Come here!'

The Russian gave Blandford a bear hug.

'You know, you're a great guy, even if you do smell like shit. You're a different man to the one I thought I knew.'

'I know what you mean. I think,' said Blandford, and then he was gone.

'SO, SAMUEL. DO YOU accept my proposition?'

'Anna, we were going to invoke the spirit of Peter Kempis. And then you come up with this . . .'

A set of plum-coloured velvet curtains was drawn around their table – the kind of thing you got in expensive Victorian brothels. They could hear and be heard, but they could not be seen.

'Of course, we can talk about Peter, his unusual life and unfortunate death. Later.'

'At best it's a form of industrial espionage. Some would call it spying.'

A frown momentarily creased Anna Barinova's brow.

'Samuel, I hate to be disappointed. How is it espionage? How spying? It is not theft. You should see it as part of a – how would you say? – due diligence process.'

'Due diligence takes place with the other party's knowledge and co-operation.'

'We're not stealing anything,' she smiled sweetly. 'We merely need to know if the technology works before we attempt to buy the company. And you'll be doing something worthwhile – something for the kind of greater good that poor Peter believed in.'

'Which is?'

'Which is something I'll gladly reveal once you've agreed to come on board. You just have to trust me on this, Samuel.'

'So, let's get this straight. You are interested in acquiring a specific piece of technology. In my capacity as a researcher for the XB Foundation, you want me to go into this company and see if the technology works. But the fact remains that you want me to deceive them. They won't know the real purpose of my visit, will they?'

'It's just a site visit, Samuel. William Barton tells me he has an interest in this company too, so you will not disappoint him. If it turns out that the technology really works, then we will pay the proper price, and the shareholders will have lost nothing. I am just wary of paying for unproven technology. Surely you can see that?'

Samuel sighed.

'I really don't think I'm the right man for the job, Anna. Thanks for a wonderful dinner. It's been great meeting you.'

'Will you do it for one hundred thousand dollars? Not bad for one day's work. How can you turn that down, Samuel?'

'How would you like my list of reasons? In order of importance – or alphabetically? I want a quiet life.'

'Very well. If you won't do it for me, will you do it for Dr Kempis?'

Samuel paused. Kempis again – a Banquo's ghost who'd been dogging him all day. Him and his damned . . . *envelope*.

Samuel patted his left breast, then his right, then hips, thighs – once, twice, three times: the phone user's pocket dance of mounting panic. But this was no missing mobile. The envelope was gone.

Anna Barinova sat back a little, crossed her smooth white legs and lit a black and gold Sobranie. She smiled.

'Looking for something?'

She clicked her fingers.

A gloved hand appeared through the drapes. The Kempis envelope held by a forefinger and thumb.

'Moscow is a dangerous place, full of dangerous people,' said Anna. 'I saw the way you kept touching your breast pocket.'

'Did I?'

'At least a dozen times. And that was before the first course. As this place is teeming with thieves I took the precaution of having whatever was so distracting removed to a place of safety.'

She took the envelope like a magician taking a prop from a hidden assistant, and called '*spasibo*'. The hand disappeared.

'Safer than my own pocket?' Samuel shot this straight back at her, in English. He took the envelope from her, and examined it. It didn't seem to have been opened, but you never could tell.

'I was merely trying to make the point – how easy it is to steal things without anyone noticing. You need protection in this country, not quite the kind of protection that some call a "roof" – that involves guns and other types of vulgarity. But you do need protection.' She touched his forearm softly. 'The protection of a friend like me.'

Samuel gulped at his drink – ice water. He'd had quite enough alcohol.

'So, please,' gestured Anna. 'Open it.'

'I will,' said Samuel. 'But not here, and not now. Thank you so much once more for a delicious supper.'

And with a short, formal bow he left Russia's only female oligarch all alone to finish her cigarette.

BACK IN THE HOTEL he closed his bedroom door and sat down on the edge of his bed.

Was Anna Barinova really such a keen student of body language? Or maybe she'd had him followed earlier, and so knew about the envelope? And had the message been opened, its contents seen – or even substituted? Impossible to say. He didn't even know how long it had been out of his possession.

He turned the envelope over in his hand. It seemed strange to see Kempis's handwriting after so long.

Well, this would be the last Kempis note he'd ever read. He ripped it open and unfolded it, then sighed: *'emptor bullarum bullam ipsam caveat! forum enim ipsum bulla sit! Iosephus Pectus non lactem sed lucem ferat.'*

Samuel stared at the paper. Yes, this really was happening. 'So typical of Peter,' he said aloud. 'A riddle – and it's in Latin.'

Samuel pondered a moment. In one way, this was good news – the authentic voice of the man. It was unlikely that Anna Barinova would have even thought of forging a Latin rhyme.

Samuel took a pen, read carefully, and roughed out a basic translation on hotel notepaper: 'May the buyer of bubbles beware! For the marketplace itself may be a bubble!'

There seemed to be a name involved; 'Josephus' was clear but 'Pectus' also had a capital letter. 'Joseph Pectus may bring light but not milk.' But what did 'Pectus' signify?

That was Kempis all right, opaque to the very last.

Samuel folded the note and placed the envelope carefully back in his jacket pocket.

As he lay in his bed, turning over the possible meaning of Kempis's last-ever tease, all kinds of things troubled him. Anna Barinova's proposal was borderline unethical, at best – although it might be fun, exciting, even. And it was a challenge, for sure. And then there was the behaviour of his male dinner companions. He switched his phone off and closed his eyes in a futile attempt to relax. It was late, but he would be up early. Tomorrow, Samuel would have some questions of his own to ask.

# CHAPTER FIVE

SAMUEL STRODE ALONG the Novy Arbat in watery morning light, and headed east along Vozdvizhenka towards the Kempinski. In the restaurant he found Blandford at a window table, greedily devouring a large plate of sausage and scrambled egg.

'Morning, Blandford. Don't get up.'

'I wouldn't dream of it,' he said, flashing a big smile.

On the far side of the river, St Basil's Cathedral glistened like a candy-striped space ship in the winter sun.

Samuel slid into a seat opposite the Canadian and pointed at a Continental breakfast selection for the benefit of a waiter, who brought him a courtesy newspaper.

The *Moscow Times* was an English-language publication read by all Anglophone expatriates, and distributed in every hotel lobby in Moscow. Blandford's eyes flicked to it a couple of times. Below the fold on page one was a blurred picture of a familiar-looking young man. The caption said, simply: 'Shamil Khamzaev – victim of latest gangland killing'.

'Why do I know this guy? Do you know him?' asked Samuel.

Blandford looked at Samuel, deadpan. Then his phone sprang into life, and he pounced. The apologetic but happy shrug of the businessman whose best friend is an incessantly shrieking phone. He began walking away from Samuel, back turned. But the opening exchange was still just audible.

'Hello?'

'You've been out the loop a while, my friend. Even for a first-use number, calling me on a Moscow network is a dick move.'

Samuel smiled at Blandford's retreating back. *Dick move* – why was that voice, that diction, familiar? He watched a waitress serve coffee and pastries to a large, swarthy man – maybe Chechen. He wore a silk suit and shades. Some gangsters had to don the uniform even at breakfast.

Blandford was pacing the corridor outside, his outline dimly visible through the hand-crafted smoked glass. The conversation was certainly animated.

Blandford's briefcase sat on the banquette seat opposite. One of its locks was already popped. Samuel slid a hand over, clicked, and flipped up the case lid.

Perhaps he shouldn't have been surprised. His own face stared up at him from a newspaper cutting that protruded from a plain Manila file. Slowly, almost reluctantly, he lifted the file cover. It revealed a mass of articles in various languages – the kind of media coverage he'd done his best to avoid after his ordeal in Paris.

Samuel's eyes scanned the pages at a furious pace. So Blandford had been researching him. No, not surprising, but disappointing. The coverage was the usual sensationalised, inaccurate stuff. Blandford had highlighted great chunks in dayglo yellow. Samuel picked up a cutting, the paper coarse and warm to the touch. Why newspapers? The technology was straight from the 1970s. But maybe that made sense, if Blandford wanted to be discreet. A mobile phone and its browser history were location-finder and personality profile all rolled into one.

His heart skipped lightly at a piece in the Swiss press. The article pictured Samuel with a beautiful, dark-haired girl – leather jacket, biker chic. They looked diffident, reluctant – and, he recalled the discomfort, the flashing of cameras. Discomfited, hunted even – that was exactly how he and Lauren had felt. The relentless attention, the remorselessness need for a 'story' after Paris had been almost worse than the escapade itself. Certainly for Lauren, who'd withdrawn entirely – from the media, from the wider world, even from Samuel. He just hoped that the beach, the glacial lake, or the mountain she was probably contemplating right then would bring her the serenity she deserved.

The Paris fiasco was chronicled in columns of banal, sub-Orwellian patois:

'. . . *a junior academic at Oxford University on a research bursary funded by William Barton's media empire, Spendlove was initially cited as a fugitive rogue trader and named by Paris police as the number one suspect in an associated murder.*

'*Following the death of Kaz Day, a senior trader at Ropner Bank, the host of Spendlove's research fellowship, the English academic disappeared for several days. This sparked an international manhunt, and the involvement of Interpol, the intelligence agencies of France, Britain, and, it is believed, the United States. In the immediate aftermath of Spendlove's disappearance, a series of trades, allegedly based on illegally obtained insider information, brought the world's financial system to the brink of total meltdown.*

'*Spendlove was cited by Ropner Bank, specifically by its star proprietary trader, Khan, whose methods Spendlove had been studying, as the man responsible for the crisis, through unlawful and unauthorised manipulation of illegal systems. Spendlove was accused of the murder of Ms Day, who had allegedly threatened to expose the trades.*'

He recalled the horror of the morgue. The brute of an inspector who forced his hands onto the cold, dead flesh of the poor woman. The skin puckered from days in the water, the flesh preyed on by eels. There could be no sympathy for Samuel. He was a murderer, right? And according to the press, also the sole perpetrator of the biggest financial catastrophe in the history of the world. Samuel shuddered slightly and read on:

*'However, investigations by the French authorities revealed that the true author of the assault on the world's financial system was the charismatic and mysterious Khan, styled by many in the media as the ultimate "Master of the Universe"...'*

Samuel shook his head in frustration. The bastards had missed the real story in favour of attention-grabbing headlines and the fun of a witch hunt. He riffled through the rest. They'd all bought Khan's story, at least at first. Why bother with the real villain when there's a convenient scapegoat to hand . . .?

His eyes fastened on to a highlighted excerpt from leader in the *Wall Street Journal*, entitled: 'Dinosaur Capitalism: Egosaurus Wrecks'. This writer was beginning to think in the right way:

*'. . . and so we have to ask the final question: "What goes on behind the locked doors of the casino economy we have engineered for ourselves in the West?"*

*'Some argue that the underlying truth of the near-meltdown of the world's financial system illustrates a deeper malaise – that we are not governed by perfectible markets whose mechanisms seek and finally reveal the true value of the assets they trade. There is a growing body of support among behavioural-finance academics that simple by-play between towering egos, the need to win, the ascription of emotional, not financial, value to an asset or a trade, can become – albeit briefly – the dominant factor in the liberal-market systems that the West have adopted.*

*'As such, the narrowly averted catastrophe that began with the trades and the death at Ropner Bank in Paris, could be seen as a struggle between a Master of the Universe and a Media Mogul who, for reasons best known to himself, entertained a grudge. Unluckily for both "big players" in this scenario, the young man they chose as a pawn turned out not to be so easily manipulable – indeed, to be outstandingly resourceful.*

*'But whether today's markets are a function of perfect pricing mechanisms or the playthings of the wealthy and the powerful,*

*immediate action is required: transparency in transaction, independent supervision, and prudent regulation are all urgent priorities . . .'*

Samuel put the leader back, and closed the briefcase lid. The leader-writer had a point. But, of course, there'd been no regulation. Nothing had changed. Khan, who'd set him up, had been nailed, after a fashion – a short time in a luxury Swiss institution that could hardly be described as a jail. But the system had preserved itself. New faces occupied old positions of power. As the father of fractal mathematics and chaos theory, Benoît Mandelbrot, had put it, the markets were frightening because people of 'great brilliance and extraordinary greed' worked in them. It was impossible to change human nature. Or very much at all . . .

'Hello.'

Medulev stood at the foot of the table. He seemed amused. How long had he been there?

'So you are a spy after all, Samuel.'

Samuel nodded at the briefcase. 'I . . . Nonsense. Blandford left his case open. Full of interesting news clips.'

Had Medulev been there a while? Did it matter? There were other issues at hand. He pushed the *Moscow Times* across the table and tapped the murder story.

'Dangerous city, as Anna was saying last night. This guy seem familiar to you at all?'

Medulev glanced at the piece, and shrugged. Indifference? Disdain? It was difficult to tell.

Blandford snapped his phone shut as he advanced on them.

'Medulev, you're here. Good. Shall we go then, Samuel? Ostankino? You up for this?'

'I'll come – but I make no promises, Blandford. I'll come, as they say, for the ride. I'd like to talk to you two.'

'The car is waiting,' said Medulev.

Blandford scribbled on a bill. 'Good enough for me! *Poyekhali!*

Let's go!'

'Yes,' said Samuel. 'Let's.'

VLADIMIR CHECKED THE MONITOR again. It was one of four in his kitchen. The monitors were the gadgets he used most in there. When he had the place built he'd insisted on having a fine, English-made kitchen, including shiny granite worktops with bevelled edges. He didn't enjoy cooking much, but an expensive kitchen was a status symbol. As was the Sub-Zero fridge he had imported from America. Vladimir used that a fair bit. He kept Swedish and French vodka, Grey Goose, in the freezer. Most of the shelving was taken up with imported beers of various sorts. They were gathered in dense rows of shiny green and brown, racked like bombs.

The door buzzer sounded again. It was curious that someone should ring the bell at night. People tended not to go out much in Grozny after nightfall. The main streets had been rebuilt rapidly enough after the two devastating wars with Moscow, but the fear of going out after dark would take a long time to die.

He went upstairs to the bedroom and checked on a much bigger bank of screens at the heart of his security system – the command and control centre, as he liked to call it. His fortress of a house was a perfect example of the dwelling of one of the *vozdushniki* – air people. Individuals like Vladimir were called air people because the peasants and fools on the other side of the high brick walls couldn't work out how they had made their money. The simpletons had decided that people like Vladimir had made capital out of thin air.

He had money because he had seen the opportunity. Vladimir had made a fortune out of the war. The conflict meant that there was an urgent and continuous demand for the sale of arms and the offer of protection, muscle in bulk, phalanxes of the brutal and the bestial. It was a good business to be in – lucrative, exciting, enjoyable.

You had to keep your guard up at all times, though. Vladimir looked quickly down into the courtyard. The Porsche Cayenne with its black-tinted windows and the S-Class Mercedes with its armour plating and bullet-proof windscreens sat quietly and unmolested. Tatiana and Igor, his two huge, semi-feral Dobermanns, were howling and snarling at the door. They didn't like strangers, or even visitors. Vladimir didn't discourage them. He felt pretty much the same.

The buzzer sounded again. Whoever it was must be very drunk or very brave. Either that, or they really wanted to see him.

He checked briefly once more. All the security cameras round the brick perimeters of his high-walled garden were working exactly as they should. The razor-barbed wire rolls atop the walls were all in perfect condition. The caller was definitely alone.

'What is it?' called Vladimir. 'This had better be good.'

'I am sorry, Vladimir. This is Sergei. You know me. Please come.'

Vladimir looked at the image of the shivering, scrawny little man. The pathetic idiot was looking round constantly, plainly in fear of his life. Vladimir peered into the monitor. This little creep was one of Khamzaev's men, if he was not mistaken. A runner, a nothing. Not even a foot soldier. He didn't even carry a gun.

'What's the problem?' asked Vladimir, complacently performing a couple of arm curls. He liked to have dumb-bells all around the house. He wasn't taking the steroids any more, so he didn't train quite as much as he used to. But he still had an appetite for pain – his own and other people's. Exercise, hard exercise and plenty of it, took the edge off the anger and tension that racked his body.

Tatiana and Igor began hurling themselves at the door. They were barking furiously and slavering now, getting into a real state.

'Vladimir, can you call the dogs off? They're making me afraid,' called Sergei.

'Shut up. What do you want, you little worm?' There was something comforting in Sergei's fear.

'It's Ahmed.'

'Ahmed?' Vladimir put the dumb-bell down. Ahmed was another matter. Not to be fucked with. 'What's the matter with Ahmed?'

'It's not good, Vladimir, not good. He wants you to come. Please come now.'

'Now? Sensible people like me stay home of an evening and play with their Xboxes.'

This was true. Vladimir had a number of particularly violent games that he enjoyed playing on the giant plasma screens attached to the wall of his private cinema.

'This is an emergency. Please come now. I have never seen him like this. He shot Rafa in the head this afternoon. Killed his own man, shot him like a dog.'

'He shot *Rafa*?'

Rafa was – had been – one of Ahmed Khamzaev's most trusted lieutenants.

'Yes, and for no good reason. He said that Rafa spoke out of turn.'

'Spoke out of turn?'

'Yes. And now Ahmed wants you. He says you are his right-hand man. Will you come?'

'Wait there,' said Vladimir, springing to his feet. Whatever it was, this was serious. Men like Ahmed Khamzaev did not behave this way.

'Ahmed says to bring weapons,' wailed Sergei. But his words were superfluous. Vladimir was already stuffing an Uzi, a semi-automatic pistol and several hand grenades into the pockets of his Kevlar-lined combat jacket. Plus a couple of bottles of steroids, just to be on the safe side.

❀

THE JOURNEY was a classic of modern Moscow. Since leaving Blandford's hotel the big, black Mercedes had spent an hour crawling northwards through the grey drear of the day. Snow was falling intermittently from low, oppressive clouds. A thick, dark canopy of cumulonimbus was strangling the life out of the sky. They still had a few kilometres to go before Ostankino.

If Medulev was the vigilant minder, Blandford was the tour guide. He'd been to the Ostankino complex before, and tried to fire Samuel's curiosity, if not his enthusiasm. The original structure was taller than the Empire State Building and the Sears Tower in Chicago, but had nearly burned down a few years ago, thanks to neglected maintenance following the fall of Communism. It was another monument to Soviet insecurity; the attempt to build something bigger – the architectural equivalent of schoolboys trying to piss highest up the wall.

Their chauffeur was a thickset man neatly liveried in black and reeking of an aftershave that seemed to have been modelled on toilet cleaner. Samuel wondered what was going through his mind. Probably not much. Nothing was free in the New Russia, including thought, and this guy wasn't paid to think.

Samuel scanned his *Moscow Times*. He was biding his time.

Eventually, Blandford lapsed into silence . . . *He'd been a family man once. A strong-willed wife, and a daughter who took after her mother – he'd had a tough time keeping up with them, but, ah . . . such fun, such good times. Their daughter was a party girl too. A year's down time before law at Stanford. That was the plan, her plan. Travel the world, learn some French or Italian. Maybe a little Arabic too, before heading for Australia and the Gold Coast, a little scuba and snorkelling.*

*Maybe she'd go out with a few guys Daddy didn't approve of. All that blonde hair. She liked dark guys – Mediterranean types. And they liked her.*

*'I'm going, Daddy, and that's final.'*

*He could see the look in those eyes, those clear hazel eyes that so resembled his own.*

*There was no point in arguing. She was an adult woman, and a very determined one at that. She was going. That was final. So very, very final . . .*

Blandford kept dabbing at his eyes with his handkerchief. Maybe it was the urban smog, though Samuel's own eyes were just fine.

'So . . .' Samuel broke the silence. 'This feels like an execution.'

'Don't be ridiculous, Samuel,' said Blandford instantly. 'The car might be bullet-proof, but . . .'

'No. *This* feels like an execution.'

Samuel threw the newspaper onto the seat beside him. 'You both know this boy. He's the one who flew us around yesterday, the helicopter pilot who was murdered last night. You've both been avoiding the picture and report of his death. Talk about pachyderm in the corner of the limousine! And I know who did it.'

Blandford shot him a look: 'You do?'

'Yes, I do . . . It was you, Marat Medulev, wasn't it? Just admit it.'

MEDULEV TAPPED on the glass divider, which glided gently down. He murmured a couple of words, and the bullet-headed chauffeur stepped out into the cold of the day.

Medulev turned to Samuel.

'I have seen this in movies and books. The great cliché of the English sense of humour. Now I experience first-hand. Please explain.'

'Well, why feign ignorance, Marat? You're not blind. We all saw the boy. And you disappeared at dinner at almost exactly the time this article says he was killed. On top of that, your gun suddenly wasn't on display any more. And you're an operative – one with military training. The 40th Army, right? Afghanistan?'

71

Medulev seemed genuinely amused: 'Sure, all true. But why? Because this is the modern world. This boy was probably in some drug deal and missed a payment deadline. I don't know. I don't care. I don't want to get involved. But the big why, Samuel, is why kill him? Why waste my time? Why even waste a bullet on this punk? I'm a businessman. I don't so much as fart unless there's money to be made. OK?'

Samuel let Medulev's words hang in the air a moment. From the corner of his eye, he could see that Blandford had picked up the newspaper. A slight tremor in his hand was amplified by gently waving newsprint.

'I think you owe Marat an apology, Samuel,' said Blandford. 'If we're going to have any hope of doing some business . . .'

'No need, no need.' Medulev held up a palm. 'Entertaining theory, but total bullshit. As for business, that's fine. There is a job for you to do – only you, it seems. We don't need to be friends, you and I.'

A tap at the window, and the chauffeur climbed back into the front of the car. Medulev took out a packet of cigarettes. This time he didn't ask Samuel's permission before lighting up.

# CHAPTER SIX

A WIDE, GREY-BROWN, concrete-and-steel mass loomed in front of them. The conical base of the Ostankino transmission tower suddenly filled the broad windscreen of the car. The Mercedes slewed round the road for a few moments, and eventually the burnished glass plates of Anna Barinova's business headquarters came into view.

The ABTV building was sexy New Russia to the Ostankino Tower's Old Motherland. Chrome and smoky glass panels were set at angles slightly off the true. The matrix of straight lines gave the impression of warm curves. It was an architectural joke, the converse of nature where the soft curves of the horizon gave the impression of mathematical straightness.

Medulev, who hadn't spoken a word since Samuel's outburst, cleared them through security, then left his companions with two curt nods. In moments, Samuel and Blandford were walking through a lofty, airy atrium, complete with Japanese miniature garden and tiny trickling waterfalls playing out onto intricately arranged displays of gravel.

'What was that about, Samuel?' whispered Blandford as they walked. 'You trying to get yourself killed? Or both of us?'

'You tell me,' said Samuel. They walked side by side. Samuel looked straight ahead. 'If I hadn't been certain you killed the boy, I know it now.'

'What?' Blandford stopped dead.

'Keep walking,' said Samuel. 'We have an appointment, remember? Do you take me for a fool, Blandford? You had just the same opportunity as Medulev. Plus, you were staring at the boy on the funeral trip in a way that I'd have thought, if I didn't know better, might have been gay. And then there was the "conference call" – that was actually to a Moscow number. The same number, incidentally, that called this morning – unless my memory fails me. Your angry friend nervous about something?'

'That's proof of nothing, Samuel.'

'Pretty compelling circumstance, I'd say. Plus there's the fact of your body language. You looked like *you'd* been shot when I accused Medulev. Remind me to fix a poker date with you some time. And then there's that greasy stain on your lapel. It could be from the scrambled egg you were wolfing down in such a life-affirming way this morning. But I suspect it's what the forensic boys call "body splatter". Bad manners not to change after doing messy work like that.'

'For God's sake! Even if all this were true, why protect me? And . . .'

A sideways look, 'Why would I do it?'

'Why do any of us do anything, Blandford? It's a hell of a question.'

They'd come to end of a cavernous hall of glass and wood.

'And as for why protect you? Well, Blandford, now you owe me. If I go along with whatever Peter Kempis or our hostess here has in mind, I may need your help.'

'Hello, gentlemen.'

The voice came from above. Anna Barinova was perched up in the clouds, or so it seemed. She was calling out from a couple of floors up. Her head was framed by the cinereous sky and the thick trunk of the tower disappearing into cloud. Her fingers, decked out in platinum and diamonds, rested lightly on the balustrade of the metal catwalk.

Samuel noticed that the fingernails were now a dark cerise colour. She had found time to repaint her nails since last night. Or maybe she had some flunky who came attend to her in the early hours of the day. Either way, it showed business sense: studious attention to the detail of presentation.

He waved a greeting, as did Blandford.

'Wait there,' commanded Anna. She took a glass-and-chrome blister lift. Seconds later, she was offering them her hand.

'So, gentlemen, we have business to attend to. I think first, though, you should see the operation we have built. We are serious people.' This last remark was addressed to Samuel. Was that a threat? Or was she just being polite but cool? This wasn't the Café Pushkin, after all. This was the heart of the business empire of Anna Barinova, billionairess and oligarch.

Immaculate in a dark navy dress with a plain band of white gold about her neck, she was briskness itself: 'So let's begin with the data divisions – radio, online news and television. They're all converged, of course. Most of the people we really want to reach watch what used to be called television on their laptops or their mobile phones.'

Barinova set off across the Italian marble floor at a high-speed clip. The message was clear: keep up, or fall by the wayside. She sustained a swift commentary and a fast, clicking pace – the Blahnik heels were high, steel-tipped, too – through the studios, sound booths, news rooms, conference halls, play or 'soft' areas, canteens, restaurants and crèches. ABTV was Portland, Oregon, transposed into a northern Moscow theme. Many of the male employees, Samuel noted, wore chinos and baseball caps. It was the west coast of the US not long after the turn of the century. Pretty cool, but just half a beat off today's pace. This was a nation still seeking its modern, post-Communist identity. For the moment, slavishly copying the United States would do.

'And this . . .' Anna ushered them down a corridor that led

to two huge doors of brushed aluminium and green leather. They were nearly as big as the oaken guardians of the Hotel Ukraina. 'This . . .' she pushed hard against them both, and they glided silently open, ' . . . is our financial services operation.'

They found themselves on what was effectively an observation platform. Sunk two storeys beneath them was one of the biggest and busiest factory floors Samuel had ever seen. The workers, though, were not welding or riveting – not a brown overall in sight. Suits and pencil skirts were murmuring into telephones, leaning into squawk boxes, or, if they were using headsets, walking round and expatiating into thin air. This was the heavy industry of communication.

The walls were alive with data. Electronic tickers flashed share and bond prices from every major Western and Asian market. Giant plasma screens carried audio-visual links to open-outcry exchanges, such as the London Metal Exchange, where traders in coloured jackets jostled and shouted at each other, and called it doing business. Which it was: millions exchanged hands every second.

In the centre of the well below them was a giant cross of desks, shaped diagonally like the saltire of St Andrew. This was the focal point of the room.

Anna Barinova followed Samuel's gaze: 'Those are my chiefs of staff. Each member of the senior management on the cross has control of a team – commodities, derivatives and structured products, stocks, arbitrage, bond plays of various sorts, swaps, foreign exchange and interest-rate trading. Some of the senior executives in the media and data-publishing businesses come and sit here occasionally. It keeps them sharp, and sometimes it's the only way to get – what is it you say? – *face time*.'

'Are you secretly Scottish, Anna?' asked Samuel.

He noted her look of puzzlement: 'I mean the way the desks are laid out in a flattened cross.'

She smiled: 'No, Samuel. If there is a model for the cross, it is the Russian Navy. The navy flag is the same as Scotland's, but with the colours reversed – a blue cross on a white background.'

Samuel saw Medulev two seats away from the centre of the configuration. Then he realised what it was: the set-up was just like the legendary cross of power that the junk-bond king and convicted fraudster Michael Milken set up for himself at Drexel Burnham Lambert in Los Angeles in the 1980s. The rule was that the closer you were to the centre, the more powerful you were. If so, Medulev was a pretty important player in the organisation. He was talking intently into a telephone. He glanced up as Samuel and Anna were talking, but did not acknowledge them.

At the very centre of the cross was a vacant desk. It was uncluttered by phones or the other paraphernalia that the trading 'admirals' had. A large, unoccupied chair of black leather sat next to it. The biggest in the room, it was set apart from the others as though it had its own aura. Samuel nodded in appreciation. This was Anna Barinova's throne, the dais from which the queen of Russia's capitalist army surveyed her men.

'LOOK WHAT THEY did to my beautiful boy.'

Ahmed Khamzaev tossed a printout of a police crime-scene photo onto the low coffee table. If Ahmed said it was Shamil, it assuredly was, but the thing in the photo was scarcely recognisable as human. There was a huge hole where the back of the head was supposed to be. Vladimir glanced at it and quickly looked away.

The old man was hugging himself, gripping his hands under his armpits and rocking back and forth. Vladimir had never seen him do anything more animated than swat a fly. That was why Ahmed ran such a successful operation. He was measured. He was cool. But no longer.

Ahmed Khamzaev was also unusual among Chechnyan mafia patriarchs in that he disliked ostentation. He loved the money

77

and the power, but he didn't drive around in cars like Vladimir's. The Bentley was parked in the compound a safe distance from Khamzaev's modest house.

Vladimir's Porsche Cayenne stood on its own in the walled court-yard beneath them. Stacked behind the mirrored windows was a riot of clothing, mostly fatigues, thick socks, a couple of balaclavas, and a spare pair of boots. There were a couple of bags of arms and ammunition, a big cardboard box full of dried fruit, tinned meat, nuts, vitamin supplements and a few small bottles of steroids. These last bore labels covered with US government health warnings. But Vladimir didn't care. He didn't speak much English, though he was able to parrot a few phrases he'd picked up from war movies such as *Full Metal Jacket* and – his favourites – the *Rocky* series.

Vladimir wondered if he'd packed everything he'd need. He'd need quite a lot, that was for sure. He looked warily back at Ahmed, who was still rocking back and forth like a professional mourner at a Beirut funeral. The legendary enforcer of Grozny was suddenly wizened, old . . . mad.

But he was still head of his clan, and Vladimir owed Ahmed; he allowed Vladimir to run his security consultancy pretty much unhindered. Providing, of course that Vladimir understood that his good fortune was something he should share with friends and protectors like Khamzaev. If Khamzaev said Vladimir was his right-hand man, that was a compliment, one that had to be accepted. He must demonstrate total loyalty and devotion. To do otherwise was to risk ending up like the unfortunate Rafa.

'Here, Vladimir. Take.' The old man abruptly stopped rocking, and tossed a big brown envelope onto the table.

Vladimir stooped to pick it up. The slow fire of the steroids was beginning to burn within him. He could feel the desire for action welling up. With it came a kind of unfocused fury, a general rage at the idiocy of the world and the weakness of its people. It would be good to punish them.

The envelope contained two thick wads of notes – roubles and dollars – and a piece of paper with two names on it.

'Who are these people?' asked Vladimir.

'I want you to be the instrument of vengeance, Vladimir. I want you to be the angel of death. You can be a one-man jihad.'

'But who are they, Ahmed?'

'One is a police officer. He emailed this atrocity this morning.' Khamzaev gestured at the photo of his dead son. 'You need to go to Moscow to see him, get all the detail you can, find Shamil's killers and destroy them, inshallah.'

Vladimir wondered whether Khamzaev was losing it. If his clan detected weakness in the old man, he would be dead soon.

'And the other?'

'The Moscow policeman gave me his name. A Westerner made a call from the place where Shamil fell, according to the police satellite trace. He must have been there. Also, he is a typical user of whores and all the decadent excesses of his culture, according to our police contact. This man should be easy enough to find, just go to the shittiest and most expensive hellhole in town. You can kill him, if you want to. I don't like Westerners.'

Vladimir turned the paper over in his hand. It would be good to get hold of one of those smug Western bastards who thought they knew everything, and sat back as Russia, whether you included Chechnya in that or not, just exploded. He would find this guy and torture him, whether he knew anything or not. Yeah, nice and slow.

But there was a problem. If Vladimir didn't speak much English, he certainly didn't read it.

'Hmm. How do you say this second one? It's not written in Cyrillic.'

Ahmed extended a hand, took the note and spelled it out – 'S-p-e-n-d . . . L-o-v-e'.

'AND THIS IS my daughter, Ksenia Barinova.'

'How do you do, Mr Spendlove? Please call me Ksenia.'

Two thoughts struck Samuel simultaneously. The first was that Ksenia Barinova was heart-stoppingly beautiful. The second was that her mother must be older than he thought. Ksenia was at least twenty-one. So Anna Barinova must be in her middle forties at least.

'A pleasure. Call me Samuel, please.'

Ksenia sat opposite him at an oval-shaped steel-and-glass boardroom table. She had eyes of a vivid, extraordinary green – emerald to her mother's sapphire. Her cheekbones were just as high, the face as devastatingly heart-shaped. And whereas her mother was beautifully preserved, Ksenia had the lustre of youth. Samuel was aware that Anna Barinova was watching him very carefully – perhaps coolly. She must have seen many men react to her daughter. Many of them must have melted – would the mother then think them weak, vulnerable, foolish?

The ceiling lights in the boardroom had an apricot glow, and the pale duck-egg blue of the frosted glass walls created a feeling of harmony and balance. Yet mayhem was just a flimsy partition away: all they had to do was stand up and look through the clear glass at the top of the wall and they would see the ordered chaos and the intensity of the trading floor below.

Ksenia took a sip of sparkling water.

'Here, Samuel.'

He picked up an embossed business card from the tabletop. Ksenia had the somewhat grandiose job title of 'President of Sustainable Investments'.

'It's my role to drag ABTV into the twenty-first century. I want us to invest in sustainable technologies and to use suppliers who have enlightened business practices in human resources – and who are sensitive to their ecological impact on this fragile planet of ours.'

Anna Barinova cleared her throat. Ksenia glanced at her sharply.

'Energy is an area of great interest to us. Russia is fortunate. We have many natural resources. We're all in agreement on that.'

Ksenia seemed to be talking directly to her mother now, almost daring her to dissent. She turned back to Samuel.

'It falls to my generation to exploit those resources in the best possible way. We need to make the most of them while paying attention to the world's pressing ecological problems.'

Samuel thought of the beautiful, toxic columns of smoke in the freezing Moscow sky, and nodded.

'We have an ancient and dangerous stock of nuclear power plants, and we are already responsible for the nuclear disaster at Chernobyl. There must be no more.'

'I think that's great, Ksenia,' said Samuel. 'Impossible to disagree with. But this company you and your mother are interested in – I don't see quite where it fits in.'

'It's actually really important.' Ksenia spoke quickly. 'They've developed a drilling technique, a new way of extracting oil. If the technology can really do what the company claims, then we've found a way of getting access to oil reserves, which previously couldn't be exploited. Drilling for oil is an ancient business by the standards of the modern world. What excites me, though, is that we can perhaps do it in a much more efficient way. If we can exploit what we've got more effectively, it means we don't have to drill more oil fields and create havoc with the ecosystem quite so soon. And, if we can extract more from the existing oilfields, then we will have bought more time to develop alternative energy sources.'

Anna pointed to the news wires and television channels on her wall-mounted high-definition screens: 'High oil prices create problems. See CNBC? "Markets toil as oil spot climbs." See AFX TV there? "Hunger marches in Baltimore." C-Span? A speech from another lunatic isolationist senator wanting to outlaw foreign ownership of US banks. The Americans sucked up spare capital from the Middle and Far East when credit was short. Now the Asians and the Arabs are flexing their muscles and the Homeland protectionists didn't like it one bit. See there? Top right? This guy gets it.'

BBC World carried scrolling quotes from US senator, Bob Zeffman, who was threatening to join the presidential campaign as an independent lobbying for lower oil prices. Oil was down from the peak of $150 per barrel, but Zeffman was saying it could and should be kept well under $100, or 'the world economy would just blow up'.

Samuel looked from one to the other. 'You make a compelling double act. Stabilise the markets – and buy breathing space to develop new technologies. But . . .'

He could see Blandford hovering in his peripheral vision. The guy had more or less confessed to murder. Medulev clearly saw lives as bargaining chips in business deals. He was done with cloaks and daggers after Paris – surely it would be better to cut and run?

Anna sensed his diffidence.

'Tell me, Samuel. After you abandoned me so abruptly last night I was left to wonder what was in Kempis's note. Do tell.'

'I'm assuming you haven't read it, Anna.'

This elicited a look of wounded innocence. 'Well, I fear Peter at the last was too obscure for his own good. He sent me a Latin riddle that didn't make much sense – stuff about bubbles and bubble markets.'

'Ha! But that's just what we want you to explore!' said Ksenia. She looked as though she'd just opened a surprise birthday present.

'I think it's what Kempis wanted you to examine, Samuel,' said Anna. 'I think we all want the same thing.'

Samuel held his hands up. Maybe Blandford was right. Maybe

he'd been wanting to do this all along, wanting the game of wit, the sometimes painful challenge of using his memory to the full, the test of courage. Maybe this is what Kempis wanted to remind him of.

'OK, OK, but I have a number of conditions.'

'Such as?' Anna was all focus.

'First, this is a one-off. We're close to the line here – legal, moral and practical. I'm not a performing animal in anyone's circus – even yours. I want a quiet life. So no more special requests. Please. Agreed?' Both women nodded.

'And second, I really don't want any money from this. I've got a bursary from William Barton and, as you said last night, he's interested in what you're doing. If you decide to take the company over, you can reward him by giving his educational foundation a slice of the deal. I'll be beholden to no one.'

'Of course, I accept your terms, Samuel. Excellent news. Deal done,' said Anna, standing up and shaking Samuel's hand.

'Not quite, Mother,' said Ksenia. 'I have a couple of conditions of my own. First, Samuel – does your memory work with Cyrillic script? There'll be a lot of that, and plenty of mathematical symbols, too.'

Samuel shook his head slowly. 'You're asking me this now? Whether I'm good enough to do you a favour?'

'Not just me.'

'Yes. I get it. For the greater good of the world and his wife. Sorry, husband.'

Samuel grabbed a desktop copy of *Izvestiya*, and frowned over it for a moment. Ksenia opened her mouth to speak, but Anna held up a silencing forefinger. Samuel then closed the newspaper. Taking a piece of paper and a pen, he lent forward over Anna's desk and began to write.

'Here,' he said, two minutes later, as he handed the A4 sheet to Ksenia. She peered at it.

'What's this?' she said at length. 'Whatever it is, it's not Russian.'

Samuel smiled. 'Maybe we should say it doesn't seem to be what it really is – pretty much like everything else. Here. May I, Anna?'

Samuel picked up a compact mirror lying on Anna's desk, and offered it to Ksenia. 'Look in the mirror.'

Ksenia picked up the mirror, as Samuel held the paper to it at an oblique angle. 'Wow!' she squealed. 'You've transcribed the article in mirror-writing! That's amazing!' Then: 'You did do it on purpose . . . right?'

Samuel raised an eyebrow.

'So what was your second condition?'

'OK. Point taken, Samuel. I'm impressed. So, my second condition . . .? It's financial. I'll take the fee you're kindly waiving and invest it in one of the companies we're incubating to develop a super-efficient solar panel system. Agreed?'

'Agreed.'

'Agreed, Mother?'

Anna sighed slightly. 'Very well. Now, Samuel, you'll need some background reading ahead of your appointment with this company.'

She reached into her desk, and produced a fat file.

'Tortoiseshell Technology – background. Please read. Ksenia will brief you later. '

'Great news, Samuel,' said Blandford. 'You won't regret this.'

But something told Samuel that he just might.

# CHAPTER SEVEN

SILVER BIRCHES. There were millions and millions of them, their trunks like shiny, skinny fingers reaching up and imploring the sky for a favour they were never going to get.

Vladimir swallowed dryly, and opened another can of high-protein vegetable juice. The buzzing, burning feeling wasn't quite so intense, but it was still there. He blinked hard, and tried to concentrate on the road ahead. He'd been plunging westward for what seemed like days. He was in too much of a rush for snow chains, and anyway the weather wasn't that bad. The heavy tread of the snow tyres had kept him on the road at a reasonable speed.

He was back on the steroids, and he'd forgotten to take his morning dose. He flexed and unflexed, flexed and unflexed his forearms. The rear end of the Cayenne began to fishtail in the snow and ice. Vladimir took his foot off the accelerator. The car's tail swung in line obediently once more.

Ahead. He had to think straight ahead. Moscow was straight ahead. All he had to do was get there, meet the policeman, find the Westerner. The rest would come easily enough.

Vladimir checked his eyes in the mirror. The pupils were still quite dilated, despite the unusually high luminosity inside the car. The snow was bouncing huge, dizzying quantities of light around. Steady now. He would get to Moscow. Straight ahead. Nice and steady.

'HERE WE ARE,' said Ksenia. She turned to the receiver set into the panel on her left and issued a short command to their driver. Ksenia's car of choice was a Toyota hybrid, but she still had the liveried chauffeur and tinted windows that every smart modern Muscovite required. They slid sleekly to a halt. 'It's just around the corner.'

Samuel looked out onto the street. They were just off Taganskya Square, in what Ksenia said had been the fashion district before the Revolution. So far as Samuel could tell, fashions in Moscow winter hadn't changed much in centuries: you trapped something feral and furry, skinned it, and then you wore the pelt. Although some of the women he could see on the street in their ankle-length sables and minks had presumably skipped the early parts of that process with clever use of platinum and matt-black American Express cards.

'So, Samuel, you are up to speed on Tortoiseshell Technology?'

'As much as I probably need to be for your purposes, Ksenia.'

Over the forty-five minutes they had spent together on the back seat of the Mercedes, Ksenia had been reading chunks of text out loud from a file explaining the basic principles of physics on which the revolutionary drilling techniques of Tortoiseshell Technology were based.

Samuel had been impressed by Ksenia's intelligence and energy. She'd quoted Bernoulli's principle, which stated that in a fluid where no work was being performed, an increase in velocity occurs at the same time as a decrease in pressure or a change in that fluid's gravitational potential energy.

Ksenia had the idealism of youth, but now that she'd got Samuel on board, she was checking him out like a veteran businesswoman.

'My mother tells me you have a fantastic memory, that you don't need to understand what you read to recall it, but I believe understanding is everything. Are you sure you were listening properly?'

'Hmm. How's this? The principle you just recited has lots of implications,' said Samuel. 'One very important consequence is that if an object moves through a fluid, and that could be air, water or oil, it is subject to drag. But if the object moves sufficiently fast, the fluid's pressure drops.'

'Correct,' she nodded enthusiastically. 'That's why marine engineers have always had difficulty driving boats as fast as they'd like. The faster a propeller moves, the lower the pressure around it. So a really fast-moving propeller in water doesn't purchase on the water as well as it might, because it actually drives the surrounding fluid away, in a sense.'

Samuel continued, 'In fact, if the propeller is shaped a certain way, it can create a bubble or shell.'

*'Let the buyer of bubbles beware.'* Kempis's Latin tease was a little clearer after his day's research. But not much. All that stuff about Joseph bearing light not milk didn't make sense at all. Unless there was some deep, hidden joke about Lucifer, bearer of light?

Ksenia was closing her file now, clearly comforted: 'And Tortoiseshell Technology has devised a drilling method based on that fact. It claims that it's found a way of super-fast drilling that allows the capture of far more oil and gas than conventional methods.'

'So it's my mission, should I choose to accept it – and I do seem to have done just that . . .' Samuel looked at her and tried to affect a certain gloominess. 'It's my mission to read and memorise the mathematics and the engineering data that is the proof of their claim.'

'Precisely. You are my star researcher.' She smiled sweetly at him.

'Ksenia, you're turning me into a spy.' Samuel smiled right back.

'Nonsense, Samuel. Freedom-fighter or terrorist? Researcher or spy? It all depends who writes the history. What we're doing is for a good cause. You give us the information, and we distribute it freely, rather than let this company hoard it for its own profit. Why should one company make billions of dollars from licenses while the planet dies?'

She looked out of the window at the eighteenth-century splendour of the former fashion district.

'Taganskaya Square used to be the cutting edge, you know. In the old days, when my mother was young . . .' Ksenia's dainty forefinger was tracing sine curves on the condensation of the window pane '. . . it was here that we got as close as the Communist Party allowed to what you would probably call the *avant garde*. Theatre directors used to put on illegal productions of old plays in a cellar underneath here. They used to make fun of the dinosaurs in the Politburo. It was bold in its way – politically and sexually. Of course, the actors and directors couldn't be openly homosexual. Nearly all of them were gay, but if it became known, they would be sent to mental hospitals or the gulag.' Ksenia sighed.

Samuel looked up and spelled out the name on a street sign: '*Bolshaya Kommunisticheskaya Ulitsa* – Big Communist Street?'

Ksenia nodded. 'Where the theatre used to be. Now it's an elite club for businessmen.'

'The theatre's become a drinking club? That's probably the best joke of the lot.'

Ksenia had stopped her window doodling. Her ice-green eyes homed in on Samuel. 'Our freedom has not bred lightness of being. That's Czech intellectual crap. What it's created is obviousness and a need to consume things as a means of feeling good about ourselves. We Russians, we are good people, but we live in an ideological and spiritual vacuum. For now, we are defined by the brand names of the things we consume – Diesel, Kentucky Fried Chicken, Gucci, Baskin Robbins, Estee Lauder, Krispy Kreme Donuts, Benetton, Zara, Thierry Lacroix . . . *Goldman Sachs*.'

'So why are you and your mother making such a big deal about this technology, Ksenia? It's not a high-street brand. It's not going to enslave the populace to consumerism.'

'I know what you're thinking, Samuel. My mother and I think differently on most things. In fact, we have competed in most areas ever since my father died, and that was eighteen years ago. But this is one thing we agree on.'

A Hummer, a Jaguar and a BMW – all with gangster-specification black coachwork, bullet-proof windows, chrome spoilers – slid along the street.

'Listen, Samuel,' Ksenia said, 'Once we have the technology, we will exploit it much more effectively than a small company would be able to – and the whole world will benefit.'

'So I'm not a spy, but an eco-warrior. Correct?'

'Correct.' A sly grin.

'In that case, why did we pull up around the corner?' asked Samuel.

'Don't you know the great rule of the FSB? That's the same as the KGB or NKVD or Cheka, or maybe ABTV in today's world?'

'Actually, no. It's not a world that interests me,' said Samuel.

'Ah, but you are part of it, my friend. You may not like it, but once you get in, you're always on the map, always surveyed.'

'Thanks for that,' sighed Samuel. It was beginning to snow again outside. 'So?'

'So don't interfere, just read the intelligence. That's the rule. You, the impartial conduit to the wider world, the innocent researcher, you don't appear at the door in a chauffeur-driven Mercedes. That would shape the reaction of the people in there. I want a full report, not just the shapes you remember.'

'There's something of your mother in you, Ksenia.'

'Maybe,' she said. 'But I say please and thank you.'

Samuel looked at her, and blinked for a moment, trying to block out the simple fact of her beauty. 'OK,' he said at length, opening the car door. 'Here we go. Mission Improbable. See you in an hour or so, all being well. And if I get this right, don't forget to say thank you.'

❧

'YES?' BLANDFORD PICKED up the phone and sat on the bed in his Kempinski hotel room. The lamp-lit bridge, the river and the jostling, multicoloured onion domes of St Basil's filled the window frame opposite. It was beautiful, but the colours and shapes had no resonance for Blandford; everything was grey, drained of splendour, meaningless.

'Kingston? Meet me in the bar downstairs. I'm ready for one of Moscow's most expensive cocktails. You should be too.'

'Marat?'

'Who else?' asked Medulev. 'What will you have? A vodka Martini made with the finest French vodka? Or maybe an Absolut Citron? Swedish vodka, French name. I recommend highly.'

Blandford looked about him. The cathedral was bathed in sumptuous golden light. Cars sped across the bridge towards the Kremlin as though fleeing the cold. His room was huge, well-appointed, and had one of the best city views on the planet. And yet none of it pleased him.

'Blandford? Are you still there?' called Medulev.

'Yes, yes. I'll be down,' said Blandford softly.

'Absolut Citron it is,' said Medulev. 'Your man has gone away to do the deed today. If he gets what we need, it's bonus time!'

'OK,' said Blandford even more quietly than before. 'See you in five.'

He replaced the receiver, and began searching for his shoes. There was a knock at his door. He opened carefully. A slender man in a suit was standing in the corridor.

'I wasn't expecting you until tomorrow. Medulev is waiting for me downstairs,' Blandford said in a near-whisper.

'Do what you have to do. I'll wait for you here,' said the man, pushing his way into Blandford's room.

THE OFFICES OF Tortoiseshell Technology were not what Samuel was expecting. Instead of a bold, chrome-and-glass statement of New Russian bullishness, he discovered an ancient chocolate box of soft browns, crushed, dark-red velvets, ornate gilded furniture, and a variety of vermilion, black and grape-purple drapes and sashes.

The reception area could have served as a museum of early twentieth-century antiques. A pale-pine grandfather clock, proclaiming its date and place of manufacture as 1915, Novgorod, ticked solemnly in the far corner of the large, high-ceilinged room. Art-deco bookcases boasted an array of literature ranging from leather-bound copies of Bertolt Brecht's plays, to the inevitable volumes of Pushkin, faded green and cream paperbacks of approved Socialist Realist writers of the 1930s, and a large and impressive ring-bound collection of the papers of the New York Geological Society. The series ran from 1945, the end of the Second World War – or the Great Patriotic War, as the Russians referred to it – to 1982, the year that Brezhnev died. Politics, Samuel reflected, was the heart and soul of Communist Russia, even affecting library subscriptions. A change of Secretary General, and an apparatchik's book funds dry up . . . Power dominated everything, intruded into every decision, just as money had always done in the West.

'Dr Yavlinsky will see you now,' said a voice behind Samuel. He whirled round.

A pretty young woman with pale-grey eyes and blonde hair tied back in a bun offered a flattened-out professional smile. She was sitting at an escritoire sandwiched between a gramophone with a huge brass trumpet for a speaker, and a bank of ancient Bakelite radios in rich, pearly clarets, marbled blues and smoky yellows.

'I'm sorry. I didn't see you there.'

'Don't worry,' she said. 'It often happens. Our visitors like to browse among the old things in reception. It makes the new technology all the more exciting.' She got up. 'Follow me, please.'

She wore a tight-fitting business suit in dark grey with a pencil skirt and padded shoulders. She reminded Samuel of old photos of the power suits of 1980s London. The overall effect would have been quite severe, were it not for her youth. She had the confident strut of a catwalk model, and a certain playfulness beneath the office mannerisms. As she walked past a harpsichord, her fingers brushed along the keyboard. She looked back over her shoulder and smiled again.

Samuel grinned back. What was it with Russian women? They were quite extraordinarily serious, but coquettish at the same time.

She pushed open the door for him, and stood aside.

Viktor Yavlinsky was tall and slim. Exceptionally tall, in fact. His long legs stretched out beneath the desk, on which he appeared to be playing chess against himself. His thin face was hardly lined, but the eyes were somewhat bulbous, magnified by a pair of thick-lensed spectacles. The frames, Samuel noted, were tortoiseshell.

Yavlinsky seemed quite young, though he dressed like a Soviet intellectual of the 1950s. He sported a yellowy-brown tweed suit, with a V-necked dark jumper of fine wool beneath, a blue-and-white checked shirt, and a narrow tie of a shiny black material that might have been woven nylon. To complete the effect of a thirty-year-old going on fifty, his hair was swept back and pomaded.

Yavlinsky rose, a motion that seemed to take a long time. When he was fully unfurled Samuel realised just how tall he was – perhaps as much as six foot seven.

'Mr Spendlove,' he said in heavily accented English. 'We are pleased you came.' *We?* Samuel glanced quickly around the room to confirm that they were alone. They were. Yavlinsky telescoped out a hand. 'Have a seat.'

He nodded at the chessboard. 'Do you play?'

'I used to. But then I realised chess can take over the personality.'

Yavlinsky nodded, an impressively large, rocking movement that seemed to come from the waist up.

'Yes, yes, it can. You are familiar with Marcel Duchamp, the surrealist?'

'You mean the bicycle-wheel exhibitor? The urinal installer? I know his work, if that's the correct term.'

'I take your point. He gave it all up to play chess, which he said was a sport – a violent sport. But it's much more than that. It is an art form, a combination of pieces attacking the opponent's king in the white fire of sacrifice . . . This is a gesture of the soul.'

'So I take it that you play regularly, Dr Yavlinsky?'

'No. Like you, I find it too time-consuming. But I do like to play through the great games of the past, to study and compare the styles of the Soviet grandmasters.' He waved a hand at a small book on the table. 'This position was achieved by one of the greats, Mikhail Botvinnik. He was not a cavalier over the board, but he was a wonderful strategist, teasing out tiny positional advantages into winning positions. I think his style was a perfect metaphor for the Cold War . . . A drink?'

Samuel noticed an exquisite art-deco cocktail cabinet of mother of pearl and frosted Lalique-style glass.

'No, thanks. I'm not thirsty.'

'Thirsty?' Yavlinsky looked at him quizzically. 'In Russia we don't drink because we are thirsty, Mr Spendlove.' Yavlinsky opened up the cabinet and poured himself a small glass of bright-green liquid.

Yavlinsky looked at Samuel, took out a second glass, but did not pour it. He crossed back to the desk and re-folded himself back into position opposite Samuel.

'Now, where was I?'

'Botvinnik's positional play, and how it was a metaphor for Cold War geopolitical strategy, I think,' said Samuel.

'Ah, yes. Well, fortunately, that's all over. In a sense, anyway.'

Samuel let the moment pass.

'The battles are different now,' continued Yavlinsky. 'No chest-beating with nuclear weapons, no annual military exercises with a build-up of troops that comes closer and closer to the frontier with the West every year. All this is good, of course.' He took a sip from the thimble of emerald liquid. 'But strategically, the conflict remains the same. In the West, there are many who want power and control over us here in Russia. We have one third of the world's supplies of natural gas and oil, yet those fools in the nineties signed most of it away.'

'And is this why you have developed this new drilling system? To enrich Russia?'

Yavlinsky paused, then laughed – an improbably high, fluted sound: 'No, no, Mr Spendlove. We are designing this to be a perfect process. This is the marriage of the intellectual and the practical. Yes, of course, we have to make *money*. But that is merely a game we must play. Our battle is to find the capital to take things further here, and to do so without giving control of our ideas and our company to the scaly-backed predators in suits who call themselves investment bankers.'

'Well, I'm not one of those, Dr Yavlinsky. Nor am I a scientist. Nor yet an engineer. But I have an interest in ideas.'

'You are better than that, Mr Spendlove. As a researcher for William Barton and the XB Foundation, yours is a voice of authority in isolation. You are the intelligent generalist. Our work is also being examined by an eminent mathematician and an internationally renowned engineer. Your opinion, combined with theirs, will carry the weight we need.'

'Which is sufficient weight to raise capital?'

'Precisely. As a quoted company on the Moscow bourse, we can either issue another tranche of shares to finance this project to completion or we can simply borrow against the future income that we are going to generate. We don't need outsiders. I'm delighted to hear that William Barton is interested in our company. Just the sort of investor we'd be happy to welcome.'

'Really? Why?'

'Well, your brief is to research, is it not? To think for a living? '

'I suppose so. Now, what are you going to show me?'

Yavlinsky considered his chess game.

'Botvinnik was a genius, you know. He used to squeeze the life out of his victims. He would crush them to death from lack of space. A boa constrictor of the chessboard.'

Samuel cocked his head to one side, a gesture of enquiry.

'Ah, forgive me. Chess . . . takes over the personality. Indeed. So . . . We have to place considerable restrictions on what the mathematician and the engineer can see, for obvious reasons. We give them discrete modules of research that are verifiable within their area of expertise, but are of little practical use without the knowledge that the other person has. It's an old idea taken from the bad old days of the Cold War – you run an intelligence cell as a series of spokes round a hub of knowledge. Each spoke hardly knows of the existence of the other, if at all. Its only connection is with the centre.

'My plan for you, Mr Spendlove . . .' Yavlinsky consulted his book and made a bishop move. 'From a series of World Championship training games in 1954 . . .'

Samuel waited quietly. If Yavlinsky wanted him to fill the gaps in the conversation, he would be disappointed. What was that phrase? That which is freely given cannot be taken. Yavlinsky had to give him what he wanted. He could not take it.

'Yes . . . You can be a weak hub, Mr Spendlove. You can be the hub that is incapable of supporting the spokes because – please forgive the frankness of my words, but the science is really quite complex – because of your lack of knowledge.'

'Which means?'

'As the intelligent layman from the big research foundation, you can see the overview and as much detail on any given area that you wish. Much of the mathematics and the engineering proposals is supported by pages and pages of interminable equations and theory. You are welcome to see these too, if you really wish.'

'As I said, I am no mathematician, nor yet an engineer. But to have sight of everything is extremely important.'

'Very well.'

He jabbed at an intercom.

'Svetlana? The big documentation, please.'

Svetlana of the golden bun hairstyle appeared wheeling a trolley loaded with four large cardboard boxes.

'Are you sure you want to read all these?' asked Yavlinsky, grinning slightly.

'I want to feel I *can* read them if I so wish,' said Samuel.

'Very well. In fact, it's not as bad as it looks. The documents are replicated in English and Russian, and the mathematics will be hieroglyphs to you, no?' Yavlinsky looked sharply at Samuel.

'Meaningless shapes, I'm afraid,' said Samuel.

Yavlinsky sucked in a large breath, then nodded.

'I must say something in a way that I hope is not discourteous: these files, they must remain here, all of them. Under no circumstances are you to take any of the papers you are about to see out of this room.'

'Of course, Dr Yavlinsky. I may ask for a pen and paper to take a few anodyne notes, which I undertake to show you. Other than that, I promise you I won't remove a single piece of paper belonging to you or your company.'

'Thank you. And I apologise for my clumsiness, but the information is sensitive. I recommend you address the executive summaries first. The supporting detail is in the various files. You'll find it's all correctly cross-referenced.'

'Excellent,' said Samuel, and began to open the first box. He had no need of pen and paper, of course, but Yavlinsky would find the request reassuring.

Svetlana had deposited the four boxes in the corner of the room, next to a chintzy, dark brown chaise longue. Something else that looked as though it belonged in a nineteenth-century brothel.

Samuel crossed to it and sat down.

'Here you are, sir,' she said, handing him a file. 'This is the first of the executive summaries.'

Samuel began to read: *'This research emerged from a case study of underwater cavitator analysis. It is a study of the changing characteristics of supercavities, whose length and shape, it has been determined, are a function of flow field as modified by cavitator nose shape and acuity. The relationship between these curves as affected by time discretization was postulated using an integral equation method . . .'*

It was difficult to understand, but not that difficult. The shape and size of the bubbles that occurred when a fast-moving object cut through oil, water or air was affected by the shape and speed of the object, be it plane or boat propeller or drilling tool. At least that's what Samuel thought it all meant. But that mattered hardly at all. He looked at the shapes of the words and drank them in.

He'd been reading for over an hour when Yavlinsky, who had been quietly whistling at Botvinnik's genius all the while, again offered him a draught of green liqueur. The Russian seemed disappointed when Samuel declined, and asked for coffee.

Samuel began reading the summary of a sub-section on vertical vortex flow at hydraulic intakes. The argument ran that fluid particles – he had to keep reminding himself that could be air, water or oil – flowed spirally from the surface of the fluid to its interior, in the manner of a screw's thread: *'If one assumes axisymmetric conditions can apply to this phenomenon, the vertical vortex would change in both radial and axial directions . . .'*

Samuel rubbed his eyes. There was a large capital Greek sigma, and couple of underscored Roman Vs – unit vectors and, he thought, a k-vector symbol that seemed . . . what? Out of place? They were last-minute additions, almost scratched in. But this wasn't Keats or Shelley, altering an ode by quill on a publisher's proof, this was peer-reviewed documented science, patented process . . . Something felt wrong. But all he could do – for now, at least – was capture the data in front of him. He leant forward again.

*'Results during tests proved this to be the case, and the formulae that were derived achieved a significant breakthrough, offering the first modern verification of the previously discounted claims of the Hungaro-Canadian pioneer of supercavitation engineering, Josef Papp . . .'*

A blue-and-white mug of steaming coffee arrived on Samuel's desk.

'Here you are,' said Yavlinsky. 'How's it going? Have you found what you want? I am impressed by your powers of concentration, Mr Spendlove. What is the word you use? Focus?'

'Well, there's a lot here, Dr Yavlinsky. It requires concentration,' said Samuel, sipping at the coffee. It was hot, black and sweet, Russian style. Samuel was glad of the hit from the caffeine and the sugar.

His eye rested on a name that made his pulse quicken for a reason he didn't quite understand. Papp? Josef Papp? Why was something telling him that this Papp, whoever he was, was significant?

Samuel shut his eyes, and called up the image of Kempis's note once more. Of course! It was all in the *casing*, Upper and lower . . . *Pectus*, indeed . . .

'Excuse me? Casing?'

'Ah. Apologies, Dr Yavlinsky. I was thinking aloud. An occasional side-effect of deep concentration.'

Samuel had made himself unpopular in more than one university library by blurting out the occasional key word, the bridge for a big association of ideas.

'If I were to go to a shrink, I'd probably be diagnosed with mild Aspergers or Tourette's syndrome. But being, like you, a fan of the marriage of the intellectual with the practical, I find it's better just to keep my mouth shut as much as possible.'

Samuel sipped at his drink once more, as if to reassure Yavlinsky that he wasn't mad.

Yavlinsky gave a high-pitched giggle. 'Yes, we citizens of the life of the mind have it hard. Giving voice to ideas is a good thing – providing you don't do it too often. Are you finding what you want?'

Samuel put his mug down. He was beginning to like this fellow, which, in some ways, was almost a shame: 'Yes, Dr Yavlinsky, I really think I'm beginning to get there.'

# CHAPTER EIGHT

'HERE YOU ARE, Mr Spendlove.'

The waitress, dressed in a Burberry catsuit for reasons unknown, stopped at their table and deposited large cocktail glasses full to the brim with transparent fluid and beaded with cold.

Blandford smiled, and handed the girl a wad of roubles.

'He's still in there – the real Spendlove, I mean,' said Medulev, snapping his mobile shut. He looked across the table at Blandford. They were in a very crowded bar. 'At least, I think that's what Anna said. It's very difficult to hear.'

'Who?' shouted Blandford.

'Spendlove. He's still in there. He's been reading for hours. Of course, he's here too, buying drinks in cash.'

Blandford nodded and shrugged slightly. The irony hadn't escaped him: the only person who'd accused him of the boy's execution was his cover name. Still, he'd keep it up for now. The man waiting for him in his room required nothing less than careful cover. Otherwise, he'd be tempted to confess all to Medulev – who saw the accusation of murder as a joke, a detail, the equivalent of a clerk mislaying a file. How many men must Medulev have killed?

They were hemmed in on all sides by the usual crowd: beautiful women with an X-ray vision for fat wallets, the male, menopausal Eurotrash business set, self-consciously trendy Muscovites and a liberal sprinkling of very thickset men in mirror shades.

Shatush, an ultra-slick restaurant and bar on Gogolevsky Boulevard, was pretty impressive even to Blandford's jaded eye. The bottom half of the main bar was illuminated by a neon blue light. The area above was cloaked in red. To look at the two blocks of colour from a distance one had the impression of a lightly electrified London bus sinking into a phosphorescent nocturnal sea.

Not that Blandford cared. Moscow felt like one big whorehouse to him – one that he and others like him were propping up with their money and false jollity. He was beginning to feel that he was the biggest whore of them all.

Just centimetres away, three women were on the bar top, gyrating to the music. Blandford had never heard of techno-funk, but he quite liked it. There was a Chinese girl wearing a tiny black bikini, her long dark hair flew in a whirlpool around her as she bumped and ground along with the music. Next to her was a black woman in a silver thong and acid-swirl patterns of gold body paint that emphasised the curves of her naked breasts; a white girl with long blonde hair was dancing nearest to the two men. The white girl at first seemed to be wearing a tight-fitting pinstripe suit. But Blandford soon realised that in fact she was naked, apart from a pair of stilettos, a large Homburg hat and body paint, artfully applied to give the impression of suit, shirt and tie. She was dancing just above Blandford. Her pubes had been shaved. But perhaps not that recently, judging from the just-discernible golden stubble. Nice touch – in theory. Blandford stared at the girl's crotch. *That*. He was supposed to want that. But it was an effort to remember.

'It's smoky in here,' Blandford shouted against the hubbub. He dabbed at his eyes again with his handkerchief. They'd been quietly streaming all night, well before they came into the hot, heavy atmosphere of Shatush. 'Shall we find a booth?'

They moved out of the bar through the main dining room. The room was divided by intricately carved Chinese black-lacquer screens, but all the more discreet compartments were taken. They moved on through the hookah hall, where tobaccos flavoured with apple, strawberry and other, stranger fruits and scents were being smoked. Eventually, they found a booth that was invitingly empty and plumped themselves down on fat, burgundy-coloured satin cushions.

A waitress came and took their order. Medulev asked her for a bottle of Absolut Citron and a bucket of ice. He had decided that this was Blandford's drink.

'Well, my friend, what shall we do? Anna is still working on her mystery deal. Ksenia is waiting for Spendlove to finish at Tortoiseshell. It seems advanced mechanical mathematics is more challenging than menus and wine lists.'

'I don't know, Marat. What do you want to do?' Blandford felt the liquor hot and viscous at the back of his throat. The elation of the kill was long gone. He had his revenge. The image of the boy's shattered cranium came back to him time and again. There was no more pleasure, but neither was there revulsion or guilt. It was just a thing he recalled, another pointless image, a picture in a stranger's photograph album.

'Come on, let's get laid,' said Medulev. 'When was the last time you had a good fuck? I'll find you a nice Russian girl. What do you say, Kingston?'

'I don't care, Marat. I'm tired. But I'll come with you if you want.'

'That's it, tovarish!' Medulev slapped Blandford's knee. 'We'll soon have you in the right frame of mind.'

Three hours later, Blandford and Medulev were sitting on a large, apricot-coloured sofa in the suite that Medulev had booked them into for a few hours. On the coffee table in front of them was a bottle of Grey Goose in an ice bucket, an array of Baltika 6 beer bottles (Medulev had ordered domestic beer, somewhat surprisingly) and two large sachets of cocaine.

Medulev had procured – there really was no other word for it – two of the dancers from the bar top. Blandford, neutral, uninterested, had already watched as the Chinese girl had carefully laid out a line of cocaine, and then snorted it with a crisp five-hundred-rouble note. They didn't have sex of any sort afterwards, just sat back and gulped down vodka. Everything seemed banal, ordinary, flattened out.

Medulev had his arm round the Chinese girl now. The black girl sat in between Medulev and Blandford. She was from New Jersey, and unlike her colleague, who hailed from Shanghai, had no particular interest in drugs, or the company of the two men, or very much at all, it seemed. Blandford liked her, in so far as he liked anyone or anything any more. Medulev had got hold of some nice New Russian girls all right – from Shanghai and New Jersey.

Medulev leaned forward and pushed a button on a boombox.

'OK, baby. Let's go,' he said in English. A thin, auburn-haired hooker standing at the far side of the room began to twist and turn to a high-tempo electro beat. She was another New Russian – from Lithuania, apparently. She started to undress, staring vacantly at the wall above her clients.

'I don't want her,' said Medulev, leaning back behind the black girl to catch Blandford's attention. 'Do you?'

Blandford shook his head.

'Well, we'll just get her to dance for an hour, shall we? Her time's paid for. Hey!' He shot Blandford a quick smile. 'Maybe if we slip her a bit more cash, we'll get her to pay a bit of girl-on-girl attention to one of these two. What do you think?'

'Whatever, Marat. Whatever. Marat . . .?'

'Ha! You want something . . . unusual? Your imagination is working? You want a girl? Maybe a nice blonde? An expensive, young American?'

Medulev smiled wolfishly, and snorted a large line of cocaine.

'No. No thanks.'

Men like Blandford and Medulev – how many? Dozens? Hundreds? – must have said something very similar before being presented with Ava, his lovely, beautiful daughter. Drugged, dull-eyed, compliant, she'd been used, used up till nothing was left. And her stupid pimp of a pilot boyfriend couldn't even protect her, so . . . she'd gone, for ever.

Blandford nodded to himself, drank a shot, and rubbed at his pink-streaked eyes.

WHEN BLANDFORD WOKE UP the room was empty. The shambles surrounding him spoke of a vigorous night. The beer was all consumed, the bottles lying in pools of warm fluid. The ice bucket was empty, apart from sour, melted ice. Two empty vodka bottles lay on the floor. A couple of ashtrays were piled high with cigarette ends of various lengths and brands. One of the sachets of cocaine had disappeared. The other was spilled across the table, half its contents had merged with the warm beer.

He got up, surprised by the mildness of the pain in his head. The boombox was still blaring out anthems of electronic euphoria. He switched it off; he could hear the cries of a woman interspersed with the deeper groans of Medulev.

Blandford moved towards the other bedroom, but sensed someone was in there.

'Hello,' he called.

'Hello, Kingston. Come in, honey.'

Blandford walked into the bathroom. The girl from New Jersey was steeping in the bath. The water was hot, and smelled of roses, but there were no suds. Her skin was a dark, glistening brown.

'I, erm, I just want a glass of water.'

'Nothing else?'

Something had improved her humour since Blandford had fallen asleep. Perhaps it was cocaine.

'Why don't you get in here with me? I'll do whatever you want for $400. Anything at all, Kingston.'

Blandford didn't answer. He was standing by the edge of the bath. She reached out an arm. Her long fingers were working his fly now. In the next bedroom, he could hear Medulev's cries intensifying. Screw it, it was only money. Screw everything. Maybe the animal organism that was his body might be interested in this. After all, he still breathed, ate, crapped, brushed his teeth . . .

'OK,' he said at last. 'I'm good for $400.'

THE POLICEMAN STEPPED into the road, almost too boldly. But Vladimir managed to stop the Cayenne just in time. He looked in the mirror as the policeman began to trudge towards him through the frozen brown sludge and the still-whirling snow. It seemed to have been snowing for days and days.

A swift, furtive glance in the rear-view mirror revealed that his eyes had a yellowish tinge. The steroids were building up in his system. The Action Man within him wanted to get out and do things. He was in a hurry.

Vladimir turned back quickly, and tugged at the cashmere Versace blanket covering the wash bag, the tins of high-protein drink and the weapons. It would have to do.

He was parked as tightly as he could into the side of the crazily busy ring road. There were no hard shoulders in Russia, no margins for error. Heavy-goods vans and huge, articulated trucks plunged noisily through the freezing filth just a few metres away. They were vast, unstoppable instruments of death and destruction, perfect for Moscow's outer ring road. Even Vladimir, who was no Muscovite, knew that it used to be known as 'The Road of Death'. Once upon a time, if your Zhiguli fell into one of the massive potholes, you'd slew across the central reservation, which used to be just a narrow strip of grass. You would almost certainly be killed by the oncoming traffic. Now there were strong central barriers, and the road was properly resurfaced. It even had an extra lane on either side, but the net result was hardly a triumph for road safety. Giant vehicles screamed around it at a lethal pace. The Cayenne with its bull bars and strengthened coachwork was solid enough, but in a collision with an articulated lorry Vladimir would have been flattened like the rest of them.

A tap on the window. Vladimir pressed a button. The tinted pane glided down.

'Citizen, what a powerful car. Impressive. Do you know what speed you were doing?'

The policeman was a sallow-faced little rat with a swagger stick. Vladimir could feel the Uzi in the pocket of his blouson. Its density and solidity were comforting. It would be so easy to blow the little fucker away. The muscles were coiling in his shoulders and the sides of his neck. He mustn't overreact. He wasn't even in Moscow yet.

Vladimir shrugged.

The puny creature in the uniform tried again: 'We can do this the hard way or the easy way. Do you know what speed you were doing?'

Vladimir could smell beer on the rat's breath. That was discipline for you. The policemen didn't drink vodka when they were driving, but they did drink beer, which didn't count in their book. Vladimir clenched and unclenched a fist inside his jacket pocket.

The little rat was beginning to take an interest in the interior of the car.

'OK,' Vladimir said, with a deliberate effort at control. 'I'll take the easy way . . . *Skol'ko?* How much?'

The rat laughed, showing an uneven set of yellow teeth.

'I see you're willing to co-operate, citizen. Very sensible.'

Then a flash of fear passed across the thin features. 'Where's your phone? You're not filming this, are you?'

Even though it was accepted practice that Moscow's underpaid traffic cops stopped drivers and made life hell for them until money changed hands, a few punters had surreptitiously filmed these encounters on mobiles. These snippets then found their way onto YouTube. It was just about the only way a cop could lose his job.

Vladimir reached into his jacket pocket, pulled out his phone, held it up, and put it back again. He put both hands on the steering wheel and stared straight ahead.

'*Skol'ko?*' he asked again.

The rat's eyes darted left and right.

'A thousand.'

Vladimir almost laughed. A thousand roubles? Thirty bucks? Dirt cheap. Not worth blowing the bastard's head off. The lucky, lucky little *cunt*. He reached into the glove compartment, withdrew a small wad of notes, peeled some off and passed them through the window.

The policeman stuffed the cash into a tunic pocket.

'Thank you, sir. Have a safe journey. You were travelling over the speed limit, but that wasn't the issue.'

'Really?'

Vladimir was staring straight ahead. This moment was over. Money had changed hands. He'd moved from 'citizen' to 'sir'.

'Yes, sir. Your number plates. They look like a diplomat's plates, but they don't register on our computer system.'

Vladimir was impressed. The police were underfunded. Why else was this fine officer on the take? They were far from having onboard computers in patrol cars, but the rat must have radioed in to a central computer in Moscow. In Grozny, he could drive with or without plates, and no one cared.

He'd taken the number plates from a car owned by an Uzbek

businessman as part-settlement of a debt – the car, the plates, some cash and the little finger of the guy's left hand. Oh, yes, and he'd forced the idiot's wife to strip at gunpoint in front of her husband and three young children. Nothing sexual, but he'd had a point to make. Vladimir wouldn't tolerate debtors, and stories like that one got around – the wife's dumbstruck humiliation, the hysterically sobbing, traumatised children. People would pay after a little incident like that. It was good for business.

'Sir?'

Vladimir unclenched his jaw muscles. He realised he'd been grinding his teeth again.

'I'm sorry. It must be because they're not Moscow plates.'

'Maybe that's it, sir. Well, good night.'

The officer turned to go, and Vladimir rolled up the window. He passed a hand across his chin and rubbed ruminatively. It could be that he'd need to do a carjack or two. The plates he'd then get would be good for three or four days, providing the bodies of the owners weren't found quickly. But he wouldn't do that unless he really needed anonymity.

The Cayenne made it into the city without attracting further calls for income from the police. He parked the car carefully out of view off Komsomolskaya Square.

Soon he was striding through the sturdy, colonnaded pomposity of Kazansky Voksal, the railway station. There were two other railway stations in the busy, traffic-congested square, but a sign proclaiming that Kazan station was the gateway to the East attracted his attention. As he crossed the main concourse a huge poster of a dark-eyed Tadzihk girl with hair piled up in coils looked down on him. Vladimir stared up at her. Moscow wasn't Russia, despite what the Muscovites thought. And Chechnya wasn't Russian.

He felt for his phone. Ahmed would be expecting a progress report soon. Well, first things first. He found what he wanted in the second bookstore he visited, and picked up the two most recent editions of *Domovoi* magazine. The westerners had *Vogue* and other tat, but none of it was as good as *Domovoi*. Vladimir wasn't into reading, but *Domovoi* had really good pictures – and it was clear: it told you what to do with your money – how to spend it, what was cool, what wasn't. That was why he knew to have granite tops with bevelled edges in his kitchen. All you had to do was look at the pictures – and copy them.

He looked up at the Tadzihk girl on the poster again as he went back to the Cayenne. *Domovoi* wasn't easy to come by in Grozny, and now he had a couple of days of pleasure ahead of him.

Vladimir fired up the Cayenne and headed out onto the Moscow streets. Driving in Moscow was a traumatic experience. The Muscovites had big-city arrogance. Any sign of weakness or incompetence was ruthlessly punished by klaxon blares and obscene gestures. Having plates that were obviously from out of town made matters worse.

Eventually he found the Donetskaya street offices he'd been looking for. The name of Ahmed's contact, Lieutenant Sergei Levitan, was good enough to get him past the bored and depressed-looking gate man and into the courtyard.

The building reminded Vladimir of his earliest school years. It was dreary and bleak and stank of bleach and chalk and low-grade clerical ink. Levitan's office was on the fifth floor. Vladimir waited a few moments for the lift before he realised it was never going to come. He climbed the staircase. The landing outside Levitan's office looked northwards over flat rooftops and dozens of construction sites. A Ferris wheel on the skyline told Vladimir that he was looking in the direction of Park Kultury, the Park of Culture. But that was New Russian bollocks. Really, it was Gorky Park. Vladimir had seen the movie.

The unvarnished wooden door opened before he could knock.

'Ah, you must be . . .' Levitan was a short, fat, balding man with flashes of black hair plastered to the side of his head. Vladimir had once had a Ford Mustang with similar things on the door panels painted to look like tongues of flame. Go-faster stripes, that was it. But you didn't see those in *Domovoi*. He had sold the car.

'Vladimir. Just Vladimir is good.'

'Nice to meet you, Vladimir.'

Levitan looked a little apprehensive. Or maybe he was sweating just because he was fat.

'What have you got for me?' Vladimir wanted to get out of there as fast as possible.

'Here is the incident report. There's no need to read it now,' said Levitan.

'I haven't time to read,' snapped Vladimir. 'Tell me what it says.'

Levitan flipped through a blue cardboard folder, turning over too many pages, then turning back. He glanced up at Vladimir.

'Um, the kid was messed up. Two body shots. The first smashed the pelvic girdle, second would have done the trick. Stomach shot, massive internal damage to the kidney and liver. Third one took away the top of the skull and made a mess of the boy's looks. There were . . . ah, traces of urine found on the victim.'

'You mean someone pissed on the corpse? Does Ahmed know this?' A familiar warm feeling was coursing through Vladimir. This was turning out to be more fun than he thought.

Levitan twitched at the mention of the word 'Ahmed', the single name by which the veteran Chechnyan warlord was known.

'Um, I have spoken to Gospodin Khamzaev. Yes, he does know the extent of his son's injuries. But not about the urine – which may be dog's urine. He wants to speak to you.'

'I'll bet he does.' Vladimir realised he would have to switch his phone back on at some stage. This was urban warfare, not the guerrilla combat he so cherished. In fact, it was a contract, a favour for the big man. Khamzaev would probably want something special now – the killer's eyeballs or testicles brought back in a bag so Ahmed could kebab and eat them, then post the video on the internet. It was to be hoped there were no specials. Even in the cold of winter it could be tricky and messy – and above all smelly – carrying bits of your victims around the country with you.

Vladimir scratched his chin then flexed his neck muscles. Levitan looked at him in open alarm. But Vladimir couldn't really help himself. Anyway, intimidating these worthless punks was good.

'Were there any DNA samples left by his attacker?'

'The lab is working on it now, but I doubt there'll be anything,' said Levitan.

'Assuming whoever took a pee on the kid was just a dog or a random drunk. Let me know if something shows up.'

'How can I get hold of you? Do you have a mobile?'

'Give me your number. I'll be in touch. Better that way,' smiled Vladimir.

'Right.'

'Anything else for me?'

'Well, there's this,' volunteered Levitan. He tossed a single sheet of paper on the table. 'Last known contacts.'

'The Westerner?'

'Westerners.'

'There are forty names here. Why did you single one out to Ahmed?'

'This guy, Spendlove, made a call from the murder scene.'

'And what does the Westerner say about that?'

'Umm . . . I've been holding off seeing him. We have a huge caseload, and Ahmed wants you to, ah . . . take it on personally. Anyway, this is where he's staying in Moscow. But you'll find him soon enough on the bar scene, and in the hooker hotels.'

'Hooker hotels?'

'Rooms by the hour. He seems to get around. You're not from town, are you?'

Vladimir looked at the list of names and addresses, and grunted.

'You know I'm fucking not.' He squinted at the list 'Who are these?' Vladimir jabbed a finger at a couple of Spanish names.

'Guatemalan prostitutes. They were taking some punters for a knee-trembler in the yard where Shamil was. They found the body.'

'Knee-tremblers in this weather?'

'What can I say, comrade? We Russians are a hardy people. Hardy enough to fuck low-grade whores in the open air if we have to.'

'I'm not your comrade, Levitan. And I'm not a Russian either.' Vladimir snatched up the contact list.

'But that's my only copy!' squealed Levitan.

'Get another one. I'll call as and when I need more,' said Vladimir. He left, banging the door behind him. 'Keep a trace on that phone, would you?'

'It's not been switched on for a while.'

'I don't give a flying fuck in a hurricane. Keep the trace on. I'll call, Levitan.'

Levitan sat down at his desk. His legs felt weak. The room was not particularly well heated, but he was sweating very freely now. He took out a large, slightly soiled handkerchief and passed it across his forehead.

It was well before lunchtime, but these were exceptional circumstances. He bent down, reached in the bottom drawer of the desk and pulled out a bottle of low-grade Ukrainian vodka. He took a quick shot from a cracked coffee mug and was pouring a follow-up when his mobile rang. He cursed quietly when he saw the caller number. Shit. It was Ahmed.

SAMUEL WAS RUNNING hard, drenched in a cold sweat. The faster he ran, the slower he moved. The ancient, rusty car was gaining, its elderly driver gurning and sneering. He glanced up into the *wintry sky. The heavy, churning sound from above was made by helicopter blades. He climbed into the empty cockpit, and began a steep descent down a vortex of swirling, dazzling white snow – which led to a thickly wooded, claustrophobic rain forest, where he was walking, covered in hot sweat now, among trees glistening with sap – waxy, podded flowers, heavy with seed – he touched one; it burst violently, spewing out tensor signs, thick-bodied serpent-like symbols of wedge products and exponentiation, copperplate parentheses, differential equations – all the hieroglyphs of mechanical maths in an endless, dizzying jackpot.*

A sharp rap at the door. A hint of impatience in this one . . . He was where, exactly? In his suite at the Ukraina, of course. His head throbbed

Samuel clambered unsteadily out of bed and padded down the pine-chevroned corridor. A glance through the fisheye in the door reassured him. He pulled and jiggled and swung back.

'Good morning.'

Ksenia marched past him before he had time to respond, and was heading into the drawing room. 'You have good taste, Samuel.' Ksenia surveyed the suite and nodded her head. 'This is the old Russia, a Soviet palace par excellence.'

'*On va casser la croûte, mon pote?*'

Ksenia's French accent was good. Just a few words of the language, purely spoken, evoked in Samuel a host of memories: times, places, adventures and lovers long gone – dinner on the Île de la Cité, the silently shouting, gigantic sculptures of the Musée Bourdelle, the sharp odour of crushed late-summer grass in the Jardin de Luxembourg, the scent of the Latin Quarter, thick with possibility, the soft hand of the biker girl in her black leather jacket.

That was what happened when he unlocked the door to his memory. The engine retrieved so much of what he wanted – and more than a little of what he'd rather forget.

'Yes,' he said, passing a hand across his forehead. Samuel sat in a hard chair opposite the sofa Ksenia had taken. 'One of the Seven Sisters. I like it.'

'You would be a good Russian, Samuel.'

'What time is it? Shall I order breakfast?'

'Noon. I've already eaten breakfast.'

'Hmm. Let me get dressed and we'll go out.' Samuel was still wearing a pair of ancient boxer shorts and a collarless shirt from his undergraduate days.

Samuel showered and shaved. The fatigue of the previous night was still with him. Yes, he had a rare facility of recall. But he knew that the slightest error could mean failure. To that extent, it was true that the cognitive – making sense of the shapes that he saw – was an important addition to his eidetic memory. He could memorise a whole page of a novel or a non-fiction book in English in a few moments. But getting the functional indicators right in a complex integral equation had no safety net. If he made an error as to one of the tiny subscripts or the power of the indices, it would take a mathematician or an engineer to spot the flaw. That might require days, weeks, or even months of work. But above and beyond that, something within him responded to the challenge. Yes, there were side effects. Yes, there was the risk of flashback to times and events he preferred not to revisit. But he didn't truly know his own capacities, and now, for better or worse, he was being tested to the limit.

Samuel and Ksenia, both wrapped up in several layers of clothes, headed out into the bright, brittle chill of the winter day. They stomped up the Arbat in the slush and turned left, right and right again onto Presnensky Val. They stopped and waited to cross the road. Ksenia laid a hand on Samuel's arm and smiled. Then she strode across the road purposefully. Samuel hurried after her.

A few minutes later, they were walking through double glass doors of a brand-new shopping arcade, stepping into a warm blast of bubble-gum-scented air. Soon they were marching past a mix of sushi bars, Mexican restaurants, interior design shops and chocolatiers. At the far end of the arcade on the left was a set of large white doors set in a gothic arch. The word 'Bed' was picked out in just-legible cream lettering at the apex of the arch.

Walking into the cafe interior was indeed like falling into bed. White linen drapes predominated, and the soft white chairs had huge butter-cream pillows. Large, black-and-white photographs of the staff adorned the walls.

'Behind us and in front of us, all at the same time,' said Samuel.

'What?' Ksenia stopped removing her layers. Lots of thin layers trapped warm air and helped fend off the Moscow winter. Ksenia didn't do fur. 'Are you feeling OK, Samuel?'

'Me? I'm fine.'

'Of course. You were saying?'

'I was thinking. About Moscow. You're catching up with us fast. In fact you're already ahead of us in some things.'

A waiter, already strangely familiar from his steel-framed photo, served them chilled water, and distributed menus.

'I think you need to eat. Try the pomegranate-and-onion bread. Unusual, but very good,' said Ksenia.

Samuel watched a waitress in a tight, white catsuit advance towards them. The photo opposite them made her look like a movie star. It was a fair representation.

'In the West, we have celebrity chefs. It looks like you've trumped us. You've got celebrity waiters.'

'That may have something to do with the workers and taking control of the means of production,' said Ksenia, laughing.

'You really think so?'

'Of course not. You British have celebrity chiefs as a way of dealing with your grief.'

Samuel shot her a quizzical look, and waited.

'It's the management of decline. You have no empire. You have a government that is a subsidiary of the United States, but does not even have the right to vote or fight for its interest in Congress or at the White House. But you do have a sense of irony. Making a movie star of the chef is a very British way of mocking the fact that none of you can afford servants any more. What is a chef? In Britain, a celebrity. In Russia, a cook.'

'Bravo, Ksenia. Point taken. But why celebrity waiters?'

Ksenia looked around her.

'At least they look good. From here, they get top modelling jobs or pick up a rich husband or wife.'

'Rich? Is that what matters? You're such a cynic,' said Samuel.

'No I am a pragmatic idealist. That is the real definition of a cynic.'

'You're probably right on all counts. But that's not going to stop me ordering something from the movie star's kitchen.'

He gave an order for pan-fried black pudding and leek colcannon with a caraway seed and rhubarb salsa. She ordered a mutton broth with a compote of garam marsala apricots and a selection of exotic warm bread.

They occupied a huge leather chesterfield. With its white and pale yellow pillows it really did feel as though they were in bed together. They lay back and Ksenia turned to him.

'Ready?'

He nodded. 'Sorry. I was really tired last night. I can go again now.'

'That's OK,' she said, and touched his arm lightly. 'You take your time.'

She handed him a sheaf of plain A4 paper and a pen. Samuel passed his hand through his hair, propped himself up on the pillows, and looked at the paper thoughtfully. After a while, he felt the inner surge, the pressure of information seeking release from his brain. He picked up the pen and began to write.

⚛

'WE'RE READY NOW!' Ksenia shouted to the waitress and then clapped her hands. Samuel had been hard at work for nearly two hours. Fearful of interrupting his flow or tampering with Samuel's concentration in any way, Ksenia had left bread on the table, but sent the food back. Now, finally, he had finished.

'*Molodets!* Well done!' said Ksenia.

She gathered the sheets of paper together. There must have been nearly fifty of them. They were covered in Samuel's tidy script, although the line-spacing and character size had grown towards the end of the transcription as Samuel had tired.

'I don't know about that.'

Samuel looked at the marks on the paper in front of him. It was as though they'd been made by someone else. It seemed difficult to believe they could be as important as all that. But then, the atomic bomb must once have been no more than a series of equations on paper.

Ksenia seemed to sense his self-doubt.

'I believe in you,' she said. Her eyes were an entrancing onyx green in the soft light of the cafe. She began to read some of Samuel's transcription, but stopped after a short while. 'So does this really mean nothing to you, Samuel?'

He hesitated.

'It's certainly well beyond my scientific abilities. I just . . .' she added.

'Mine too. The more advanced technical language and the equations are, um, all algebra to me.'

Ksenia nodded, deadpan. 'English humour. The only weapon you have in the modern world – a conventional weapon, but a dangerous one.'

Samuel took a mouthful of the pomegranate-and-onion bread. He was suddenly ravenous.

Ksenia began to scrutinise the transcripts, while Samuel tore at a mustard-seed roll and dipped it in a mix of sesame oil, lemon juice and balsamic vinegar.

'So what does Tortoiseshell Technology actually have?' she mused aloud. 'We start with the premise that objects that cut through water, air, or oil can actually change the nature of whatever it is they come in contact with. How they do that depends partly on the shape of the object – let's call it a propeller or a drilling blade in the case of Tortoiseshell.

'The other thing that matters is the speed at which the object moves. The faster it moves, the lower the pressure of the fluid around it. When the fluid pressure falls below a certain point it vaporises and creates a vacuum, a cavity in the fluid itself.'

Ksenia stopped to nibble on a morsel of bread. 'I remember watching my mother make cakes as a little girl. One time we acquired a prize toy – an electric whisk. I used to love the way it worked through the mix. It mixed it, but created a space round itself.'

Samuel nodded. 'I think that's pretty much relevant. Cake mix is a rather special kind of fluid, and you're beating air into the mix. That makes it stiffen. But the idea of a blade moving at speed through fluid, lessening pressure, simultaneously driving the fluid away and changing its state – I think that's basically right.'

'But I still don't see what Tortoiseshell has done with this. What's the application?' asked Ksenia. She went back to the thick pile of words, equations and crude sketches.

'Well, it's not a million miles away from cake mixing,' said Samuel. 'As far as I understand it, it's all to do with beating and bubbles. When fluid reaches what you might call vapour pressure it forms small bubbles of gas within itself. That's always been a problem for marine engineers trying to get a propeller screw to get maximum purchase on water, for example.'

'Because the faster the screw turns, the more likely it is to create a bubble?'

Kempis's Latin note and its warning – *Let the buyer of bubbles beware* – floated up into the back of Samuel's mind. With some effort, he managed to put it to one side.

'Partly that,' Samuel continued, 'but also because the bubbles themselves are unstable. If the pressure changes – for example if the propeller slowed down sharply – they would tend to implode quite violently and cause damage to the blade of the propeller or drill. There have been instances of imploding bubbles causing damage to the hulls of sea vessels.'

'Well, I have to say, this cavitation sounds pretty useless to me,' said Ksenia. 'Either the fluid runs away from the blade or it attacks it.' She broke open another roll of bread, and smiled slowly. 'Though when I think about it, maybe this is a little bit like love.'

'Maybe,' said Samuel. One day he'd like to interrogate Ksenia about her theories of love – running away and attacking, indeed. 'But what Tortoiseshell and its proprietor, the clever Dr Yavlinsky, have done is use that bubble against itself. Yavlinsky reckons to have found the optimum speed for oil drilling, based on the density and viscosity of the oil. It uses a drill that's got a cutting edge which changes the vortex of the radial and axial directions.'

'I think I saw a diagram about that. Is this the one?'

'I think, so. They reckon they can create this self-inverting bubble that creates a vacuum within a vacuum. The bubbles don't then implode, but they go in a kind of figure-of-eight shape round the blade or propeller, and drive the rest of the fluid in whatever direction you want.'

'So they're using the bubbles against themselves?'

'Yes. It's as though they've invented a cake mixer so efficient that it scoops all of the mixture out of the bowl. There's nothing left to lick.'

'Shame about the cake mix. But not if you're extracting oil from the ground.'

'The really clever part is they do it using an allied technology, called Version Thirteen. It uses ultrasound to create an oasis in which the cavitation effect is virtually suspended.'

'I thought ultrasound was a safe form of X-ray?'

'That's just one of its uses. Ultrasound creates an image by measuring the frequency at which sonic waves bounce off an object. Yavlinsky has used very high-level ultrasound to impart a tiny input of energy to the molecules in the fluid, and change the nature of the molecules themselves.

'Imagine bouncing a tennis ball against a wall. If you bounced a million tennis balls against the wall at the same time and you knew how to listen for the sound of the balls, the length of time they took to come back to you and so on, you'd be able to build an image of the wall – its dimensions, distance, and so on. Agreed?'

'You're talking about principles similar to radar, correct?'

'Exactly. Now imagine if those million tennis balls were wet when you bounced them. You'd get a different reading for the return journey of the balls, and the sound they'd make. But if you adjusted for the fact that the balls were wet, you'd still get the information you wanted. But you'd also end up with something else.'

Ksenia considered. 'I guess you'd end up with a wet wall.'

'Precisely. By measuring and observing the data you change the quality of the data observed. Heisenberg's uncertainty principle.'

'I thought you weren't a scientist.'

'I'm not. I studied those papers as well as memorising them.'

'So the point is that Yavlinsky has a drilling technology that subtly changes the nature of the fluid by bombarding it with ultrasound?'

'Correct again,' said Samuel. 'A wet wall would conduct an electric current in a way that a dry one wouldn't. His ultrasound device imparts some sort of kinetic energy to the fluid that effectively suspends the cavitation effect, or at least means that Yavlinsky can change it.'

'So this is beginning to make some sort of sense,' said Ksenia.

120

'Instead of creating a vacuum that you can't drill into, the cavitation effect is being suspended or warped by this new technology, and used to push fluid onto the blade itself and wherever you want after that.'

'That's about it.'

'So that's the science that underpins the executive summary in the early part of all this. The process called Version Thirteen is a super-efficient way of cleaning out oil wells. The ultrasound waves travel vast distances in a fraction of a second. So whole fields can be made susceptible to the technology quite easily, and very little of the fluid is dispersed or driven away. Genius!'

'Yes,' Samuel. 'That would be Yavlinsky. He'd been working with a series of matrix models for the bubble-flow, and different types of ultrasound generators used at different frequencies for years.'

'Ha!' Ksenia poured them both some water. 'And I'll bet the thirteenth experimental model was the one that worked. Hence – Version Thirteen.'

'Yavlinsky believes that only sixty per cent of oil is being recovered at the moment,' said Samuel. 'If the maths is right, this technique can increase it to ninety-five per cent.'

Ksenia whistled softly. 'Let's take a cautious approach. If we say oil recovery only increases to seventy-five per cent, that still means Russia's oil reserves are effectively increased by twenty-five per cent from where they are now.'

'Yes,' said Samuel. 'At least that. The topographic nature of much of Russian oil reserves is ideally suited to this technology. The ultrasound is most effective in large, flat spaces. At least, that's the claim.'

'Do you believe it?'

'It's not my job to believe in anything. It does make sense, of a sort. And Yavlinsky's eccentric enough not to worry about the economic implications.'

'The economic implications are that Russia has a trillion dollars more wealth – and the environmental gains I was hoping for should be there too. Samuel, I will never be able to thank you enough.'

The bill arrived and Ksenia deposited an American Express card. Matt black, of course.

'I hope you can stay a bit longer, Samuel. You seem to have a good relationship with Dr Yavlinsky. It would be good if you could pay him another visit.'

Ksenia was smart, idealistic and fabulous to look at. Was she the only thing in Moscow that was what it seemed on the surface? Was it just coincidence that she was part of the chorus – Blandford, Anna, Kempis's ghost – all pointing him in the same direction? And what about going no further? He'd been the one who insisted on that before taking the commission. Last, beyond all these, were the echoes of Paris and Lauren. He knew the kind of thing that might happen if he took the next step – a causal chain of the uncontrollable. Events, people, markets, media morphing into monsters; emotions sliding into the miserable dark places where broken hearts go to die.

Ksenia's green eyes, her radiant smile: 'I forgot to say "please" – and I promise I'll find a proper way to thank you.'

Samuel knew he should say no, firmly and immediately. But he didn't say anything.

KINGSTON BLANDFORD OPENED the door of his hotel room. He felt dishevelled and dissolute after his night out with Medulev. He had would strip off and get straight in the shower. Or not . . .

'Where the fuck have you been?'

His visitor was sitting in an armchair looking out at the Moscow River. When they'd first made contact, it was business. Hard-core, brutal stuff – information for a price. Now, the man in his room had no reason to be there. At least from Blandford's point of view, it was over.

Outside the window gulls shrieked and swooped for the booty carried by vast, slow-moving refuse barges heading for landfill. They would stink of shit, but they would be warm enough. If only he could climb in to that thick, dirty mountain of crap and go to sleep . . .

'Well? I'm waiting.'

Anton Miller passed a long, bony hand through fine, grizzled hair, then interrogated a Chopard wristwatch – a luxury item somewhat at odds with the plain white, Brooks Brothers button-down shirt and matt black, dime-store suit.

His face was narrow and lined, but he looked remarkably fresh. Scarcely a crease in the suit. It was as though a dental appointment had run slightly over schedule. But he must have been there for several hours – sitting, watching, waiting.

'Sorry . . . I forgot.'

'You forgot.'

Miller spat the words quietly, slowly. 'Lucky I only sleep four hours a day. Fuckwit.'

Miller rose from his chair and stood still, eyes fixed intently on the river, like a heron scanning the shallows for a minnow. The morning sun streamed in from the enormous window. Miller was luminous, lightly electrified by the light. He turned.

'Well, Mr Forgetful, now it's time to remember.'

The hooker had been receptive, surprisingly so. He'd responded briefly, a momentary stirring – then the moment was gone, the excitement usurped by the image of the dead boy, the sense of himself, sweating on top of a hooker, using her as the others had used Ava . . .

Blandford blinked the images away, kept his voice flat, even.

'Can we talk later, do you think? I need a shower.'

'A shower? I've been waiting all fucking night. You owe me.'

123

'OK, OK.' The two men sat in the armchairs near the window and Kingston Blandford leaned forwards, throwing himself into the charade.

'Spendlove spent the entire day with Yavlinsky.'

'So he's memorised the formulae!'

'He's not sure. It's complex, difficult stuff.'

'What's he expect? A spinning top?' Miller rolled his eyes. 'And is Spendlove intending to give this information to Anna Barinova?'

'The daughter. Medulev calls Ksenia her mother's secret weapon. But she's a different generation. Different agenda. It's not money with her.'

Miller shook his head. By the river, two gulls fought, black-eyed, deadly, over a gobbet of putrid flesh.

'She wants to save the world, of course she does. When your mother's a billionairess, what else is there to do? So . . . Spendlove? He's spewing it all out for her benefit now?'

'You know Spendlove from Paris, right? A man with brains – but when he starts thinking with his penis, the lobotomy is terrible to behold.'

Miller stood up.

'Keep close to him, Blandford. You had your date with destiny. Now finish this job, and then get on with your life.'

'Can I have the pictures? You said I could have the pictures.'

'What? Of your little girl? Do you really want them?'

'Yes. They're all that's left.'

'Jesus, Blandford.'

Miller withdrew a battered paper wallet from his jacket pocket, and handed it to Blandford. The Canadian leafed through the images – that blonde-haired girl, yes, that was his daughter. But these men? All these men, with their leering, twisted faces. Who were they? And was he, honestly, any better?

Miller's cool grey eyes were not without pity.

'I can take them away, Blandford. You've seen them now. Isn't that enough?'

Blandford shook his head slowly. Maybe not in direct response to Miller's question.

Miller patted Blandford softly on the shoulder, once, and left.

SAMUEL TOOK THE CALL two hours later.

'Blandford. You're bright and early. Calling to protect your investment? Or have you got something to tell me?'

'No, not really – on either count. Just stepped out of the shower and was wondering how it went, is all.'

'Well, *it* went fine. But you don't know what you're asking. Unlocking memory is . . . Well, I'm wiped out.'

'I'm sorry to hear that Samuel, I truly am. I empathise, I really do.'

'I hear you.'

Samuel hung up. He'd heard Blandford all right. And . . . if he was right, he recognised a certain caller, the one who'd accused Blandford of making a *dick move* over breakfast. Maybe that was a voice from Paris. Maybe Blandford wasn't just in it for the money. He could sense all kinds of problems lurking beneath problems, all sorts of dangers swimming beneath the surface.

He shut his eyes, and tried to think of something neutral: a sunny meadow, a snatch of Lucretius opining on the nature of things, a simple glass of beer back at The Eagle and Child in Oxford. But all he got was a swirl of symbols and diagrams, images of more innocent times in Paris never to be relived, and the smiling face of Peter Kempis inviting him to a game of chess. He would play now, wouldn't he?

**PART TWO**

*'HERE. EAT.'*

*'Whuh?'*

*He looked into the eyes of the man slumped on the sofa. He slapped him on the cheek, just hard enough to penetrate the fog of drink and drugs. The party was in full swing around them. A rapid, swirling pulse of electronic euphoria issued from huge, flat speakers attached to the wall of the enormous, parquet-floored penthouse.*

*Teheran, with its minarets, office towers, dusty yellow and dull red dwelling houses sprawled extravagantly before them. Dawn was just breaking. Colour was slowly insinuating itself back into the day.*

*He pushed aside a pickle dish full of a yellowy-white powder. He put down the bowl of food, licked a fingertip and delicately rubbed a few grains of the powder on his tongue. Cocaine, premium strength. He'd taken plenty in his early, foolish days as a trader. But that time was long gone. He got his kicks elsewhere nowadays. Well, maybe just one, tiny toot – for old-time's sake. Hell, he wasn't long out of house arrest in Lausanne . . .*

*There were around forty people in the room. Young girls gyrated in miniskirts, their long, silky-soft legs moving in perfect unison. They all had slightly different versions of the classic Persian beauty – long, heavy, jet-black hair, almond eyes with massive lashes, and full, sensuous mouths. They were in the groove, all dancing together, entranced by the music, their experience enhanced by the cocaine.*

*All except one. A blonde-haired girl called Ava with a pretty snub nose and sparkling hazel eyes danced next to the other girls. She was next to them, but not one of them. She wore a tiny toga-style dress, no underwear, no shoes, no make-up. She didn't need any of that. Her skin glowed, her hair shone, her body swung in perfect unison with the music. Every man in the room – apart from himself, and the drugged, and the comatose – devoured her with his eyes.*

*Most of the men were sprawled on floor cushions and sofas. They loved the floor show, the mix of young girls and older men with money. It was the same the world over, the classic party cocktail. True, the source of the male partygoers' wealth was generally rather dubious, but what did the girls care?*

*He had made – and lost – a fortune on something much rarer, much more precious: his talent. But that talent hadn't been respected. Once he'd been feared and respected. All that was going to change back. And in the changing, scores would be settled. Those who had disrespected him would pay.*

*They had called him Master of the Universe once – and they'd been right. He'd been at the centre of the system, doing favours for heads of state of smaller countries, finance ministers of big ones. His opinions, his contributions to the global debate – the universal yes or no, buy or sell, that was the global market – formed part of the market, helped shape it. What was it that sanctimonious hedge fund guy had called it? 'Reflexivity' – ha, yes. Just shorthand for having so much influence that if you told traders they'd make money by jumping over a cliff, they'd do it.*

*But then the good and the great had turned their backs. They said he'd overdone it, that he'd put the system at risk. The fools. If they'd kept their nerve, if they'd had faith in him, he'd have brought the Americans and the Brits to their knees. He'd have reduced the markets to rubble, bought for nothing, sold for plenty. And the new system would have had his friends, his happily* dirigiste *technocrats in Paris and Berlin in charge. Well, more or less. He himself would have been at the centre of it all – master-builder, architect of the new order.*

*Well, after it had all gone wrong, he'd got out of Switzerland and its useless legal system thanks to the efforts of a couple of fantastically expensive lawyers, and favours from very influential friends who didn't want it known quite how much they enjoyed the company of very young boys and girls. This time, he would start with a blunter instrument of power.*

What do you call a peasant with a machine gun? 'Sir.'

*Not that he was dealing in guns, not unless thermonuclear devices were available in hand-held format. Come to think of it, that probably day wasn't too far off, given the pace of miniaturisation. There'd be a great market in gadgets the size of a cellphone with the capability of destroying a city the size of Baltimore. Until someone actually destroyed a city the size of Baltimore – at which point there'd be what you'd have to call a disrupted market. But he knew those markets, they were his, after all – and they'd settle, and even after a few hundred thousand dead and thousands of square miles uninhabitable for a millennium or so, there'd still be an opportunity to make money. For the markets to function. Which was comforting, very comforting.*

*He shook his head. One tiny line of that coke, and his mind was racing. Not all of it was nonsense – but he needed a clear head, and quickly.*

*He padded over to the kitchen. His dark jeans emphasised the narrowness of his hips; his olive-coloured silk shirt lent him a somewhat oriental air, accentuated by a short, silvery crew cut. His hair seemed to shine against the faint sheen of his tanned skin. Or was that colouring natural? Was he a Malay? A Eurasian? A*

*Maori, even? Impossible to tell. His unlined, almost elfin face gave no sign of age or suffering.*

*He drew a glass of water, found his companion and shook him – hard, this time. He tried to make him drink, but the man was far gone, out of it. One of the girls sidled over towards them, and rested a small hand on his shoulder.*

*He looked up. The dark eyes narrowed.*

*'Can't you see I'm not interested? Go away.'*

*The girl recoiled as though she'd been bitten. He shook his companion by the shoulder again, then slapped him across the face. The second hit left the raking imprint of his fingers on the man's cheek. A response, at last. He picked up a bowl of food.*

*The girl he'd sent away was already entwined with one of the other men. Another, the oldest of the lot, wore a thick, grey beard. Now greybeard was dancing with the blonde girl, mouth to mouth, groin to groin. She was emitting little cowboy-style whoops. The girl was drunk – and high on something else. Her eyes were all glazed now, and she'd lost that perfect rhythm. Probably heroin, then, rather than cocaine. Not that he cared. She was just another whore.*

*'Here. Eat,' he urged. His friend was slowly resurfacing. 'Halwa Puri Cholay – spicy chick peas, hot crunchy puris and sweet halva. One of our Pakistani friends brought it. The most delicious breakfast food there is.'*

*'I don't feel well,' said the man in thickly accented English. But he could see the focus slowly returning to the dark eyes and the colour flowing back to his cheeks.*

*'Nonsense. Eat. You will feel better. I need you to be wide-awake, Medulev. My Farsi is simply not up to the job. They could do it in French, certainly, and English. Maybe even Russian – but they're insisting on Farsi. So eat. Then we'll find the minister and all will be well.'*

*Within a few minutes Medulev had identified the minister he sought. He was Mr Greybeard.*

*After a short discussion, he and his friend were ushered into an anteroom through a succession of doors. The minister and three companions listened intently as Medulev spoke in perfect Farsi. The minister took a call on his mobile. He snapped his phone shut and smiled. He grunted a command to one of his aides, and a briefcase appeared from beneath a sofa. He popped the locks, flipped the lid – dark green, banded stacks – used American dollars. He closed the suitcase, flashed them all a quick, brilliantly white smile. The case was satisfyingly heavy in his hand.*

*'I'll see you later,' he said.*

*They ran down the stairs from the penthouse, clicked the door shut, and didn't look round. The two men walked quickly at first, but soon slackened their pace. The streets were deserted. He hailed a cab and gave the name of his hotel. The first call to prayer of the day issued across the rooftops through hundreds of tinny loudspeakers.*

*He smiled to himself and patted the briefcase. He would move to a safer place later. The young helicopter pilot, Shamil, would take him across the border tonight.*

*It was all rather dangerous, rather too high-speed for his liking. But it was lucrative, and he had to start again somewhere. For now, this was a good area – a good business, a volatile but manageable location. It was a space and a place to operate from. The connections were strong. Maybe it was worth investing a little time in learning Farsi to add to the English, French, Russian and Italian he had mastered, in some cases, almost as well as his native tongue. He didn't like being reliant on others.*

*But that mattered little for the moment. He ran his hands against the sleek leather lid of the briefcase and sighed contentedly.*

*He was back.*

# CHAPTER NINE

'WELL, WELL, WELL, Anna. You've done nicely for yourself, my dear.'

'Thank you. I do my best,' she said, with some effort.

She crossed the room quickly and looked down onto the trading floor from the glass wall of her office.

'Would you like a drink? Water? Tea?'

'Nothing for the moment, thank you.'

He was very close to her, her back turned.

She started like a cat at his first touch, but soon relaxed. He stroked her cheek thoughtfully, caressing her face with the middle part of his forefinger.

'You know, Anna,' he breathed, 'for all this finery and these minions below us, you're not much changed from your student days. I remember you as a pretty, heavily pregnant girl running a market stall. I'd watch you heaving cases around. You wouldn't accept a hand from any of the men. And you could shout the patter better than any of them. You were a natural.'

'I was, wasn't I?' she murmured, almost dreamily.

'You know you were. Talent and determination like that – making a market out of nothing, out of the ashes of other people's misery – that's rare, Anna. But tell me, do – why ever did you marry Igor Barinov?'

'The child needed a father.'

He moved his mouth closer to Anna's ear. She could feel his breath. 'I'll tell you. Because I know. I know you. Far better than you know yourself.'

'Igor Barinov must have seemed like a catch – you married a pentathlete and a university goalkeeper. As a prominent, well-paid athlete, he would have had state housing and an income for life once he was too old to compete. But then the Soviet Union fell apart. The whole state apparatus ground to a halt. And yet Igor Barinov wasn't like you, was he? The collapse of the old system that had favoured him was way too big a loss. It must have been very difficult to live with an alcoholic. It must have been a relief when he died.'

'It's so long ago. This is a new era.'

'One that you created. One that set you free to trade, to do what you do so very well.'

The screens on the trading floor below them flashed the stories of the moment – looting and food rioting in New Jersey; the National Guard called into Missouri, where a state of emergency had been declared. A national workers' council had been set up in Spain, offering guidance and leadership in opposition to the government. Bond prices around the world were rising. Shares were tumbling, yet again. In the US, a newly formed motorists' lobby group had thrown its weight behind Senator Bob Zeffman and his campaign for cheaper oil.

He paused for a moment, and surveyed the screens flashing blue and red – mainly red – below them.

'Tough day on the market today, right? But insignificant compared to what you've been through. A tough day back then might have finished you. The young mother who left Ksenia with her grandmother and went to the local market. You traded whatever there was to hand; cigarettes, chocolate, blue jeans and training shoes with English labels on them, even if they were made in Poland. The more money you earned back then, the more popular you became in the Barinov household. It was very generous of you to buy Igor's parents a bigger property when you could afford to.'

Khan teased and stroked Anna's hair with one hand. The other still described slow, deliberate circles on her cheek.

'So kind – and the perfect way to humiliate them. Money is a weapon in the New Russia. And who understands that better than you, Anna? '

Khan's finger rested for a second against her mouth. An eruption of some kind on the floor below. A minor triumph. Maybe a defeat. He looked down and smiled.

'Traders, brokers, salesmen – worker ants, at best. But you're my queen, in whom I've invested so much – time, money, knowledge. I have waited patiently, Anna. Now I want some return.'

WHO *WERE* THESE people? Vladimir pushed through the morning crowds milling about the Frunzenskaya Embankment. What were they all doing? Another little idiot bounced into – and then off – his thick, leather-jacketed torso as he marched along the street.

Rising up in front of him was the Cathedral of Christ the Saviour. It was undoubtedly a grand building, if hardly an elegant one. Five golden onion domes glistened palely in the winter light. The highest was some seventeen stories high.

He could see the cathedral from his hotel room. The previous night Vladimir had checked into a Novotel less than a kilometre away. His room was on the same level as the top of the highest dome. The view was spectacular, but the ceiling height in his room was so low he could touch it with his outstretched hand. The hotel architects had clearly been intent on cramming as many rooms as possible into the space available. Space was an unbelievably expensive commodity in Moscow, and getting dearer every day.

This damned crowd! A young couple bounced into him now. They sprawled backwards from the impact. Stupid bastards had linked arms, and wouldn't unwind themselves from each other. Serve them right. Street justice. It was a happy, warm, righteous feeling.

Vladimir strode on, but could hear them cursing. He turned and grinned at them, then raised his middle finger: *'Na khui!'* he called, to the horror of a couple of old ladies laden with shopping bags.

'Suck my dick!' he added – in English, the language of the sophisticate. Vladimir continued on his way. It was getting on for noon, and he realised that these were the first words he had spoken all day.

He spat messily on the pavement. The hunt was not going smoothly. He'd registered at the hotel last night as a Mr Kelvinov, using one of his many passports. That had been easy enough, but tracking down the Westerner was proving a lot more difficult.

First, there'd been the muscle on the door at the Hotel Ukraina. They didn't like the look of Vladimir. The bulges in his jacket spoke of more than just hard work in the gym. Then there was his demeanour. The security guys could sense danger, and they weren't going to help him.

He'd fared even worse with the Guatemalan hookers. Their mobile phones weren't responding, so he'd had to call Levitan, who'd been more concerned to get off the phone than to give him proper information. But eventually the policeman had done his stuff. It seemed that Angelina and Gabriella liked to work the tourist trade at the Cathedral of Christ the Saviour during the day. What lovely girls they must be.

Vladimir pushed his way into the grounds of the cathedral. For some reason, the Muscovites had always regarded this site as a spiritual home, a natural place to convene at times of crisis – even during the Communist years. Had he asked one of the scores of tourist guides, Vladimir would have understood the iconic significance of the place. Commissioned by Alexander I in 1812 to commemorate the defeat of Napoleon, it had been looted and desecrated on Stalin's orders. It took three rounds of dynamite blasts to raze the building to the ground. Even under the baleful and hostile gaze of the Party hardliners, hundreds of tearful citizens had gathered to watch; they dropped to their knees proclaiming the cathedral as sacred and imperishable. Perhaps that really was the case, though their faith must have been tested when Stalin replaced it with the world's biggest swimming pool.

And then in the earliest days of the New Russia, Mayor Luzkhov had ordered the reinstatement of the Cathedral of Christ the Saviour and her golden domes. She had risen again, in record time. Uzbeks and Ukrainians and scores of nationalities from the East made up the workforce that laboured twenty-four hours a day, sweating in the sun, shivering under the arc lights of the night. When Muscovites saw their cathedral, they saw a symbol of resurgent nationhood, the precious, proudly restored centre of the city's pride.

Perhaps that was why they'd banged up those screaming Pussy Riot lesbians – they had to be lesbians, right? – who'd staged a 'protest song' in the cathedral. Vladimir was no Christian, but it served the disrespectful dyke bitches right.

Vladimir wasn't a tourist either, and he certainly wasn't a Russian. He was a Chechnyan who couldn't understand this country, and didn't want to. All he saw was a big, ugly building that was far too tacky ever to be in *Domovoi*. So far as he could tell, it was just a money trap for the gullible, a big retail outlet – factory-sized, now he thought about it – for the fools who believed in the Russian Orthodox Church's version of God. There were always money changers and food sellers outside Christian temples. Money changers and prostitutes. Maybe he shouldn't have been surprised that the Guatemalan girls found a demand for their trade at the cathedral.

Vladimir couldn't see anyone who might be Guatemalan outside. He almost stopped a black woman, but realised just in time that she was with her husband and that both were American. It later occurred to him that the Guatemalan girls were not of African race, but that hardly mattered. Even in what Vladimir regarded as the racial cesspit of Moscow, dark faces, unless they were identifiable types from the east, still stood out. Guatemalan, African-American, they were all the same to Vladimir – creatures who would be referred to back in Chechnya as 'black asses'.

He stripped a couple of twenties from the fat roll in his pocket and paid to enter the cathedral. He resented paying the forty roubles, but he had to find these women. Soon he found himself part of a closely packed, irregular crocodile of sweaty, steamy religious tourists. They were trudging round the aisles and gazing up at the mosaics on the ceiling and the marble panels depicting the great military victories of Russia.

Vladimir knew he had the right girls as soon as he saw them. The two of them were hanging round the exit of the cathedral, where postcards and other bits of God-tat were most unashamedly hawked. Their clothes were a bit too bright, especially against the cool darkness of their skin. Their manner was a bit too professionally cheerful. When they asked punters for change for their imaginary purchases – and they only asked men, of course – the eye contact was way too long. These were girls looking for trade.

Vladimir cut away from the crocodile and brushed past a couple of women who were rocking silently in prayer before dazzling iconic depictions of saints that Vladimir had never heard of. Still, he admired the workmanship that had gone into the icons. If the Christians were going to worship a god, they may as well worship one with well-heeled saints.

In his enthusiasm, Vladimir had inadvertently broken the reverie of one of the women, who tutted after him. He spun round – almost told her to go fuck herself, but that would be to draw attention; it would be a mistake, especially after the Pussy Riot incident – and when he was so close to his goal . . .

'Hello.'

Vladimir stood in front of the smaller of the two girls. They were quite slight, with big brown eyes and skin the colour of dark honey. Both wore headscarves. All the women in the church covered their heads. But it would be a foolish move for these girls to retain the headscarves outside. The scarves and their dark colouring gave the pair a gypsy air, and Moscow was not noted for its tolerance.

'Hello. You help me?' said the girl in the red headscarf.

'And me too,' smiled her companion, who had a bright green piece of cloth stretched tight across her head.

Vladimir looked at the recklessly grinning pair.

'You need a little money, I think?'

The girls looked at each other.

Vladimir sighed. They clearly didn't understand Russian. He tried again in English.

'Oh yes. We need help. We help you too,' said the one with the red headband.

'We help you very much,' giggled the other.

Vladimir reckoned the girls' English was about as bad as his own.

'It depends,' he said.

The girls looked blank.

'Maybe,' he said.

Two nods.

'Where you from?' asked Vladimir.

Another blank to fill.

'What country you from?'

The tourists in the aisles shuffled endlessly past. Had anyone noticed a man picking up two prostitutes in a cathedral? Did anyone care?

'We are from Guatemala. Is Latin America,' said the girl with the red headband.

'Yes, Guatemala,' echoed her friend. 'You help us?'

'Yes, I help you,' smiled Vladimir. 'I help you, and then you help me too. Come.'

Vladimir indicated the exit with his hand, and Angelina and Gabriella – he'd find out which was which later – stepped out after him into the cold air, and back towards the waiting Cayenne.

IT HAD PROBABLY been a mistake to walk, but Samuel wanted the exercise, the sense of freedom. Walking kept him on the outside of himself. With lots to observe, the random floods of images and incidents could be held in check. Usually.

Yavlinsky had said it wasn't far, and he was almost certainly right. But Yavlinsky had probably been expecting Samuel to take a taxi. Still, the wind had dropped, and it wasn't snowing.

He'd walked the length of the Novy Arbat, past the casinos and the Irish pubs and the windowless bars, sirens to the desperate.

The city's building work continued, as always. Another day, another new complex of luxury apartments for Moscow's *vozdushniki*, the air people of the capital.

He eventually came to the teeming junction of Novy Arbat and the Nikitsky Boulevard, and took a left. After three blocks he came to an apartment building that announced Yavlinsky not just as an air person, but as an inhabitant of the stratosphere.

The last time Samuel had seen anything like Yavlinsky's building it had been abutting Central Park, complete with lime-green awning and a doorman in matching livery. But Yavlinksy's doorman was rather different. He wore a bulky, armour-plated vest beneath his bright red cloak. Samuel guessed that the differences between New York and Russia did not stop there.

He asked for Dr Yavlinsky in his best Russian. A polite request to look into a security camera, an insect click, the soft, bright pop of a security photo. Yes, Dr Yavlinsky was expecting him.

Samuel took the lift to the seventh floor. The landing had polished, chevron-style flooring of pale pine slats, a nod of homage to decor like the warped but beautiful floor of Samuel's hotel room. This however would never warp. The wood was biscuit-thin; it was laid out like a jigsaw on a flat wooden tray overlying a functional concrete floor. The moment the wood began to spoil it would be replaced. The whole place reeked of newness and the incoming culture of obsolescence, use-once-and-dispose capitalism.

A matt black wooden door opened silently to reveal a grinning Yavlinsky.

'Good of you to drop by. Come in.'

Samuel followed Yavlinsky into a living room that was as self-consciously modern as the Tortoiseshell Technology office was American-retro. The place was festooned with fake zebra-skin rugs, funky lamps, and contemplation balls of creamy white plastic. An egg-shaped cocoon chair hung from the ceiling. Small, purple flames smelling slightly of methylated spirits, flickered over a set of white pebbles in a large fireplace. The fire was neither warm nor luminant, merely decorative – another interior designer's joke. The large window was dominated by the biggest lava lamp Samuel had ever seen. It must have been fully two metres tall. Bright orange lava morphed in a hippie heaven of pseudo-amniotic fluid: doughnuts the size of a man's head became irregular fire extinguishers; mutant rugby balls turned themselves into giant frankfurters oozing up and down, slowly transmuting into hour-glasses that eventually stretched themselves apart, the umbilical nexus between the globes finally snapping, creating more and more continuously evolving life forms.

'The interconnectedness of things,' said Samuel, momentarily transfixed. 'One form becomes another, becomes another . . .'

Yavlinsky cleared his throat loudly. Then: 'Here, let me take your things.'

The Russian was no longer in work gear, but was still firmly trapped in 1953. The hair and tortoiseshell glasses remained un-changed, but he now wore a huge, baggy cricket sweater, and voluminous trousers that tapered sharply at the ankles. The look was completed by a pair of Jesus sandals and grey socks.

Samuel handed over his coat and a couple of fine woollen sweaters to his host.

'Now, what can I offer you? A vodka perhaps?'

'Actually, having just trekked here through the cold, I thought perhaps a cup of tea.'

'Of course, my friend.'

Yavlinsky retreated into a galley kitchen. Ivory and black chess pieces clashed in crowded, mid-game conflict on the glass coffee table in front of Samuel.

'More Botvinnik?' he called out.

Certificates and photos hung like hunting trophies on the wall behind the chess game. Doctorates and diplomas from Moscow State, St Andrews, Brown; an array of endearingly foolish Yavlinsky grins and squints into camera flashes – some academic gowns, many beards, conference groups, or maybe trade junkets. One shot featured a rifle-shaped AK47 vodka bottle, and a bunch of dimly lit, dark-skinned men in suits clustered round the beaming inventor, but not quite looking directly into the camera.

'I thought I might be able to persuade you to change your mind,' said Yavlinsky, setting down a frozen bottle and a couple of shot glasses.

'This is unusual, isn't it?' said Samuel.

'Yes. This is Korchnoi, not Botvinnik. An eccentric genius. Perhaps the only truly eccentric Swiss citizen.'

'Not the game. I meant the photo behind you. Recent, to judge from the Kalashnikov on offer. And . . . not an awards ceremony.'

'No, a trade conference. Defence issues. I thought to see if propulsive screw-propeller technology might help with my own project.'

'And did it?'

'Some of the delegates there seemed to think I might help them, at least. I had plenty of offers of funding.'

'Which you didn't accept?'

'No, no.' Yavlinsky picked up a bishop and moved it from its fianchettoed haven on g3 into the centre of the conflict. 'I don't want to be tied to a system, even if I can make it work for me, like dear old Botvinnik did with Communism. I want my freedom.'

'But I thought you were a Botvinnik fan?'

'I am, Samuel. But when I'm at home, Korchnoi is my private vice. He was a cavalier. He fought rigid systems in chess, as in politics. However, I prefer not to revel in the life and works of an apostate Russian in public.'

'An apostate even now? Aren't the days of thought control over?'

'The politics are different, but the sense of being Russian endures. Never underestimate the patriotism of a Russian. Korchnoi chose to leave Russia. That was understandable. Fleeing Communism was understandable. Renouncing one's status as a Russian and turning one's back on Mother Russia? That's something else.'

Samuel picked up a glass, nodded, and drank the shot. It was fiery and soft at the same time, wonderfully relaxing after the walk in the cold.

Yavlinsky grinned at him. 'We'll make a Russian of you yet.'

'But not an eccentric Swiss.'

Yavlinsky laughed: 'Nevertheless, you're neutral. Or at least people think you are. That makes you valuable.'

He picked up a pile of folders and an old book covered in red cloth, then dumped them on the table next to the chess set.

'These,' he said, reaching behind his chair and dropping two more buff folders on the table. 'These are all the materials I have on the man you asked about.'

Samuel picked up one of the folders. It was a mish-mash of press cuttings from the 1960s. Some were in Russian, some in English. One name stood out in all of them – in both English and Cyrillic script: Josef Papp.

'It's strange you should ask about him. I studied his work when I only had a germ of an idea. The ultimate result was Version Thirteen.'

Samuel silently mulled over the note from Kempis. The translation of the first part was fairly unambiguous: *'Let the buyer of bubbles beware of the bubble itself. For the marketplace itself may be a bubble.'*

But the second part had initially defeated him: *'Iosephus Pectus non lactem sed lucem ferat.'* His first translation was too cryptic to make any sense at all: 'Joseph Pectus may bring not milk, but light.'

He'd spent some time pondering a Satanic reference, Lucifer the light-bearer, but it still didn't work. He recalled the image of the note in his mind. The name was the problem. *Pectus* was the word for the chest, the breast, sometimes figuratively used for the heart or soul. But 'Joseph Breast'?

Kempis had loved corny jokes. Samuel remembered how he would refer to the composer Giuseppe Verdi as Joe Green. Seeing the name 'Josef Papp' in Yavlinsky's documents had been a moment of revealed truth. 'Pap', like 'dug', was an archaic word for a woman's breast, hence the reference to milk. This was just the kind of semantic curiosity that Kempis treasured. So Josef Papp was a reasonable rendering. Kempis's note was pointing straight at the man.

Samuel glanced through a number of articles written in English. His own research meant that he'd read some of them already. A Canadian of Hungarian origin, Josef Papp claimed to have made extraordinary breakthroughs in the field of supercavitation. Samuel wondered if Yavlinsky had told anyone about his request for the materials. It might look like an innocent enough scientific enquiry, but he had to assume someone, somewhere would be watching.

Yavlinsky sat back and ruminated aloud, the fingers of each hand spread wide, tips conjoined to create a cage of meaning.

'In my view, Samuel, either Josef Papp was a genius whose work was stolen by the authorities because it was too valuable for one man to own or control, or he was a complete fraud.'

Samuel put down a file, and picked up the cloth-bound book. Its title was *The Fastest Submarine*. The author was Josef Papp.

'And which is it – genius or fraud?'

'I'm not sure, Samuel,' said Yavlinsky with his Cheshire Cat smile. 'Why don't you take all this away and read it properly? Then we can discuss.'

'An excellent idea, Dr Yavlinsky.' Samuel stood and began to load the files into the rucksack he'd brought with him. 'I'll read, digest, and call.'

'Very good. Perhaps you might also give me a considered opinion as to Version Thirteen?'

'The initial impressions are excellent, Dr Yavlinsky, though as you know I'm no scientist,' said Samuel. He rather hoped that Tortoiseshell's patents were secure. Yavlinsky, like many scientists, seemed to be unaware of the true worth of his discovery. But then again, maybe Ksenia was right. Maybe this was too important a discovery not to share.

'Good,' said Yavlinsky again, and slapped Samuel on the back as they made their way to the door.

Samuel braced himself for the cold as he left Yavlinsky's apartment building. The street temperature had dropped, casing the pavement slush with a crunchy, fragile layer of treacherous frost.

IT TURNED OUT that Angelina was the one with the green headscarf. She and Gabriella were now tied to chairs facing each other.

Vladimir wondered whether he'd overdone it. If you used a decent quality of pillow, placed it over your subject and then beat hard, you could cause a great deal of damage. Vladimir was especially good at applying a car jack to the liver, and he could do so without leaving so much as a bruise. Vladimir also liked to use a pillow. The victims looked better that way, even after a long session. When he was fired up, he tended to get carried away, to live in the pleasure of the moment for a little too long. He had to try and remember that the main purpose was not exercise – these sessions could be a serious workout, after all – but to procure information.

Gabriella was now sobbing uncontrollably.

Her eyes were huge and round with fear. The crying seemed to have made her face swell. The hand and feet bindings hadn't been too tight when he'd put them on – as part of the little sex game that the girls had suggested. But now it seemed as though they were cutting into the flesh. There was no question of loosening them. That was just the bitch's hard luck.

Vladimir was naked from the waist down, wearing only a leather jerkin that showed off his abdominal muscles to excellent effect. The steroid-fed penis, though, was annoyingly shrunken and withdrawn. But that didn't really matter. Vladimir glanced over his shoulder at the mirror, and flexed those abdominals once more. Perfect, almost.

The interrogation hadn't been subtle. That was partly because there was no common language between them. But once he'd got the girls tied up he obtained what he needed fairly quickly, although he'd had to force it out of Angelina. The left side of her face was heavily swollen from the broken jaw.

The girls had indeed been in the alleyway that night. They'd seen a Western man in a suit with floppy, light hair walking away. Servicing their clients, they'd not noticed the body at first. Then came the gruesome discovery. Vladimir wanted more information. What could they tell him? They shrugged and shook their heads.

He would finish up here, leave the Do Not Disturb sign up, and Gospodin Kelvinov would disappear. The passport that hotel reception would give to the police wasn't even a particularly good fake, and the photo was laughable – nearly a decade out of date; it showed a wimp with dyed blond hair and no proper respect for body muscle. He had much better-defined musculature now, a strong neck to be proud of, and short, close-cropped dark hair. Almost unrecognisable – nothing to worry about there. And anyway, Sergei Levitan would work it all out pretty quickly, and put any kind of investigation right to the back of the queue.

Now he had to find the Westerner, but first there was the mess in the room to attend to. He took a gun with a silencer from his jacket, walked across the room and stood with his back to Gabriella momentarily. He turned from the window towards her, the golden domes of Christ the Saviour framing his bulky, sweat-glistened torso. The sobbing stopped, but the breathing was almost as loud. The girl's chest was heaving, the eyes even larger than before. But any message, any plea for mercy was lost on Vladimir. He pulled the trigger. Angelina screamed. Vladimir moved quickly, put his hand over her mouth, then injected two more shots into her head.

Vladimir grunted, and glanced at his watch. What next?

MEDULEV WAS LATE. Blandford stepped out of the anteroom in the Ostankino complex, and poured a tiny portion of super-chilled water into one of the conical paper cups provided. He sipped at it, and pushed against the giant doors opening onto the observation platform.

The ABTV operation hustled and bustled as brusquely as usual. It looked like a good day in the markets, judging from the predominance of blue on the screens. There was Medulev sitting at his station, close to the centre of the giant cross of power. He was talking on his mobile phone, but Blandford soon caught his eye. The Russian nodded, and raised his eyebrows – not a gesture of apology, more an intimation that the call was important.

Blandford quickly became absorbed by the activity beneath him. And then the void engulfed him again. Blandford watched these busy, purposeful people filled with desire and appetite. What did he have?

He felt a soft tap on the shoulder.

'Ah, Medulev. I was a million miles away.'

'Do not be lost, Kingston. Come with me. Apologies for my lateness, but we would not have been able to see Anna before now, anyway.'

'Is she so busy?'

'Anna is always busy. But this last couple of days must be something special.'

Medulev led them from the observation platform down a couple of corridors and through the dove-like whirr of two sets of automatic doors. Eventually, they came to a large meeting room. Through the glass-walled corner, the busy floor – the crackle of the market lines, the rasping of scores of voices executing trades – was still visible. But all the noise was gone. They were left with a gentle, air-conditioned hum, a chrome meeting table with a military parade of perfectly sharpened pencils and notepads all bearing the ABTV logo, black leather chairs and a walk-in, glass-fronted fridge filled to the brim with mineral-water bottles of bright blue and red.

'Anna was very disappointed that she couldn't go with Samuel to Tortoiseshell.'

'Would she really have wanted to supervise the visit herself?

Doesn't she trust Ksenia?' asked Blandford as Medulev handed him a tall glass of sparkling water.

'You have met Ksenia, Kingston. She is very capable, but she is blinded by the idealism of youth.'

'Isn't idealism good?'

'Of course it is.' Medulev's face was deadpan, but his eyes glittered.

'But Anna has a more commercial outlook on life, let's say. I want to thank you, Kingston, for introducing us to Samuel. As you predicted, he has been most useful. The early indications of his work are good. When we meet with Anna, I believe you will be rewarded . . .'

'Maybe.'

The two men whirled round. Anna Barinova was standing in the doorway, hand on hip. She wore a tight-fitting black dress of shot silk that would have worked well at a drinks party. A single band of pearls adorned her neck. Their creaminess set off the paleness of her skin.

Blandford moved over and instinctively kissed her on the cheek. She – at best – permitted the intimacy.

'It is too early for celebration, Kingston,' she said.

'Yes, of course.' He flushed slightly.

'But the early indications are good. My engineers are studying the transcript now.'

'In any event,' said Anna briskly, 'Your introduction has been most useful, Kingston. Now you have a choice to make.'

She pressed a buzzer. In an instant, a young, sleekly dressed male assistant arrived carrying a battered, red leather attaché case, and two envelopes. He laid them out at one end of the meeting table.

Anna Barinova rested a hand on the leather case. 'This is the old-fashioned way. There are dollars in here. Fifty thousand of them, all used notes.' She flipped open the lid, the diamonds and the white gold on her fingers twinkling and flashing.

'This one is a bearer bond for $50,000 of Venelikon stock,' she touched one of the envelopes with a forefinger.

'So they're both basically cash,' said Blandford.

'How so?' asked Medulev, looking between the two of them for answers as though he were watching a game of tennis.

'Surely you know what a bearer bond is, Marat,' said Blandford.

'I run a media business, Kingston. I may sit on a trading floor, but I've no idea what the people around me are actually doing.'

'A bearer bond is redeemable by any bank, no questions asked,' said Blandford. 'It's in effect a giant bank note for the value of the bonds.'

'And in the last one,' said Anna, holding the envelope gently between thumb and forefinger, 'is the user name and access code to a Cayman Islands offshore trading company. It currently holds just one security – shares in a publicly quoted company, invested to the value of $50,000 at yesterday's market price. At today's prices . . .' She briefly consulted a chrome-plated BlackBerry. 'The shares are worth $49,980.76. A trading loss on the day of not quite 0.04 per cent.'

'So I have a choice. Traditional cash – always a good thing,' said Blandford. He picked up the briefcase to weigh the notes. 'And liquidity in a different form. Bearer bonds. I love bearer bonds. Money in an easy-to-lose format.'

He barked out a laugh. Medulev and Anna exchanged a quick glance. Where was the joke? This was money, serious stuff.

'Finally, there's a Cayman Island offshore trading company, complete with an investment portfolio of one share. Could I ask what that is?'

Anna Barinova looked at him, a billionairess's stare. Blandford could see that he was expected to guess. 'It's Tortoiseshell Technology. It has to be.'

She gave a tiny nod.

'You choose your form of payment. You are based beyond the sovereign territory of Russia. It is for you to determine how you wish to be paid,' she said.

Blandford looked down. This should have been one of the most exciting moments of his life. If the technology worked, this could turn out to be a real pay day. Once upon a time he would have opted for the most conservative options, the bearer bond or the cash. Probably the bearer bond, as it was much easier to carry and wouldn't create problems with airport security. The money could have been so useful – he could have set Ava up in her own apartment.

But that had been then, and this was now.

*Tic-Tac-Toe* – he dabbed a finger at each of the options, and finally began to reach for the offshore envelope. But Anna picked it up.

'Not before we can independently verify that the information brought to us by your contact is accurate.'

'That's a bit unfair, Anna. Why let me look but not touch?'

'There is an old Russian phrase, Kingston. In English you have the carrot and the stick. We Russians have *knut i pryanik* – the whip and the gingerbread.'

'So this is the gingerbread, right? Where's the whip?'

'Not here, Kingston. I merely wanted you to understand that the gingerbread is so very, very good . . .'

'And that the whip would be very, very bad?' said Blandford.

'You are a logical man, Kingston. I like that,' she said, and moved across to the glass door of the fridge for a fresh bottle of mineral water.

Blandford smiled. This woman and her metaphorical whips couldn't touch him. But he was curious.

'Something tells me you aren't going to crack any whips if the intelligence Samuel has regurgitated for you doesn't produce the goods. I'm acting in good faith, as he is. I think we can all see that.'

He turned to Medulev, who remained expressionless.

152

'No one's questioning your good faith, Kingston,' she said, with the same icy reasonableness. 'But . . .'

'Fire away,' said Blandford.

'What's the connection between Samuel and the British secret service?'

'And the CIA, come to that,' added Medulev. 'We understand that he had some involvement with them in Paris.'

Anna Barinova looked at Medulev sharply. She would lead the question-and-answer session.

'Well, surely you know some of this? You were both at Dr Kempis's funeral. He was buried with military honours for his services to the Soviet Union and the Russian Federation. He was a spook. Not just a spook, a double agent.'

'We are asking you about Samuel, not Dr Kempis.'

'In this world, there are people who don't know, and people who know that they don't know. I fall into the second category. You wanted someone to do a very specific task for you, and I found the right person.'

'So you don't know why Samuel Spendlove was chased down Alexander Gardens by two Communist sympathisers?'

'Samuel didn't even tell me about that until hours after the event.'

'But you knew Kempis yourself?'

Her eyes were steady and cold.

'He taught a summer series of seminars at my old school.'

'Kempis was not a school teacher,' growled Medulev.

'Did you learn your English in Britain, Marat?' Blandford was beginning to get bored of this process. ' "School" often means "university" in North America. I'm an alumnus of Princeton, and Kempis spent a few summers there. It was through him I met Samuel.'

'So, Kingston, your connection with Dr Kempis was purely educational?'

153

'And social. Anna, I travel a lot. I know the best bars in most cities in the world where business is done. But Kempis never tried to recruit me for British Intelligence, nor for the Russians. If he had, I'd do a better job of convincing you otherwise, wouldn't I?'

Blandford brushed back his quiff. It was a pointless charade.

'We have observed you, Kingston, and we do not think you are involved in the knowledge game. But Samuel? We are not so sure. And what kind of job is this? This *research* he does for William Barton? It seems he can decide where to go, what to do and, indeed, whether to work or not.'

'I take your point, Anna. I guess William Barton owes him big-time after what happened in Paris. I really don't know.'

'Is it Barton or the British government that pays him?'

'I don't know anything about Samuel's personal finances, Anna. But if the Brits are anything like Uncle Sam, they'll want bang for their buck. Samuel wouldn't be able to travel around the world on taxpayers' money. There'd be some guy in Whitehall wearing a cheap suit and wanting a weekly report, irrespective of whether or not there was anything worth reporting.'

Anna sipped pensively on her mineral water.

'What you say fits with what we have observed, Kingston.'

'So you believe I'm telling you the truth?'

'I'm saying this: what you say is consistent with the facts that we have observed.'

'Well, let me ask you both something. May I?'

Anna looked at Medulev, then at Blandford. She shrugged her indifference.

'What, in the name of sweet Jesus, does a new drilling technique for oil have to do with the secret services of Russia, Britain, the US – or Abyssinia, come to that?'

'Blandford, what sort of a businessman are you that you ask such a question? If the Tortoiseshell invention works, billions of dollars will be generated almost literally out of a bubble. Empires rise and fall on the back of such events. The oil industry will become even more powerful.'

She took out one of her black and gold Sobranie cigarettes, which the young attendant lit for her.

'Where there is money, there is power. Where there is power there is intrigue. The path to power is never straightforward.'

'Anna, I accept that there could be billions and billions of dollars involved here. I asked Samuel to come and meet you. He was coming to Moscow for a funeral. He knew nothing about you or your business. I saw the moment, made the introduction. That's what you've been paying me for.'

'Yes, Kingston, but you forget why he was in Moscow in the first place.'

Blandford let the blue, blue eyes lock on to him. He waited.

'Yes, he came for a funeral – and we all agree that Kempis was a spy.'

'That may be so, Anna, but I don't think Samuel is a spook.'

She considered. A blue-grey ladder of smoke rose from her cigarette. Abruptly, she shattered it with a diamond-glitter wave.

'In that case . . .' Swan Lake, a trance mix, issued from the chrome-plated phone on her desk.

Anna snatched up the phone and turned towards the window. Blandford could not understand Russian; he had no idea what Anna was discussing. He thought he heard her say *Kamchatka*. Wasn't that a city – no, a region – a far-eastern one?

'Are you sure? OK. Yes. Soon. Bye.'

She gave out a deep breath, and turned back to them.

'Forgive me. As far as Samuel is concerned, we can only act on the observable facts. The rest is conjecture. My apologies for troubling you in this way, my dear Kingston. Now . . .' She gestured at the table. 'Which do you choose?'

'Well, I guess I'll take the Tortoiseshell shares. It's got to be the most interesting option.'

'Very good, Kingston. Very good.' She smiled. 'Now, if you'll excuse me, I have a number of things to attend to.'

The young servant gave him an envelope. Blandford pocketed it, bowed to Anna and Medulev, and left.

'SO?' SAID MEDULEV, as soon as the door was closed.

'I'm thinking, Marat,' said Anna.

She sipped her water once more. 'How many men do we have on Kingston?'

'The usual. Two, including me.'

'Two, twenty-four hours a day?'

'No. In relay. And when it's me, like it was the night we had dinner at the Pushkin Café, I don't follow him to the men's room. I have some real business to do – and Blandford? He's harmless, a low-rent Western schmoozer who does a little commerce because there's nothing else. '

Anna Barinova frowned. 'I'm not so sure. I believe him when he says he's not a player, but there's something not quite right about Kingston Blandford. We must wait – and watch.'

# CHAPTER TEN

YAVLINSKY WAS EARLY. Samuel could see the tall figure in his dark grey, military-style overcoat stomping up and down outside the main entrance of the Tretyakov Gallery in Pyatnitskaya Ulitsa. It was an easy, if chilly, walk from Samuel's hotel. He was getting used to the cold now. In fact, he enjoyed it, in a perverse sort of way.

Yavlinsky spotted Samuel and waved. He was standing in front of a statue of the founder of the gallery. The Pavel Tretyakov icon was mounted on a high plinth; arms folded, Tretyakov glared down with the icy superiority of the professional aesthete. Japanese and American tourists, come to marvel at the museum's treasures, scurried about the courtyard in happy oblivion.

The facade of the building was quite unlike anything Samuel had ever seen before. It was as though someone had made a huge model of a nineteenth-century artisan's house using materials of pink-and-amber marzipan, stuck an onion-dome tower in the middle of it – and then cut the whole thing in half.

'Ah, Samuel,' said Yavlinsky with his customary grin. 'Punctual as ever. Shall we walk as we talk?' He unfolded his arms and gestured towards a pair of large wrought-iron gates leading to spacious gardens beyond.

Samuel stood for a moment before the frontage. A two-metre-thick band of white stone filled with dense Cyrillic lettering perched on top of the walls of pink-and-red stucco brickwork. It looked as though the facade was an unsuccessful piece of camouflage for a giant greenhouse.

'Unusual, isn't it?' smiled Yavlinsky. 'I used to loathe it, but now I like it. Designed by Victor Vasnetsov in 1902, in what they call the revival style. Not that it revived the fortunes of the house of Romanov in any significant way. Please.'

Yavlinsky gestured towards the gates once more. He and Samuel fell into step on the tired, impacted snow. Moscow had not seen a significant fall for days.

Samuel looked at the lettering on a large yellow rectangle on the gates, his eyes screwed up in the effort of translation.

'The Garden of Sculpture of the Era of Totalitarianism,' offered Yavlinsky helpfully. 'After the fall of the Romanovs we threw them and their gods out. This is where the Communist icons are to be found. As you know, we are fond of icons in Russia.'

They passed through the gateway and Samuel saw himself confronted by a huge, heroic-looking figure.

'Kalanin,' said Yavlinsky, nodding towards the fierce-looking four-metre-tall statue exhorting the main picture gallery to rise up and seize control of the means of production. 'Over there you will find a Lenin or two, and a Dzerzhinsky. We have discarded their ideology, but they are not forgotten.'

'Why not?' asked Samuel 'I thought this was the New Russia.'

'It is. But the values are eternal: strength and stability. Peter the Great, Lenin, Stalin and our modern leaders – they share a great deal. The difference is that some tolerate private enterprise, others do not. The big similarity? None tolerates opposition.' Samuel and Yavlinsky sat on a bench underneath a huge bust of Lenin.

In the middle distance, some thirty metres away, a young man in a shapka was wandering among the statuary. There was something furtive in the way he moved. There was something too dutiful about the young man's scrutiny of the statuary, something faintly sinister about the way he constantly sidled out of Samuel's line of sight.

Samuel felt a sudden wrenching feeling in the solar plexus – acknowledgement, but not recognition. He looked over directly now. The softly glistening shapka was nowhere to be seen.

Samuel exhaled slowly, a dragon's breath that gradually dissolved and merged with the gelid air. A slow blink, and the kaleidoscope in his mind's eye turned once more. Yes! He *had* seen this man – at the Pushkin Café. He was one of Moscow's *jeunesse dorée* who'd disapproved of his examination of the books. His girlfriend had been wearing a yellow satin dress, and . . . Samuel blinked again, closing down the riot of images.

He hadn't heard from Anna Barinova for days. He hadn't heard from Ksenia either. They'd got what they wanted when he regurgitated the Version Thirteen formulae. As Lenin would have put it, he'd been a useful fool. Perhaps he should tell Yavlinsky that he'd looted his scientific treasure trove? But if he did, what then? How would he get any closer to solving Kempis's riddle? Better, perhaps, as Ksenia had said, not to interfere with the intelligence.

Before he could speak, the Russian broke the reverie.

'We have much to talk about, Samuel. I am interested to hear how you think that the XB Foundation might be able to help my company. Plus, of course, we need to discuss supercavitation techniques and my friend, Joe Papp.'

Samuel glanced at him.

'I never met the man, of course. He is dead, dead since many years – but I think of him as my friend. Will you go first, or will I, Samuel?'

Samuel stood up, stamped his feet and clapped his arms about his chest to beat out the cold. He looked towards the copse of silver birch; the Pushkin Café observer had disappeared, but he'd still be there, no doubt. Samuel placed his hand on Yavlinsky's shoulder, and they began to walk again.

'So far as I'm aware, Dr Yavlinsky, the Version Thirteen technology looks good.'

The Russian gave a small, satisfied sigh.

'I'm no scientist, but I subjected the documents you gave me to an exhaustive and exhausting analysis.'

Yavlinsky looked at him uncertainly.

'That is to say, I was as thorough and rigorous as I could be, without having the detailed engineering and scientific background to subject the theory to the most rigorous analysis. But I can say that my report to the XB Foundation will certainly be positive. If my colleagues are impressed by your company, I'm sure Tortoiseshell Technology will get its endorsement.'

'Excellent news. Your foundation's investment will make me very happy. I like to do business with people I can trust.'

Samuel stopped for a moment and looked at Yavlinsky. The Russian's eyes seemed bigger than ever behind their thick glasses. Trust? It was conceivable that this man was the only person in Russia he could truly trust. All the others – even Kempis, now under the ground – seemed to have their own agendas, an ulterior motive or two for every single act. Yavlinsky might just be a naif, a citizen of the life of the mind, who wanted little more than a bit of money to support his consuming passion of detecting patterns on the chessboard and in the physical world.

Another sigh dissipated on the cold air.

'So, Dr Yavlinsky. I wish I could say more, but I can't for now. Other than to wish you well.'

Yavlinsky looked at Samuel carefully, then smiled. He extended a hand, and they shook.

'Now, tovarish, we are brothers in the pursuit of knowledge. You've read the papers on our friend Joe Papp – what do you think?'

Samuel nodded, pleased to be moving on.

'You told me Papp and his work were the starting point for

Version Thirteen. His story reads like a *Boys' Own* adventure, but I couldn't really see the connection with Version Thirteen.'

'*Boys' Own?*'

'It's an expression. It just means people who like adventure for its own sake, people who explore.'

'Ah, yes. People who explore are also people who invent,' nodded Yavlinsky enthusiastically. 'Joe Papp was both. He was a man way ahead of his time. It's difficult to imagine how primitive the technology was in 1966 when Papp achieved his feat.'

'Or claimed to achieve it,' added Samuel.

'Or claimed to achieve it, granted. But think of the immensity of the claim – to cross the Atlantic in just over half a day in a submarine that he built himself. And to do it all at a speed of up to 480 kilometres per hour. In other words, at a speed to compare with the average commercial airliner of the era. This was more than just a triumph of engineering. Papp realised a scientific principle in machine form, and then backed his own intellectual judgement and engineering skill to risk his own life. This is confidence in one's applied intelligence.'

They had come to a vast concrete block on which the sharp, lightly idealised features of Bakunin gazed eastwards towards a copse of silver birch and conifers. Yavlinsky brushed snow off a bench with a gloved hand. They both sat. Samuel took off his gloves and rummaged in layers of clothing.

'From what I have read, the press, especially the Canadian press, were extremely sceptical about Papp's claims.'

Yavlinsky took out a small hip flask from the inside pocket of his overcoat and a thick metal medallion with a Red Army logo.

'Papp had been missing for days from his home in Canada and was then discovered bobbing along in a life raft off the Brittany coast,' said Yavlinsky. He twisted the circumference of the medallion; it was a metallic heliotrope that grew into a large shot glass.

'Another triumph of human ingenuity,' smiled Yavlinsky. 'We Russians are very clever when it comes to finding ways to drink. This little device is ex-Red Army. A tank commander probably drank from it in the field. Vodka and death in the great outdoors. Care for some?'

'Just the vodka, thanks.'

Samuel knocked back the shot. He closed his eyes and contemplated. Somewhere behind all this, he sensed Kempis. Was he warning Samuel of some danger?

'There's much that doesn't make sense, Dr Yavlinsky,' said Samuel slowly. 'Yes, there was evidence of a traumatic journey. Papp's flight helmet was battered. There were bruises and abrasions all over his body. The goggles had a cracked eyepiece, and all the rest. But it was circumstantial. No one ever found the one-man submarine.'

The vodka was trickling down the back of his throat in a flurry of hot, white fire. 'What they did find, though, was a return plane ticket from Montreal to Paris. When you add in the fact that a man who looked like Papp was seen in Montreal boarding a flight to Paris, it's not surprising that the Canadian press thought the whole thing was a hoax.'

Samuel offered photocopies of ancient newspaper cuttings to Yavlinsky, who waved a languid hand at them.

'I too thought it incredible, Samuel, just as the Canadian journalists and the French authorities did. That a man could make a solo crossing of the Atlantic in just thirteen hours, touching speeds of 480 kilometres per hour – this was inconceivable. The self-built machine was never found, as you say. Who could believe such nonsense?'

'So you *didn't* believe Papp's claims? I thought you said your research began with Papp?'

Samuel handed the cup back to Yavlinsky, who poured himself another hit of vodka.

'A toast: to science, and the furthering of human knowledge,

162

our understanding of this wonderful universe and our own very unimportant place in it,' said Yavlinsky. He downed the shot in one. 'I didn't say I *didn't* believe Papp's claims. Merely that I can *understand* why some didn't.'

'Who did believe him?'

'The Russian naval authorities. I think also that they were most annoyed. How could a single man working in his garage outdo them in both hull design and fuel technology? They looked like fools, amateurs.'

Samuel remembered the pictures in Papp's book, *The Fastest Submarine*. The craft looked like an eighteen-foot gaming dart.

He closed his eyes for a second. *What an incredible journey it must have been. Papp, strapped into an underwater missile, its engine packed into its fat back end. He could imagine the craft tapered down to an almost perfect point, its sharp nose surrounded by three propeller-like flights, and Papp piloting the thing like some crazy, underwater Baron von Richtofen, for thousands of kilometres through the dark blue waters, over continental shelves, through shoals of fish – surfacing in the creamy cold of the Brittany shoreline.*

'If Papp did make that crossing, he was . . . incredibly brave,' said Samuel. A solitary flake of snow drifted onto the photocopied newspaper cuttings on his lap. He brushed it off with a forefinger. 'But the ship, and let's assume there was a ship, was scuttled off the French coast.'

'Was it?' Yavlinsky was examining some indeterminate point on the skyline. 'We both know the official version of events. The Western press decided that Papp was a paranoid hoaxer. The plane tickets were strong circumstantial evidence of this. The lack of a craft, more so. The unfortunate Papp said that the craft became unstable towards the end of the trip, so he had to scuttle it, and bail out, battered and bruised. The official line is that he was lying all the way.'

Samuel's phone beeped urgently. He glanced at it quickly. A text message from Blandford. That could wait.

'And you believe he was telling the truth?' asked Samuel.

'You were a journalist once weren't you, Samuel?'

'Sort of – by accident, really.'

'You have a way of – how do you say this in English? – putting words into my mouth. I associate this habit with journalism.'

'Only bad journalists do that kind of thing. It's never really been my thing. Was I putting words into your mouth?'

'You assume that I believe all of Papp's story, or none of it. I think he mostly told the truth, but the real story lies somewhere in the middle of things. Papp was a proud man whose dream went badly wrong. You see this picture?'

Yavlinsky pulled out one of the cuttings. Samuel nodded.

'This is a replica of the original craft. Papp was made to *seem* like a liar by the Western authorities. In his book, he claims that the craft itself was made of plywood. This is laughable, and deliberately so. The Americans and the Canadians did not want imitators, and they wanted to portray Papp as a crank.'

'But surely wood was ideal? After all, if the submarine was operating in a bubble it wouldn't have got wet, would it? And why would the western authorities want to humiliate Papp?'

'I believe that the authorities wanted to humiliate Papp because they were furious with him,' said Yavlinsky. 'It was also possibly an attempt by the West – futile but an attempt nevertheless – to put the Soviets off the scent. As for the material of the hull, you are right. Essentially, the submarine was a kind of dart, flying in a bubble of its own making. In this sense, the material of construction is almost irrelevant. It could have been made of paper, and it would have worked even better – a wonderful power-to-weight ratio. But things go wrong. I believe that the original craft was made of aluminium.'

'Aluminium?'

'The papers you have speak of aluminium. This would have been the material of choice. Papp would have wanted this. If the bubble was breached for some reason – temporary engine failure, freak turbulence – a plywood hull would have been crushed by the water pressure.'

'So what about the picture?'

'As I said, it's not the real craft. The pictures seem to have been just convincing enough to satisfy the amateur scientists out there. They could see something that allowed them to admire the idea, but they still thought Papp was a flawed genius, a man whose imagination and vanity got the better of him. The wooden piece of stage kit that you see in the pictures is *like* the real thing, but not viable.'

Yavlinsky reached again into his overcoat pocket for the hip flask. 'I see, by the way, that we have a fan club out there. I assume our young friend in the fur hat is interested in you rather than me?'

'Ah, so I wasn't imagining it.'

'He's been looking at that statue over there for several minutes longer than I feel he really wants to. I fear he must be getting rather cold.'

Samuel laughed quietly.

'Well, why don't you put him out of his misery, Dr Yavlinsky, and tell me what your understanding of all this is? Then he can follow us into a tea room and warm up a little.'

'We have our own central heating,' said Yavlinsky, passing Samuel the military shot glass once more. 'Let him suffer a little longer.'

Samuel drank.

'Good. Now, where was I? Well, it transpires that Papp was on to something. I have tried hundreds of variations of this nose-fin design,' said Yavlinsky, tapping the paper on Samuel's lap. 'What you see in the picture does not work, or at least I could not make it work for a drilling blade. I believe however that Papp did create a viable prototype, and tested it without the permission of the Western authorities. This was why he had to be discredited.'

'But the prototype sank.'

'I believe that too. Either it is rusting on the sea bed off the coast of Brittany, or the Soviets found it and stole the technology.'

Samuel looked again towards the mixed copse of fir and silver birch. Beyond the first few trees his eyes met an impenetrable darkness. 'You are sceptical. Papp was a Hungarian native, don't forget,' said Yavlinsky. 'He would have been a very young man at the time of the 1956 crushing of the Budapest uprisings. He would never have given his work to the Soviets. They would have had to find it for themselves.'

Samuel nodded. Was there something moving out there? Had a piece of darkness changed tone or shape? The shapka spy was still shivering in front of his statue. Was there *someone else* out there? Or was he beginning to imagine things?

'. . . and I was able to obtain theoretical work done in this country that seemed to assume that Papp was on to something,' Yavlinsky finished with a quick flex of the lips, half-grimace, half-grin.

'Ah yes,' Samuel said, sitting straight up once more. Some of the physics texts he had been so ardently tutored in by Ksenia before his first visit to Tortoiseshell Technology flashed into the front of his mind.

*'Cavitation,'* he began to recite, *'in sharp contradistinction to supercavitation, is a phenomenon that is typically unwelcome in the arena of hydrodynamics. The bubbles resulting from this phenomenon (as work is done on the ambient fluid – see preceding note on Bernoulli's principle) are intrinsically unstable. They implode as both bubble and the ambient fluid (water, oil, air) slows down. This in turn generates a sudden rise in ambient pressure. The implosion of such bubbles may cause damage to the agents doing the work on the ambient fluid (e.g. drills, propellers) and*

*related equipment (e.g. boat hulls and other superstructures).'*

Yavlinsky looked at him with some alarm.

'I thought you weren't a scientist, Samuel?'

'I'm not. Just a little textbook learning,' said Samuel quickly. 'When you're as ignorant as I am of these matters it helps to cram a bit.'

'Cram?'

'A strange, old-fashioned expression. It means to learn without understanding. The English education system specialises in it.'

'You English are a strange lot. You send your little boys away from their mothers to be beaten and sodomised and have their heads filled with things they don't understand. That is a terrible system, no?'

'It's not that bad, Dr Yavlinsky.'

'Really?'

'Well, from the little boys' point of view, some of them come to enjoy the sodomy. And where would Soviet intelligence have been without male homosexual English spies?'

Yavlinsky laughed and slapped his knee.

'Very good, Samuel. Very good. Anyway, now you have your answers.' Yavlinsky nodded in the direction of the man in the bearskin hat, who had re-emerged from behind a statue. 'It's time to put your minder out of his misery.'

'Do we have any answers? I'm not sure.'

Samuel rose and began to follow Yavlinsky out of the park.

'The answer, Samuel, is that I'm not sure either. But the Soviets had a lot of research on imploding bubbles and the border between cavitation and supercavitation. It's all about making the bubbles work for you. If you want to have a super-fast submarine, you create the perfect bubble. If you want to have a super-effective drill, you create bubbles that implode the way you want them to. As I told you, Papp's story was the perfect starting point for the research that led to Version Thirteen.'

They were almost out of the main gates now. Yavlinsky offered his hand in a gesture of farewell.

'Just one thing,' said Samuel after a quick lighthouse survey for the bearskin hat. 'When you say "the Soviets", whom do you mean, exactly?'

'It ought not to take much guesswork. The interior ministries have specialist information wings, and then there are certain units of outward-looking ministries. The FSB has the power. In the old days, they just had knowledge. Now they are learning how to turn that knowledge into money.'

'Modern-day alchemy,' said Samuel.

'You're beginning to sound like the oppressed masses. Those who don't understand the knowledge economy think money comes from nothing. But you know how it works.'

Yavlinsky took Samuel's hand, shook it, and turned to go.

'What about your documents?' called Samuel. 'Don't you want them back?'

'Of course. I shall come to your hotel tomorrow, if this fits with your arrangements. I have a long day and a dinner at the end of it. Investors, you know. Perhaps we can meet later in the evening. Toasts. What do you think, Samuel?'

'That would be just fine.'

The trademark reflexive grin, and then Yavlinsky was on his way, soon swallowed by the evening gloom.

Samuel turned and headed in the other direction, back towards the Hotel Ukraina. Twenty-five metres away, the young man in the shapka waited for Samuel to get to a safe distance. Then he took out a mobile phone and spoke into it softly and urgently.

# CHAPTER ELEVEN

'MR SPENDLOVE, PLEASE.'

The hotel clerk looked up uncertainly.

'It's a little early for visitors, sir.'

'I know. He's not expecting me. But I'd like to surprise him. We have a meeting that's long overdue.'

A wad of roubles landed on the counter. The clerk quickly checked the reception area. No one was about. And the pile of notes was just in front of his midriff, so his back was a direct block for the security cameras. One quick movement, and the notes were in the inside pocket of the receptionist's grey jacket. He scribbled a three-digit number on a compliments slip.

'That's very good, sir. Be sure to ring down if you want anything.' The clerk mimed the action of telephoning for the benefit of the all-seeing eye behind him.

One of the desk phones rang. It was that over-ambitious concierge with another question about petty details. By the time the clerk had replaced the handset and looked up once more, the reception was empty again. It was easy enough, and probably better, to believe the visitor had never been there.

A FEW FLOORS above, the lift doors sighed open.

Quiet steps on the softness of the four-star luxury carpet, a gentle tap on the door.

'Who is it?' The inquiry from within was muffled.

'Room service.'

'But I didn't order anything.'

'Room service.'

A short delay; a slow, cautious opening of the door.

'Ah, Spendlove. At last.'

TO SERGEI LEVITAN the gravel-grey clouds outside his Donaskaya window seemed impossibly low. Soon they would break through the glass and wrap him up in a chilly charcoal shroud. Soon . . .

His mobile burst into a shrill electronic rendering of Mozart's 40th Symphony. The lieutenant jumped in his chair, and peered anxiously at the display screen. He had a tiny chrome-plated Prada phone, the height of gangster chic. Levitan wasn't quite sure of its provenance – almost certainly retained as 'evidence' from the body of some worthless hoodlum found tortured and mutilated in the docks at the port in southern Moscow. They were all punks. Screw them, screw the evidence.

The ring tone got louder and louder. Blessed Mary and all the saints. It was him. Ahmed, father of another useless piece of shit stowed in a morgue drawer. But a powerful father, one who had paid much for his hold over Levitan. The third time that morning. This time he would have to take the call.

'Hello?'

'Levitan? Is that you?'

'What can I do for you, sir?'

Levitan hated being called by Ahmed, especially on his mobile. The networks were notoriously insecure. Calls were routinely monitored by the FSB or, worse, the private security forces of one of the corporations owned by the oligarchs. The biggest corporations had political and industrial clout and autonomous security forces; they were states within the state, everyone knew that. Powerful, but unaccountable, you didn't mess with them.

But Levitan had to take the call. To ignore Ahmed again would be tantamount to suicide. Still, Levitan couldn't bring himself to address the gangster by name, especially in the Donaskaya station.

'Where is he? Where's Vladimir?'

'I . . . I don't know. Hasn't he called you? I gave him all the help I could.'

A bead of perspiration ran down the back of Levitan's neck, further moistening his collar. His office had always been warm in the winter, but not too hot. Yet ever since Vladimir's visit Levitan had spent a lot of time shivering and sweating.

'You gave him the contact list for Shamil's murder?'

Levitan cringed. Was he being so explicit on purpose? Did Ahmed want him hauled up on some perfunctory corruption charge by the authorities? Half the police force was corrupt and lived off slush payments, but that wasn't the point. The evidence was always there to nail you if you pissed off the wrong person. Nevertheless, explicit discussion of handing over official investigation documents on a mobile phone was like holding a loaded gun to the head.

'Well, did you? Are you there, Levitan?'

The old man had some cranky Chechnyan dirge playing in the background.

'Yes, yes, I'm here. Vladimir was given all the help I could offer. He said he'd call if he needed anything.'

'Well he hasn't called *me*, that's for sure. I want results, Levitan. From him or from you. Is that clear?'

'Yes, yes it's clear.'

Levitan could feel an urgent rumbling in his stomach. His career might be over. His life might be over. But he would take a mighty dump first.

'What about you? You making progress catching Shamil's killer?'

'We're making every effort, sir, every effort. Our workload . . .'

'Workload! You have no workload! Your only work is to find my son's killer. Do you want me to review the situation, Levitan? I can assess your usefulness. You need to show me you are *useful*. If you can't find Shamil's killer, at least find Vladimir. The stupid ox must call me. You don't want me to send more people, do you, Levitan? They'll find him and then they'll come to see you and help you prioritise your . . . *workload*.'

'Yes. I understand,' said Levitan. But the phone was already dead in his hand.

Levitan reached for the bottom drawer of his desk. The sweating and the trembling abated considerably after the second shot of the Ukraine's finest. He pushed the vodka to the back of the drawer. The bottle was still more than half full, which would mean less than three bottles that week. If he could just keep his office drinking down to that, and get through this Chechnyan crisis, he'd be fine. Early retirement and a modest living, maybe in private security, beckoned. A prosperous male Muscovite in his fifties could attract a decent-looking young wife from the provinces. Third time lucky, maybe. It could all yet work out for Levitan, if they'd only leave him alone.

But that would certainly never happen unless . . . Levitan sighed and rummaged among the large pile of beige folders on his desk. He knew exactly where the Shamil Khamzaev file was. One up from the bottom, just above the documentation on the two prostitutes found dead in the Novotel.

No one had been particularly excited about the deaths of the two hookers. The Russian-language press had largely ignored it. There'd been a short piece on the killings in the *Moscow Times*, run as it was by decadent Western scum who'd never known hardship in their lives; the journalism in the paper displayed their cultural prejudices. The girls were South American, a curiosity. If they'd been US nationals there'd have been a fire storm.

These hookers had to have been killed by Vladimir. He picked up the bottom file. A passport photocopy from the hotel showed someone called Kelvinov, who looked like Vladimir's son or nephew. And the photos of the girls themselves . . . Levitan winced. Vladimir seemed to enjoy his work.

There was now a bomb quietly ticking under what was left of Levitan's career. He had been relying on Vladimir to find Shamil's killer and take revenge on behalf of Ahmed. But Vladimir was making things worse, not better. Why had he felt it necessary to kill the girls? The girls had claimed that they'd seen someone walking away from the scene of Shamil's murder, but no one could get information out of them now. Far from dealing with the issue for him, Vladimir had fucked things up. Vladimir was now lying low, leaving Levitan to deal with Ahmed and the urgent requirement for answers. If anyone discovered that he'd given Vladimir a copy of the Shamil file, Levitan would be fired and disgraced. More than that, he could end up standing trial for aiding and abetting two murders. But if he could not find Shamil's killer quickly, Ahmed would deal with him before the system of justice did.

Levitan had buried both files at the bottom of the large pile of unresolved murder cases. Given the steady flow of murders, there was a pecking order of targets. Western politicians were top of the list, but they typically came with their own security. Next on the list of priorities came the Western bankers and businessmen. Then came assassinated Russians, whose cases were less intensely delicate and political – unless they were journalists or oligarchs.

The Russian nation had gone into mourning a few years ago over the death of the ubiquitous television presenter and producer, Vlad Listyev. The newspaper journalist Anna Politkovskaya's death was another classic of its kind. She had been a critic of the government's connections with business. She'd alienated too many people. One of them had her killed outside her apartment.

Paul Klebnikov, the editor of *Forbes Russia*, had been shot too – he was a Westerner, but the death of a Western journalist, perversely, caused less of a furore. True, the foreign press tended to get upset, but the Russian people saw foreign journalists as part of the machinery of mockery that the West put in place after the fall of Communism. So there were plenty of headlines, and lots of apparent action, but nothing really happened. Everyone knew that foreign journalists were expendable. Klebnikov's assassins and their paymasters would never be found.

Levitan was now going to have to activate the files – and actually investigate them. Incredible it should come to this. He needed Vladimir to find someone or something to satisfy Ahmed's blood lust.

Levitan pulled out the two files, stuck them into a nasty black plastic briefcase he'd been meaning to replace for years, and strapped on his shoulder holster. He was heading for the Novotel to try and find Vladimir, or at least something he could present to Ahmed as progress.

As things were, Shamil's death was a low-grade clubland incident. Easily forgotten. But if Vladimir went after the Westerner, life would become intolerable – spooks, diplomats, press attention. Better to chase the chaser and then get back to the chaser's master. Crazy, crazy, crazy. But then what did you expect from Chechnyans?

Levitan searched for his car keys. This was serious stuff – make or break. He would stay off the vodka for the rest of the day.

THE HOTEL DOOR opened a crack. But a crack was enough.

The blow was swift and well-aimed. The knuckleduster jabbed at Blandford's temple, just visible behind the chain lock, with speed and precision. He dropped to the ground where he stood, like a wet towel hitting a bathroom floor.

When he came round he found himself in a dark, cold room.

Panic! He couldn't breathe! He tried the nose, not the mouth. Slowly, slowly . . . A little better.

Where was he? An attic, perhaps? No, it was clammy and dank. More likely to be a cellar. He was bound to a chair by skeins and skeins of packing tape. The plastic bit painfully into his legs, arms and chest. There was something in his mouth, something about the size of table-tennis ball. It must have been inserted before the creature in front of him applied the gag.

And what a creature it was – dark and swarthy, though not particularly tall, with an absurdly muscular V-shaped torso that might have been splurged out of a giant tube of toothpaste. Atop its massive neck sat a tiny-looking head. It wore tight, belted jeans. The huge bulky thighs met a few centimetres above the knee. It was more dinosaur than man, except for a spark of something – intelligence, or at least a vivid meanness – that glowed in the hollows of dark pupils set in yellowy corneas.

'So, Spendlove. Speak Russian?' it asked in thickly accented English. He popped open a can of Heineken from an ice chest.

Blandford shook his head vigorously.

'No? Shame? My English not good.'

He stripped off his T-shirt and flexed his pectorals.

'It feels good to do this work.' The creature crossed over to Blandford. Rancid sweat had met and mated with a chemically engineered primrose deodorant. Blandford retched.

'You are wanted man, Spendlove. But easy to find for me. Yes, easy for me. I am Vladimir.'

Vladimir tossed the contents of the beer can down his throat, crunched the metal to a small ball in his paw, and threw it on the concrete floor.

'Nice hair, floppy hair,' said Vladimir, ruffling Blandford's long, silvery-brown locks. 'You big man, yes? Drinks? Girls? Big spender in town. But you make mistake, Spendlove. Using phone. I also have phone.'

Vladimir held up a chrome iPhone with an engraved copperplate V. 'I have – how you say? – *app*. Foolish to call when you kill boy. Now you pay.'

Blandford scanned the dark, dilated pupils and their jaundiced corneas. There was nothing there he recognised as human. *Nothing*. But this brute had tracked him down for an act Blandford really was responsible for, bar and room bills he'd really racked up – just not in his own name. Poor Spendlove. He should never have implicated him in this mess. But back then – a million years ago – the person who'd been Blandford had had a crazy life, done crazy things . . .

'Hah! Calm man, brave man, Mr Spendlove. Time for movie show!'

Blandford looked about the windowless room. It was just dark and dank and gloomy. He had no idea how long he had been unconscious.

Vladimir withdrew a small DVD player from the bag and set it down on a dresser opposite Blandford. Next to it, he carefully placed what looked like a small Bunsen burner and an implement with a wooden handle and a triangular steel head that was vaguely familiar to Blandford. Memories of a happy summer spent decorating a cabin in the countryside near Toronto suddenly came to him. It was a wallpaper scraper. The final element of the line-up was a big jar, perhaps half a litre, of acid. The heavy smell alone would have told him what it was – almost like a cake in the oven, but with a searing, unmistakable layer of sharpness at the top of it all. But the label, in Roman lettering, gave it away – $H_2SO_4$, sulphuric acid.

Blandford blinked slowly. He had moved on from the mild panic and the soreness he had felt on coming round. It was impossible to tell what this brute wanted. The cretin didn't even know who he really was, so it was highly unlikely Blandford would be able to satisfy him. What followed would be pointless and painful.

'You watch, then we see. Bad news. Burner is very, very hot. Good news. Not take long. Chefs make cream puddings with it.'

*Crème brûleé*? This creature was mad.

The DVD player flickered into life. A home movie began. Blandford recognised Shamil. He was sitting by a pool and grinning into the camera. Another boy, probably his brother, came into view and Shamil pushed him away. This was his show, his moment of screen glory. Then there was a shot of Shamil in a dinner jacket. The camera zoomed out and there was a pretty girl in a wedding dress standing next to him. This was his wedding. He suddenly lifted the girl, his wife, in the air. Then there was a still image of Shamil's crumpled body in the alleyway.

Blandford felt the bile rise in his throat. Shamil had a wife, a brother, a family. He was, what, five years older than Ava? And now they were both dead. To his astonishment, something in him wanted to laugh: *An eye for an eye!* Ha, so much for that. It just made things worse . . .

Vladimir flicked off the DVD player and moved to the back of the dark room.

'Now you get to be star. I remove . . .' He made a gesture indicating the release of the gag. 'I take off. You speak. Speak, but no shouting.'

Blandford nodded. For the first time he noticed a red dot of light at the back of the room. He was being filmed.

'You tell me what happen with boy in movie, Shamil. He . . . helicopter driver. You know him, Spendlove?'

Blandford nodded once more.

'Not scream, not scream. If you make noise, you will be dead. See that?' Vladimir pointed at the jar of sulphuric acid. 'You tell me all. Not scream. If you do, this goes here.'

Vladimir's hand touched his own groin. 'Acid. See? I put here. Soon – no balls.' He laughed uproariously at this witticism, and undid Blandford's gag with a swift, delicate movement.

Blandford shook his head and drank in a deep draught of air. Then he looked hard into the cold fish eye of the camera lens, glinting darkly beneath its tiny glowing red light.

ANNA BARINOVA WAS sitting at her desk, wrapped in thought. She'd spent time on the trading floor earlier. A moderately busy day always delivered the occasional quick-fire spate of shouting and gesticulation. The opening of the New York municipal bond market caused a ripple of activity on the far right-hand arm of the cross, but the frenzied waters of trade soon closed over the agitation. The tide of commerce crept on; the unexpected opening offer prices were soon forgotten in the police-blue and the cherry-red of the screens, the ebb and flow of profit and loss, knowledge and risk, party and counter-party, dollar, yen and euro.

A gentle knock at the door – Ksenia.

'So, Mother? Does the formula work? Did Samuel do his job properly?'

Ksenia sat down in a leather and chrome Barcelona chair at the far corner of her office. The daughter returned the mother's look, sharp, green eyes locked into ice-blue.

'I should go back down to the trading floor. The troops will be missing me.'

Anna Barinova referred to her 'civilian' employees as troops with good reason. They were the crack forces of the New Russia, appropriating profit, snaring inaccuracies in other people's calculations. If their judgements were better than those of the equities trader in Philadelphia, the foreign exchange dealer in a Singapore boutique, or the lumbering juggernaut of a global bank laying off debt at discount prices because someone in the boardroom had got nervous, they would re-sell or buy back within hours, minutes or seconds. The margins were tiny, sometimes a hundredth of a percentage point. But the base figures were inconceivably large, billions and billions of dollars, and the agglomerated margins were what translated into huge slabs of profit.

'We've all been missing you, Mother. Where've you been?'

Anna contemplated the trading floor. The scene had its own structure, a kind of music, almost, if you let its rhythms and cadences embrace you.

'The guys down there are wondering what's happening. They need your guidance. Me too,' persisted Ksenia.

She took her mother's bejewelled hand. Nowadays, it was rare for them to touch. The business world Ksenia had so recently entered had mediated their contact down to a couple of air kisses a day.

'Don't wonder, Ksenia, my darling,' she said at length. 'We will get to know the real value of Spendlove's work shortly. Sooner or later, everything that happens in the world is reflected by the markets, by what happens down there.'

Anna placed a petite palm against the glass. Was there a dark angel of the markets? If so, how would he trade today?

'If Pakistan drops a nuclear bomb on Bangalore, it will be revealed down there. On the Bombay exchange the price of put options – the right to sell at prevailing prices – will soar, share prices will crash at the same time because the economy will go into meltdown; the dollar will jump in value as investors go for safety, and they will buy gold for the same reason. Everyone looks for comfort in a crisis.'

'But, Mother, there's no rhyme or reason to that. If you just go by the numbers, numbers will take over the world. There has to be a better way, a sustainable way not just to make money, but to make sense of things.'

Anna broke her daughter's gentle grip, smiled, and held a forefinger to Ksenia's lips.

'Hush. You sound like an old-fashioned Communist. If only

you knew how it was back then. You can never know what our generation had to do to get to this.' She gestured down at the pulsating screens. 'Come with me.'

Anna and Ksenia called the lift and descended to the trading floor.

'But this is a stupid world of ones and zeroes,' continued Ksenia. 'One man making money at another's expense . . . this is not a real business. There are no machines; we are not making things that we can sell. As you said, when the world gets worried, people want physical assets. You can't touch shares, derivatives or foreign exchange contracts.' Ksenia was cut short by a frenzied cry from the floor.

In the jungle, as on the trading floor, there are special sounds that speak an unmistakable truth. The alarm call of the baboon when it sees a leopard; the throaty, triumphal growl of the male lion when the pride has made a kill. These both have simple and direct equivalents: the high-pitched wail of panic when the market moves the wrong way against a position calibrated to win or lose millions of dollars for each tiny fraction of a percentage point. Or the open-throated roar of the trader whose bet has paid off – big time. This was the cry of a big kill.

The head of domestic equities, a prematurely bald, chubby man, was standing up and shouting a double-fisted bellow of joy. Four or five of his team, sober-suited young men and women, were clustered round him, peering into his screen. They all had the same information on their own desks, sited out in the wings of the vast floor, of course. But that was absolutely not the point: this was a moment of victory to be shared with the tribe.

Anna looked down on the frenzy. Only Medulev seemed completely unmoved by the celebrations. He was at his desk looking up towards her.

'I think we may have an answer to one of your questions,' she murmured.

'What is it?' Ksenia could see one of the tickers on the rolling band of domestic equity prices appearing with a forty-five per cent mark-up, then a few seconds later a seventy-eight per cent increase. 'Which share is TST-R?' she asked, guessing the answer before it came.

'Tortoiseshell Technology. It seems our friend Kingston made a good choice of payment. His shares have nearly doubled,' said Anna.

'So this means that Samuel got it all right?'

'The market clearly believes that the technology works, but this is bad news for us. We'll have to pay more, much more, to purchase the company.'

'Do you think Samuel has double-crossed us?' asked Ksenia.

'My dear, you came up with the plan!' Anna offered Ksenia a long look. 'Didn't you think through the market implications? About the potential impact of this technology on global oil reserves? Now there's a risk it will be subtly copied so as to get the best of the extraction technique, but using just a slightly different method. Tortoiseshell will claim patent infringement in the courts, of course, but it's too small to fight such a suit, and will probably go bust before it gets justice. Either way, the share price plummets and the big guys steal the idea.'

'Well, yes, I can see there's a risk of that,' said Ksenia hesitantly. 'But we couldn't bid for Tortoiseshell before making sure that there was something worth having.'

A high, warbling sound issued from a BlackBerry. Anna monitored the caller ID.

'What time is it in London?'

Ksenia turned an elegant wrist to expose a slim band of white gold and a Patek watch face encrusted with diamonds.

'The correct answer is that it's the same time there as it is here, Ksenia,' her mother reprised putting her hand over the BlackBerry. 'And it's the same time in New Delhi, New York, Vladivostok and Sydney. It's thirty seconds after the market's decided that Tortoiseshell Technology has an earth-shattering product, and that's the only time it is.'

'Hello?' she called into the BlackBerry, 'So what do you want to do?' she asked, and disappeared into the office anteroom.

⚛

KSENIA SURVEYED THE mayhem on the trading floor. Tortoiseshell Technology had more than doubled now. The oil price was off five per cent, with trading suspended for the day. It always was if there was a five-per-cent shift up or down in a session – a precautionary measure to stop really huge swings in the price of such a vital commodity.

Ksenia supposed a falling oil price made sense if the Tortoiseshell invention had suddenly increased the global supply of the commodity by forty per cent. She just hoped that cheap oil wouldn't mean an orgy of demand: yet more jet-skis and baby Bentleys and private jets. Ksenia went back to her mother's office to collect her bag.

Odette's theme from *Swan Lake* suddenly started playing on her mother's desk. Ksenia picked up the shiny chrome phone and flipped it over. A Kamchatka number?

The anteroom door was shut. Ksenia pressed a green icon.

A male voice, a crackling sense of distance.

'Hello?'

Ksenia dropped her voice half an octave to add a little age: 'Yes?'

'Anna? I still have it. What do you want me to do? Anna . . .?'

'What I said. Do what I said.'

'So you want me to do what *he* said . . .?'

The phone was snatched from her hand, and the line cut. Medulev looked at the number, and glared at her.

'How dare you!' cried Ksenia.

'This is your mother's phone. And that call was none of your business, I'm betting.'

'Who the hell was that? And what's mother's connection to Kamchatka? Don't tell me she's a geologist all of a sudden?'

Medulev put the phone in his pocket: 'As I said, it's none of your business.'

'Well, I'll make it my business then.'

'That would be a mistake.'

He turned and walked out of the office.

'ROOM SERVICE? I definitely didn't order anything,' grumbled Samuel. He opened the door, shut it immediately – then opened it again.

A slim man in a grey suit and open-necked polo shirt stood waiting patiently. He had the youthful figure of a fit forty- or even thirty-something. His litheness, though, seemed incongruous with the deeply lined, hang-dog face of a near-seventy-year-old. The man wore an expression that looked as though he had a mild but persistent toothache – one that had been bothering him for most of his adult life.

'Well, are you going to let me in?' asked the man.

Samuel blinked.

'I . . . Yes, yes. Come in, Mr Barton.'

'So you do recognise me? Most of the people on the payroll only recognise the signature on the cheque.'

This was untrue and inaccurate, and they both knew it. Barton and his media empire were world famous. He had been *Time* magazine's Man of the Year not once but twice. The Americans were obsessed with him and his Japanese wife, Reiko – his fourth spouse, and less than half his age – ever since he had taken a controlling stake in the Washington Post. Barton's smiling face was all over the society pages of glossy magazines, the cascading wrinkles creased up in happiness next to the smooth oval demureness of his socialite oriental wife. The British media, where Barton also had extensive interests in various websites, television and radio stations and newspapers, loved the fact that the crabby old sexagenarian had rediscovered his youth and the joy of sex so late in life. Barton made a great subject for lampooning satire: part global media mogul of incredible gravitas and power, part pussy-struck boy scout.

And he'd once sent Samuel to Paris on a 'research' bursary that had nearly cost Samuel his life. In Blandford's briefcase, Samuel had skim-read a dozen press cuttings, many of which featured pictures of himself and the media mogul. Of course Samuel recognised William Barton.

He opened the door wide and stood aside.

'Quite a place you've got yourself here,' said Barton, nodding at the oak-chevroned floor and the large, high-ceilinged rooms in Samuel's suite. 'Is the XB Foundation paying for this?'

Samuel felt the famous icy glare, the look that had allegedly caused reporters to faint in news conferences.

But that was fine. All the man could do was sack him, Samuel reasoned. And anyway, he very much doubted that he would be presented with a bill.

'Absolutely not, Mr Barton. A business associate, a Canadian who claims acquaintance with you, by the way, booked this suite. Kingston Blandford. I expect him to pay for it.'

Samuel was standing by the piano in the drawing room. Barton had placed his slight frame on the sofa opposite.

'Are you sure?'

Again the glare.

'Why, yes,' said Samuel, somewhat bemused that a multi-billionaire should take such a close interest in a minor item of expenditure. But then the rich were supposed to be mean. 'We came to the funeral of a mutual friend, and Blandford arranged the flights and accommodation.'

'Why would he pay for all this?'

Barton's voice was quiet, but the words hung in the air.

'Well . . . I did him a favour, and now I think he stands to collect a fat commission. Why wouldn't he?'

'Hmm. That was quite a favour you did him, I believe. Do you know where he is now?'

'No, I don't. Blandford gets around.'

Samuel offered Barton a chair. Why was Barton looking for Blandford? It couldn't be connected with the boy's death, surely?

'He prides himself on his contacts.'

'I'll bet he does. The smarmy little bastard has been stalking me for years. Must have given me his card a dozen times. Have you got something for this, by the way?' Barton pointed at the bulge in his cheek.

'Ah, gum. Yes . . .'

Samuel produced a waste bin. Barton spat the gum into a paper napkin and disposed of it.

'Ever smoke, Samuel?'

'No, never.'

'Well if you ever do, don't give up. Otherwise you'll find yourself addicted to abominations like this.' Barton gestured to the bin. 'Nicotine gum. Cherry-Coke flavour. The final indignity. My wife hates cigarettes. And I head back to New York tomorrow. So that's that.'

A watery smile creased Barton's features for a moment.

'Now, Samuel, I'm not your direct employer, but I do know the trustees of the XB Foundation rather well. Very well, in fact, as I happen to be one of them. I wouldn't expect you to be impressed by financial arguments, let alone any threat of withdrawing your bursary. But I do expect you as a former lawyer to be familiar with the doctrine of corporate opportunity.'

'The notion that anything one does or discovers in the course of

185

paid employment actually belongs to the corporation and not the employee? I would have said that doesn't necessarily apply in the case of an educational trust,' smiled Samuel. So that was it – like everyone else, he wanted the technology.

'In strictly interpreted case law, perhaps not, Samuel. But let me make an unusual but perhaps appealing argument to you.'

The ravines in Barton's face appeared to split in the middle – the media mogul's version of an ironic grin. 'What about in equity, not law? What about the moral case for divulging to the educational trustees the work done and discoveries made while in receipt of a generous bursary?'

'I don't deny that the bursary is generous. I wasn't expecting anything more from the trust after the events in Paris . . .'

'I apologise, Samuel.' Barton held up his hand. 'It's hardly right to point out one's own generosity – most ungenerous, in fact. I'm not used to making visits like these, and I'm certainly not accustomed to asking for things politely.'

Samuel bit the inside of his lip gently.

'Yes . . .' Barton put a pensive hand to his jowly chin. 'More to the point, I did acquire one of the world's great publishing houses. That would have been impossible without your efforts.'

Barton stood up, and looked out over the Moscow River. Night traffic crawled along the Krasnopresnenskaya embankment opposite.

'And now I appeal to your reason and your sense of what is proper.'

'Tell me more about the favour that you so famously did for Kingston Blandford, Samuel.'

'Famously?' queried Samuel. 'It was done in circumstances of total discretion.'

'Oh really?' Barton laughed quietly.

'I did the work on a totally confidential basis. I took no payment because I'm already being paid by the XB Foundation.

I did say that the Foundation should be allowed into any deal if Tortoiseshell's process worked.'

'There's something about you I rather like, Samuel. You're direct. You've got balls. You try to do the right thing. I probably shouldn't be surprised at that.'

An ambulance siren wailed loudly in the night air down on the embankment. Barton watched its progress.

'Another rich man has had a heart attack. I don't intend to be one of them, Samuel,' he said turning back to face him. 'You look pretty fit, but you'll do well to do as much as me in the gym. I'm the king of the running machine.'

'My association with you is keeping me fit, Mr Barton. I seem to be constantly on the run.'

Barton laughed again.

'What you don't realise, Samuel, is quite how unusual this is. I have people to do this kind of thing for me.'

'What kind of thing, exactly?'

'I'm here to conduct a negotiation. Not with you, but you've now become part of it. You're implicated.'

'I've just explained that I tried to keep the door open for you. I don't think it would be right for me to give you Tortoiseshell's secrets, but I hope you can strike a deal with Anna Barinova.'

'You are absurdly naive, Samuel. There's business to be done, a personal negotiation. There are times when things need to be done face to face.'

Barton spread his fingertips over the arm panels of his chair. 'I was in Bergen recently, chatting to Bob Zeffman. Heard of him? Kissinger, when he was still a player, Schmidt, Merkel, Attali, Mandelson and every other Mandarin you've ever dreamt of. Every Bilderberg meeting – at the Trianon in Versailles, the Dolder Grand in Zurich, every glorified Women's Institute meeting at Davos – I've been there because I had to. And now I'm here. Barinova isn't the keeper of the secret. You are.'

187

'So you're interested in Tortoiseshell?'

'I want you to commit the formulae that you memorised to paper for me as soon as possible. You work for the Foundation.'

Barton turned away from the window and the fast-fading sounds of the rich man's heart attack. The pale eyes directed a keen, sharp coldness straight at Samuel: 'Now, Mr Spendlove, will you do that for me?'

Samuel shut his eyes for a moment. The inner world flicked into vivid life – *the antipodes of mathematics, of helter-skelter submarine rides veering past shipwrecks, reefs and giant stingrays, the vector diagrams, the tangled undergrowth of equations slipping in and out of focus.*

He looked up and found Barton staring balefully at him. Samuel didn't ask whether he had a choice. The answer was clear enough.

BLANDFORD QUICKLY WORKED out that his captor was a steroid-fed moron – Blandford didn't know much about these things, but he could tell that Vladimir was definitely not a normal human being in any significant sense. The cretin clearly couldn't understand most of what Blandford was saying.

The prospect of death lent Blandford's thinking a marvellous clarity. There was a kind of serenity about it all. The coming pain would be no more than a distraction. He was ready.

But there was one thing he could do. Samuel didn't deserve to suffer the same fate. The brute would eventually discover that, bar bills and phone calls notwithstanding, Blandford really wasn't Spendlove. Blandford had confessed several times to the camera – yes he'd killed the boy, and why. Vladimir's English was limited. Blandford was pretty sure that he didn't understand what he'd said. But sooner or later, someone would see that Blandford had squared the circle: he'd killed the man who'd effectively taken his daughter's life.

But all this was an unimaginable subtlety to Vladimir. He began to amuse himself by pouring a little of the sulphuric acid into a small beaker and burning Blandford's hands. The pain was excruciating.

This was thirsty work, and his captor was now searching for another beer can.

But the restraints had also been burned by the acid. Blandford pushed hard. It was difficult to get leverage with his arm strapped to his body. Vladimir would be back any second. The door banged open, just as Blandford managed to free his left hand.

Vladimir walked up to his prisoner, smirked and turned away.

The small beaker of acid was just within Blandford's grasp. He reached out and took it, trying not to look at the ravages wrought by the acid on his own flesh. He held the beaker behind his back and waited for his captor to drink his beer and get on with round two of whatever it was he had planned.

Vladimir tossed back his beer can, wiping foam from his mouth with the back of a stinking hand. He approached Blandford again, and put his face up close. The combination of halitosis, beer, sweat and sickly deodorant was masked a little by the smell of his own seared flesh.

'OK, nice-hair man. Now we have fun, real fun.'

Vladimir checked that the camera was running, and went to light the blowtorch. He stood a couple of metres away as he did so. Just a bit too far away.

'Hey!' called Blandford.

Vladimir laughed.

'No good, brave man. No good. Vladimir have fun now. Nothing you say good. Not money. Not nothing. Just fun for Vladimir.'

He turned the flame to a cruel spike of blue and red.

'But I never told you the most important thing. The most important thing of all, the thing you must know. If you want the real truth about Shamil,' said Blandford.

'What must know?'

'Must know. Shamil. I whisper the secret. Not for the camera, OK?' Blandford lowered his voice. 'I whisper the secret.'

Vladimir laughed and shrugged in an almost childish way.

'Secret? You tell Vladimir secret?'

Vladimir approached and bent his head in close. Just close enough.

'The secret, Vladimir . . .'

'Yes?'

He was nodding and smiling as though they were complicit in a nursery game.

'The secret is you're a total fucking arsehole.'

Blandford whipped his left hand out from behind his back and threw the beaker of acid into Vladimir's face. Vladimir pulled away sharply, but not quite in time. Two thirds of the beaker hit his face on the right hand side. He fell to the ground and began to scream and curse, holding one eye.

Blandford jiggled the chair over to the main jar of acid. It was the matter of a few seconds to burn through the remaining plastic bindings. Vladimir was still shrieking and groaning. He had a talent for inflicting pain, but none whatsoever for suffering it.

Vladimir looked up to find Blandford standing not quite over him with a nearly full jar of sulphuric acid in his hands. Blandford was just far enough away not to be jumped. Vladimir, backed up against a wall, had nowhere to run.

'So . . .' said Blandford, smiling. He let a drop of acid splash on the wet floor. It hissed and spat, reacting angrily with the moisture.

Vladimir was curled up into a ball now, whimpering like a puppy that knows a thrashing is due.

Blandford looked at him with contempt. It was all so pathetic, so shallow, so worthless. Was it even worth killing this brutal, sadistic piece of shit?

'Vladimir? You understand this?'

The muscle-bound monster looked up at Blandford, fear filling his good eye.

'You, Vladimir, you and I are very different.'

Blandford smiled and nodded, and Vladimir instinctively copied the action.

'You . . . are . . . a dog turd. Something not even worth stepping on. But you are alive. I . . .'

Blandford held the jar of acid up high, eliciting a small squeal of terror from Vladimir.

'I, on the other hand, Vladimir . . . I . . . am already dead.'

And then, to Vladimir's utter astonishment, Blandford grabbed a plastic funnel, and poured the entire contents of the acid jar straight down his own throat.

The tidal wave of pain was overwhelming. As Blandford fell to the floor he realised his whole body was dissolving. It was a huge tsunami of agony and despair, searing, terrible pain. But then, suddenly, it wasn't so bad after all.

Blandford saw, for a brief moment, Ava's smiling face – and his wife Deirdre, beside her. They were healthy, happy – and beckoning him to a bright, bright light of perfect whiteness.

SAMUEL WAS IN mid-gargle when the doorbell rang. He spat quietly into the sink, and crept into the drawing room of his suite. The bell rang again. It sounded deafening in the still of the night.

Samuel cautiously put an eye to the tiny spy hole embedded in the tall front door of the suite. The bell sounded for the third time.

'Hello?' called Samuel. He stood to one side of the doorway. He realised that Barton's talk of gangsters had got to him. Maybe someone was about to blast the door open with a shotgun.

'Mr Spendlove? Special delivery.'

Samuel reflected for a moment. Barton had told him not to open the door.

'Please leave it outside. I'll get it later.'

'Very good, sir. But . . . please to sign receipt.'

A piece of paper and a pen appeared under the door. Samuel signed a docket covered in a riot of Cyrillic lettering, and pushed it back, together with the pen. The sound of the delivery man's retreating footsteps soon faded to nothing.

Samuel sat down on the floor next to the door. His heart was pounding hard in his chest. He would quit Moscow the next day. That was it. He would do as Barton requested, then go back to London.

He made himself wait ten minutes. Then, pulse still thick in his ears, he opened the door as quietly as he could. Samuel snaked an arm out and took the small package from the mat. He pushed the door shut again quickly, then locked and chained it. The whole operation had taken three seconds.

Whatever it was had been pushed into a Manila envelope with his name and the name of the hotel written on it in a nondescript blue ink scrawl. The contents seemed to be vaguely cylindrical, and quite light. Whatever it was, it certainly wasn't a bomb.

Samuel held the package to his ear and shook it. It rattled. He ripped open the top of the envelope and wiped the back of his hand against a weary eye. He was holding an oval receptacle. Samuel probed the container. Inside it was a small brass key, with Chinese style carvings on its head. Circles within circles. The key to what, exactly?

# CHAPTER TWELVE

'SO YOU DIDN'T take a credit card imprint from Mr Kelvinov?'

The young girl in front of Sergei Levitan sat with her hands in her lap. She began wringing them in slow motion. A slight creature from some village near Sergiev Posad to the north and east of Moscow, she had yet to learn that make-up had moved beyond the Cleopatra era. The receptionist had huge blocks of turquoise eye-shadow plastered over her eyelids – Soviet-hooker chic. It almost made Levitan feel like an urban sophisticate.

'No, sir. No credit card.'

The girl's thin hands were moving a little faster now. She was pale and frail, and the hotel uniform was practically falling off her. The cheap white cotton shirt beneath a plain blue smock gave her the look of a schoolgirl at a poorly produced annual play. And this one had forgotten her lines.

'Why is that?'

'Well, sir, as my boss says, Moscow is a cash economy.'

'So Kelvinov paid in cash?'

The two of them were sitting across a small desk in the manager's office, which for some reason was sited right at the top of the Novotel. It was a tiny box of a room in a narrow annexe just off what passed for penthouse suites. The manager, a nervous, sandy-haired fellow, was from Tula in the south. He clearly resented Levitan's presence, but had nonetheless allowed his office to be used for the interview. He irritated Levitan by walking past the door every three minutes and flicking curious glances at him and the girl through the small porthole in the door.

Lying on the desktop between Levitan and the girl was the file on the murder of the two prostitutes who'd died so horribly on the seventeenth floor. The Shamil file was safely in Levitan's decrepit briefcase. He didn't even want to think about where that one might take him.

'Yes, sir. He paid in cash.'

'And how much of that cash went to you?'

The girl looked up fearfully.

'It's all right,' said Levitan gently. He took a soiled handkerchief from his pocket, dabbed at the patina of cold sweat on his brow, and tried to manufacture a reassuring smile.

'Your boss is right. This is a cash economy. No one can blame you if you took your share. You're poorly paid. It's expected in the hotel trade, one of the perks of the business.'

The girl peered into Levitan's twisted features and glanced nervously at the door. Then her bony little hands moved to the top button of her blouse. She had reached the third before Levitan realised what she was doing.

'No, young lady. You misunderstand. That's not what I'm after. You just need to tell me as much as you can remember about Kelvinov. He's a dangerous man. He must be caught,' said Levitan.

There was a knock at the door. It was Aksyonov – tall, fair-haired, and – something that was almost becoming a rarity in modern Moscow – a true Muscovite, born and bred. There was something reassuring about Aksyonov. He was solid, dependable, smart without being too clever. The poor bastard couldn't be too clever, because he seemed to like the work. One day he'd discover that being a policeman in modern Moscow was an impossible job. Till then, he was a damn good bag man to have around.

'Sorry to interrupt, boss,' said Aksyonov. He looked at the girl re-buttoning her blouse – not for too long – and tossed a tiny data stick onto the desktop.

'What's this?' growled Levitan.

'The security camera shots. Inside and outside.'

'No tapes? No discs?'

'No, sir. Just put this in your laptop. It's just a question of trawling through and finding the right images. The manager tells me that Kelvinov drove a Porsche Cayenne with diplomatic plates.'

'I don't have a laptop, Aksyonov, in case you hadn't noticed,' said Levitan. 'The trawling will be your personal pleasure, not mine. When that's done, get onto the traffic division. It's unlikely, but it's possible this maniac was stupid enough to get pulled up for a traffic violation. Diplomatic plates turn normal people into idiots and they don't realise that no one is immune in this city. Remember the history lessons in school? Ivan the Terrible driving a coach and four through a hedge of blackthorn? How he always drove his carriages in the middle of the road at top speed as a demonstration of his invulnerability, just like gangster warlords in the early Yeltsin days?'

Aksyonov pursed his thin lips.

'Ha. Probably not,' said Levitan. 'You're too young.'

'Maybe not, sir. But I do remember the gangsters treating the city like their own personal racing circuit. I'll call traffic.' Aksyonov headed off.

Levitan waited till the door was quite closed and twirled the tiny data stick in his fingers. 'So, we have everything on record.' He was now striving for gravitas and cool competence. This was a real struggle; Levitan's stomach was complaining volubly again. He really must go to the doctor.

There was a sharp rap on the door. Aksyonov was peering in through the small round window. Levitan beckoned him in.

'What is it, sergeant?' he asked impatiently. 'I'm conducting an interview here. This is the second interruption. It'd better be good.'

Aksyonov had worked with Levitan for a while. He recognised the different moods, and when to ignore them.

'The station called, sir,' he said calmly, 'It's all a bit puzzling. The desk said there was a new case for us, as we weren't doing anything.'

'Did they?' asked Levitan. 'What did you say?'

'I took the details and said I'd pass them to you.'

Levitan considered. Aksyonov knew that Levitan had two files, two active cases. But Aksyonov also knew that what Levitan kept in his briefcase might not tally with official records. There were all kinds of reasons why it was good to be able to work away from the official register of record. One of them was financial. Sometimes it paid not to jump to the obvious conclusion about a potential perpetrator.

Not jumping to the obvious – and correct – conclusion about the perpetrators of a restaurant killing in Chekhovskaya a few years ago had been lucrative enough for Levitan. There was no way he was going to find the two members of Ahmed's clan who'd been seen outside the restaurant moments before. The money had been good, but there was always a price to pay – as he was now discovering.

'Well, we'd better finish up here quickly then.'

The lieutenant's hand instinctively went to the handle of his briefcase. He opened it and scooped the file off the table and into the case, where it joined Shamil's file and a couple of bottles of warm Baltika 6. Warm beer was fine. Levitan tended to drink less when the beer was warm. The good news was that no one at the station had discovered that these files were missing. But the depressingly bad news was that Ahmed wanted results fast.

The lift was glass-panelled and operated on the external walls of the building. Levitan considered this to be an extravagance, a security risk, and an unnecessary provocation to his queasy stomach. The cold Baltika 6, sister to the tepid ones in his case, had seemed like a good idea at breakfast. Less so now.

'So what information do we have on the new case?' asked Levitan wearily. 'Don't tell me. It's another gangster execution.'

The golden onion domes of Christ the Saviour Cathedral seemed to be floating upwards over Aksyonov's shoulders as the lift descended.

'I'm not sure, sir. There seems to be some confusion over the identity. Male. Possibly a foreigner.'

'Let's hope so. If only it turns out to be the supposed diplomat Kelvinov, at least some of my problems will be solved,' muttered Levitan. A spark of hope sprang up within him. Maybe, just maybe, somebody had taken out the appalling Vladimir. That would at least make life simpler, although he would still be left with the problem of finding Shamil's killer. Or at least convincing Ahmed he'd found him. It seemed too easy that this Spendlove had killed the boy and then made a phone call to position him at the time and place of the crime. Something wasn't right.

'The station says we can't say for sure yet, sir,' said Aksyonov, flipping open his broad-feint reporter's notebook. 'The details at the scene indicate that the deceased is either named or connected with an American or a Brit – some English-speaking Westerner, anyway. The name is . . .'

The lift was newly installed with a sharp gear ratio and a brutal braking system. It came to an abrupt halt at the sixth floor. An elderly woman dressed in a sable coat and carrying a dachshund in a scarlet travelling bag stepped in. Levitan passed a handkerchief across his clammy brow. He noticed that the unfortunate dachshund had been dressed in a miniature pink silk bow tie. The three shared the briefest of eye contact to acknowledge the enforced intimacy. The lift lurched sharply downwards.

'Yes, sir,' said Aksyonov, quietly carrying on where they had left off. 'Either named or directly connected to a Western name.'

Levitan looked down at Aksyonov's notebook.

'Spendlove,' he groaned quietly, then – it was too much, too sudden – he vomited, mightily, over a very surprised old lady and her dog.

❦

WHAT A MORNING it had been. Anna Barinova sat with her troops at the very heart of ABTV's operations. Makarov, her equity chief, had been building a position in Tortoiseshell Technology – nice and slow, so the prices didn't rise too sharply and draw attention. The next phase was trickier, as TST.R featured prominently on the price ticker, and the news wires began to highlight it as a fast-mover. Within minutes there was a worldwide scramble to get into the shares, which seemed to be jumping five per cent an hour. There were 'corrections', of course – occasional dips in the price, as early buyers took quick profit. The corrections provided Makarov with the opportunity to buy more, building a powerful stake in the company. The management would need to take account of this shareholder's views.

Anna had spent the morning carefully monitoring the Tortoiseshell operation. The information leak about the significance of the technology was premature. It had cost her money. That was the thing about information, though. You tried to control it, but you never could – not with so much at stake. Blandford was one who had plenty to gain. His $50,000 of stock was now worth $125,000. But Yavlinsky stood to make the most.

Medulev had been sitting just a few feet away, watching the action. Barinova was like an orchestral conductor, a maestro, at the height of his powers. Despite the preoccupation with Tortoiseshell, the troops had benefited from the general turmoil in the markets, thus making even more money. The bond desk had bought US government bonds heavily on the view that a fall in oil prices would ease inflationary pressure, leading to a fall in interest rates. Falls in interest rates meant higher bond prices.

Medulev knew little about the various markets, but he understood that the little Moldovan guy opposite had done well, judging from the hand gestures and the smiles. With every little wave of approbation from Anna, the Moldovan fingered his greasy Wharton Business School tie.

There was one period of ten minutes or so when the floor became a Mexican wave, whooping market coup after market coup. After the bond team, the domestic equities desk stood up to acclaim and be acclaimed, then the international equities desk got a wave from the centre of the cross.

Ksenia strode onto the floor during a relatively quiet period. The hooting and the tongue-clicking that customarily marked the entrance of an attractive woman onto the floor were more muted than normal – just one or two whistles, a smutty joke, a catcall. Not only was this woman the boss's daughter, but also the boss was present.

Anna was speaking into a video link with Frankfurt, and registered Ksenia's arrival with a flicker of her brow.

'OK, I'll speak with Erich Halberstadt about it. See you, Clarkson.'

She looked up, then sat back in her large black leather chair. Ksenia stood close to her desk, demanding attention.

Then came a new round of screaming and chest-beating from the international equities desk. A major Wall Street firm had raised its profits forecast for Maple Bages, one of the giant American banks, by ten per cent. The US market was surging. A new wave of triumphal adrenaline swept across the floor, and beyond.

Bond positions were being switched into equities around the world. The screens showed managers in Kuala Lumpur barking buy orders; the urgent crackle of squawk boxes connected to Tokyo, Milan, New York and Sydney all recorded a global move to surf the tide of euphoria.

Anna Barinova took it all in, swivelled silently from side to side, her hands resting on the arms of her luxurious throne. Ksenia hadn't moved.

'Have you come to invite me to lunch, dear?'

'I'm not interested in lunch. What's this game you're playing with Tortoiseshell?' hissed Ksenia.

The rest of the floor continued to go about its business. But everyone could sense the boss was about to have an argument with her daughter. Juicy gossip would have to wait for the end of the session, though. There was money to be made – or lost – in the seconds following the Maple Bages upgrade. The market kaleidoscope was turning, and everyone had to concentrate, to make sure of perfect alignment with the new pattern, a new world order that might last ten minutes or two months.

'Makarov has been buying the stock all morning. We now own fifteen per cent of the company.' Anna's voice was soft, the cornflower-blue eyes ultra-cold.

'But what about the technology, Mother?'

'Well, the market seems to believe in it, and in Tortoiseshell's ownership of it. What more can I say?'

Ksenia shook her head, and looked about her at all the measured mayhem. She reached over and plucked her mother's packet of Sobranies out of the tiny handbag on the desktop.

'Why don't you have a cigarette break?' asked Ksenia. 'Because there are one or two things I'd like to say to you.'

She marched off the trading floor, clutching the cigarettes. Quiet cheers could be heard from the gossips and the many confrontation-junkies across the room.

SAMUEL TRIED BLANDFORD'S mobile again – the fourth or fifth time that morning. Still no response. He'd called the Kempinski earlier. No one had seen Blandford for nearly two days. The manager had come on the line to ask if Samuel were a business associate of Blandford's. There was a bill to settle.

It was getting late in the morning. As yet, Barton's car had failed to materialise. Samuel wandered listlessly around the huge suite. Invariably he found himself drawn to the large windows of the sitting room; he stared down at the river and the vast expanse of the city unfolding before him. Blandford must be down there somewhere – walking the streets, or sunk in the depths of the river. Samuel tried to shake the image from his mind.

Life had a different value in Moscow. It was a bargaining chip in the deal-making process. You could openly discuss who'd killed whom, as this was an occupational hazard of a forceful negotiating position. It was all a question of how much the bargaining chip was worth. How much for the boy's life? And Blandford's? And – a small, involuntary shudder – his own? So much for the grand plan to save the world. It was time to get out, whatever the rest of the world wanted. Barton, the Barinova women, Blandford, Kempis? Goodbye to all that.

The bedside phone rang – a long, high-pitched warble. Samuel sprinted into the bedroom and grabbed the handset.

'At last.'

'Excuse me, sir? This is reception.'

'I know. Mr Barton has sent a car for me. I'll be right down.'

There was a short silence followed by a rapid exchange in Russian that Samuel didn't quite follow. The name 'Gospodin Barton' was mentioned a couple of times.

'There is no Mr Barton here, sir,' said the receptionist. His accent was strong, but his English was good.

'Mr Barton said he was sending a car for me.'

Another exchange in Russian.

'There is no car for you, sir,' said the receptionist eventually. 'I have a Lieutenant Levitan of the Moscow City police department. He wants to see you, and asks that you wait in your room.'

'I see.'

Samuel replaced the receiver and drifted back to the sitting room window. There was no snowfall; the sky had a low, grey intensity, the flatness of Moscow sunlight. The White House opposite was positively iridescent. But the vista gave Samuel no pleasure.

The local police, with their local concerns. What else should he have expected?

The doorbell rang. The door spyhole revealed a small dark, balding man and a taller, younger fellow with pale-blond hair. Suddenly Barton's admonition not to open the door to anyone came back to Samuel.

'Who is it?' he called.

'Police. Lieutenant Levitan and Sergeant Aksyonov. Moscow City police.'

'May I see your identity cards, please?'

The two men held up plasticised photos superimposed on an emblem of the Moscow police department and the two-headed eagle of the Russian state. Samuel opened the door.

'You speak Russian?' asked Levitan.

'A little.'

'We'll try in English, but I'm afraid I don't speak well. Sergeant Aksyonov speaks good.'

The fair-haired man nodded.

'Quite a place. I've always wanted to stay here,' said Levitan. 'I couldn't afford. Too expensive for ordinary citizens.'

Levitan shot Samuel a look that struck him as decidedly old-fashioned – a hybrid of Communist dogmatism and materialist envy.

'So, what can I do for you?' asked Samuel.

'I'm afraid I have some bad news for you, sir,' replied Aksyonov.

'We're the investigating officers in charge of the murder of an acquaintance of yours. As you were one of the last people to see him, we have a number of questions to ask.'

'Murder?'

Samuel had already seen too many dead bodies. It couldn't be happening to him again.

'You don't seem unduly surprised, sir, if I might say so.'

Samuel ran a hand through his hair.

'Well, I'm not. I was told he'd gone missing.'

'Really?' Levitan and Aksyonov exchanged a glance. 'When was that, and who told you?' asked Aksyonov.

'Last night. Quite late. I had a visitor.'

'A visitor?'

'Yes. It sounds strange, but I got a late-night personal visit from William Barton. Have you heard of him?'

'Yes, sir. I've also heard of Bill Gates and Mark Zuckerberg. William Barton owns two television stations and at least three newspapers in this country alone. Are you serious?'

Levitan picked twitchily at his hair.

'Yes, lieutenant. Never more so. Barton told me he'd gone missing. They had an appointment and he failed to turn up for it.'

'An appointment? Really?'

The two policemen again looked at each other, then back at Samuel with intense interest.

'We have his business diaries. There are several entries featuring your name, but not William Barton's. Most unusual.'

'Have you informed the embassy?' asked Samuel.

Levitan's eyes widened slightly.

'The embassy, sir? Which embassy?'

'The Canadian embassy. Kingston Blandford was a Canadian national.'

'Kingston Blandford, sir? Who is he?' asked Aksyonov. 'We're here to investigate the murder of Piotr Ivanovich Yavlinsky. He was found dead in his apartment just a kilometre's walk from here this morning.'

A chasm opened beneath Samuel. That goggle-eyed amiability,

gone? Yavlinsky was a drinker of bright-green liquor, vodka and tea, a chess player, an innocent, What had he done, other than unearth a beautiful secret? In his mind, Samuel riffled through the endless stream of images and equations. Poor Yavlinsky, he'd unearthed a secret that was too beautiful, too valuable for him to live.

'How could this be, Lieutenant?'

Levitan was looking less and less well. 'He's dead, sir. That's all you need to know. And I have to inform you that not only were you one of his most frequent associates in the days leading up to his death, but we also understand he had a package delivered to you last night. Would you mind showing us that package? Its contents may have a material bearing on the case.'

KSENIA WAS SITTING in her mother's chair, behind the high altar of her desk, high up in the chief executive's office.

Anna entered without knocking.

'Make yourself at home, why don't you? Mind if I have a seat?'

'Only a little. What are you doing, Mother?'

'What we planned.'

'We! You're playing your own sordid game! We should release the technology to the world, right now.'

'But that would be theft – theft of the intellectual property of Tortoiseshell Technology. The best way to release it is to acquire the company, and then do what we see fit with its main asset.'

'You mean pay for it, and then give it away?'

'Not quite. You'll see.'

'We didn't get sight of the plans to make money! Can't you see that making Version Thirteen available to the world is the right thing to do?'

'It's also breaking the law – it's stealing, Ksenia. And please don't lecture me. Do you think I want a daughter who's a pillar of moral rectitude – bullshit moral rectitude?

'You know, Ksenia, you behave as though profit is a bad thing. The Communists didn't differentiate between making a few kopeks on a bag of potatoes and selling your body in the streets or bars for hundreds of dollars. Turning a profit was absolutely and uniformly evil: there was no difference between potatoes and prostitution. We are in a new era. Companies make profits, which are taxed. The tax is used to build a better life for everyone. Better schools, better health provision, better roads – that's what capitalism is about.'

'But you say profit is all there is. You say profit is absolutely good.'

'No, Ksenia. I say money is absolutely neutral. Profit will always perpetuate itself if it can. What we must do is harness some of that power for our own benefit. We must have our share. Everyone in Russia will benefit if we can grab a larger slice of global wealth.'

'If you take too much now, there'll be nothing left for tomorrow.'

'For you, you mean?'

'No, Mother, I mean for your grandchildren, and your great grandchildren. Sustainability.'

'If my generation gets it right, Ksenia, there'll be much more for future generations. That's the point.'

Anna reached into a desk drawer, withdrew a packet of cigarettes, and quickly lit up. She tossed the packet onto the desk, within easy reach of Ksenia.

'Quick hit, darling?'

'I don't.'

'No. Of course not.'

Anna emitted a rich cloud of smoke.

'Why don't you behave sensibly, Ksenia? Is it so difficult to support me in what I'm trying to achieve? Instead, you undermine me constantly.'

'You disgust me.'

Ksenia's lower lip trembled very slightly. Anna inhaled deeply, extinguished her cigarette with unnecessary force, and leaned forward.

'I must be such a disappointment to you, darling – your flawed, imperfect mother. Don't take any responsibility for the damage you've caused. That's what a good spoiled, rich girl does. Why not do something really useful? Go to a few polo matches. They have a better class of criminal there. Go pick up a rich husband. Now that would change the world.'

'Why are you doing this, Mother?'

'Why?' Anna leaned back in her chair. 'Because you're my daughter, and I love you.'

The *Swan Lake* theme suddenly issued from Anna's handbag – the last time Ksenia heard that ringtone it had been Kamchatka calling.

'Wait here. I'll be back,' she said, suddenly all plain business. She strode from the room.

As soon as the door was closed, Ksenia sprang up, checked her mother's desk drawers for anything that might help. Nothing, of course, just fountain pens with inks in exotic lavender and scarlet. Ksenia slammed the drawers shut and stalked out. If her mother had a plan that she wasn't prepared to divulge then Ksenia would just have to come up with a better one herself.

VLADIMIR APPLIED THE wad of lint to his cheek, and winced. Soaking the dressing in milk had been a big improvement, but the burns and the scars from the acid splash were still very painful. Initially, he'd drenched a piece of lint in water and then applied it. This had only made things worse. The pain had cracked inside his head like summer lightning. He'd spent so long building his body up, and now a few drops of liquid were eating away at him, chewing him down to the bone.

Vladimir glanced in a dirty, cracked mirror on the wall at the back of the dank cellar. He looked away again quickly. The figure he saw resembled a cartoon pirate.

By some miracle, there was an eye patch in his first-aid kit; he wore the patch over his right eye. It held down another piece of milk-soaked lint. Vladimir hadn't been able to see out of his right eye since the little runt of a Westerner had thrown the acid over him.

How could he have been so stupid, so careless? Vladimir certainly wasn't stupid. Such people did not survive in Vladimir's business, let alone make money and build a reputation like his. So this was bad. It was an embarrassing blemish to both his reputation and his looks. The face in the mirror was a mess.

The only consolation was the truly excellent definition of his abs, pecs and triceps. Vladimir swallowed another couple of steroid tablets. Then he took alternate sips of a vegetable protein concoction and his favourite low-calorie chocolate milk drink. The steroids might not dull the pain, but it would soon matter less.

After a few minutes, the nervy aching was still there, but his body was dealing with it better. Vladimir gulped down some water, and looked ruefully at the stinking package on the floor.

He would dispose of the body of Samuel Spendlove and then drive back to Grozny in the Cayenne at a sedate pace. Cruising, careful driving. That's how it would have to be. Vladimir was down to his last set of number plates. The Uzbek diplomatic plates were now in a plastic bag at the bottom of the Moscow River. So there could be no more mistakes.

Vladimir poked a toe at the thing on the ground. It was probably still fair to call it a corpse. Bagging up the body had been exceptionally difficult. There were cracks in Vladimir's ancient rubber gloves, the only ones in his kit. The acid had seeped through and scorched his fingers. He was normally too professional to feel queasy, but the thick stench coming from the remains was sickening.

It was all wrapped up now. The remnant parts had looked older than he'd expected, but maybe the Westerner didn't take care of himself the way Vladimir did. Anyway, none of it mattered now. Job done, once he'd disposed of this package that had the look and dimensions of a large, curious-smelling bag of fertiliser.

By the side of the bag was a photo, half-eaten by the acid. Vladimir picked it up delicately. He didn't want any more acid burns. Vladimir could just about make out a young blonde girl leaning forward to snort a line of cocaine, surrounded by several men, all dark-haired, some bearded. So his Westerner used whores. No surprise there. They all did. He threw the photo in the bin. That was the last detail taken care of.

Soon it would be dark enough for Vladimir to get his parcel out on to the street and into the boot of the car. Vladimir turned his head and caught a sniff of himself. He hadn't showered in days. His personal odour was a cocktail of sweat from the frequent exercise sessions and the effort of bagging up the corpse, the acid and its reaction with human flesh, and the plastic bag he'd used for the body. It was truly repellent.

He touched his eye anxiously and then the confidence and the aggression kicked back in. He would have surgery on the eye back home. He had enough dollars to have the best plastic surgeons flown in. Or he could fly out if he really had to. The savage scarring of his cheek would be remedied. But underlying all the confidence and the steroid-driven chemical surges, something told him that the smell of decay came partly from Vladimir himself. He had to get out of there, and he had to get out quickly.

He checked his commando diver's watch. It would be getting darker outside, and Vladimir would just be a big guy carrying a large, heavy parcel in a twilight street. Once he was back above ground, Ahmed would call. Ahmed would probably have called a dozen times while he had been in the bunker. He would be happy now. He'd email Ahmed the video of Spendlove's confession.

Shame that he'd not kept things under control so as to capture the moment of death. Still, that was a detail, no more. Things were looking up.

THE MAGENTA CEILING strips from the underground car park in Ostankino filtered corpse-grey light through the tinted windows of the limousine. His skin, lustrous and faintly tanned in sunlight, took on a greenish hue.

'Yes, it's a difficult road to follow. But true excellence is self-isolating, Anna. You know this.'

Anna clicked off her phone. The deadened silence of her bullet-proof, bomb-proof limousine had an almost religious feel – to her, at least. She had her mobile cathedral in an underground car park, and she had her renegade priest.

'Use the business thinking that's got you this far. Kamchatka is a long way away, and there are other factors to consider, as you say. Yet you know the answer as you ask the question: use the simple verities of focus, control, ruthless objectivity. People think you're a sorceress – whatever you want to call it – because you apply simple, ruthless logic to all situations. Very few can do this. Let the herd believe that it's all magic, so much the better.'

Anna watched, listened, nodded. Let the masses believe in magic and let Khan believe in control. It was all the same to her.

'Now,' he said, checking the chunky TAG Heuer on his wrist before shooting her a quick smile. 'What's the state of play with our friend Samuel Spendlove?'

'YOU DO NOT seem to measure the gravity of this situation, Mr Spendlove. It is your situation, and it is serious. Or is there a mis-understanding?' asked Aksyonov.

It had been a while. Questions, no answers, more questions . . .

Sergei Levitan and Aksyonov were still sitting with Samuel in his hotel suite around an ornate coffee table with an inlaid mosaic composed of mother-of-pearl and flat, lustrous chips of stone. A silence fell, tempered only by the soft sigh of embankment traffic far below.

Samuel breathed in deeply. Once, twice. Yavlinsky? Dead? Blandford was missing, according to Barton. He hadn't heard from Anna Barinova, Ksenia or anyone from ABTV. His breath formed a cloud on the windowpane.

Samuel seemed to have been in a vacuum ever since he had completed the work that they had asked him to do on Tortoiseshell Technology. Or maybe he wasn't in a vacuum. Perhaps the stillness was orchestrated by Kempis as part of his message, or the preface to some swift, terrible assault from a hidden predator – a viper, a hawk, a giant spider. For the moment, the damage was being done to others. He would use the space and time to analyse before the blow – and there must be one – finally fell.

'No, no. There's no misunderstanding, Sergeant. I'll get the package for you now. It's in my bedroom.'

Samuel let the door of his bedroom close behind him. He picked up the padded envelope and shook it gently. A soft rattle. He weighed it in his hand. He couldn't keep the policemen waiting.

Samuel returned, withdrew the container from the package and set it down on the table. He glanced at one man, then the other. The tall blond one was impassive. The short sweaty one looked angry, or unwell, or possibly both. Silence descended.

'As you can see, Sergeant, Yavlinsky is a strange man. I mean *was* a strange man. He sent me an empty container. Why? Only he would know,' said Samuel.

He kept his words even and his face straight enough, but as he spoke he couldn't help himself fingering the small brass key in his trouser pocket.

⚛

'ARE YOU SURE you're sure, Alexander?'

The figure on Anna Barinova's phone screen broke up into a pixellated mess again. That was a side effect of encrypted data channels; they carried less data as a recognisable voice pattern. But the frustrations of image-freeze and the like were minor indeed. Absolute security was essential for conversations like this.

'. . . as I can be, yes.' The white-coated figure crackled and spat back into life. Behind him, the lights of some desolate Azerbaijani town were beginning to assert themselves on the twilight. 'The drill is less efficient than conventional technology. In fact, it's dangerous, because of the unstable bubbles it creates. We've been testing it for . . . what, three days? We've lost three rig shafts already; they've buckled because of the supercavitation effect.'

'So you're saying that the Version Thirteen technology doesn't work?'

'Yes, Madame Barinova. We have the best engineers in the country here, and we used exactly the specs you sent. It's far worse than existing drilling systems – way less efficient, unstable, and much more dangerous.'

'Very well, Alexander. Thank you. Have a drink on me.'

Anna saw the mini-image of herself wave in the bottom right corner of her phone screen. Alexander waved back, and the connection was cut. She snapped the phone shut, and looked at her troops on the floor below. The glass felt cool against her forehead.

The funny thing was, this didn't have to be bad news. She had the only thing that mattered – more information than the rest of the market.

A FEW MOMENTS later, Anna stalked out of her office, took the lift down to the trading floor, and strode to her desk at the centre of the cross. The waves of trade parted once more, just for a moment, and she received applause – claps and cheers and shouts of approval.

This was ABTV's record day in the history of its market trading, for sure. At the head of it all, the leader of her crack troops, was the diminutive, agelessly beautiful, utterly ruthless Anna Barinova. She was the perfect embodiment of the market itself, all wrapped up in a black cocktail dress: cool, sexy, endlessly energetic.

And then she climbed on top of her desk and held her hands high and wide.

'Ladies and gentlemen . . .' Her voice was calm and authoritative. 'Please forgive my interruption. I know how busy you are – and what a great day we're having.'

There was a small wave of cheers at this, but Anna stilled them with an outward turn of her palm.

A look, a raised hand – the applause died. A moment of stillness.

'But – but now we are going to change strategy, and I mean *completely* change strategy.'

Total silence from the traders. Phones rang against a backdrop of unanswered electronic voices and static from squawk boxes. 'My instruction to you all is to close out your positions on everything – shares, bonds, derivatives, swaps. Everything. Especially oil puts.'

Gasps all around the crowded room.

'Sell, sell, sell.'

An instant of hushed shock.

'Are you saying that the miracle drilling technology doesn't work after all?' called a trader from the back of the floor.

'No.' her voice was loud, clear, certain. 'I'm saying *we're saying it doesn't*. Oil will bounce back up once the market sees where we're putting our book, so sell the puts and buy call contracts – get the right to buy oil at cheap prices. Oil's going back up and just about everything else will tank. Think of what you did a few minutes ago, and do the opposite. Are we clear?'

Stunned incomprehension. Then, a short, fat man at the back who'd stood on his desk to get a better view of Anna clapped loudly, then cheered. Seconds later, the entire trading team of nearly a hundred people was standing to applaud her. She was going to make them all rich.

Anna accepted the applause for a moment, then called loudly, 'Back to work!'

The whole team scrambled back to their desks and began to close out their positions, causing further mayhem in an already confused and turbulent market. Suddenly, the activity of a brutally frenetic day stepped up several gears. This they understood – you drive something up (or down), and you make money. Then you drive it down (or up), and you make money. All that mattered was that you were doing the driving, that you were ahead of the game. You had to be the Smart Money, not Other People's Money, which never benefited from the best information. *To work!*

The screaming and shouting reached a new level of intensity. Standing in the middle of it, Anna could almost believe that the sheer level of passion and will – the concerted, concentrated effort – could lift the trading floor off the ground. Anything was possible. Capitalism had come to Russia.

And then a truly massive roar went up. The wires were carrying a news story whose import the journalists didn't quite seem to understand.

BMB 10244/39912 – 16.53 GMT FLASH:
RUSSIAN INVENTOR MURDERED. DR PIOTR
YAVLINSKY, FOUNDER OF TORTOISESHELL
TECHNOLOGY, FOUND SHOT DEAD AT MOSCOW
HOME. More follows –

The shares in Tortoiseshell, which the floor had been driving down anyway with aggressive bets, now began to plummet. The salesmen were pushing the house position that the technology didn't work anyway – and sure enough, oil prices rose sharply (and the right to buy, the call options, soared in value). All the beneficiaries of cheap oil – industrial sectors, whole countries, if reliant on natural resources – fell back sharply. The index on the next day's opening of the Nikkei Dow in Tokyo was showing an estimated five-per-cent fall. This level of volatility might precipitate a crisis of confidence in the system. But Anna Barinova's troops didn't care about that: they'd made money on the upside, and now they were playing the downside for all it was worth.

It was all so intense, so frenetic, that no one, no one apart from Medulev, noticed the departure of the chief executive. Medulev sat at his desk monitoring the battle cries, the wild price fluctuations and the general excitement that surrounded him. He surmised that Anna Barinova had gone back to her private office. He was right.

Anna looked down at the mayhem, the rippling threads of energy that the machine she had created was weaving into profit. It was a shame about Yavlinsky. If pressed, she'd have said he was a man well out of his depth who didn't realise what was at stake. But the unfortunate Yavlinsky was far from the front of her mind just then. As she turned from the window and paced her office, Anna was silently cursing. She had an urgent call to make, and the Kamchatka number kept ringing out.

# CHAPTER THIRTEEN

IT WAS TIME to go. Vladimir grabbed his holdall and bounded up the dozen or so wooden stairs at the far end of the cellar. The heavy oak door unbolted easily enough. He closed it behind him, fumbled in his bag, found the medieval lock and fitted a huge iron key, some thirty centimetres long. Vladimir smiled briefly. He felt like a character in one of his own Xbox dungeon games.

There was no snowfall, but a frozen wind whipped in off the river, cold but still scorching to his wounded face. Within a couple of minutes, he had retrieved the Cayenne.

After unlocking the door and returning to the cellar, Vladimir carried the body up the steps and placed it in the boot of the car. No call from Ahmed yet, and no missed calls on his phone. He drove carefully through the courtyard of the gated tenement building.

The windows of the lower flats were broken, and the place was generally filthy and dilapidated. A pale yellow shard of flame guttered and spluttered in an unattended brazier at the far side of courtyard. He glanced in the rear-view mirror, wound the car windows down and searched the deep, dark pockets of blackness in the doorways and the jagged stairwell apertures – again, and again, and again. The fire was the only moving thing that Vladimir could see.

❁

'IS THIS THE famous English sense of humour, Mr Spendlove?' asked Aksyonov. He had first seen the Yavlinsky file that morning, after the station called him at the Novotel. He and Levitan had paid a fleeting visit to the murder scene, which was still being examined by a couple of harassed-looking creatures from the overworked forensic department, but the trail to Spendlove seemed direct and hot. He and Levitan had come straight to the Ukraina.

Neither of the officers had known who Yavlinsky was until a few hours ago. Much less did Levitan care. It was Vladimir who was supposed to take care of Spendlove, and it was surprising that the Westerner was still in one piece. Vladimir had clearly fallen down on the job; Ahmed would be furious. Yavlinsky's case was attracting a great deal of publicity, and it would now be difficult for Vladimir to dispose of Spendlove quietly.

'It is most certainly not a joke, Sergeant,' said Samuel. He waved at the item on the table between them. 'Does this say anything to you?'

'It says to me that it might be grounds for bringing you to the station and charging you with impeding my investigation,' said Levitan. 'I am looking for clarification of the events surrounding Dr Yavlinsky's death. What is this?'

'I'm as mystified as you, I promise you. You're welcome to keep it, obviously.'

'Why did he send you this . . . this useless thing, Mr Spendlove?' asked Levitan, waving a dismissive hand at the table. The container, Samuel realised for the first time, was an empty yogurt pot.

'As you know, Lieutenant Levitan, I am a researcher, and a certain part of Dr Yavlinsky's work was of interest to me.'

'You are scientist, Mr Spendlove?' asked Aksyonov.

'No, a researcher for a William Barton foundation, as you know. I had an academic curiosity about an inventor who sparked Yavlinsky's interest in a special drilling technique.'

'Yes, the drilling technique,' said Levitan. 'The shares in Dr Yavlinsky's company are all over the front pages of the newspapers. This is a great Russian invention, and Yavlinsky was about to become a very rich man. A very sad time to lose his life. Were you a shareholder in his company, Mr Spendlove?'

'Absolutely not. I was what's called an insider, Lieutenant. I had access to special, confidential information that could have affected the share price. I wasn't allowed to hold shares. If I'd bought any before the general market had access to my information I could have been jailed.'

The two policemen looked long and hard at Samuel.

'Your special information certainly seems to have worked magic on the share price,' said Levitan, eventually. He withdrew a copy of the *Kommersant* financial newspaper from his briefcase. A headline screamed 'Tortoiseshell Chief Dead!' The article said that after a precipitous raise, the shares checked back sharply on news of Yavlinsky's death and persistent question marks over whether the technology worked . . .

Could that be Samuel's fault? He was confident the transcription was faithful, even with its late additions and changes. But he couldn't be certain. Had an error in the transcript led to all this speculation – and ultimately Yavlinsky's death, killed by Samuel's error? The bigger error had surely been to agree to the damned assignment in the first place.

Samuel swallowed thickly. 'Yavlinsky could have made a lot of people rather rich, including himself. Why would anyone want to kill him?'

'Yavlinsky had his fingernails pulled out, one by one, then he was shot in the back of the head, Mr Spendlove,' said Levitan. 'Definitely, it was not suicide. Someone wanted something Yavlinsky was unwilling or unable to provide. Where were you between the hours of nine o'clock last night and four o'clock this morning?'

'I've already told you. I was here, Lieutenant. I was visited in the late evening by Mr Barton.'

'Ah yes, Mr Barton. We shall check that with the reception desk. No doubt this world-famous business tycoon had himself announced before coming to see you?'

'I expect so.'

'So, you met with him and for the rest of the evening you were here, and then the package was delivered?'

'That's right. Barton stayed for a while. We talked.'

'About what?'

'Business. Everything is business with Barton.'

'Yavlinsky business?'

'Yavlinsky was mentioned, yes. But mainly, general business. William Barton's got into the habit of making me offers I find I can refuse.'

'You refuse offers from someone so rich? You must be a wealthy man, Mr Spendlove.'

'Only because I'm not interested in money.'

'So you say. How long did Barton stay?'

'An hour or so. Then I got ready for bed. Just as I was drifting off – another knock at the door. When the package was delivered, I thought it really might be Yavlinsky in person. He'd told me he was going to a dinner and might drop by for a nightcap.'

'So you took delivery of this stupid little pot at what time exactly?'

Samuel blinked.

'I don't know. Late. Very late, come to think of it.'

Levitan and Aksyonov looked at each other, then back at Samuel.

'Obviously, we'll be checking all this with the staff,' said Aksyonov. 'Did you get a good look at the person delivering the package?'

Samuel shrugged slightly.

'No, I didn't. I made him leave it outside. I signed a receipt, which he put under the door, though.'

'I see.'

'As I said, we shall make the routine checks,' continued the sergeant. 'So why was Yavlinsky coming to see you, Mr Spendlove?'

'To pick up his papers,' sighed Samuel. 'One second, please, and I'll show you.'

Samuel disappeared into the hallway and came back a moment later with a large box of documents.

'I must impound these while the case remains open. You understand.'

Samuel nodded. Both policemen stood. Aksyonov picked up the box of documents. 'For the moment, that is enough. But please do not leave the country. Is your passport at reception?' Levitan asked.

'Yes. You're not going to take it, are you?'

'No need.' Levitan produced Samuel's passport from his jacket pocket. 'You weren't planning to go home soon, were you?'

'Actually, I was . . .'

'Well, don't. Little is certain in this world. But you can be sure we will need to ask more questions.'

Samuel closed the door after the departing policemen and walked slowly into the sitting room. He picked up his mobile and called Blandford again. The phone didn't even ring this time. The image of Blandford's grinning face flicked off the screen.

He was stuck in Moscow, no passport, a sitting target. He was almost reluctant to go to the window and look down on the winding river. Blandford, the guy who'd brought him, the one person he had some control over, had disappeared – or worse. He conjured up Yavlinsky's endearingly barmy giggle, his love of chess, the bug eyes. He was arguably the one seemingly genuine person in this concoction of venality – and he was gruesomely murdered. And then the twin queens of glamour – the Barinova women – had disappeared. Down below, a doorman stamped his feet in the cold. The flare of a match attended to a cigarette. Ah, Medulev and his favourite habit . . . He had also disappeared.

His phone rang. Samuel saw the picture ID and snatched it up with a small cry of triumph. His caller poured an excited stream of words into his ear. Samuel nodded, let the energy dissipate a little. After a few seconds, he interrupted:

'I agree, I agree. Funnily enough, Ksenia, you're just the person I want to see too.'

THEY COULD SMELL the dark, rich odour of diesel minutes before she reached the stadium. Ksenia wound down the window by just a fraction, but even so, the brutal cold of the evening blew in sharply. Out of the black of the night came the sound they were listening for – a repulsive, throaty roar, a dark angel gargling before spitting up the juices of the planet.

Ksenia had dispensed with her customary driver before she picked Samuel up at the hotel. That suited Samuel too. Neither wanted her mother's employees around. Still, Ksenia seemed withdrawn. And after the enthusiasm the Barinova women had shown, followed by elusiveness, he wasn't going to play the first card.

After a few minutes, Ksenia, inevitably, started in on the technology.

'. . . so, Samuel. You agree?'

She closed the window and turned a corner.

Samuel took it all in: Ksenia's focus at the wheel, the intensity of the grip and the night vigilance.

'Does it matter? You'd do it anyway, right?'

'Yes, of course. Because it's the right thing to do. You acted in good faith, and so did I.'

'And you don't want Barton suing you, either. He thinks the formula's his.'

'I don't care about that.'

'Well you should. But even if you don't, there's another problem. Version Thirteen doesn't work.'

'What!'

She stamped on the brakes. The car's snow tires shrieked. They slid to a halt on the cusp of a deep ditch.

'According to the police and the media, anyway. And there's no chance of the inventor ironing out any faults.'

Samuel explained Levitan's news, and the *Kommersant* media report. He'd checked the online world before Ksenia came by the Ukraina. It was full of speculation about the murder. A favourite theory was that Yavlinsky had been punished for producing duff technology by disgruntled investors.

'Unless, of course, you deliberately falsified the information?'

'You think I'd do that? For what possible reason?'

'For your own protection, perhaps.'

Ksenia bent her head for a moment, then looked up and re-started the engine.

'Do you want to carry on?' asked Samuel.

'Do you?'

'You bet.'

They breasted a hill, and there it was, bathed in a bright, buttery glow of floodlights. The Devil's Basin, as the locals called it, was a massive concrete stadium, used for football and many other sports. Russian soccer did not attract the same enormous television revenues as the English or Spanish leagues. In a bid to raise extra income, the owners of the Devil's Basin staged other events.

They parked and climbed out of the car. The lot was dominated by a banner promoting tonight's spectacle – *Monster Truck Car Killer, Stock Car Racing.*

'This is just so depressing, don't you think, Samuel?'

The red asphalt of the car park was pocked with holes – large puddles in the spring and autumn, dust bowls in the summer. In winter, they were treacherous traps beneath a camouflage of snow. Ksenia shuddered, but not from the cold.

'Is this really what people find entertaining?'

'Seems so,' he muttered. He had more immediate problems to deal with.

The oppressive stench of motor fuel was suddenly dispelled by the welcoming aroma of fried onions, caramelising on a griddle. A couple of Uzbek vans were selling kebabs and little pies to the crowds.

Samuel saw her looking over, and suddenly shared her hunger. He took off his coat, draped it over Ksenia's shoulders and marched up to the nearest van. He bought two kebabs, and they munched on them in the night air. Tiny gobbets of grease escaped onto Ksenia's chin and hardened quickly in the cold. Samuel produced a handkerchief and wiped them away. It was good to eat in the night air. The weather might be cold and hostile, they might face trouble ahead, but the food was warm and comforting.

'*Niet.*'

A burly fellow in a woollen bobble hat sat at the turnstile of the Drivers' Entrance. Ksenia's card, as an executive of the sponsoring ABTV, was good enough to get her in. But the steward wasn't going to do Samuel any favours. From the machine-gun volleys of Russian, Samuel could see that Ksenia tried charm, threats, and charm again. All she got was a series of *Niets*.

After a final fruitless exchange, Samuel put a hand on Ksenia's arm.

'It's fine. You go in. I'll wait for you in the car.'

'But . . .'

'Just do it. I'll see you later.'

Samuel turned and headed back into the parking lot. He watched until Ksenia made her way inside, then he turned, back towards the arena.

❀

WITHIN A FEW moments Ksenia had found her seat. The spectacle was not so much enraging as depressing. The first part of the entertainment consisted of men dressed in aviators' suits and crash helmets walking out to the accompaniment of loud American rock music. Ksenia didn't know what it was exactly, probably something from the 1970s, well before she was born. The men proceeded to accept the applause of the crowd, just about all of whom seemed to be drinking the beer sold by the numerous stadium attendants. The drivers greeted all corners of the Olympic-sized bowl with their arms uplifted in salutation, in the manner of gladiators in ancient Rome. But instead of lions and tigers, their foes were ancient cars – Fiats, Zhigulis, Škodas from the Communist era. Their weapons were huge 'monster trucks'. So far as Ksenia could determine, the monster trucks were turbo-charged armoured cars with improbably large wheels at least a couple of metres in diameter. The drivers climbed into the cabs of the monster trucks and simply drove over the old cars until they had reduced them from three dimensions to two. This orgy of consumption was entertainment.

The animus of the spectators towards the old cars surprised her. It seemed that the crowd really hated the ancient vehicles. The beery oaf next to her was drinking with a steady enthusiasm and cheering loudly as an antediluvian Zil was attacked by a bright yellow monster truck. The whole stadium roared as the giant black tyres rolled the ancient limousine into thin, tinny oblivion. Perhaps this was revenge against the old Communist system. The man next to Ksenia snapped open another can of Baltika 6 and gurgled happily as the monster truck rolled back and forth. She watched him carefully. No, it probably wasn't anything as sophisticated as politically motivated revenge, even if the Zil was an ancient symbol of Communist power and privilege, the sedan chair of the apparatchik. It was simple stuff: a kind of blood lust, the pleasure of consumption and destruction.

The last act of brute demolition featured a green-and-orange monster truck. A sad-looking Zhiguli played the role of tethered goat. As the rite of destruction neared its end, Ksenia made her way down to the trackside tunnel, which was full of ancient, souped-up cars preparing for a race. Most of them were revving their engines. The noise and the stench and the waste almost made Ksenia sick.

SAMUEL SOON FOUND what he wanted. A big American gas-guzzler, a customised General Motors Crossfire, pulled up in a reserved parking space.

Samuel marched forward as a dark, thickset driver got out. His right fist was thrust into his jacket pocket, fingers tight around a roll of one-rouble coins. Samuel flashed a grin, and with his left hand mimed smoking a cigarette. The driver hesitated a moment, then nodded and ducked into his car. As he emerged, holding a packet of Lucky Strike, Samuel connected cleanly with the side of his jaw – a perfect right cross. The driver fell backwards, unconscious, into the car.

It was the work of seconds to remove his kit bag, don his helmet, and head for the Drivers' Entrance once more. Samuel flashed his stolen pass at the steward, and headed inside.

THE RACE WASN'T quite the revolting spectacle she'd expected. Well, it was. It was all *those things*, those things she hated. Noise, waste, stench, roaring idiots, brute destruction, the dense, dark smell of masculine sweat, what the illiterate might imagine to be testosterone. But at the bottom of it all, there was some place she couldn't quite locate inside her that got the rhythm and the music of it all. Something about all this rawness appealed to her. It was elemental and ugly, but weirdly sexy – she felt like a lioness watching a testosterone-fuelled jungle fight – to the victor, the spoils.

After a few laps of raucously cheered recklessness she worked out that the driving was aimed largely at destroying the opposition, not completing the course. The goal wasn't to win, but to have sharper elbows than the next guy. You proved that by utterly annihilating his car.

After a dozen or so laps, apart from the two leaders, the field was down to one ancient Lancia, painted in zebra stripes, a Toyota truck, with just chassis and wheels left; it looked as though it had been at every marine landing in the Second World War; and a large Massey Ferguson tractor, painted matt pink. With a top speed of under thirty kilometres per hour its only strategy was to block and destroy the other vehicles. The two leading cars were actually racing each other. One was daubed in yellow and green stripes. The other, a big American car from the 1970s, which might have been a Buick, was painted matt black. Its driver was kitted out in black too – black helmet, black leathers.

Ksenia was no petrol head, but she could see that these two didn't like each other. The yellow-and-green truck kept trying to sideswipe the black car every time they were running in parallel – which they often were, as the driver of the black car seemed hell bent on chasing the tail of the other.

Twice the black car just escaped from being sandwiched between the truck and the concrete wall of the central reservation. The red digital scoreboard was showing three laps left when the black car slowed as the truck tried to ram it again. The truck bounced off the concrete wall, and, using its momentum as it span, the black car nudged it into the reach of the deadly pink tractor, which mashed it up against the barrier.

The crowd went berserk as the black car finished the race with a two-lap procession of triumph.

Now was Ksenia's moment. The driver of the green-and-yellow truck was clambering out of his vehicle. He was clearly angry, and remonstrated with the stewards who tried to help him.

Ksenia removed her shoes, took a deep breath and vaulted the barrier dividing spectators from the track. A posse of men in dayglo yellow safety bibs ran towards her, but she was too quick. She ran to the driver, and blocked his path, hands on her hips.

'Well?' she enquired.

Two stewards had caught up with her now; one tried to take her arm. She shook his hand off angrily. The driver signalled to the stewards that all was well, then took off his helmet.

A few people in the crowd had seen the confrontation and were beginning to cheer, assuming that one of the drivers had been cornered by an angry wife or girlfriend. This was extra entertainment.

'I didn't realise you were a motor sports fan, Ksenia,' said Medulev. 'What do you want?' he asked, putting his driver's helmet under his arm. Sweat plastered dark hair to his head.

'I want answers,' said Ksenia, standing her ground.

'Just one moment.'

The driver of the black car was walking towards the winner's rostrum. Medulev sprinted towards him. Within seconds he confronted the black-suited driver.

'What the fuck, man?' shouted Medulev. 'You trying to kill me, you fucking asshole?'

SAMUEL LIFTED UP his visor, then removed the black helmet from his head. Sweat was pouring from him, but the adrenaline from the race still coursed through him. The crowd, he knew, was cheering wildly. They loved confrontation. Head-on collision of any sort was their thing, the reason they came.

But a calmness had settled on him, a kind of reverie. It was as though he was watching himself, as he had been ever since he'd strode into the changing rooms, read the brief, and settled into the car.

*The open-throated roar of the engine, the thick smell of grease, oil, sweat-drenched leather; the animal surge of power at his feet, the screams of the waving, baying, crowd, and the constant roaring in his ears – not the car, not the people, but the creature within, the beast that had no memory and vision. No vision other than the prey, the car in green and yellow. A heavy, dark pulse hammered relentlessly in his head. He had his quarry, right in front of him.*

Medulev looked at Samuel, open-mouthed.

And the inner roar was gone, replaced by the noise of thousands – loud, but way less intense. Samuel bowed briefly, a gesture of mock-courtesy.

'Am I trying to kill you, Marat? I rather think that's the kind of question you should be asking of yourself, don't you?'

Ksenia rushed up.

'Samuel! What the . . .?'

'Oh, he's with you now?' Medulev looked from one to the other.

'I wouldn't know about that,' said Samuel. 'Why don't we have a nice shower and a chat, Marat?'

'I've got nothing to say to you.'

'I think you will, you know. When you hear the topic of my conversation.'

Medulev grunted at the effort of regaining his composure. Eventually, he nodded, and beckoned them to follow.

THE THREE OF THEM climbed a flight of stairs and walked along a cold, carpetless breeze-block corridor. This was functional architecture at its most Spartan. Medulev opened a small white door set deep into the wall, and they proceeded into a dank, windowless changing room. The stench of male sweat and engine oil intensified.

'So, let's be polite. What the fuck, Spendlove?'

Medulev nodded, then deliberately turned away from Samuel to face Ksenia. He must have had training in legal process. The witness turns from interrogating counsel, and addresses the judge, who must form an impression as to credibility.

Medulev unzipped his driver's suit and fixed Ksenia with his dark brown eyes. His body was taut, well-muscled and firm; the chest was covered in dark hair with a hint of grey. He was wearing a small pair of white cotton briefs. Without moving his eyes from hers, he reached down and took them off.

Ksenia crossed her arms, and tried to stare firmly into Medulev's eyes. All she got for her pains was a sneer.

'Nice displacement activity, Medulev,' said Samuel. 'But I know what you've done. I know you killed Yavlinsky.'

Ksenia gasped. Medulev simply laughed, continuing all the while to stare at Ksenia.

'Haven't we heard all this before? Wasn't I supposed to have killed that gangster pilot scum?'

'But you made Yavlinsky an offer for Version Thirteen, didn't you?'

'It's a piece of junk. It doesn't work.'

'That's not an answer.'

The photo in Yavlinsky's apartment flicked up again into sharp focus in Samuel's mind.

*Yavlinsky was grinning into the camera – to one side a bottle of vodka shaped like an AK47, to the other, a group of men.*

He concentrated – zeroed in on the mental image. Yes, no doubt, the group included Medulev.

'In fairness, that's not much of a question.'

'Oh, no? You were one of the guys chasing Yavlinsky at the defence contractors' fair, weren't you? He said he's had a lot of interest. But I'll bet you weren't working for ABTV, were you?'

'Fuck you, English. You're not so smart as you think you are.'

Medulev was still standing in front Ksenia, his legs splayed.

Two more drivers came into the changing room. They saw the three of them, and exchanged a couple of softly spoken words.

'You want this technology. You killed Yavlinsky because he failed you,' said Samuel. Medulev's deflections – his refusal even to look at Samuel told him he was right.

'And I have a question for you, Marat,' said Ksenia.

'Well, spit it out. I'm getting cold here.'

'What's Kamchatka got to do with all of this?'

'Kamchatka?' said Samuel. 'Where the hell is Kamchatka?'

He saw Medulev's face break into an absurd grin. Then everything very suddenly went bright white – then pitch black.

# CHAPTER FOURTEEN

VLADIMIR WAS HEADING due east. He would dump the body, then take a couple of days to recover from his wounds before tackling the long drive home. He kept a steady pace; the Cayenne was handling well. It was built for long trips. The pain from the acid burns was persistent and unpleasant, but it had begun to abate slightly.

He hadn't taken the steroids in a while. Things were calmer, and that helped. Vladimir had found a couple of extra back issues of *Domovoi* magazine on a newspaper stand the day before. They were full of beautiful images. The *Domovoi* magic was strong; through the magazines he could escape to a pain-free world with ease.

As he drove, the mobile rang. Vladimir fumbled for the phone. He wasn't wearing his bluetooth ear clip; he groped for the speakerphone. Almost fatally – the car veered to the wrong side of the road, towards an ancient bus with the logo 'Grundig' stencil-sprayed onto its rusting coachwork. The bus hooted furiously. Vladimir swerved just in time, and pulled into the side of the road. The Cayenne came to a slushy halt in a snow bank just past a small stone bridge over a frozen stream.

'Vladimir?'

'Yes, Godfather?'

Vladimir killed the engine. He picked up the mobile and pressed it to his ear, even though it was still on speakerphone.

'Vladimir! Where are you?'

'I am outside Moscow, Godfather.'

'Why are you outside Moscow when you have not avenged Shamil's death? I need you to get back there and deal with Spendlove. Levitan tells me his name is written in blood across half of the files in his stinking police cells. Spendlove is a high-level criminal. Don't you read the papers, Vladimir?'

There was a brief silence. Vladimir looked about him. The road was free of traffic. Silence flooded in, punctuated only by the starved cawing of rooks, dotted about the high skeletal twigs of silver birch and black elm. The world seemed a vast, desolate place.

'The man is dead, Godfather. Soon he will disappear completely. Nothing left.'

'Ever heard of *Kommersant*?' barked Ahmed.

'Is it a magazine?'

'No, Vladimir. It's a newspaper, one of many – and they're all full of stories about the criminals that plague the world. Spendlove is one of these.'

'That is impossible, with the greatest respect. The clip I sent you shows his confession, and the corpse. The murderer is dead.'

'Utter horseshit. They were the rantings of a fool! Drivel! Nonsense. Did you understand more than two words the man was saying?'

'I am sorry, Godfather. My English . . .'

'English is the language of the infidel, of Great Satan and Little Satan. But it is a useful tool to help us engage with the enemy. The man you questioned so brutishly would have said anything. Whatever he said, he wasn't Spendlove.'

A gentle but audible thump of a keyboard in Grozny made itself heard in the rural outskirts of Moscow. A few more taps and bumps came down the line. 'Ten seconds on the Western internet would have revealed that.'

'But, Godfather, I was working in conditions of the greatest secrecy. I avoided even internet cafes . . .'

'If you're going to work for me again, Vladimir – if you want to stay alive in this hard world – you need to be informed, twenty-four seven.'

A horrible shriek came through the speakerphone.

'My God! What's that?'

Ahmed chuckled. 'Goat. Rashid is making the sacrifice in the courtyard right now. Goat meat is good, Vladimir. We shall eat well tonight.'

Another series of taps at the keyboard: 'Now, here we are . . . The crimes of this monster, Spendlove. It says in today's edition of *Kommersant* that Spendlove is involved in a big oil scam.'

'An oil scam?'

'Hundreds of millions made and lost on the strength of this man's lies. These are the real criminals, Vladimir, the ones in suits. He is involved in everything, Vladimir. He is still alive – and he must die.'

Vladimir leaned forward and rested his head on the dashboard. Its coolness offered little comfort. His whole body ached; his eye was now hurting again.

'But, Gospodin Ahmed, I am injured. I must rest before I go and find the other Spendlove.'

'The *real* Spendlove, Vladimir! I don't know who the dead man is, and I don't care. Levitan has contact with him, but is talking to him only. So . . . it will be easy for you to find this snake and kill him. Only then shall Shamil and I have vengeance. Only then will justice be done.'

'I appeal to you, Ahmed, my benefactor. I am unwell. I need medical treatment.'

'You are a warrior, Vladimir. Finish the task, and you will be given the honour and respect due to you on your return. I am taking personal care of your dogs. They are in my house, Vladimir, under my roof. When it comes to their well-being, no detail will be overlooked.'

232

Vladimir sat bolt upright. Igor and Tatiana. Ahmed had care and control of the two creatures he loved most in the world. *No detail would be overlooked when it came to their well-being.* Or lack of it.

'So, Gospodin Ahmed, of course. I shall finish the task. I shall find this Spendlove creature, and I shall kill him,' said Vladimir.

'Good, Vladimir, good. Bring me his balls on a kebab stick.'

'Really, Gospodin Ahmed?' Vladimir would enjoy the process of castration, but he really didn't want the stench of body parts in his car.

'No, you fool,' spat Ahmed. 'Just send me a video clip. I wish you swift success in this just quest. Inshallah.'

Vladimir contemplated the road and its eastward aspect for a few mournful seconds. Then he reached over to the back seat for his holdall, and rummaged in it until he found what he was looking for. There it was. He took two steroid tablets, plus an extra one for good measure, and gulped down a mouthful of low-calorie chocolate milk. He selected a CD – not the Chechnyan folk songs, but the Westerner, James Blunt. Blunt was a giant talent, a true poet, one of Vladimir's favourites.

He cranked the Cayenne into gear, swung it round, and headed back for Moscow. After a few minutes, that familiar warm feeling began to take hold of him again. It was fuelled by something dark, animal and angry, but that was good. He slipped a couple of sticks of strawberry gum to take away the dryness in his mouth, and give him something to masticate. Otherwise the inevitable jaw-grinding would be a problem.

And a little later, the notion of 'problem' seemed pathetic, limp, unmanly. He had a job to do, something to attack, hard. What more could he want? Ha! But not a speeding ticket. He eased off the accelerator. All the same, the Cayenne was travelling towards Moscow at a considerable rate.

❀

SAMUEL OPENED HIS eyes. He was reclining on a sofa of soft, lilac-tinted leather. His head hurt. It was a sharp, light-sensitive pressure headache; the tension over the front of the eyes was the kind of ache he'd get from working a succession of long days to finish an academic monograph – or spending hours memorising and regurgitating data.

He didn't recognise the room, but the muted lighting and the decor felt familiar. A soft knock at the door settled the question.

'Would sir care for a drink? Some water?'

This from a solicitous, smooth-faced young man in ABTV livery. ABTV, of course . . . How long had he been out, he wondered.

'Yes, thanks. Still.' His voice was thick and croaky. He felt terrible – a banging, thick grogginess. But the pain, searing as it was, was behind his eyes. And he'd been hit over the back of the head. Hadn't he?

A single tap at a wall socket, and a leather panel slid silently back to reveal a shiny phalanx of red and blue mineral-water bottles. The attendant brought him his drink on a tray, lent over and smiled.

For a second, he was back in the Tetryakov gallery, beside Yavlinsky. They were drinking vodka and laughing at the man in the shapka, this man, in his fur hat, staring like a bored schoolboy at sculpture he had no interest in, stamping his feet in the cold.

Samuel did his best to stop his hand shaking, took the glass, and watched the attendant slip out of the room. The door shut behind him with a gentle smack of its lips. Was he in a sealed room? Was it soundproofed? And where was Ksenia? She was the one who had taken him to Medulev. Had she brought him here, also?

Before he could collect his thoughts, the door in the opposite wall opened, and a pair of fine sapphire eyes fully engaged with his.

'We live in a dangerous world, do we not?' said Anna Barinova simply.

234

She sat in a chair opposite him.

'You said I needed protection, Anna, and you were right. I need protecting from *you*. I take it the nice young fellow who just served me water, the one you sent to spy on me and Yavlinsky, was also the one who smacked me on the back of the head?'

'Ivan? No, no. He's a loyal employee, no more. He looks out for me, that's all.'

'I've had enough of this,' said Samuel. He got up sharply. Too sharply. The room swam and tilted around him.

'I wouldn't do that if I were you,' said Anna.

She jabbed at an intercom. 'He's awake.'

Seconds later, Ksenia came through the door at a trot, her brow twisted with concern.

'How are you, Samuel?'

'I'd like to say all the better for seeing you, Ksenia. But my headache is telling me that ours is not what you'd call a healthy relationship.'

She come over and placed a cool hand on his forehead.

'I'm so sorry about Medulev. They're animals, his driving friends. When they discovered you'd taken out our one of their own, it was all I could do to get you out of there. I called ABTV, and they came at once. '

Samuel addressed himself to Ksenia: 'So you saved me from Medulev and brought me here?'

Ksenia offered to help him up. But he shrugged her off. Now was the time to focus. Play the innocent and get the hell out. Alone.

'So, before I go, Anna, my apologies for the damp squib. It seems the information I gave you isn't a superior technology after all. I must have got it wrong.'

She laughed softly. 'I don't believe you made a mistake. It's just that Tortoiseshell's model didn't work. Our laboratory tests showed it didn't work, so it was time to destroy the prototypes and walk away.'

'I'll bet you walked away with billions.'

'If I have made money, it's because the markets have simply reacted to the information available. If the information is wrong or faulty, the markets find out just as surely as water flows downhill.'

'I know how markets work. I learnt that in Paris. There's more to this than you claim.'

She examined her fingernails for a moment, then spoke in an urgent semi-whisper.

'You really should not seek answers so fervently. There may be no answers worth having. There may be other forces at work. Either way, let it be, Samuel.'

'And you don't care if the technology doesn't work, Mother? You've made some cash – and *that will do?*' Ksenia was standing up, pale with fury.

'*If*? The Baku tests showed it didn't work. Simple. The money? That's what I do – one of the things I do.'

'Here.' Ksenia rummaged in her bag and produced a Perspex case, the size of a small make-up bag. She opened it, and a black spider, half the size of her little finger crawled out on to the top of the desk. On the top of the ventrum was an hour-glass marking of bright red, nature's warning of danger.

'You know what they call you, Mother, your loyal troops?'

The spider lay still for a moment, then began to crawl, slowly, towards Anna.

Ksenia turned to Samuel. 'They call her *the Black Widow*. Get too close, and she sucks out your energy. She eats you up. *It's in her nature.* That's what they say, Mother.'

Anna stared at the creature as it approached. 'Get rid of that thing!'

'Do you see yourself in that thing at all, Mother?' Ksenia sat back, a smile on her face. 'I never realised you didn't like spiders. I plan to keep her. Maybe I'll call her Anna.'

Samuel could see Anna gripping and ungripping her fists,

fighting to control her breathing. The Black Widow – dark, sexy, dangerous, was that was her? Undoubtedly.

This, surely, was Samuel's moment. He had a hunch. He'd play it.

'And when you go hunting, Anna, how far does your web extend? Forget about the Baku tests for Version Thirteen. What about the Kamchatka tests?'

Was that a second's hesitation? He couldn't be sure. But the moment of indecision, maybe even fear, whatever it was – was already over. The Black Widow pressed hard, twice, on the intercom, and the door opened.

LEVITAN AND AKSYONOV merely nodded to Anna Barinova. So she *knew* them, and she was *expecting* their arrival here, in her office. Black Widow, indeed. Samuel sat down on the lilac sofa. This would be interesting.

Levitan cleared his throat, as though making an announcement: 'We are here to ask you, Mr Spendlove, to come to the Donaskaya station. We have questions concerning the murder of Piotr Ivanovich Yavlinsky and financial felonies concerning the theft of information from Tortoiseshell Technology – and insider dealing in its shares.'

An attendant appeared in ABTV livery, and began the delicate process of trying to shoo the spider back into its box.

Samuel sat still. There was an ugly familiarity to the feeling; the jaws of some invisible apparatus were closing on him. Shades of Paris, with its intrigue, treachery and poisonous financial lures. Spiders, though, that was a new one. Let ice flow through the veins. Let the rest of them show their hand.

'What's changed since our interview this morning, Lieutenant?'

'Much, Mr Spendlove, very much. For example, the package you say was sent by Yavlinsky and delivered to your hotel.'

'Yes?'

'The hotel has no record of any such delivery. Also, the concierge service does not operate at the time of day you say this package was delivered.'

'I said I thought it was strange.'

'Correct. And so is this.'

Levitan was struggling to extract something from the inside pocket of his jacket. Eventually, he produced a cellophane packet containing a piece of paper and handed it to Samuel.

It was a beautifully embossed piece of paper, covered in images and Cyrillic script. The Russians still loved their gilded receipts. Often an average meal or a visit to a museum would yield up a beautiful paper memento.

'Don't pretend you don't know what it is, Mr Spendlove. It's a share certificate relating to a holding in Tortoiseshell Technology,' Levitan bowed towards the Black Widow.

'So, Mr Spendlove,' continued Levitan. He took back the cellophane specimen bag and held it up. 'Isn't *this* what was delivered to your room the other night?'

'No. That's ridiculous.'

'Not so ridiculous,' said Levitan with a slow smile. 'We found it in your room at the Ukraina.'

'That's impossible.'

Samuel shot a look at Ksenia. She came and sat next to him, and took his hand. Samuel gently unhooked his fingers. He wouldn't be caught so easily. Ksenia had brought him here, to her mother. As what? A prize? A bargaining chip? A sacrifice?

'One moment, Lieutenant,' said the Black Widow. 'I gave a certificate for precisely this number of shares to an associate of Mr Spendlove's, a Canadian citizen – Kingston Blandford.'

'This is totally preposterous, Anna, and you know it!' said Samuel. The eyes he looked into were unblinkingly steady. He turned back to the policeman. 'In any event, Lieutenant, did you search my room without my knowledge? Did you have a search warrant?'

'Oh, Mr Spendlove, do you feel your human rights have been breached? This is Russia. Sergeant Aksyonov and I just happened to be paying a chance visit to your room, one which happened to coincide with the maid going in to clean up. So we thought we'd go in behind her and surprise you.'

'But you weren't there, Mr Spendlove,' said Aksyonov.

'So we looked hard for you, Mr Spendlove,' said Levitan. 'Under the bed, in your suitcase. We just couldn't track you down. But when we found this piece of paper and saw the name of the company that's been all over the newspapers and on the television, we really thought we'd like to talk to you about it. Especially as you promised us that you weren't an investor. What was it you said, now?' asked Levitan with counterfeit forgetfulness.

'That if he invested in Tortoiseshell Technology he would be an insider dealer, I think it was, Lieutenant,' said Aksyonov. 'I'll have to double-check in my notebook, but I'm pretty sure that was it.'

'So there you have it, Mr Spendlove. It all becomes even more interesting when we discover that you are in possession of the share certificate that Madame Barinova says she gave to an associate of yours who hasn't been seen for two days. I think we need to have a chat down at the station, don't you?'

'And if I refuse to come?'

'Well, I could arrest you. I have enough to do that on several counts already.'

'I want to call the British Embassy.'

'Please do,' smiled Levitan. 'On your mobile. In my car. Whenever you like.'

Samuel stood up.

He turned to the Black Widow. 'You were expecting them, weren't you, Anna?'

She shrugged. 'The lieutenant called about the share certificate.

He seemed anxious to meet with you as soon as possible.'

'I wasn't difficult to find, once I'd been rendered unconscious,' Samuel snorted. 'How did this share certificate of Blandford's get into my room?'

The Black Widow looked away.

'Time to go, Mr Spendlove,' said Levitan.

Aksyonov placed a guiding hand on Samuel's shoulder. He moved to break free, resenting the gentle pressure, then exhaled.

'All right. I'll come now.'

'I'll come with you, Samuel,' said Ksenia. 'Our family, if family's the right word, has treated you disgracefully.'

Ksenia directed a furious stare at her mother, who gazed back, deadpan.

'Do as you will, Ksenia.'

'I'm afraid there's no room in the car, Miss Barinova,' said Levitan.

'Really, Lieutenant? What are you driving? A motorbike and sidecar? And it's Madam, to you.'

'I'm sorry, Madam. We can't carry civilians.'

'Don't worry. I have my own vehicle. I'll follow you. And I'll call a lawyer, Samuel. One that's not compromised by ties to my mother.'

'As you see fit, Ksenia,' said Samuel. He marched through the open door without waiting for a response.

A few moments later Samuel was sitting in the back of Levitan's police car as it nosed through the freezing car park. The car stank of stale tobacco. Now that they were in an enclosed space, Samuel could smell rancid beer beneath an odour of cheap cigar on Levitan's breath. In the rear view mirror he could see Ksenia creeping along behind them.

The setting sun was bleeding the colour out of the day. Everything was magenta with streaks of dark orange and black. Soon it would be night. He craved sleep, the comfort of oblivion.

He'd call the embassy, maybe – but they'd only care about calming things down, minimising embarrassment. Barton? No, he'd run far and fast. Blandford? Disappeared. His best hope was Ksenia – if he could trust her. Could he? That, he simply didn't know. Life had turned bloody and brutal.

The security guards waved the two vehicles through, and away they went, heading towards central Moscow, negotiating their way through the ever-present, ever-aggressive evening traffic.

Ksenia almost lost them a couple of times, as she didn't have the invulnerability of police markings, nor Aksyonov's super-assertive driving style. Samuel watched her progress through the traffic. She was determined to keep up. But no one noticed a third car, somewhat erratically driven, even by Moscow's standards. The third vehicle in the informal procession was a Porsche Cayenne.

# CHAPTER FIFTEEN

LEVITAN'S POLICE CAR was some sort of old-fashioned Fiat. Samuel guessed it was a product of the long-standing commercial alliances between the Soviets and the Italians, where the industrialists had needed to side with various socialist hybrid governments for decades after the Second World War. Aksyonov held the slim black plastic rim of the steering wheel in steady hands, and thrust through the traffic on the inbound lanes of the road into the centre of the city.

Aksyonov needed to be a good driver. Despite the best efforts of the Moscow City Police mechanics, the gearbox of the ancient Fiat had the smoothness and coherence of a bag of spanners in a spin drier. Every now and then the car lurched forward as Aksyonov reached for a bit of gearbox that had simply gone missing. Nevertheless, they were making progress.

In the back seat, Samuel clicked his tongue at his mobile screen. Still no signal. He'd tried and failed to get through to the British Embassy several times. He looked over his shoulder. Ksenia was still in sight.

Samuel's custodians seemed remarkably relaxed. Levitan had taken his jacket off to reveal a crescent-shaped swathe of perspiration round each armpit. He was smoking some sort of cheroot, which at least masked the body odour. Samuel was relieved not to have been handcuffed, but then he hadn't actually been arrested. Legal process, though, was hardly the issue. The guns that Levitan and Aksyonov had in their holsters – they were the issue.

Levitan was now in expansive form, chatting away about the good old, bad old days under Communism.

'Once upon a time, I tell you, people used to be scared to walk in front of the Lubyanka. There was an invisible force field of fear. If you were a total stranger who didn't know it was the headquarters of the KGB, you'd guess pretty quickly. It didn't matter how busy the pavements were, no one would go within ten metres of the entrance. When we get a call in the district now, what is it, I ask you?'

'Some prostitute beaten to a pulp by her pimp?' offered Aksyonov, swerving expertly to avoid an obviously drunken manoeuvre from the Maserati in front. He glanced across at his partner.

'Want to stop that pisshead?'

Levitan shook his head. 'A Maserati? You kidding? How much money and power does that fucker have? And how did the bastard get them? Too much trouble.'

'So straight to the Lubyanka district?'

'Precisely,' growled Levitan. He reached into the glove compartment and took out a can of beer. 'Nightclubs in KGB Land!' muttered Levitan. 'Felix Dzerzhinsky, old Iron Felix, he'd be reaching for his revolver, I tell you.'

'My wife wants to send our little girl to the school for super-models in Rybalka Street. Can you believe that, Lieutenant?' Aksyonov checked his mirror. Samuel rubber-necked in the back: Ksenia was still following doggedly. She was doing well. 'The fees are in dollars,' moaned Aksyonov. 'It will bleed me dry.'

'And the street names are all changed,' said Levitan. 'Red Guard Boulevard, Red Guard Street, Red Dawn Street, Red Student Street, Red Army Street – all renamed overnight. I didn't know where I was half the time in the early nineties. Kalinin Street is the New Arbat, Kirov Street's not Kirov any more. It's Meat Traders' Alley. "Like it used to be," they say. Well it was always Kirov in my time. As a matter of interest, who are "they" anyway? The Westerners with their dollars and their overbearing ways, that's who. Well, the day of reckoning beckons.'

Levitan finished his rant with a swig of beer and a venomous look directed at Samuel, as though he personally had renamed the entire city centre of Moscow and piled shame and ignominy on all of its people through his superior access to credit cards and luxury goods.

A moment's silence – into which Aksyonov spoke.

'Could we make a little detour, Lieutenant?'

Levitan looked at his watch.

'Would you mind explaining why?'

'My wife. She's an obsessive. If our little girl isn't going to be a supermodel, then she can be a tennis star.'

Levitan grunted and took another swig of beer.

'So she's been having tennis lessons out at Le Méridien Moscow Country Club,' said Aksyonov, smoothly changing lanes. 'She left her racket there last time. If I don't pick it up, she won't be able to practise between lessons. There'll be hell to pay. '

'How old is your girl?'

'Seven.'

Levitan laughed and slapped the dashboard.

'You poor bastard, Aksyonov. I don't know who to feel sorrier for, you or your daughter. Why am I thinking of remarrying? It's a mystery.'

Aksyonov waited for Levitan's mirth to subside.

'If we head west now I can pick up the racket, then we can come into town on the Tverskaya.'

Levitan was mopping his face with a stained handkerchief. He glanced back at Samuel and checked his watch.

244

'Gorky Street, you mean. All right, but I hope the traffic's not too bad. We've got a lot of questions to ask our friend here.'

Aksyonov nodded. A couple of minutes later he swung the Fiat off to the right. The road to the country club was a minor route; the lighting soon petered out, leaving the motorway from Ostankino as no more than a distant backdrop to the copses of birch and pine. The road took them through a dense wood, one of a series outside the city limits. The halo of orange around the Ostankino highway soon gave way to an inky darkness. They seemed to be rushing forward at quite a pace, hurtling into the night.

Suddenly a massive shock hit the side of the car from the left. It felt like a huge hammer blow. Aksyonov shouted something incomprehensible and wrestled with the steering wheel. The old Fiat left the road, which was heavily cambered. The wheels crunched through the narrow track of gravel on the shoulder of the carriageway.

'Shit! Shit! Shit! What the hell was that?' screamed Levitan.

They plunged into the forest. The Fiat's headlights picked out thinly spaced trees. Samuel tensed in the back, searching for handholds, though he knew that a single impact would be fatal.

Then the car's headlights went out. Still they hurtled forward.

'Oh my God! Oh my God!' wailed Levitan.

Each tree loomed huge in the windscreen, but then disappeared at the last second. They evaded trunk after trunk after trunk and, miraculously it seemed, finally threaded a way through.

Aksyonov sat very still once the car had come to a halt. Silence reigned for a brief moment as they contemplated the extremity they had just visited – death's precipice. There then came a soft murmuring from Aksyonov – the Orthodox Church's version of the Hail Mary.

'There's a time for prayer, Aksyonov, and this isn't it,' said Levitan. He was visibly shaking. 'You all right, Mr Spendlove?' he asked in English.

'Mother of God, defend and preserve us!' shouted Levitan, in a prayer all of his own. 'He's gone. Quick, out of the car! Let's find him.'

Aksyonov remained motionless.

'I wouldn't do that straight away, sir, if I were you.'

'Oh really, Aksyonov, and why's that?' asked Levitan, his hand on the lock.

'Because we were knocked off the road by something enormous. Whoever or whatever it was, was after us. That's why I switched the lights off.'

'You switched the lights off? You nearly killed us, you fool!'

'Standard evasion tactics, sir. If I'd left them on, I think we'd all almost certainly be dead by now. The prisoner's gone, sir, and good luck to him. I intend to sit here nice and quiet for a little while – with my gun drawn.'

They waited in the darkness for a few moments listening to the sound of their own breathing subside. As the adrenaline began to depart, they started to shiver.

A shot rang out somewhere in the impenetrable deepness of the forest with a soft, echoless thump. It was followed by a startled cawing of jackdaws and rooks and the flapping of wings. A deer bolted, running fast and fearful. And then the commotion began to subside, replaced all too quickly by a drained silence. Its eerie completeness was matched only by the impregnable blackness enfolding them.

A FEW METRES AWAY, Samuel lay on his side in what seemed to be a shallow ditch. The bottom half of his body, so far as he could tell without the benefit of sight, was covered in a clotted mulch of leaf and rotted fern. It was a heavy, thick smell, but not unpleasant – a kind of physical manifestation of the dense, velvet darkness. Samuel held his left hand in front of his face. He couldn't see anything. He moved the hand closer until he touched the tip of his nose. He waggled his fingers a centimetre in front of his eyes. Still nothing.

It felt curiously comfortable in the ditch, far warmer than it had any right to be. Perhaps the composting effect of the leaf mulch was creating a residual heat. As the excitement of escape began to wear off, Samuel realised that his right knee hurt. He must have damaged it when he took the chance of opening the door and rolling out onto the forest floor.

Samuel knew he could have been killed, but now at least he was master of his own fate. He could contact the British Embassy and get them to pick him up. To do that, he had to find his way out of the forest and evade the attentions of Levitan and Aksyonov.

Samuel rotated his head. All about him was blackness. Perhaps the policemen were dead, in which case it had been a very smart move to get out of the car. Or maybe they were simply lying in wait. The first one to move would reveal himself, and the game would be lost.

Samuel was reasonably well placed to play that game. He extended his right leg very stealthily, testing for pain. It was unpleasant, very sore in fact, but not too bad. He moved a hand down and felt the kneecap carefully. It was probably just bruised. He would give it a few more minutes, then move.

Samuel was attempting to stay completely still and make absolutely no noise, but he became increasingly aware of the loudness of his own breathing. He tried to quell the sound, but still it came, a slight but distinct sound of respiration. It seemed like some deafening crash in the bitumen silence. Samuel held his breath for a moment. But the noise was still there.

He realised to his horror that someone or something was next to him, right there with him. He could not tell exactly how near, it might have been metres or even centimetres. The instinct to get up and run was strong. He could feel the flood of adrenaline and the rush of blood through his veins. Fight or flight – the classic choice.

With the greatest difficulty, Samuel resisted the urge to shout out and run at whatever it was. It was most likely to be an animal. After all, he hadn't heard any approach steps, and he doubted that the policemen were skilled stalkers or hunters with an aptitude for stealth.

Whatever it was had reined in its breathing or gone away. Samuel listened intently. There was now no question of moving any time soon. He let himself sink a little further into the comforting mulch.

Then he saw it. A tiny flash of pale-silver light, perhaps torch light, about a hundred metres away. And then he was immersed in the infernal blackness once more. Samuel had heard that the human eye could see the flare of a match fifteen kilometres away in darkness such as this. He could believe it. He stared in the direction he'd seen the light and tried to make his breathing utterly inaudible. The difficulty of contemplating the unknown and the steadily dropping temperature were making him shiver slightly now. This too was something he had to control. He mustn't, he couldn't, give himself away.

He blinked into the darkness. Samuel was beginning to wonder whether he had imagined the flash of torchlight when he saw it again – a silver feather, a little further to his left, but no nearer.

Immediately there was a response from close by. Some five metres away from Samuel came a sharp gunshot. He wasn't looking in the direction of the shot, but in the microsecond of brilliant white light his peripheral vision caught a huge beast of a man wielding a very large handgun.

The shot was followed by a soft oath in a language that Samuel didn't understand. It sounded like a variant of Russian.

Engulfed once more in darkness and silence Samuel focused on controlling his diaphragm so that the breath came with no discernible noise. He was almost overpowered by the instinct to scream and run at the gunman. He dug his nails into his palms, trying to focus on the pain.

His mind flipped endlessly over the possibilities. The armed man may have been the reason the car had left the road. Samuel hadn't been paying particular attention to the traffic. He'd just assumed they'd been hit by a huge truck and concentrated on making the most of the opportunity to escape. Maybe it was this man who'd forced them off the road. But why should he want to kill them?

Samuel sank even lower still into the mulch. Of course, it was entirely possible that their assailant wasn't interested in all three of them, rather Samuel himself. Ever since he'd agreed to meet the Black Widow and procure the drilling technology, he'd found the world beating a path to him. Even William Barton had knocked on his door. Yavlinsky was dead. Blandford was missing. Would he be next?

He should never have agreed to any of this – Blandford, the Black Widow, Kempis. He should never have done their bidding. And then he remembered – Ksenia. Her face flashed into Samuel's mind: her beautiful eyes, her mother's smile. Where was she? Had she been forced off the road too? Was she the innocent party in all this? Or had she led this predator to them?

Samuel suddenly stiffened in terror. Something was approaching. He could hear human footfall as twigs snapped, making sounds like tiny firecrackers. Heavy boots landed cautiously on the crisp bracken. The man was close now, very close.

Then stillness and total blackness descended once more.

Across the cold night air a sickening stench assailed Samuel's nostrils. Whoever it was seemed to have soiled himself. Faeces, sweat, something sharp and chemical, and beneath it all something really alarming, the foul odour of something rotting, something corrupted. It must be the man with the gun. If Samuel could smell him, he was definitely within touching distance.

Should he simply lash out? He would have the advantage of surprise, but he couldn't even see his opponent. Once he had revealed himself, he would be lost. His foe was undoubtedly heavily armed, and would be more used to fighting than Samuel.

Then he saw what he was up against. A very faint phosphorescent blue light licked against the contours of a huge bulk of a man about ten metres away. Fortunately, his back was three-quarters turned to Samuel, who lay dead still where he was. He shivered at the size and obvious physical power of the commando – for that was what he was, with heavy swathes of ammunition draped over his huge torso. Grenades and knives were slotted into countless pockets in his combat fatigues.

All the commando needed to do was glance to his left and catch sight of Samuel, and that would be it, the end. Thank God, he hadn't tried to hit this creature earlier. The man was a muscle-bound munitions dump.

But there was little chance of the commando looking anywhere other than into his own lap. He was searching intently for something on the ground and then lifted his head and pulled gently at a large grenade attached to the left epaulette of his fatigues.

There was a moment more of quiet and blackness – suddenly punctured by what started out as a gentle fizzing sound. After a couple of seconds the fizz multiplied itself a thousand-fold into a huge roar. The figure of the commando was momentarily visible again. He was half-kneeling, and over his shoulder he supported what looked like a vacuum cleaner with a metre of pipe extending from the body of the contraption.

A trail of red and yellow sparks spat from the commando's shoulder, scoring the woodland blackness. Samuel could feel the shock of impact before he saw the flames or felt the wave of heat from the exploding car.

Levitan's Fiat was thirty metres away. It crackled and roared with an intense white light. It was clear there could be no survivors. Just as the flames were beginning to lose their intensity, the petrol tank exploded. Warmth and fierce orange light flooded over Samuel.

He realised with a start that they both were mesmerised by the hit on the car. Now was the time to slip away. As soon as the commando turned, Samuel was surely dead.

He began to creep away – slowly, slowly. The burning wreck still had the rapt, childlike attention of the commando. Samuel began to ease himself from the ditch – almost out of earshot now, inch by inch . . .

He had no real idea of where to go, other than away from the incandescent wreck of the police car. Once back in darkness, he would be invisible once more. He desperately wanted to be invisible.

Samuel's peripheral vision now came to his aid. As he crept, only half-erect, towards the cover of a silver birch, he saw it – a flickering fishtail of silver light again. If the commando had been shooting at it, there was at least a chance that whoever was wielding the torch could be an ally.

He was crouched down, taking step after agonising step, his progress hampered by his injured knee. The fire that had engulfed the car was beginning to abate and the comforting darkness was just a few seconds away.

A few seconds too far. Something thumped into a tree trunk in front of him. Instinctively, Samuel knew from the percussive thwack that it was a bullet. Then came another, and another. The last missed him by millimetres. He actually felt the rush of air before it smashed into a silver birch.

Samuel put his head down and ran. He wasn't looking for the torch bearer now. He sought the darkest part of the forest – blackness, refuge and oblivion.

Brambles clutched at his legs and arms. Thorns tore at his clothes and flesh, but he plunged on. Behind him he could hear the commando crashing into the forest in pursuit. Stealth was finished with now. Samuel's heart was beating wildly. He was fighting against panic. He scrambled up a steep bank and clawed his way through thick curtains of creeper and bramble. It was a race against death. And he was losing it.

The commando hadn't fired a shot in Samuel's direction for a little while, but the sound of pursuit was getting closer. The crashing footfalls were getting louder and louder.

Samuel pushed on grimly. Had it come to this? Was he going to perish in some nameless forest outside Moscow? Out of nowhere an ancient phrase echoed in his head: *'Perspicacity and perseverance, dear boy'* – Kempis, twinkling eyes, Amontillado in hand, Radcliffe Camera over his shoulder – *'Perspicacity is nothing without perseverance.'*

Samuel breathed in deeply, and forced his way through a dense thicket of thorn, and stopped himself just in time. A gibbous moon had extricated itself from thick, greedy fingers of cloud. It cast just enough light for Samuel to see that he stood on the edge of a sharp drop. He was at the top of an escarpment, a mini precipice. It was impossible to say just how steep the drop was; the moonlight's grey gruel wasn't bright enough for that. But it was certainly several metres deep.

This was his chance, his last chance.

Samuel drew himself behind a black elm trunk, and waited. The next six or seven seconds were filled with ever-louder crashing and trampling. There was a swishing, percussive nature to the sound. The commando had a machete.

Then the commando was through the thicket of thorn. He was a huge, stinking, sweating beast of a man. In the pallid moonlight Samuel saw that he was wearing an eye patch on a face marked and pitted by thorn scratches, and something else he couldn't identify, maybe some kind of pox.

Samuel's mental snapshot of the commando took a third of a

second. Now, just a metre away, he was teetering on the edge of the precipice. The commando had considerable momentum, but there was just enough moonlight for him to see the danger and attempt to check himself.

But it was too late. He began to fall. Then, just as he was disappearing down into the dark void beneath them, he whirled round, dropped the machete, and flashed out a mighty forearm to grab at a bush next to where Samuel was hiding. The commando had managed to latch on to a frail-looking branch, halting his descent.

Samuel watched with horror. The branch bent – but did not break. The commando began to haul himself up. His boots had made some sort of purchase on the face of the escarpment. He had stabilised his fall and was slowly making ground towards the summit, using little shuffling steps in a reverse abseiling technique.

Samuel emerged from behind his tree. He could not allow the commando to regain the top of the hill. His adversary saw him and fixed him with his good eye, then redoubled his efforts.

Samuel was no more than a couple of arms' lengths away. All he had to do now was push the commando and he would disappear into the abyss. But something prevented him. All it would take was a simple, vigorous movement; his adversary would be at the bottom of the ravine. If the commando didn't die immediately, he would almost certainly break a limb, and then suffer a slow death from exposure and loss of blood.

Samuel stood in front of the commando. The physical effort, the will to survive were etched on the scarred and pock-marked face. The good eye pleaded. The commando offered his other hand to Samuel. Samuel couldn't quite rely on gravity to do his job for him. He reached out and pushed against his adversary as hard as he could.

A bad mistake. At the instant of connection, the commando grabbed at him. The grip from the commando's left hand began to crush the bones in Samuel's right. He was immensely strong. He was trying to leverage himself up and cast Samuel down to the bottom of the void now, in one single, violent movement.

But Samuel acted just in time. The commando was about to transfer his weight up and pitch Samuel into the ravine when Samuel used his forward momentum to crash his forehead into the commando's eye patch. There was a shriek of agony. The grip was broken. Samuel was free. The commando toppled back – into the abyss.

The shrieking stopped after the second thump on the escarpment face. Then, after a few more small sounds of settling rock and shaking shrub, there was silence.

The moon, Samuel's saviour, disappeared back behind its screen of cloud. The now-familiar darkness embraced him again.

Then he saw it once more, the subdued flash of silver. It was a torch, certainly, but it had been taped or shuttered in some way to give it a restricted tunnel of light – a battlefield tool.

'Hello? Hello?'

A female voice. Ksenia? Samuel checked for a moment. The Black Widow's daughter might just have a gun in her hand. He said nothing, swathed in comforting darkness.

The silver light flashed again, seeking him out. It was distant, perhaps fifty metres away, though it was difficult to tell exactly because of the thickness of the foliage and the dense grouping of the trees.

'Hello? Samuel?'

Friend or foe, she was coming towards him. He had to do something.

'Ksenia? Is that you?'

He hid behind a tree, the better to observe her.

'Samuel, are you all right?'

'I'm fine,' said Samuel – the polite, reflexive lie of the Englishman. 'Keep coming this way.'

After a couple of minutes of scrabbling through stubborn shrubs and thorn Ksenia stumbled out into a clearing. He watched her for a few seconds. He couldn't see a weapon, but he couldn't be certain of anything.

He broke into the open.

'Over here!'

She ran to him, holding out her arms. Samuel allowed himself to fall into her embrace.

'You're all right, thank God!' she exclaimed, still hugging him tightly. He could feel her breath, hot on the corner of his neck. They remained locked together for a moment.

'You are well, Samuel Petrovich. This is good.'

Samuel wheeled round. A trap, after all. The deep male voice belonged to a rotund, bearish man with a thick white beard.

'Who are you? Who are these people, Ksenia?'

But even as he phrased the question, he realised he knew the answer. The man's companion was a woman of similar age with tight white curls clinging to her head. They were both *shestidyesatniki* – the sixties generation.

And, yes, he had seen them before. The Lenin lapel badge, a military decoration peeking through the coat: the messengers from Comrade Kempis. He could picture their faces fraught with tension, behind the windscreen of the ancient Zighuli in Alexander Gardens.

'I suppose I should be surprised. But that's not going to get me very far, is it?'

'I see you recognise us now,' said the man, smiling.

'I lost control of my car, and they pulled me out,' said Ksenia. 'They helped me look for you in this place.'

'Easy to look and get killed,' said the man. 'Not easy to look and live.'

'Nothing is easy. As all friends of Peter Kempis will appreciate.'

'Comrades,' said the woman. 'Comradeship is more important

255

than friendship. But, yes, we were also friends of Comrade Kempis.'

'Samuel Petrovich – son of Peter. Not his natural son? No? But it makes sense, of a sort I suppose,' said Ksenia.

'And they were following us?' Samuel asked Ksenia. She was shivering now, holding on to him hard. If this was an act then she was damned good at it.

'We have been following you every day of your visit to Moscow,' said the man, evenly. 'We are not always obvious. We had to be when delivering Comrade Kempis's note to you; we feared you might leave the next day. Drastic action had to be taken.'

'You were following the police car from Ostankino?'

'The police car, and your friend, and the mercenary. These people are such amateurs. No finesse, no sense of what is obvious, what is necessary and what is discreet. You have attracted much interest in Moscow, but the mercenary was new. He is a dangerous man. I mean to say he *was* a dangerous man. I told Ksenia only one of you would come out of that wood alive. He is dead, yes?'

For a second, Samuel saw him again: hand outstretched, that eye staring out of the darkness, the body, falling away from him. Samuel's shivering increased.

'I assume so. You are Gospodin . . .?'

'My name is immaterial,' said the old man. 'Comrade is sufficient. I am a comrade of Comrade Kempis. To seek more is the cult of the personality.'

'But why are you doing this, comrade?'

'Because Comrade Kempis asked me to. He was good man. He said you would come to Moscow on his death, and he asked us to give you the messages we gave you, and to watch over you – and your friends.' He nodded at Ksenia.

'I'm sorry. I'm confused here,' said Samuel. 'Messages? You almost ran me down in the street, Comrade, and gave me a note.

What other message have you given me?'

'You have it with you, Comrade. Unless I am much mistaken.'

'Excuse me?'

'In your trouser pocket. A brass key. I hope you have not lost it, Comrade. This is the important message. It was Comrade Kempis's wish that you have it some days after the first note.'

Samuel reached into his pocket and produced the key.

'Good,' said the old Communist. 'Comrade Kempis said that you were the perfect man to entrust with the key and the responsibilities that go with it.'

'But wait a minute, Comrade. I thought that package was from Yavlinsky.'

'It was. Yavlinsky was one of us. He too knew Comrade Kempis.'

'So who killed Yavlinsky?'

'We hoped you might know.'

'I might. But even if I'm right, I'm not sure why,' said Samuel, standing stock-still. 'Do you know what the key is for?'

The old Communist couple shrugged. 'It has responsibilities, as we said. Perhaps Comrade Kempis thought you might work out what they were for yourself.'

'I'm sure we'll discover what it's for,' said Ksenia. 'Come on, Samuel.'

'Come with us,' said the woman. 'We will give you shelter.'

Samuel looked dubiously at the old couple, then at Ksenia.

He was injured. He was exhausted, he needed to rest. And he needed to be safe. A sworn allegiance to Kempis's memory was as good a surety as any. And Ksenia? Whatever she wanted, whatever her allegiance, better to keep her close.

Samuel peered into the darkness of the thickets. It was eerily quiet. Whatever animal life they hadn't scared away would be watching from the undergrowth. He sighed, and moved towards the road, and what passed for civilisation.

The moon scudded out from behind its dense cloud cover once more, veiling the group in the softest, palest silver. Far away, deep, deep in the mountains beyond the woods, a wolf howled.

*SAMUEL WAS CLIMBING stair after stair. He was trapped in an Escher drawing, a victim of perspective, condemned to trudge endlessly upwards, but never reach a stopping point . . .*

With a painful effort of will, he blinked himself to consciousness. Of course – the room at the top of the giant concrete skyscraper, the heroic people's housing project of the 1960s – whose lifts didn't work, and whose stairwells stank of urine.

He climbed out of the camp bed – standard Red Army issue, by the look of it. Some things he didn't remember. His clothes, for example, were a mystery. The coarse cotton of a dark blue shirt irritated his skin. And he was wearing dungarees, in a tasteful shade of chocolate brown. Unless he was still trapped in an unpleasant dream, these clothes were not his own.

Mounted on the wall opposite was a huge black-and-white picture, illuminated in the watery winter morning light that flooded into the small, dingy room. The plain black frame contained an image of two dark-haired men shaking hands; one was quite young, the other in his early middle years. They were clasping each other with both hands; bear hugs surely would follow. The picture was huge; it occupied an entire wall.

Samuel rubbed his eyes and yawned. He felt achy and rather cold. The small room in which he had slept was not well heated. Beneath and to the right of the vast photograph was a chest of drawers and a framed photograph of a dog wearing a huge, loose collar and some kind of fancy dress.

'Klinkov.'

Samuel turned. Ksenia was standing in the doorway, watching him, her expression unreadable.

'Excuse me?'

'Comrade Klinkov. That's the name of our host. This is his spare room. He really must have known how to work the old system. A spare room was an unheard of luxury in his day.'

'Klinkov?' repeated Samuel blankly. He thought back; Kempis had never mentioned the name.

Samuel looked again at the photograph. Of course. Klinkov was the older man. And the young man beside him was a hero of the Russian people. Yuri Gagarin, the astronaut.

Ksenia strode over to the picture and gazed up at it.

'Klinkov was a respected engineer in his youth,' she said, 'and the dog was the first living creature in space. A true triumph for the Soviet Union.'

She stroked the dog's photograph tenderly.

Samuel reflected on how unfortunately for Soviet technical triumphs, the dog had not in fact munched its way through various canine treats while orbiting the earth at several thousand miles an hour. The creature, Laika, had made it into space all right, but had died painfully from overheating within few hours of blast off – thus becoming the fastest dead dog in history. The irony of this historic event being referred to in this present moment did not escape him.

'Where's Comrade Klinkov now?'

'At a Party meeting with his wife. They are conveners of the local branch.'

'The Communist Party?'

'It's not illegal to be a Communist in this country, Samuel. The meetings tend to be full of old people, and some very young ones.'

'Younger than you, Ksenia?'

She nodded. 'They're typically confused and struggling for a sense of identity. Who are they? What is Russia? That sort of thing. They're not all diehards like the Klinkovs.'

Samuel scratched his cheek slowly, and gazed out of the window. You could probably say Kempis was a diehard: an intellectual, an ideas man – a Communist. Ideas could get you into trouble.

'And anyway,' added Ksenia brightly, 'a lot of them just like the free food you get at the meetings. Not everyone has benefited from market reforms.'

'You mean not everyone has benefited in the same way as your mother?'

'I'm not like her, Samuel.'

Samuel held her gaze, but said nothing. She shrugged her shoulders, as if his opinion did not matter.

'And even if I am, you've got more important things to worry about.'

Ksenia gestured to the coffee table beside him.

There, ranged in neat, ribbed rows, like a breakfast display at a fancy hotel or a smart St James's gentlemen's club, were all the newspapers of the day. And their front pages screamed about a story of deception, market manipulation and murder. *Kommersant* led on the disorderly oil market, with a big picture of Yavlinsky. The *Argumenti I Fakti* took a more ideological view. The market in Russia's most precious natural resource, oil, was being manipulated by the West. The notorious industrial spy – he gulped at the sight of his own picture – Samuel Spendlove was sought by police, but had escaped after a fire-fight in a forest outside Moscow. *The Express Chronicle* ran pictures of the Black Widow, Ksenia and Samuel next to a story about the manipulated oil market. Samuel's Russian wasn't quite good enough to decipher the story accurately, but the implication was clear: Ksenia had gone missing; Yavlinsky was dead; the oil market was in disarray, and Samuel, conveniently, was responsible for the lot.

Images of the previous night began to tumble through his mind. The Devil's Basin, the Black Widow, the police, the darkness and terror of the forest, the fire-bombed car, the commando. Dear God, he had killed a man. He'd had no choice, true. The psychotic brute was hell-bent on murdering him. But now Samuel had blood on his hands. He had taken a man's life – and it felt ugly, brutal, coarse.

He glanced again at the headlines. This was Paris repeated, but far, far worse. Was there any truth in the propaganda? Was this what he was becoming?

Samuel got up and stumbled slightly. His right knee, which he'd banged in escaping the police car, had swollen up in the night. It nearly gave way. Ksenia reached out and Samuel put his arm over her shoulder.

'Be careful,' she said. 'You had an eventful evening.'

'We all did, from the little I remember,' said Samuel.

But Samuel could remember all too clearly. And he didn't want to.

Ksenia walked him to the window and opened the curtains. They seemed to have landed in some cockpit in the sky. Fat, voluptuous plumes of smoke from a dozen factory chimneys formed a beautiful, faintly sinister flotilla amid the cloud bank.

Samuel pulled out his mobile phone and dialled a number.

He got through to the British Embassy on the second ring.

'One moment please,' said the voice on the other end after Samuel had announced himself. An interminable series of clicks followed. Samuel began to wonder just how many ears would be listening to his conversation.

'Hello? Mr Samuel Spendlove? Laverock Windlesham of the British Embassy speaking,' boomed a male voice. The sonorous baritone had an accent straight out of the BBC Home Service of the 1950s. Samuel could picture this guy wearing an immaculate suit and sitting bolt upright at his desk.

'Good morning, Mr Windlesham. I need your help.'

'We'd heard, Mr Spendlove. We'd heard.'

'I hesitate to think what you've heard,' said Samuel guardedly.

'Well, what haven't we heard?' said Windlesham. He had the authoritative joviality of a public-school prefect. 'The police, among others, have been on to us about you. People appear to think you've been rather a naughty boy. I understand you didn't return to your hotel last night, which means you're wandering round without a passport – definitely not recommended over here. Then, of course, there's the whole business of bodies, a number of bodies, falling to the floor in your wake, not to mention accusations of insider trading.'

'I think I need a ride home.'

Samuel looked at Ksenia. She flinched and shook her head.

'Well, obviously, we'd be glad to lend a hand if you're in a spot of bother, old lad. That's what we're here for.'

'Great.'

Samuel saw Ksenia's bruised disappointment – *real or counterfeit?*

'So just tell me where you are, and we'll send a car,' purred Windlesham.

Samuel started slightly. He didn't want to get Comrade Klinkov into trouble.

'That's very kind, but I'll get to you under my own steam. There's no need to bother sending a car.'

'No, really. It's no bother, no bother at all,' said Windlesham. Did Samuel detect tightness in his voice?

'Well, that's very kind,' said Samuel after a short pause. He could almost hear the other parties to their conversation – there'd be dozens of them – waiting for his next words.

Samuel recited an address. Windlesham thanked him and repeated it carefully to make sure the details were correct. They bade each other farewell with bogus cordiality.

Samuel shut down the phone and turned to Ksenia.

'So that's it, you're just going to run back home?'

'Not home, no,' said Samuel.

He let his words hang in the air between them for a moment.

'I didn't like the sound of the guy at the embassy, and I'm pretty sure the line was tapped. I bet they have no intention of "lending me a hand".'

'What address did you give him?'

'A meeting place with Yavlinsky – the Tetryakov Museum.'

'They're not stupid. They probably had a satellite trace on your phone.'

'I'm sure they did. Which is why we've got to act fast.'

'We?'

'The world thinks I'm a killer. A violent psychopath. Why not use that to our advantage?'

'I don't understand.'

'I'm abducting you and taking you to Kamchatka.'

Ksenia narrowed her eyes and studied him closely.

'What do you know about Kamchatka, Samuel?'

'Well there's something there, for sure. Your mother flinched when I mentioned it, and I'm guessing it takes a lot to make the Black Widow flinch. Why, what do you know?'

Ksenia shook her head. 'I've never been, but I know plenty about the place because of our sustainability division. The Soviets had the grand plan of harnessing the energy of the volcanoes for heat and energy. That would have been one of the few ecologically sound Communist plans. Sadly, they never followed it through.'

'Do you have a name? A person we can find?'

Ksenia shrugged. 'I've got a number. That's all.'

'It's a start. And who knows, your mother might just be prepared to trade more information in return for her daughter's safety.'

Ksenia laughed, but Samuel played it deadpan. Maybe it wasn't such a joke. He was discovering things about himself every day. He'd just killed a man, after all.

**PART THREE**

*'OK, GRISHIN. TAKE her up.'*

*He shot his cuffs – a quick check on one of his very few luxuries in life. Perhaps the diagonal-cross cuff-links were his only luxury. The navy blue crosses on a white background were an emblem of honour, one that he wore, he hoped, with dignity.*

*To some it might have seemed like vanity to wear a dress shirt on the fifth day at sea. Dressing up was the kind of thing British naval officers did in the decadent days of their dying empire.*

*But for him, the dress shirt was a simple necessity, as everyone on board knew. His wife washed and pressed his uniform for him. The navy couldn't or wouldn't do it. The navy, or the bastards who administered it in Moscow, couldn't or wouldn't pay him, or his men. They hadn't been paid for months the previous year. It seemed to be getting better now, but there was no mention of when their back pay, pitifully small as it was, would come to them. Still, they were all in it together. The men knew he shared their conditions and sought no favours.*

*The truth was that he only had two white shirts, so he had to take the dress shirt with him on manoeuvres. It had become something of a talisman for the men. When they saw the dress shirt and the cuff-links bearing the insignia of the Russian navy, they knew that they were on the final leg of a voyage. The cuff-links and the smart shirt beneath the clean but frayed sleeves of his dark-*

*blue uniform meant that they would soon be back at base. Spartan as it was, their home port was just that – home. After five or six days beneath the sea, the prospect of breathing clean air was a huge boost to morale.*

*'Grishin? Are you asleep?' he barked into the intercom.*

*'Absolutely not, Commander. We're at thirty metres and rising.'*

*'Thank you.'*

*The commander fingered the cardboard package. It was about the size of a shoebox, and surprisingly light. But then perhaps it wasn't so surprising. Titanium was super-strong, but weighed very little.*

*'Mochanov, take over,' he ordered. 'I want ten minutes up there.'*

*'Yes, Commander,' came the instant response. Mochanov was from Magadan, the eastern Siberian port. He was a natural sailor. Though sometimes, after days beneath the sea, you had to wonder if there was such a thing as a natural submariner.*

*The commander walked purposefully off the bridge to a flurry of salutes and greetings. Morale was good, even after the long days of manoeuvring in the Sea of Okhotsk and then heading south and east to cross the tip of the Kamchatka peninsula into the icy, dark-blue waters of the Pacific. They all loved to see the cuff-links and the dress shirt, no doubt of that. One or two cast curious glances at the package he was carrying, but none looked too closely. He was the commander, the leader, the most trusted man on the vessel.*

*The Osprey was an Antyey class submarine, and still in pretty good shape. Although the cretins in Moscow couldn't work out how to pay, feed or clothe the men on whose loyalty they relied so heavily, they did recognise that the naval Pacific shield wouldn't be much use if the vessels weren't maintained. So there was fuel, if nothing else, although The Osprey was nuclear-powered and only needed refuelling every couple of years.*

*As he made his way up to the Conning Tower, he could imagine the sight at the surface of the chilly, blue-black Pacific. The water would bruise and bulge as though some giant dolphin were emerging, and then the Osprey would pierce the surface, cutting into the air with a swish and a soft roar, amid avalanches of creamy white foam.*

*Within a few seconds Grishin's voice crackled on the talkback. They had surfaced. A junior rating saluted and cranked open a couple of hatches before bobbing back down.*

*The commander levered his slim frame onto the tiny deck of the tower, and stood on the grey metal cross-grill. The tang of salt, the droplets of spume and the cawing of gulls were food, drink and music all at once. Behind him was the impenetrable depth of the Kuril trench, more than 26,000 feet deep at one point. Ahead lay the city of Petropavlovsk-Kamchatsky, dominated by the still-active Koryakskaya volcano.*

*Beyond that, lay the naval base that had barely existed during The Great Patriotic War, though it had come to prominence later. Civilians had not been allowed into the area until after the fall of the Soviet Union. The final step of his journey would take him home to Olga and the children.*

*It was a fine day, exceptionally so for the time of year. There was little breeze, and the ambient temperature of minus two was pleasurable for a short time; the engine had been cut to dead slow. He drew his threadbare uniform about his shoulders and screwed up his striking emerald eyes to squint into the vanishing point between sea and sky.*

*Little Maria and Kolya gave him a true sense of purpose, a real perspective. This was Russia's Pacific defence. This ship, these men, himself. They were there for Russia, the Motherland. They remained loyal to the navy despite their own good sense and the efforts of the pitiless bureaucrats in Moscow.*

*So – he reached inside his jacket and took out the box – what was this damned thing? Despite all the frantic calls from Moscow, he was tempted to cast it into the sea. Was that the proper thing to do? He had to think of Maria, Kolya, Olga, and his role as front-line defender of Mother Russia. Someone had to.*

*He opened the box and weighed the object within in the palm of his hand. It was a curious shape, like the snout of a Bottlenose Dolphin. The apertures in the side of the nose were exhausts, but looked alarmingly like eyes. The tiny grills were full of sonar equipment. The engineer in him was tempted to pull the thing to pieces and work out the principles of its design.*

*But time was running short, that much was clear. So should he, or shouldn't he? He tossed the thing up in the air and caught it a couple of times.*

*Maybe, maybe not. The consequences were so hard to work out. If this thing had only civil applications, the only banal little fact at his disposal, why give it to a naval man? Because he was so far away from the rest of the world? Because he knew how to give and take orders? Because there was a boot at his throat? He would be home in less than twenty-four hours. He would see his family, and then decide.*

*He was getting cold. Time to go back down. He put the contraption back in its box, and began the descent. Within a couple of minutes he was back in his cabin, and moments later on the bridge giving orders to dive. The crew, highly trained submariners who loved their excellent commander, knew how to take orders. They responded with perfect, unquestioning discipline.*

# CHAPTER SIXTEEN

KSENIA SMILED AND reached out and grasped Samuel's hand. A gesture of control, complicity . . . or just the instinctive reactions of a nervous passenger?

Samuel wasn't a nervous flyer. Not normally, anyway. But the Tupolev 96 did not inspire confidence. New Russia had made its mark in the salons, restaurants, clubs, bars and, of course, banks of Moscow. Aviation, however, was the kind of thing that took a while to change.

The aeroplane rattled – and took off with the laboured inelegance of a goose scraping itself into the air from the surface of a lake. The Tu-96 was a reminder of the way things had been for so long. It was a long-range craft, perfectly suited for the flight to Kamchatka, but it didn't compare with the modern fleets of Western airlines.

Once they were airborne, Ksenia admired her cheap wedding ring and gently withdrew her hand. Samuel pretended not to notice, and looked about the cabin with its threadbare brown-and-orange aisle carpeting and dingy, matching curtains that separated them from business class. The curtains were drawn back for take-off. They were sitting two-thirds of the way back in a cabin adapted to accommodate some 150 passengers.

Samuel jammed down a plain black baseball cap, sat back and sipped a mineral water.

At worst, this trip would buy them breathing space. The Russian or British authorities might or might not guess they were going to Kamchatka. But it would take them time to get there. The Brits wouldn't have a hope. There were no direct roads – a throwback to the Soviets and the super-secret military era. At best, they might get some answers. With real information, the road ahead might be clear. There was always a first time.

Ksenia, hair hidden under a cloche hat, was now playing with her phone. 'Kamchatka's actually bigger than the whole state of California, you know, but with just 80,000 people outside the capital.'

'And we're headed for a crowd scene? The throbbing metropolis of Petropavlovsk-Kamchatsky?'

'No choice. There are a third of a million people – it's the only civil airport on the peninsula. Otherwise, it's basically a huge military and naval base. Everything's secret and off-limits,' smiled Ksenia. She seemed happy and excited.

Samuel pulled out the American passport she'd given him the day before. For good money, and Ksenia had plenty of that, good-quality fake US passports were quickly and easily obtainable. 'Unless, like us, you're vulcanologists with the right permissions.'

'Exactly, Dr Jack and Mrs Karina Daniels.'

Samuel flashed her a grin. 'Whoever supplied you with this, Ksenia, has a feeble sense of humour. Jack Daniels?'

'They're very convincing, and all done in twenty-four hours. I think that's pretty impressive.'

'It's impressive enough, and I'm grateful, believe me. Of course, I wanted to get away from Moscow, its helpful diplomats, its ugly police force and its giant mercenaries.'

Ksenia looked at him. 'Kamchatka has its own danger – for a start, 160 volcanoes, thirty of them active. It has hot geysers, and the most unbelievable flora. As for the wild animals – mink, brown bear, wolf, wild cats of all sorts. It also has nuclear missile silos, 150,000 conventional troops, including tank divisions, two submarine bases, and at least one nuclear base.'

'But does it have the answers we're looking for, Mrs Daniels?'

She smiled tightly. 'The first task is to get in. As you can imagine, security is tight at the airport. You may well be questioned about the purpose of your visit and your spiel on thermal conduction will have to sound convincing.'

'OK, OK,' said Samuel. 'Pass me the notes. I'll read them now.'

Samuel had a couple of hours to get a basic grasp of the extraordinary geography that he, as a supposed geologist, was going to study. He had a notional specialisation in detection and analysis of volcanic drill core containing adenosine tri-phosphate (ATP), and lipopolysaccharide protein. Klyuchevskaya at 15,584 feet was the dominant volcano, with the relatively stable Kamen, (last eruption pre-1900) a close second at 15,197 feet. Other volcanoes included Bezymyannaya at 10,121 feet and Tolbachik at 12,080 feet. Even for a non-geologist, it looked like a fascinating place.

As president of sustainable investment at ABTV, Ksenia was trying to revive the old Khrushchev-regime plan of harnessing the steam and energy of the volcanoes for heat and power. Once an underground pipe system was installed, the energy would be cheap. This idea had attracted the Communists, and it would be 'natural' – which pleased Ksenia. She had a quota of standing permissions to take geologists out there when she wished.

Ksenia had fallen into a drowsy sleep as Samuel read. She rested her head on his shoulder. Her mouth – plumply angelic – was turned up towards him.

He reached over and turned her face towards him, his crooked forefinger lifting her gently so gently – by the chin. Then he kissed her delicately, full on the mouth. They were a married couple after all, it was important to play the part.

Ksenia opened her eyes. Had she really been asleep? She smiled, and turned away from him to sleep.

Samuel refocused. Time to brief himself, to give this plan some sort of a chance. He leafed through a little background on scoria, then ploughed into the ATP-meter notes that Ksenia had given him. But the material had a sedative effect.

He woke up as the Tupolev landed bumpily at Petropavlovsk-Kamchatsky.

Samuel peered out of the window, eager to see the terrain that was so isolated, so sparsely populated, so special. All he saw was an impenetrable fog. The captain announced that the outside temperature was minus eight – normal for the time of year.

They clambered out of the plane, down a narrow metal staircase glistening with de-icing fluid. A quick walk across the greasy tarmac took them to the freezing, cavernous arrivals hall. The small airport terminal building had the trappings of capitalism. There were advertisements for the staples of modern Russian life: beer, vodka, cigarettes, and banks. But the placards were pinned to cold, plain concrete walls. The floor was covered in linoleum that, if not from Stalin's era, had probably not been upgraded since Khrushchev was forcibly retired as Secretary General of the Politburo.

The luggage belt ground into action. It struck Samuel that the thing could probably double as a hay baler. Their fellow passengers, most of whom looked as though they had connections with the navy, began to gravitate towards it. The hay baler produced the bags soon enough. Samuel grabbed them and, one in each hand, followed Ksenia to the exit.

As they came into the tiny arrivals hall, a large, red-bearded man in a nondescript grey uniform approached them. In the background, half a dozen Military Policemen lolled in chairs and smoked cigarettes that stank of pine resin. Through the haze Samuel detected an air of bored vigilance, heavy with latent aggression.

'Papers please,' said the bearded man. His Russian had a strangely guttural quality.

Samuel handed his passport over. He would let Ksenia do the

talking. Neither of them would be able to stand up to any sort of sustained questioning. They'd be exposed as fake geologists in a minute, and they'd be caught in just about the worst circumstances. A civil police car now pulled up outside the arrivals hall, its lights strobing blue.

The man looked at both documents, then at the two of them in turn for a long moment.

'Very good. Come with me. We'll get these back to you after we've taken copies,' he said at length.

He then grabbed their bags from Samuel and led them towards an ancient Toyota. Samuel wanted to laugh out loud. So the big bearded guy was the hotel's welcoming committee. But maybe it wasn't surprising that it all felt so military; this was supposed to be Kamchatka's identity, after all. And this was where the Black Widow's web extended to.

Samuel got in the front and Ksenia hopped in the back. The smooth airport road soon gave way to a rougher, pot-holed surface that took them through a cityscape almost completely invisible through the dense, freezing fog. The occasional square-set Soviet-era building loomed into view, then dissolved back into thick grey nothingness. Apparently, they were heading for the *Avacha* Hotel. Samuel stared out of the window raptly. Out there, a burgeoning civilian life rubbed shoulders with the military, all nestled together under the shadow of the most impressive range of volcanoes on the planet. Some dormant, some not.

THE ROAD OUT to the Kirov family home was scarcely worthy of the name. It was a shallow streak of tarmac of variable depth and width – a thick, solid spillage of hard core and tar – as though someone had knocked over a giant wine glass full of stones and boiling pitch, and then walked away.

Hundreds of millions of tons of volcanic ash had dumped

themselves down near the tiny village that was home to the Kirovs, and a number of other naval families. It was, just sometimes, slightly unnerving to live so near an active volcano. But Kirov comforted himself that eruptions only happened every forty years or so. The last eruption had happened ten years earlier. If he did what was expected of him he would be retired long before the next one. The family would be back in Moscow. They would be safe . . . and rich.

The rest of Russia knew little of Kamchatka. It was a long way away from the centre of power. Few people lived there, and its military significance guaranteed a patina of secrecy. Even the occasional volcanic eruption went largely unreported in the Russian media. At the time of the last eruptions, the Communists were in power, and Kamchatka was almost totally closed off from the rest of the Soviet Union, let alone the rest of the world. Geologists knew that something had happened; a few small articles had appeared in the Western press. But there was no locally sourced information, so it wasn't 'real', not a big story. The military and naval personnel of Kamchatka were left on their own to do their best, as they always were.

The city of Petropavlovsk-Kamchatsky sat by a perfect natural harbour. Kirov's village was also near the sea. There were whales and dolphins to be seen in the summer along the wild coastline. Although it was home to the majority of the peninsula's population, Petropavlovsk-Kamchatsky was no rookery of metropolitan sophistication. Kirov and Olga had decided that it was better for the children to live outside the city. There was a good naval school in the village, and they had so much more freedom living within the confines of a small community. There was no need to lock the house if they went to visit neighbours; everyone left their keys in the ignitions of their cars.

But even this small, close-knit community could not ignore the fact that it was located in an area fraught with the risk of natural disaster. It wasn't just the possibility of a volcanic eruption that hung over them; there'd also been gargantuan earthquakes in previous centuries. Some thought another quake was imminent. The residents of the village accepted this as part of life. Everyday, they observed the wisps of smoke emanating from the nearby volcanoes; they no longer noticed the smell of sulphur in the air. Although, on occasion, Kirov could feel a dangerous heaviness, an atmosphere pregnant with the possibility of the random and the terrible.

Kirov tried to set an example for his men without judging them. He could have decreed that private trade – the little markets that sold food and other items procured from the naval stores – was not compatible with his sailors' the solemn oath to protect Russia from invaders and aggressors. He could have said their sole aim and focus should be Russia, to keep her safe and to shield her.

He could have, but he did not.

He could also have left the navy and become a consultant. Kirov's knowledge of seafaring, and the naval hardware he handled, plus his fine education (after Moscow State University, a second degree at the globally renowned Moscow Institute of Engineering and Physics), could have secured him a fat consultancy on the west coast of the United States. He could have been earning thousands of dollars a month, but he choose not to.

They were approaching the village now. The outlying dwellings were little more than *domeeks*, or huts, with wooden walls and simple, slanted roofs. Inside, a wide wooden ledge ran around three of the four walls. Single men lived in these, and kept their bedding and their food on two sides of the wide shelving. One shelf served as a larder, one as a bed, and the third would often boast a small television set, which, in addition to the Russian national channels, sometimes picked up grainy images from local Magadan television across the Sea of Okhotsk, or strange and incomprehensible programming from the northern islands of Japan.

A few minutes later the jeep slowed, and Kirov jumped lightly to the ground. His athletic, slender figure with its wide shoulders and head of dark brown, slightly greying hair was shortly to be seen walking past the Kirov family's vegetable garden. Leafy clumps of fast-growing, hardy Russian tarragon peeped above a shallow covering of snow. Beneath the ground, beetroot and potato were waiting for spring.

This month he had again opted to take part of his wages in goods from the Osprey's store. He had packets of buckwheat, some dried chickpeas and several tins of tuna in brine, which ought to fulfil the protein requirement, plus – the big prize – a plastic bottle of Heinz tomato ketchup.

He thought of little Kolya's face and the joy this delicacy would bring to his eight year-old son. Kolya had acquired a taste for ketchup at the big hospital in London.

'Daddy! Daddy! Daddy!'

A small, heat-seeking missile dressed in trainers, jeans and a Barcelona soccer shirt with legend 'Messi Kolya' on the back, launched itself at Kirov's knees.

'Whoa, big boy!'

Kirov dropped the kit bag and scooped up his child in a single movement. The little boy hugged his father as hard as he could. Kirov could feel the child's soft cheek against his own stubble-coated face. Against Kirov's chest, the beating of Kolya's little heart pounded out a tattoo of excitement and exertion. The long hours and days at sea melted away in that instant. And they also made sense. This was what the sacrifice was for. There was a reason for the separation and the sadness it caused. It was this – the love of his family, and their protection.

'Hey!' called Kirov. A second soft, loving missile honed in on its target. Kirov's girl-child slammed into his other thigh. With a little groan, he bent down and gathered Maria up in his arms. She was dark-haired like her mother, whereas Kolya was golden-haired, very like Kirov's long-dead father. How he wished his father could have seen his offspring. 'Well, who's home, I wonder?'

Olga, slight, dark-haired, still girlishly pretty, stood smiling at the dilapidated door frame.

Kirov strode towards his wife with the two children in his arms. They were kicking and squeaking with pleasure and mock-protest as he crossed the threshold and set them down.

Olga embraced him with a different tenderness, a womanly love. She kissed him on the cheek and held him to her, her arms enfolding him. It was always like this when he was away for more than a couple of days.

'Anatoly Nikolaievich, my darling, I do believe you've lost weight again. You're so thin!' she said.

'I'm perfectly fine, my dear,' he said, engaging with his wife's near-black eyes. Kirov occasionally teased her that she was really an Azeri, but that was just a sure-fire way of getting a punch in the ribs. Olga was a pure Slav from Volgograd, and that was that.

'You look emaciated, Anatoly.' She watched him carefully. 'Are you worried about something?'

Kirov threw his kit bag on the bed and laughed.

'Of course, not. I'm home, with you and the kids. I have leave. I have food – not great, but it's food.'

The family meal was full of happy and animated table talk, and Kolya eventually accepted that he would never be allowed a sandwich made exclusively of bread and tomato ketchup.

Eventually the children were tucked up in bed. They were exhausted, and went to sleep halfway through one of their favourite stories, Kirov's tale of derring-do under the seas. He had hardly begun to chase the American submarine away from Russia's territory under the Bering Sea before the sound of gentle, rhythmic breathing filled the room.

Kirov kissed them both gently on the forehead – the golden-haired boy and the dark-haired girl. They were each so different, but so beautiful, and both his. Kirov looked upwards and gave thanks to whatever it was – God or Providence – that had allowed him to know true love.

He cast a last glance at Kolya as he turned out the light. Through force of habit, he put his ear to his son's chest. The breathing was even, steady and peaceful. The lung condition that had so nearly killed him seemed a thing of the past. The doctors said it would be perfectly all right, so long as he kept taking the drugs. Soon he would be over it completely. His first-born would turn into a fine, robust young man, like Kirov – but even bigger and stronger. It was a fact that still astounded Kirov; a fact he could not put a price on.

The lovemaking with Olga that night was wonderful: tender, passionate, needful, hungry. They knew that they could take whatever they wanted from each other in the certainty that really they were not taking anything at all. It was impossible to take that which was so freely given, and with so much love. They fell into a deep sleep in each other's arms.

It was still the middle of the night when Kirov woke up. The falling dream had come to him again. He'd had it several times now. He was walking through a field of windmills, enjoying the sound of the grinding stones as they made the flour. Then he was suddenly caught up by the wind, almost like a kite. He could fly, and it was an exhilarating feeling. And then the ability to fly began to drain from him, and he was falling, falling, falling back down to earth, with a dark, black hilltop rushing up to greet him. It was then that he would wake up, covered in a chilly patina of sweat.

Kirov sat bolt upright and looked at his watch. 4.23 a.m. Next to him, Olga's breathing fell out of rhythm for a moment, but she turned over without even a murmur, and the regular pattern resumed. Kirov suddenly panicked. Where was his kit bag?

He crept out of bed and looked in the small wicker wardrobe. There was his bag. Empty. Olga had unpacked all the food and the clothes and left the large canvas bag at the foot of the cupboard among Kirov's meagre collection of shoes.

Ah yes, there it was.

He reached for the shoebox that Olga had placed next to an old, much-cobbled pair of boots. He picked up the box and placed it under the bed. He had promised to guard it to the utmost, sworn on the life of Kolya. He felt much happier with it close to him.

Kirov stared up at the ceiling then out of the window into the dark, dark sky. He was worried; that much Olga had picked up the second she saw him. He could almost feel the presence of the thing under the bed; it was like another living being in the room. Like all living beings, it would have needs. And he had no idea what they might be.

# CHAPTER SEVENTEEN

THERE WAS NO need for time travel. Not when you had the Hotel Avacha.

Samuel tramped down the dingy, dog-breath corridor, trailing in the wake of Ksenia. It felt as though he'd landed in the early 1950s, right into the heart of Soviet-era austerity. The bedroom was an amalgam of dismal orange, ochre and dusty brown, the colours of ploughed earth.

'So, Mrs Daniels,' said Samuel. 'I have a question.'

'I understand your impatience. I'm impatient too. We'll take the next step tomorrow, first thing in the morning.'

'First thing in the morning?'

Ksenia began making up a camp bed.

'Yes, we have a date.'

Samuel scratched the back of his head. 'So we do. With our mystery man in Kamchatka.'

'Exactly. Sleep tight.' She switched off the light, and Samuel lay on the camp bed in the dark, listening to her undress. Soon her breathing assumed the hypnotic rhythm of sleep, and Samuel eventually followed, his dreams full of nodding oil derricks, and the big, ever-changing bubbles from Yavlinsky's lava lamp.

HE AWOKE EARLY with musty taste in his mouth, and a sore back.

The mattress in the Ukraina had been bad enough, but the Avacha had to take the prize. It was like sleeping on a table. And there'd only been one pillow, which had compressed to a sweaty lettuce leaf.

Ksenia was still asleep. Samuel went into the bathroom and turned on the light. A dingy, opaque shower curtain hung around the shallow bath. He turned on the water and a trickle came from the shower head. Well, what could he expect? They were at the ends of the earth. It was a miracle there was anything here at all. He gave up on the shower and ran a bath instead.

As he lay in the tub, he pondered their next steps. All had been pleasingly quiet since their arrival. A new identity, and a new phone – purchased, but not used, by one of Ksenia's girlfriends months ago. Samuel assumed it worked, but he didn't want to take the risk of turning it on. There'd probably be no signal most of the time, anyway.

So he was cut off from the outside world. He couldn't even browse the news websites on his phone. Sooner rather than later he'd be reported missing. The deaths of the policemen, surely, would mean he was a wanted man. Yavlinsky? His gut still told him that it was all too much of a coincidence, that Medulev was the killer, or at least involved in some way. He didn't need to spend time surfing the internet to know that his absence would be just too convenient, and that he'd be the number one suspect for the killing. As the French said – *les absents ont toujours tort*. You ain't there, you get the blame. The commando? He snorted. He'd bet no one, certainly no one who'd raise the alarm, would know about the commando. So the one crime he *had* committed would be the only one he wouldn't be accused of. The machinery of justice, in perfect action.

Then, of course, there was the kidnapping. The media would be having fun with that, for sure. His willing victim and pretend-wife was still sleeping next door. He'd had to trust her, up to a point.

The passports, plane tickets, and phones were all from Ksenia. And she seemed truly angry with her manipulative mother. But ... there was something that didn't quite fit, some quirk, some kink somewhere that kept playing a false note at the back of his mind.

*Kolkumi-Nomizu product . . . ebullio . . . dark-skinned men . . . lava bubble . . . asymptomatic equivalence . . . Sobranie cigarette smoke . . . dissonant vector tagging . . . snowflake on a cold lip . . . Something . . .*

But this was just conjecture. Samuel climbed out of the bath, wrapped a towel round his middle and opened the threadbare curtains. The fog of the previous evening had rolled away, and the sky was clear. The day was just beginning.

LOW PRESSURE ROLLED in at the end of a fine day, filling the troughs of the valley beneath them with a gently undulating sea of grey mist.

'I give up,' said Ksenia. The phone in her hand rang out for the twelfth time that day. 'Let's try again tomorrow. Either it'll be answered or it won't.'

'Your logic is impeccable,' said Samuel. He was tired, but wary. A day's backpacking had put respectable distance between them and the rest of the world. They'd come to the middle of nowhere to make a phone call, and whoever it was on the other end wasn't picking up. Ksenia seemed inexplicably cheerful about it all. Did she know this was a dead-end? Maybe her self-possession came from a secret agenda. Maybe the plan was really hers, not his.

'So, tomorrow is another day. Let's enjoy this,' she said. 'Beautiful, no?'

Samuel looked about them. She had a point. Terrifying, extraordinary, beautiful at a stretch. Tolbachik, one of the most active volcanoes in the range, surged out of the thick bed of mist like the fat conical nose of a vast, dark spacecraft. The volcano was to the north west of them, snow sprinkled like icing sugar over its top. The light was fading fast, but for now the roseate hues of the sinking sun bounced off the surface of the mist, and refracted in a gorgeously bruised, infinitely broken sky.

'Look, another bomb, a big one,' said Ksenia. 'Feel this. It's incredible.'

Ksenia was standing next to a huge needle of rock. Samuel walked up to it, and guessed its height at sixteen feet. How big must it have been when it plunged upward, spat high in the air by the angry Tolbachik, before hurtling down into the earth and boring into the ground?

OK, he'd go along with her gambit. No better way of seeing whether she was playing games or not. He copied Ksenia's stance and braced himself against the bomb, both palms flat to its rough surface. After a few moments, heat began to flow through him.

'You're right,' he said. 'Incredible. They're the most remarkable hand-warmers I've ever come across.'

The main valley of the geysers was much further south from their position, and when they went there the next day, they would roll straight past the far-flung geyser outpost site that Samuel and Ksenia were heading for.

They were carrying enough food for three basic meals and emergency bivouac materials, which would be essential if they couldn't find the *domeek* marked on their map.

Now, after hours of hard trek, here they were, on opposite sides of a huge natural monolith. It was as though they were playing push-me–pull-you with the vast, black stone. The colour was now draining rapidly from the sky in a silent protest of deep, dark coagulating reds and violets.

Ksenia peeped round at Samuel.

'They're warming, these stones, but, oh, so very dangerous. Look.'

She pointed upwards. Samuel squinted against the eastward aspect of the sky, which was already plunged into dark blue.

'Here. See.'

Ksenia came round to Samuel's side of the bomb and took his hand, then pointed upwards. A crude wooden notice board in English and Russian commemorated the deaths of two scientists who had been caught in the last Tolbachik eruption, decades before.

'What a horrible way to die,' said Samuel.

'It's not recorded here, but I know that a helicopter was caught in the last Tolbachik event,' said Ksenia. 'There were deaths in the air as well as on the mountainside.'

'Human life is so fragile. I suppose it's all about survival of the fittest,' said Samuel.

'Don't be so morose,' laughed Ksenia. She looked about her at the dark vermilion sky. Beneath them the mist was gently simmering. 'I don't think we're far away now, Dr Daniels. What do you think?'

'I'm not sure.'

Ksenia was still holding his hand.

'What is it you Latin scholars say? *Carpe diem*?'

'Well, yes. It depends on the occasion, of course,' said Samuel. 'Seize the day.'

'Yes, seize the day. Come, the map tells me we're close. We can do just that.'

Ksenia, still holding Samuel's hand, began to head down the hillside. She seemed to be following some sort of run, made by the local fauna – feral mountain goats, cats or sables perhaps, but not man. Samuel chased after her, watching his every step.

The sun was finally engulfed in blackness. The night sky stretched and yawed away into an infinite ocean of twinkling white astral jewels, some faint, some brilliant in the moonless sky.

Ksenia switched on her mobile phone, using the minimal light from the display screen to illuminate the narrow, winding track. Samuel cursed quietly. If one of them fell and broke a limb, or even twisted an ankle, that could be the end of both of them. The temperature was dropping sharply, and the mountain, even if they didn't stumble to their doom, had an abundance of animals that would gladly take them for supper. There were supposed to be bears everywhere, although they were yet to see one.

'Here it is! The map was right!' cried Ksenia. 'The best natural bathing in the mountains.'

An oval-shaped pool lay below them, shimmering in the starlight. It was wreathed in steam; the exotic miasma of volcano – sulphur, loam, silt, fern, conifer – rushed up to greet them.

Ksenia broke her grip, and bent to touch the surface.

'Mmmm. Perfect. It's like a hot bath. About forty degrees, I'd say.'

Samuel stood stock still, his mouth very slightly agape.

'Bathing, Ksenia? You've brought us out here in the pitch black with wild animals running around just so we can take a bath?'

'You had a plan, and I had one too. I've always wanted to jump into one of these pools. Don't forget. We're officially thermo-physicists here, developing plans to tap the energy beneath the permafrost. If we have plans to run power stations using the steam from the Kamchatka volcanoes, we have to test the water.'

Ksenia began gathering dead wood, which was in abundant supply. Dried branches of birch and other deciduous trees had fallen victim to the sulphur in the volcanic waters. Ksenia called over her shoulder towards Samuel as she bent to create a series of small piles.

'Oh, come on, Samuel. Lighten up! You going to help, or just stand there?'

Ksenia continued to gather wood. With Samuel's help she soon created half a dozen mini bonfires. She rummaged in her backpack and produced a stick of solid paraffin, which she unwrapped and broke into several small pieces. She then distributed the waxy shards among the heaps of fuel. Samuel realised that she'd come prepared. She had planned this.

'OK, I give up,' said Samuel. 'What's the aim here? We light beacons in the middle of the wilderness? To make sure we're visible?'

Ksenia threw a handful of kindling onto a pile of wood.

'Isn't it obvious? I'm an FSB spy. I've lured you out here, away from the clutches of my mother, so the Russian people can take full control of everything it rightfully owns.' She laughed, produced a cigarette, and lit it.

'My big, secret vice – this, and betrayal.'

Samuel stared at her, dumbfounded.

Ksenia threw her cigarette to the ground and stubbed it out.

'I am what I am. Some people are, believe it or not. We're in the middle of nowhere; in a situation we've taken immense care to contrive, the two of us. And I've facilitated the whole thing – documents, money, safe phones. If I were going to betray you, I'd have saved myself time and trouble and made a quick phone call in Moscow. I believe in you, Samuel. Or I thought I did.'

Samuel looked around him. She was right. They were definitely in the middle of nowhere.

'So . . .' she smiled. 'All I'm doing is what you see. I'm inviting you to bathe with me. And I happen to like bathing by firelight.'

Ksenia struck a match, which she cradled in her hand against the cold force of the hillside wind. In a couple of minutes all the mini bonfires were burning fairly well, although one had a sharp, smoky odour from yew wood that was green and moist.

Ksenia walked quickly right up to Samuel, then stopped abruptly. She was deliberately, provocatively close.

'Well, Dr Daniels? I think the fires will last for about fifteen minutes, maybe even twenty. Are you coming in with me?'

Ksenia reached up and drew Samuel's face towards her. They stayed a fraction apart for a second, then kissed. Samuel opened his eyes and glanced over her shoulder. There was nothing beyond the fires, save utter darkness. Soft and delicate at the start, the enquiries they made of each became more and more urgent, until, at last, the enquiries were all he could think of.

A gentle chill guttered through the cluster of dark orange flames by the side of the natural pool. Ksenia's fingers were cool on his face. They began to trace a pattern on Samuel's chest. He shivered as she moved to the belt of his trousers.

Soon they were both clothed only in the gentle, flickering light of the fires. Samuel held his body against Ksenia. Her skin was soft, white, flawless. The tautness of her stomach felt cool against the heat of Samuel's excitement.

'Come,' she said with a smile. She stepped delicately into the pool, and then dived under, resurfacing just a couple of metres away. Ksenia tossed her shining black hair back over her shoulders. She beckoned to Samuel.

Samuel stepped in, then immersed himself and stood shoulder-deep in water against a flat rock at the side of the pool. Ksenia was right. The volcanic outflow was the perfect temperature for a warm bath. The only sounds were the wind ruffling the foliage and provoking the fires to crackle and snap. Smoke drifted across them, mixing with the steam and the brutal, exotic odour of the volcano. Ksenia moved towards him, her eyes glittering in the firelight. She put her arms around his neck and kissed him hard, drawing him towards her. Then Samuel felt a different warmth and wetness as she moved over him and hooked her legs around the back of his hips. He threw his head back to look up at the stars – so close, so impossibly distant.

AS THE LAST FIRE reduced to a fat lozenge of embers Ksenia kissed Samuel softly on the nape of his neck where she had been cradling his head. Slowly, she withdrew, and they swam to the edge of the pool and clambered out. Ksenia produced two micro-towels from her backpack.

'OK, time to go, don't you think?'

Ksenia hurriedly began to dress in the fading light thrown out by embers that offered an occasional, grudging pulse of amber in the irregularly gusting wind. Once the fires were out, there would be blackness, emptiness. Samuel would have no choice but to hold Ksenia's hand and – for the moment at least – trust her.

As they scrambled down the mountainside, the last guttering flame finally died.

# CHAPTER EIGHTEEN

SAMUEL AND KSENIA awoke to another fine day. The hike back to the cabin, where they'd spent the night, had been exhausting. Although the facilities were basic, Samuel had slept far better than the night before. They were sharing a tiny room with bunk beds.

Samuel got up and dressed quickly. It was freezing cold outside the cocooning warmth of his sleeping bag. Ksenia was still fast asleep. He opened the door of the *domeek* and stepped outside. Nearby was a forest. New saplings and green shoots were beginning to pierce the light covering of snow. Plant life was forcing its way back as winter approached its end. New life, new beginnings. Nature replenished herself, might Samuel not try? For a moment he allowed himself to believe that he and Ksenia could stay here, like this, forever. Never return to Moscow and remain safe from the Black Widow, from the police, from Barton. Their lives could be their own. They could, perhaps – he flinched at the ambition of it – be happy.

Samuel forced himself back into the present moment. He had a plan. He couldn't afford to be distracted from it. He walked away from the cabin towards the beginnings of the forest. He looked around him. There was no one in sight. It seemed that he and Ksenia had been the only guests staying at the *domeek* that night. Most people waited for spring to establish itself properly before going trekking in this area. He was about fifty metres from the building when Ksenia called.

'They have a satellite phone here. Let's try again.'

Hand-in-hand, they walked back and entered the tiny office of the man who ran the place. He gestured towards the phone.

Samuel dialled the now-familiar number.

'Yes?'

Samuel hung up, grabbed Ksenia's hand, and marched out to the forest. He fished in his pocket for the phone Ksenia had given him, and dialled.

'Who is this? Why do you keep calling me?' A well-modulated voice. The Russian, so far as Samuel could tell, was precise.

'My name is Samuel Spendlove, you will have read about me in the newspapers.' And now was the time to play his hunch. 'Here, speak to your boss' daughter, my prisoner.'

He passed the phone to Ksenia.

'Hello. This is Ksenia Barinova. I've been kidnapped. Please do what he says,' she begged. 'He's capable of anything. He has a twisted mind, an *English* mind.'

She pronounced the last words with horror, and then gave the man the co-ordinates she and Samuel had agreed on the day before, before begging him not to tell her mother. If he did, her kidnapper had threatened to perpetrate even greater atrocities on her. She emitted a little whimper, and handed the phone back to Samuel. He clicked it off and nodded. She'd given quite a performance, which was great. But actresses were dangerous. How much of the night before had been an act?

Well, he could be reasonably certain of a few things. One, the man was working for the Black Widow. Two, he'd definitely tell the Black Widow about his conversation with Ksenia's kidnapper. Three, whether or not this worked, whether the man turned up or not, would all depend on how much Anna Barinova loved her daughter.

Samuel turned and looked at Ksenia. Suddenly, she seemed small, vulnerable, standing there at the centre of this strange and hostile landscape.

OLGA RAN HER HAND lovingly though Kirov's hair, caressing the grey streaks at the temples. He was sitting in his favourite armchair with his wife draped adoringly over him. The children were safely in bed after a day of non-stop play and laughter with their papa.

Kirov had returned from manoeuvres a refreshed and invigorated man. He had finally finished the children's tree house; the long days at sea and the constant demands of the job somehow didn't matter any more. He'd rediscovered the joys of a family he already loved.

The lovemaking that night was shot through with a new passion. Kirov was always a driven man, but this was so special, this hunger, this avidity, this desire for the moment. They made love once, slept briefly, then fell on each other again. Olga wept silent tears after the second time. The passion of their congress was so overwhelming; to be able to give and give and give – and know that your generosity is known, understood, honoured, treasured. This was to know love.

Olga was still unconscious to the world when Kirov slipped out of bed, kissed her very gently on the forehead and got dressed. He stopped briefly on the landing and stroked his children's hair, then kissed the tips of each of their tiny, perfectly formed fingers.

And then Kirov took the box from under the bed, crept downstairs, quietly unlocked the door and walked out into the chill of the night.

# CHAPTER NINETEEN

EVENTUALLY THEY EMERGED from the deep shadow of the gorge to the west and south of the dominating presence of Kronotskaya. Samuel dropped the backpacks to the ground. They were on a plateau, less than half a kilometre below the summit of the volcano. It was a flat, more-or-less circular area of some thirty metres in diameter. Birch, hardy elm and conifer played irregularly stationed sentries round the perimeter. It was close to the middle of the day, and the weather, having threatened murk and gloom in the early morning of their departure, now offered a fine view of the valley of the geysers to the west. A river sprang, seemingly magically, from halfway up a major hill, several hundred metres above sea level. There were no tributaries that Samuel could see. It gushed outwards and downwards and, presumably, seawards.

Then he looked to the north; the mystery was solved. The source of the river was a huge, glacial lake that must have pushed and bored its way through the rock to spew itself out of the mountain many kilometres away. Samuel gave a thousand-mile stare to the south, but he could not make out the sea that he knew must be there.

'Well, I'm done. Shall we bivouac down and get some sleep?'

'But it's still the middle of the day. And anyway, we have a rendezvous.'

'But that might not happen before it gets dark. I thought we could rest now, so we've got energy for later.'

The sun was a pallid, buttery gold, as big a force as it was going to be that day.

'OK, let's have a rest.'

They made a rough shelter using ropes and tarpaulins between two birch trees at the edge of the plateau, laid a ground sheet, and then unfolded their sleeping bags.

'They zip together,' said Ksenia. 'It will be better if we undo them and then zip them together. Body heat.' She looked at Samuel very seriously.

SAMUEL AWOKE TO a sulky, darkening sky. Ksenia was wrapped in his arms. He pulled open the cord of the hood that protected them from the elements. There were a few clouds, but the temperature was dropping fast.

How long had he been asleep? He had one way out of this mess, and one way only – to think his way out.

*'Intelligent awareness is a redundancy, dear boy.'* He could almost reach out and touch the commented monograph Kempis was offering him. *'What use is acuteness without vigilance? Even for the most brilliant, work is essential. Always guard against complacency.'*

Samuel rubbed his eyes. He'd have to do better.

'Hello,' said Ksenia sleepily. She kissed him gently. Samuel instinctively held her to him. She searched for him with her lips. They kissed again.

As they made love once more, Samuel felt he could have been anywhere. He had never dared believe that he could feel transported again, taken out of himself in this way. He had Ksenia, the wilderness and the moment: its taste, its smell, its vibrant, pulsating touch. That, and nothing else.

Afterwards, they both slipped back into a dreamless, peaceful sleep. When they awoke for the second time, darkness had enveloped them; the stars had returned. A large, cantaloupe moon gave off a powerful light.

Samuel heard a noise in the undergrowth, and sat bolt upright. A revolver was pointed straight at his head – the dark mouth of the barrel was about one metre away.

'Am I early? Tell me, when does the kidnapping take place?' asked the visitor.

Ksenia screamed. Samuel fell painfully back to the stony ground.

The visitor was a dark, slender man. He handled the gun with a chilling, casual expertise.

'Perhaps I will kill you now, Mr Kidnapper, and leave your body for the carrion crows.' He looked at Ksenia. 'You I can take to your mother, and claim a prize.'

Samuel tried hard to talk to the man, not the deadly black mouth of the gun.

'OK, it was a game, a foolish game. But we had to get you to come. I think we may be able to help each other.'

The man considered, his finger on the safety catch of the gun. Then he laughed, not unkindly.

'OK, I'll leave you to get changed. It's good that you have no gun.'

Samuel raised an eyebrow.

'I checked, of course, while you were asleep, or otherwise engaged. You make a very poor violent criminal. But I'll be watching. No tricks.'

He retreated twenty metres or so, and turned his back, whistling softly.

'This is . . . just embarrassing,' hissed Samuel, as he pulled on his jeans and boots.

'You said it,' muttered Ksenia. She was looking for an extra sweater in her rucksack.

When they were dressed the man approached again. There was no sign of the revolver. The man radiated confidence and competence. Samuel didn't have the training himself, but he could easily spot the economy of movement and expression. This guy was a professional. If it had been Ksenia's plan to wrest control from Samuel, she'd succeeded in putting their fate in this fellow's hands. For the moment, at least.

Tall, slim, dark-hair, flecked with grey at the temples, he had an air of natural courtesy and deference about him. He offered a firm hand to Samuel and then to Ksenia. Samuel looked at him as he introduced himself to Ksenia. And then a double-take. Was his mind playing tricks? He had no time to consider it.

'Commander Anatoly Kirov of the Russian Navy.'

'We have much to discuss, Commander,' said Samuel.

'Not least the fact that you got me here under false pretences,' said Kirov.

'Apologies for that. You really shouldn't believe what you read in the newspapers. But you wanted to come, Commander, didn't you?' said Samuel. 'And you brought it?'

Kirov nodded, and inclined his head backwards, towards his backpack. Samuel waited, and Kirov produced a box. From it, he withdrew an aluminium gadget the size of a large bicycle seat. Samuel recognised its basic shape from the many diagrams he carried inside his head.

'Excellent, thank you, Commander.'

'Is that what I think it is?' asked Ksenia.

'I think so,' said Samuel. 'Version Thirteen. The only prototype left in existence.'

## CHAPTER TWENTY

THE LIGHT WAS FADING fast; a chill evening wind was getting up.

Kirov rubbed his hands and then spoke. 'First, I have a practical suggestion. It's getting cold, and dark. Let's quickly gather the fuel for a fire. There's plenty of wood here. We can make tea and have vodka.'

'An excellent idea, Commander. A Russian way forward,' said Ksenia.

Kirov wrapped the Version Thirteen box into his jacket and headed off in the direction of the largest copse on the perimeter, but he kept the two of them in his peripheral vision at all times.

Samuel and Ksenia also made sure they could see Kirov as they acquired several armfuls of wood and brought them back to the centre of the plateau.

'How did you know he had a prototype Version Thirteen?' whispered Ksenia. 'I thought they were all destroyed after the tests.'

'I didn't,' said Samuel. 'It was an educated guess. Your mother doesn't strike me as the type of person who would invest all that time and money and then destroy the technology at the first sign of failure.'

'But why him? And why here?' she murmured, dropping some dry branches of elder.

'Let's find out,' said Samuel, and waved at Kirov, who was approaching with a large bundle of fuel.

Now they had enough for a sizeable bonfire. Kirov rummaged in his knapsack. Out of it came a large bottle of vodka, a billycan and a Red Army field cup. Samuel thought of Yavlinsky and the museum. Drinking from a Red Army field cup was one of the last things Yavlinsky had done. A simple pleasure now denied him by the product of his own genius, the thing that presently lived in Kirov's box. The wind gusted cold and hard. Samuel shivered.

Soon the flames were crackling, spitting empty defiance at the velvet-blue night. Kirov had taken some of the larger logs and arranged them in a triangle round the fire as seats. He then opened the vodka, which had taken on the ambient temperature; it was perfectly chilled. The billycan produced piping hot black tea; Kirov added honey. The Red Army cup was passed round until they'd all had two shots and could feel the warmth seeping through their bellies.

They were all staring into the fire, taking comfort from its heat. Each was waiting for the other to start in. Kirov was watchful; he had the lean and hungry look of a green-eyed fox. Tiny tongues of flame danced in his eyes.

'Very well,' said Kirov. He sipped at an enamel mug of tea and honey, and looked from Samuel to Ksenia, and back again. He withdrew the box from his jacket and placed it down by his foot. 'You were right, Spendlove.' Kirov gazed moodily into the fire. 'I wanted to come when you called. I was glad.'

Samuel nodded: 'You wanted to rid yourself of the burden.'

Ksenia laughed. 'The burden of what? Carrying a shoe-box containing a piece of technology that doesn't work?'

'It could be that I got it wrong in Moscow,' said Samuel. 'I saw the research, and my memory was flawed. Or it could be that my recall was accurate, and the technology doesn't work. Or it could be that I was given bogus data.' He turned to Kirov.

Kirov threw the dregs of his tea into the base of the fire, which hissed and spluttered in complaint.

'Maybe. I believe that no one knows the true secret of this

machinery you call Version Thirteen. I think no one has been allowed to know the truth. I'm a sailor, not a scientist. What is this damned thing supposed to do?'

Ksenia explained the industrial and ecological benefits she'd hoped for. Then added, bitterly, 'But the technology is flawed. According to my mother, the lab tests prove it. She and ABTV have bet billions on that.'

Kirov's head fell forward slightly. The orange firelight gouged dark holes in his eyes. He suddenly looked very tired.

'But even if it did work, would it save the world?'

'No,' said Samuel. 'But it would buy us a reprieve. We'd have years and years to find clean, efficient technologies not based on fossil fuels. What we're considering, Commander Kirov, is a fourth possibility. That the technology works, but there's no record of the correct formula. And that the inventor was murdered for withholding that crucial piece of information.'

'And you will tell me he wasn't murdered by you, despite what the media say about the ruthless, homicidal, hostage-taking Englishman,' said Kirov.

'I will,' said Samuel.

'I knew as much,' Kirov reached for the vodka. 'I can judge these things, Spendlove. You're no killer.'

The fire cracked and popped. Samuel blinked and looked away, banishing the image of the commando falling slowly to what must have been a horrible, slow death.

'In any event,' he could feel himself rallying, 'the fact is that the Black Widow's effectively keeping it under your guard in conditions of massive security. May I ask what your day job is?'

'A number of things. The short version is captain of a nuclear submarine.'

'And Anna Barinova trusts you, doesn't she? Something tells me you go back a very long way – at least twenty years.'

Kirov nodded appreciatively. 'You're good. The newspapers

got that right. Even if they said your genius was criminal. So, yes, Anna does trust me. We go back a very long way. All the way to Moscow State University. Twenty years and a few more.'

'Also,' he added, 'we have a commercial arrangement.'

'That makes sense. A trusted friend – but the modern bond is business and money.'

Kirov looked up into the night sky. 'I care nothing for business, Spendlove. But money is useful. Especially on the rare occasions when it pays my men to defend our country. Especially when it buys medicine for sick children.'

Kirov tossed another log on the fire, which spat its anger, throwing up a stream of amber fireflies into the night.

Samuel accepted another shot. He and Kirov were getting somewhere. There was something about the man, something likeable, something that commanded respect. 'All the evidence I can see says that what you have must have potential. Why else send it all the way out here – to the world's biggest, high-security compound, entrusted to an old friend?'

'OK, I hear that,' said Kirov. He got up and began pacing back and forth, concentrating hard. 'But answer me this. If this thing could work, why did I get a call yesterday? I was given strict instructions to destroy it.'

Samuel's world shook a little. This was crazy. Why go to such trouble to cosset, control and protect – and then destroy Version Thirteen? He looked to his left to see what Ksenia made of it all.

She was gone.

The two men looked at each other – and then all around. Version Thirteen had gone too.

Kirov cursed quietly, ran to his knapsack and withdrew a contraption Samuel took to be a night-sight. He swept the terrain, jaw muscles taut.

'Can you see her? Has she got it?' asked Samuel.

Kirov scrabbled frantically in his pack.

'Christ's bones! She has my gun too!' With that, he set off at a run.

Suddenly fearful for her safety, Samuel called out.

'Ksenia! Ksenia! Take cover! He's coming after you.' And Samuel ran through the darkness after Kirov, stumbling into the black night.

He had to track Kirov from the sound he made as they scrambled up the mountainside. Samuel fell painfully, twice, but each time picked himself up, grim-faced. There was an animal trail of some sort that Samuel, now on all fours, used as a tactile guide, a kind of nocturnal Braille.

Ksenia was leading them right to the top of the volcano, it seemed. The night-sight was a big advantage. Samuel had no chance of keeping up, and after a while just followed the trail, as best he could. As he gained height, the sulphurous smell of the guts of the volcano became stronger and stronger.

Samuel scrambled up and over a promontory of solidified lava. It hung down over the lip of the volcano like the grease from a massive candle. Eventually, he came to the very top, the shattered cap of Kronotskaya. The lip of the volcano crater formed a walkway, roughly two metres in width. The thick fumes from the interior were almost overpowering. Samuel jarred his knee on a small rock and shuddered at the thought of what a fall would mean now. He picked up the rock and tossed it into dark interior of the mountain. Nothing. No sound. Just the ever-hungry void.

Samuel feared he might have lost Ksenia and Kirov for good, when the beam of Ksenia's torch picked out their shapes in the darkness. He could see Kirov, standing a few metres beneath Ksenia, like a supplicant. She was perched on a high point of the rim, and was looking down at him defiantly.

'Ksenia!' called out Samuel. The two hardly acknowledged his presence.

He edged closer, in a moment he was within earshot.

'So, Miss Barinova, will you give it up?' asked Kirov.

Samuel could see that Ksenia had the box under her arm.

'No, Commander. You want to destroy it.'

'I was entrusted with its safekeeping.'

'But you want to destroy it? If it works, that would be a crime against humanity, and against the planet. I cannot allow that.'

Samuel was still well below them. He shouted up, desperately. But they were playing out their own drama. Samuel cut his hand on a sharp rock, cursed and crawled forward again.

Ksenia withdrew Kirov's revolver from her tunic. It looked heavy in her hand. She was trembling.

Kirov took three quick, lithe steps up the rock, and in a second overpowered Ksenia. The gun slipped down into the fiery abyss, which didn't so much as belch in appreciation. Ksenia screamed, kicked away from him, and rolled to the very edge of the volcano. In her left hand she held the box, away from Kirov. He was on top of her, but still she held Version Thirteen over the edge.

'No, Kirov! No!' cried Samuel.

'Stay back!' called Kirov. 'I'll roll us both over if anyone comes near. I'll kill her. I'll kill myself. I'll take this damned thing with me. There are bigger issues here. You don't understand.'

But Ksenia still refused to yield.

'If I give you this, I give up the hope for the future. Whatever my mother is offering you can't be more precious than that.'

'You're right,' said Kirov. 'There is nothing more precious than the future.'

The volcano disgorged a huge bubble of sulphurous gas beneath them. The stench and the heat poured over them, momentarily suffocating, almost overpowering.

'I have a son, a sick son. He needs expensive medical help. The only way I can get that is keeping my bargain. If I have to kill myself, and you Ksenia Barinova, to safeguard the life of my child, then I will.'

He looked into her eyes. The two seemed posed strangely like lovers, bedded on the edge of the abyss.

Samuel at last dragged himself up to within a few metres. The momentum of their struggle had taken Kirov and Ksenia to the rim of the volcano walkway. One pulse of energy, one reactive push and they would both fall into the seething lava.

Samuel was almost too exhausted to speak, but he gathered his strength.

'Stop! Stop, Kirov, stop! There's something you must know!'

Kirov stared back at him. His grip on Ksenia's wrist was firm. One flip, and he could take Version Thirteen and the two of them into hellfire. 'And what's that, exactly?'

Samuel could scarcely get the words out: 'The health and well-being of your children . . . you should know that Ksenia is one of them.'

'What?'

'Ksenia is your daughter.'

Both Ksenia and Kirov froze in the moment. They peered through the darkness at Samuel.

'I've spared your life once today, Spendlove. I may not be so kind a second time.'

'I'm not lying.'

Kirov relaxed his grip on Ksenia slightly, but still held her tight to him. They moved back slightly from the rim's edge.

'Commander, I didn't even know your name until today. But the moment I saw you with Ksenia, I knew you were father and daughter. Ksenia, you share a bone structure with your mother, but you have your father's eyes. And there's something about the way the two of you hold yourselves. So that was how I knew you must be an old, old friend of the Black Widow's, Commander. You had to have more than twenty years' history with her – long enough for your daughter to be conceived.'

Kirov and Ksenia looked at each other in astonishment.

'You've never seen your father, have you, Ksenia?'

Kirov released Ksenia, who scrambled to her feet.

'He died when I was a tiny child, swept away by a tide of alcohol.'

'Except he wasn't your father. He was the man you mother married. And Kirov, you had a student fling with Anna at university?'

Kirov too stood up. 'Yes, yes . . . then she broke with me in favour of a brighter prospect. I . . . had no idea Anna was pregnant.'

Father and daughter looked at each other for the first time, and smiled.

'I think it's time we went back down and had another go at a fireside chat, don't you?' said Samuel.

# CHAPTER TWENTY-ONE

MEDULEV SAT ON the edge of a 1960s cocoon chair and cursed. You couldn't sleep in the fuckers, you couldn't relax in them, you couldn't work in them. Why on earth Anna Barinova paid any attention to the various faggot designers she patronised, he'd no idea.

Still, this was among his favourite ABTV investments. A little stake in Sports Universe on the Novy Arbat was a money-maker, and a useful foothold into a wider world. Medulev sat on his intensely irritating and impractical perch and smoked pensively before an array of security screens.

All the good things in life were there: compulsive gamblers shovelling coin into slot machines or pissing away fortunes on the roulette and blackjack tables, while drinking overpriced, watered-down cocktails. Overweight businessmen lay down in velvet-draped 'privacy' (did they really think they weren't being filmed, the dumb fucks?) as harridans from Uzbek and the Steppes ground their crotches a centimetre above faces taut with the agony of lust; the punters knew they'd get beaten to crap if they so much as laid a finger on the girls without paying an extra 10,000 roubles. On the top left of the screen bank, the footage of the VIP rooms played out. An industrialist with a penchant for Asian and Philippina hookers, two at a time, was getting himself blown and blindfolded at the same time – which seemed to Medulev to defeat the object somewhat. But what did he know about what made people happy? The only woman he might ever love had no interest in him, only money, so far as he could see. The Black Widow, indeed . . .

In another suite, a screen portrayed Admiral Borzov. *Again*? Medulev looked at Borzov's huge, flabby white back, thickly covered in dark hair. The admiral was trussed up in a pair of tight leather crotchless underpants that cut cruelly into his walrus hips. Medulev inhaled meditatively as he watched Borzov's sweaty bald head bob up and down energetically. The admiral was kneeling in front of a large, black male prostitute. Paulie, known as Mr Hollywood to his clients, was American, and very popular with male and female punters, apparently. Two small mysteries presented themselves to Medulev. Why did Admiral Borzov love to suck black cock so much (he always choose black trade)? And how could the stud get it up when confronted with the overpowering ghastliness of Borzov in his obscenely tight thong? You had to hand it to the hooker, he was a real pro . . .

The best thing of all about being an investor was access to this private room, where he could smoke as much as he liked. Moscow was too fucking cold to smoke outside, whatever the tobacco fascists said. In fact, as he stubbed out his last smoke, he decided to have another, straight away. Just because he could.

And then his day was ruined. The screens at the top right were 'floaters'. Depending on who was in the control room, they might be patched in to a sports channel, a Dutch porn station – whatever. Today, he'd come on his usual day, but with a special request.

The screen at the top right showed indistinct, inky blurs. This was the readout from one of ABTV's commercial satellites. The signal wasn't that great, and the image of the terrain beneath the satellite would need the kind of expensive visual enhancement you only got in high-level defence projects. So he switched to graphic representation of what the satellite was tracking. A dozen or so different-coloured lines swam across the screen, some of them offered a little digital burp. And the one Medulev didn't want to see was trilling away in green. Fuck! What was the point of all this stuff, this serious business, if other people couldn't be relied on to do the most simple things?

His phone flicked into life.

'Hi. Yes, it's me. Bad news.'

Medulev panned reflexively across the bank of screens. Borzov, mission accomplished, was prostrate on the floor, sobbing.

Phone to his ear, Medulev looked on in distaste. It was Madame Borzova he felt sorry for. Her husband obviously wasn't throwing much of a fuck into her, and it was rumoured he liked to give her the occasional slap. Certainly, he was known for his brutality among the men in his command. Still, it all paid, and it paid cash.

Medulev heard out his interlocutor with some concern.

'No, no doubt. Kamchatka. Coming though loud and clear. Version Thirteen still exists. What do you want me to do about it?'

Another ten-second burst from the other end.

Medulev grimaced.

'But isn't that why you picked Kamchatka?'

This got a shorter, sharper retort.

Medulev grunted assent, and switched his phone off. He'd realised the stakes were high, but he hadn't reckoned on starting a fucking *war*.

He reached for another cigarette. As he lit it, his hands were trembling.

'DO WE HAVE a fix on the target, Lieutenant?'

'Aye, Commander.'

Mochanov read out the co-ordinates. You had to give him credit, thought Samuel, Mochanov was acting as though he and Ksenia weren't there. Which, officially, they weren't. Coming with Kirov had been the obvious choice among relatively few after the incident on Kronotskaya. They all needed more time to work out what it was exactly that they had, and then what to do with it. Ksenia and Kirov needed time together. They kept sneaking glances at each other. Samuel suspected neither one could quite believe in this late-arriving good fortune. It was a comfort that something positive was coming out of all the mayhem and horror surrounding them. And as for Ksenia, her desire to do the right thing – and it surely was the right thing – had been proved on pain of her life. Samuel hadn't trusted the Black Widow's offspring, but Kirov's daughter was another matter entirely.

They'd boarded the *Red Kite* early. In the cramped officers' mess, they'd eaten a breakfast of salt biscuit and tea sweetened with a metallic jam. Kirov had introduced them as 'observers', and the officers had nodded acceptance. Not belief, as Samuel registered it – but acceptance. He sensed that this was Kirov's personal fiefdom. If Kirov wanted to bring 'observers' – clearly not military and hardly even political – then that, Samuel guessed, was clearly well within his gift.

The commander looked down at his console. Samuel and Ksenia had been invited onto the narrow bridge. To keep them out of harm's way – or under observation? Kirov had retaken custody of Version Thirteen in this period of mutual truce. And now, after a few hours at sea, the manoeuvres had begun.

The sonar readout showed that the vessel was about one hundred and sixty kilometres east of Karaginsky Island, still well within Russian territorial waters.

'Prepare torpedo one for launch, Mr Mochanov.'

'Aye, aye, Commander.'

Mochanov issued a couple of curt commands, and clicked busily at a keyboard. The Shkval 2 torpedo appeared in digital wire-frame form before their eyes. Its health and well-being were duly checked. A full-body scan completed, they were ready to go.

Samuel felt privileged to be there. The professionalism and

dedication of the crew were obvious to see. It felt like they were all part of a living organism. The *Red Kite* wasn't just a means of locomotion but a life-support system, very much part of the entity. He began to see why sailors loved their craft so. To be part of a team, to be working towards a common aim had an air of simplicity and nobility about it. In that moment, loner that he would probably always be, it was a life he envied.

'Feed her the co-ordinates, please, Mr Mochanov.'

The lieutenant dutifully entered the data.

Over breakfast, Kirov had given them a basic briefing: the *Red Kite* was a new vessel that Kirov and his crew had been called in to trial. It was a super-class version of the Bars submarines, not an Antyey, like Kirov's regular craft, the *Osprey*.

From the comments of the crew in the early hours of the voyage, Samuel sensed that the new craft handled well enough, even though it was unfamiliar. The submarine was super-quick at sea level and underwater.

Samuel sat and watched the commander at sea. Operational decisions were the stuff of his being.

'Torpedo one primed and ready, Commander,' said Mochanov.

Ksenia had shown no great interest in her father's briefing at breakfast. Even though it was the defence of Mother Russia, and even though it revolved around the principle of supercavitation, the basis of Version Thirteen, Ksenia seemed to have dismissed it all as just Boys' Toys.

Samuel, however, had drunk it all in. Yes, it was peripheral, but maybe, just maybe, it would have some relevance to Version Thirteen. So he and Kirov had gone into a huddle: the torpedo was new, a special design. The fastest speed the old torpedoes could reach was five hundred kilometres per hour. They had a range of one hundred kilometres, but once they were launched there was no proper guidance system. A target on the edge of the range would have twelve minutes to manoeuvre.

'Simple avoidance tactics work easily with the old generation,' Kirov had said. 'They are fast, but difficult to manoeuvre, as easy to avoid as a roaring drunk in an empty ballroom. You hear and see them coming, and just let them run at you. Then you sidestep.'

Samuel now got out of the way of a rating who was heading for Mochanov. Soon he'd see some naval sidestepping in action.

'Fire torpedo one, please, Lieutenant,' said Kirov quietly.

'Aye, Commander.'

There was absolutely no sensation of the missile leaving the vessel, but the two officers, Samuel peering over their shoulders, tracked its bright yellow digital path on the monitors as it honed in on the target.

'I wonder what the Americans will make of this,' murmured Mochanov.

Kirov looked at his number two, but said nothing.

Samuel tried to make sense of what he saw on the screen. They were firing a very noisy, super-fast missile towards American territory. The Shkval 2 was capable of over seven hundred kilometres per hour, an ultra-fast supercavitating missile. Not only that, it could slow down, or even switch to the conventional propulsion systems the Americans used, and then reprogramme and redirect. These Shkval 2 torpedoes, with their titanium-edged nose-cones and depleted plutonium payloads, were very difficult to avoid, apparently. And deadly on impact.

They all watched on the screen as the torpedo closed in on its target. The ship's captain would have plenty of notice. Even at seven hundred kilometres per hour, the torpedo would need more than sixteen minutes to travel the distance. Sure enough, the sonar alarms seemed to have done their work; the target ship, a red dot on their screen, took a sharply different course. The frigate had been bowling along at 119 degrees, heading for the closed naval township of Pakhachi. Now it set a 270-degree course, doubling back towards the cover of Ossora, a fishing village on the western edge of the Karaginsky Gulf. The old Shkval torpedo would have had to be detonated in mid-course, as the evasive action of the frigate would have seen the missile run aground on Karaginsky Island, possibly self-destructing on a beach.

But the Shkval 2 was a different animal. Neither Kirov nor Mochanov moved a muscle. They just watched as the torpedo slowed itself down, and then curved round the northern tip of the island, its course marking out the shape of a yellow digitised question mark. The frigate tacked back and forth, but the torpedo slowed again.

'Is the missile still in supercavitational mode?' Samuel asked Kirov.

'The speed will tell you,' he said quietly, and pointed. 'See, the torpedo has slowed considerably, but only to two hundred kilometres per hour, a speed still way beyond any conventionally propelled missile.'

So yes, still supercavitational. Samuel felt something almost physical within him. There was an idea taking shape somewhere, some connection being made.

The game of cat-and-mouse was shortly over. The frigate had suffered the manoeuvres equivalent of a direct hit. The torpedo was carrying no payload, and self-destructed two hundred metres away from its target. In combat, the vessel would have been atomised.

Kirov and Mochanov looked at each other.

'I take it you're impressed?' asked Samuel.

'Yes, indeed I am,' said Kirov. 'The performance was excellent, but it will certainly have been monitored by the Americans, who still favour the 'run silent, run slow' method of naval warfare.'

'And this craft is all about noise and speed?'

'Exactly.' Kirov motioned to Mochanov, who took over operational direction. 'The US missile guidance technology is pretty incredible. It is an exaggeration to say they have torpedoes that can check in a hat and coat, and order a meal before strolling into the main restaurant to explode. But not much of an exaggeration.'

Kirov laughed. Samuel saw the easy confidence of a true master of his environment: 'What we're doing here is the "run loud, run fast" method of supercavitational warfare. We make such a noise we give away the position of our vessel as we fire the missile, as well, of course, as the position of the missile itself.'

Samuel looked at the screens, drank in the low-level cacophony of radar blips, digital cries, the clanking of ratings on the gangways, murmured conversation, and the thick static of open radio channels.

'So this manoeuvre will have attracted attention?'

'Naturally it will have,' said Kirov. 'We've just witnessed the Russian navy demonstrating several steps up in sophistication. We are showing off the manoeuvrability of our latest weaponry off the Alaskan coast before the vigilant eyes and ears of the American defensive shield.'

Kirov gave the instruction to head back for base, and Mochanov set to issuing the orders. The new vessel was harboured at a small, closed naval island not far from the fishing village of Ust Kamchatsk, about a hundred and fifty kilometres north of Kirov's home.

As Mochanov busied himself, Kirov came and sat next to Samuel.

'So you get the military implications of all this?'

Samuel nodded. 'But I sense you're troubled, as I am, by another question. Why on earth would you do such a manoeuvre right here, right now? In essence, it's a question you and your men probably ask yourselves a lot: what on earth is Moscow thinking of?'

MEDULEV HAD A FLUNKY from Sports Universe bring up a couple of canvas chairs to the control room. He and Spavinski sat in them while Borzov was exiled to the cocoon chair, which soon swallowed him up. He lay back, blinking impotently, like an oversize mole trapped in an onion bag.

Medulev pointed at the screen at the top right corner of the bank.

'Let's get going.'

Spavinski was a thick-set rear admiral with oblong-lensed spectacles that lent him an owlish demeanour. But he was a warrior. He'd seen action – in war and in black operations. Medulev, as an Afghani vet, respected that. You weren't a man till you had blood on your hands. He glanced briefly and contemptuously at Borzov, the overgrown baby in the cocoon chair.

'Comrade, is it secure?' asked Spavinski.

'Nothing is secure. But I represent the owners. What can I say? Careless talk will cost lives.' Medulev directed the last remark at the room generally. There might be some idiots listening in. These places were riddled with covert surveillance devices. A generalised death threat could only help. Medulev turned towards Spavinski and made an encouraging gesture. *Comrade* – he liked that. Old school.

Spavinski took out a walkie-talkie.

'Old-fashioned, but encrypted,' he explained. 'Just so long as no one's bugging this room.'

'If they are, they're fucking dead!' snarled Medulev. 'Let's get some friendly fire going, shall we?'

'All done at this end,' Borzov called out. 'Can't compromise the golden goose, can we?' he chortled.

'Obviously not,' said Medulev. He wondered how much these two made out of all this. Probably much more than he did, and he did his fucking job properly – and only blew a bit of it on hookers and drugs.

The three of them settled to watch what might have been a very boring screen-saver program from the 1980s. It was a simple encrypted patch-through from a naval administration facility in a western suburb. Borzov would regularly monitor routine manoeuvres from home or wherever he happened to be, via an encrypted connection.

What came through on the screen looked to Medulev maybe more like a bad piece of internet gaming – Tetris without the nice graphics. The fact that hundreds of billions of dollars and the lives of several human beings – many of them his brother warriors – were at stake, however, certainly commanded Medulev's attention. That, and the fact that if the Americans took it the wrong way, they might be starting the Third World War.

Medulev reached for a light, and settled to watch a series of increasingly angry bleeping dots begin to converge on each other. The nearest land mass was some godforsaken place called Garaginsky Island. He sat back, and tried to relax, hoping he wasn't witnessing the beginning of the end of the world.

KSENIA HAD GONE to get some rest in Kirov's cabin. Samuel was settling in the officers' mess at Kirov's invitation when three separate alarms went off.

'What the . . .?'

Kirov closed his file and put the top back on his fountain pen. Samuel noted that the exercise log of the most modern submarine in the Russian navy was filled in by hand.

'OK, OK.'

Samuel could see Kirov gathering himself, analysing the situation.

'This new vessel has a sonar alarm for unfamiliar objects or obstacles. That's helpful for navigating polar icecaps and dealing with unexpected sub-sea ice formations. And that's the highest tone we hear. The second – the one that's like a police siren – indicates we're under attack.'

'And the third?' asked Samuel, trying hard to keep his voice steady.

'It's the emergency dive alarm.'

They were hurrying back to the bridge well before Machanov's voice requesting Kirov's presence there came over the vessel's talkback address system. Kirov almost fell over on one of the catwalks on the way. Samuel stumbled in his wake. Sure enough, they were plunging into an emergency dive.

When they got to the bridge, Mochanov was issuing urgent instructions to the engine room.

'We're not supposed to be under attack, Commander, are we?' asked Mochanov.

Ksenia arrived, wide-eyed and panicked, straight from sleep.

'Attack? We're under attack?'

'No. No, we're not,' said Kirov.

'Not under attack?'

'No, daughter. Not supposed to be under attack.'

If any of the crew had registered the relationship, they didn't show it. The volume of the alarm was relentless, an impediment to thought, Samuel felt. How could people think clearly with these mad sirens in their ears?

'The mission briefing is clear.' Kirov announced. He was thinking things through, out loud. 'The manoeuvres have been successfully completed. All we have to do now is return the vessel to base.

'Sir,' said Mochanov, his voice flat, professional, 'You need to see this.'

On the radar screen, a small green trail was making its way directly towards them.

'What is it? The Americans? Did they take the exercise as a hostile act?' asked Kirov. He quickly answered his own question. 'No, they wouldn't be that stupid.'

'Well?' Mochanov was looking at a sonar engineer who was

listening to the sound in his headphones.

'It's one of ours, Commander,' said the rating. 'The sound signature's unmistakable. It's a Shkval 2. Closing fast.'

Kirov scanned the screen: 'How long have we got?'

'About six minutes, Commander. This is an exercise, isn't it?'

Kirov ignored the rating's question.

'The missile. It's tracking our movement, I take it?'

'Yes, sir. Sharp movements make it slow to near-conventional speed, then it redirects.'

Kirov and Mochanov exchanged glances.

Samuel was monitoring events carefully. 'So if the earlier exercise is any guide, clever manoeuvring might delay the outcome by a few minutes. But if this torpedo is live, then the outcome is certain death.'

Ksenia put her hand to her forehead. Kirov gave Samuel a look of sardonic thanks.

'No word from Ust Kamchatsk?' barked Kirov.

Mochanov shook his head. 'They say they don't know what we're talking about.'

Kirov cursed quietly. 'But they must see the torpedo. What about the other command centres? Kronokai? Petropavlovsk?'

'They can't understand it either, sir.'

'OK,' said Kirov. 'Well, if this is an exercise, the torpedo will self-destruct within a few hundred metres of us.'

'Yes, Commander.'

Mochanov's jaw muscles flexed.

Samuel understood the real meaning of the exchange with Mochanov. The torpedo might well turn out to be battle-primed, and fired in error, a piece of friendly fire. Deadly, friendly fire.

Ksenia was holding on to a rail. She was pale and drawn.

'And to think, all this is because of Version Thirteen.'

And then the thought gave birth to itself within Samuel. He kissed her hard, for half a second.

'You're wonderful! Of course!'

He clapped a hand on Kirov's shoulder.

'Version Thirteen! Where is it?'

'Here. I carry it with me at all times now.'

'Give it to me, Commander.'

'What?'

A shout from a rating on the sonar. 'Closing rapidly now, Commander. Impact in four minutes thirty-four seconds . . .'

Samuel was shouting now. 'Jesus Christ, Kirov! What am I going to do, steal it and swim to the surface? Give it to me.'

Kirov withdrew the box from his tunic. Samuel grabbed it.

'Four minutes and closing, Commander.' The rating's voice was calm, measured, professionally level.

'Kirov, listen.' In all the mayhem, there was a moment of clarity between the two men. 'I need to get to the flotation tanks, the place you fired the missiles from. Will you come with me?'

Kirov nodded. He turned to the bridge.

'Do the flotation tanks have explosive bolts, as on the Anstey class, Mochanov?'

The lieutenant paused for a moment.

'Aye, sir.'

Kirov looked back at Samuel: 'And you need to get into the tank itself?'

Samuel passed a hand over his head, as the drawings, the algebraic equations and the narratives sped through his mind. He was back in Yavlinsky's office, working through that stack of papers.

'Yes . . . Yes, that's our best chance.'

'Good.' Kirov took Mochanov by the shoulder and spoke quietly now. 'Well, keep manoeuvring to slow this thing down as much as possible, and, as it closes for impact, blow the tank.'

'Aye, Commander.'

'Now, take command, and for God's sake, get your timing right. I'll be back shortly.'

'Aye, aye, Commander.'

The sonar engineer was staring into his screen.

'How long have we got?' asked Samuel quietly.

'Under three minutes, sir. She's closing.'

'Come on!' shouted Kirov.

He sprinted across the catwalks and down a corkscrew stair, Samuel following close behind. They ran hard along deck two, then pounded down a second and a third ever-tighter staircase to the belly of the vessel. They stopped on a half-landing, both breathing hard.

'You do know, Spendlove, that an explosive bolt is a tactic of last resort? It could compromise the strength of the fuselage. If it leaks, we'll all drown anyway.'

'Trust me, Kirov. It's our best shot.'

Kirov looked at Samuel, shook his head in disbelief, and snatched at a gantry handset. He spoke urgently into the talkback system.

'Lieutenant, is the launch pod for torpedo one pumped out?'

Samuel could hear the rating in the background, calmly counting down the time to impact. They were manoeuvring hard, surging this way and that, but the torpedo was still closing.

Less than a minute left now.

'Yes, Commander. Pumped clear automatically post-launch.'

'Very good. If this torpedo misses us and doesn't self-destruct at a safe distance, open launch pod one, please.'

'Yes, Commander.'

They ran down another deck level and waited outside the door to launch pod one. Samuel's heart was pounding. His pulse roared in his ears. Kirov picked up a monitor and they listened to the countdown up at the bridge.

'Forty-four seconds and closing . . .' said the rating in the same unflappable voice.

Samuel put his hand over his forehead and tried to concentrate
. . . *axisymmetric conditions . . . the fat, candy-striped onion dome*

319

*of St Basil's in the winter sun . . . steeped in a delicious, sun-ripened tomato broth . . . Tverskaya, Okhtony Ryad stations . . . radial and axial directions . . .*

'Forty seconds . . .'

He could feel the pressure of the ocean, the vast weight of water, bearing down on them all inside their fragile craft . . .

'Thirty-five . . .'

The images were shooting back and forth in his brain, sliding out of control . . . The problem wasn't the recall, it was the exclusion, the filtering out of the irrelevant. His brain was being bombarded, assaulted from within, a random crowd of ideograms, pictures, phrases, symbols – all bursting to get to the front of his consciousness, screaming louder and louder for his attention . . .

'Thirty . . .'

'Preparing to blow ballast tank bolts,' said Mochanov.

'Twenty-five seconds . . .'

Samuel jerked his head up. Kirov was shaking him by the shoulder.

'What now, Spendlove?'

Samuel shook his head, and closed his eyes . . . *vertical vortex . . . athermic capacitance . . . wedge product . . . limited parameter set . . . exponentiation . . . instrument panelling, ultrasound function . . .*

'Twenty . . .'

'Jesus, Spendlove, come on!' Kirov punched at the craft wall, barking his knuckles.

'Fifteen . . .'

'Blow ballast tank doors,' said Mochanov, neutrally.

A dull thud, followed by a sickening lurch downwards.

They waited a second. The fuselage was holding. Kirov grabbed a nearby handset. 'Mochanov? Your report?'

'The torpedo overshot us, sir. It's now slowing and looking to redirect. It didn't self-destruct.'

'Open pod one, please, Mochanov.'

'Aye, aye, sir.'

The pod doors opened with a gentle belch as the vacuum within the chamber was broken. The only barrier between the two men and the intensely hostile ocean was the outer door of the launch pod. The floor of the pod smelled of brine and algae – an odour that humans were never meant to experience. This was life lived thousands of fathoms beneath the surface.

The procession of blurred images in his head slowed, and stopped.

*Functionality – Supercavitation Drill Modality A . . .*

Samuel looked up.

'I have it. I think . . .'

'You *think*?' cried Kirov.

Samuel ripped off the lid of the Version Thirteen box, and they dashed into the pod.

'Here, help me!' shouted Samuel. He held o  an upright, one of the supports for the Shkval 2 torpedo. He handed Kirov Version Thirteen. Then he shut his eyes, seeking a diagram . . . Careful on the detail . . .

'Its nose should be pointing outwards, towards the sea door, Kirov.'

Expert seamanship saw Kirov secure the equipment in seconds.

'And then . . .' Samuel opened his eyes, walked to Version Thirteen, and pressed two small dimples either side of its nose. A piece of metal, not unlike a small radio mast, flicked up from the body of the equipment. Ultra sound.

The rating was counting down again over the talkback system.

'Thirty seconds to impact . . .'

They stepped back into the main body of the vessel.

'Twenty seconds . . .'

Samuel picked up a handset: 'Close the pod door, please, Lieutenant. And then immediately open the launch door, as though you were launching the first torpedo again.' His voice was as emotionless and flat as he could make it

A moment of agonising hesitation.

'Fifteen seconds . . .'

'Beg pardon, sir, but this vessel is under the control of Commander Kirov . . .'

Kirov snatched the handset: 'Just do it, Mochanov!' he screamed.

'Yes, Commander,' said Mochanov. The inner door closed instantly, and then the outer sea-door opened. Samuel could sense the vastness of the ocean, the imminence of doom, just a few centimetres away.

The submarine yanked itself hard to port and sharply down – a desperate manoeuvre. Samuel and Kirov stumbled and grabbed the handrail nearby.

'That was a narrow one. She's turned again now . . .' They could hear the voice of the lieutenant, as unperturbed as before. 'But she's heading our way, getting closer every time.'

'How long to impact this time, Mochanov?' asked Kirov

'Twenty-five seconds, sir.'

'Very good,' said Kirov, and turned to Samuel, who withdrew the remote control device from his pocket.

'This is it, Spendlove, the final pass. We're done sidestepping.'

'Twenty seconds . . .' said the rating.

'Fifteen . . .'

There were three buttons on the device, which seemed to be correctly positioned. But there was one vital detail left. Samuel searched and searched in his memory. *Which button activated the sonar?*

'Ten seconds . . .'

The three buttons: green, red and yellow.

*The kaleidoscope in his head turned, turned, turned again. Yavlinsky's lava lamp: morphing, endlessly changing, fluid shapes*

*and patterns of mathematical formulae, infinitely malleable instrument diagrams . . . a large capital Greek sigma, and couple of underscored Roman Vs – unit vectors and, he thought, a k-vector symbol last-minute additions, almost scratched in. But if, in his mind, Samuel could scratch them out . . .*

And it slowed to a stop . . . *Yes! That one! So if it wasn't really a k-vector, shown in red . . . then the correct button must be . . .*

Samuel pointed the remote at the pod door, and pressed green, hard.

A huge explosion. The submarine rocked up on the crest of a massive shockwave. Samuel and Kirov were hurled to the ground. Every alarm on the submarine went off at full volume, screeching and wailing as the craft shuddered and rocked uncontrollably. She would surely break in half at any moment. The lights flickered and failed – all was total darkness. Samuel and Kirov held on to each other – in that moment, brothers in arms, waiting for the freezing black waters of the Pacific to come and claim them.

But the waters never came. The lights flickered back on, soon to be followed by the sound of cheering from the crew. The explosion had been outside the vessel, not inside. The Shkval 2 had indeed been primed on a war footing, but it had self-destructed.

The two men made their way back to the bridge and accepted the rousing cheers of the crew. The roars of joy bounced back and forth inside the narrow hull of the submarine. Samuel, awash with the elation of survival and the fatigue of extreme recall, gave a small smile. It was a great way to go deaf, after all.

Ksenia hugged Samuel and her father in turn. Then she rounded back on Samuel and gave him a long slow kiss on the lips, one that had the crew cheering and whooping even louder. Samuel smiled again, shook his head, and sat down on a bench. Ksenia came and put her arm round him.

Kirov put a hand on Samuel's shoulder as he gave the command for launch pod one to be pumped out and the sea doors shut. Later,

Kirov would retrieve the device himself. Mochanov was already speaking volubly to the command and control centres on the peninsula. They wanted explanations. No, they demanded them. Through the fog of Samuel's fatigue it was difficult to tell what sort of excuses were offered.

After a few minutes, and to Samuel's great relief, Kirov offered to take them back to his cabin. He sat them on his bunk bed, while he positioned himself behind his tiny desk.

'My formal duty is to write up the log. But that's a bit of problem, Spendlove. I have no idea what happened.'

'Do you think the incoming missile was a mistake – friendly fire?' asked Samuel.

Kirov shook his head slowly, regretfully.

'No, no I don't. It was ours, all right. But only technically 'friendly'. Too much radio silence. Too little explanation since. That, I will deal with – as best I can. But what I really don't follow is this: what happened down there? How did you blow up that torpedo?'

Samuel shook his head, he was almost beyond exhausted.

'I'm not certain I fully understand myself, Kirov. But I'm destroyed by the events of the day. Can I get some rest? I promise we'll discuss it tomorrow.'

'Be my guest,' said Kirov.

Samuel lay on the bunk, Ksenia snuggled beside him. As he drifted into a dark, deep sleep, the last sound he heard was the soft scratching of Kirov's pen on the pages of the exercise log. Just before consciousness ebbed to nothing a sharp pinprick of fear probed him. He might feel content, protected, safe for the moment, but outside the confines of the submarine . . . He had cracked Yavlinsky's code. He had information that people would kill for. Had already killed for. But for now, he could do no more than embrace the welcoming darkness.

'YOU SHOULD HAVE given Spendlove the same treatment you gave that stubborn bastard scientist.'

Medulev had the phone clamped to his ear. It was an unpleasant experience. The voice that issued from the speaker was distorted and high – as though the caller had just had a hit of laughing gas. That was scrambled audio for you – you got annoying side-effects now and then.

Medulev's main concern was to clear the room, get things back to normal operations as quickly as possible. A young girl in the tartan tunic that, for some inexplicable reason, was the uniform of Sports Universe employees, was shepherding the admirals out of the building via one of several off-street doors. The screens had gone back to relaying the good news of carnality and profit, instead of the depressing shit they'd just seen. How come the submarine had escaped? The admirals were muttering about consequences, and the cost of a cover-up – basically asking for money, when all they were doing was protecting their own income stream. Still, Medulev would probably have done the same. Thank Jesus H. Christ on a rubber blanket that the Americans hadn't waded in. There'd have been more than a bit of explaining and covering up to do then.

Which made this call all the more perplexing. An angry Khan was one thing. An unreasonable one was another. He was beginning to break his own cardinal rule: that logic was all. Khan had always said that once things got personal, people made mistakes. All this was definitely personal, and probably a mistake.

Medulev waved a silent farewell to Spavinski, and sat back down on a canvas chair.

'You said there was no need, Khan. He never had the information, so he couldn't use it.'

'Well, if he didn't, he does now.'

'You think?'

'I think,' said the weirdly high, animated voice. 'Find the kit, and destroy it. And the same goes for Spendlove.'

Medulev rang off, and sat in contemplation for a moment. This wasn't the old, ultra-cool Khan that he knew. He was under pressure from someone or something.

Interesting . . . but that could wait. He had a couple of practical things to do first. Instinctively, he patted at the comforting bulk of his shoulder holster.

# CHAPTER TWENTY-TWO

A FORLORN CLUSTER of orange lights winked dimly at Samuel. They were two, maybe three knots away. It was difficult to judge distance at sea, especially at night. The tiny fishing village of Ust Kamchatsk was just beginning to set about its business. Small trawlers edged around the dock; their mast lights rocked drunkenly in the swell.

Their submarine was heading for the tiny island and its deep-water harbour just offshore. The *Red Kite* slipped into her moorings silently, like a beaten dog. Kirov took Samuel and Ksenia up to the conning tower. Together, they took in the ordered chaos of disembarkation.

'So, Spendlove?' said Kirov, when the quay was finally quiet. The first glimmerings of a silver-grey dawn were beginning to paint themselves into a crack between sea and sky.

'Are you asking me what you should put in your log?'

Kirov laughed, and looked out towards the horizon. 'So I can explain to my masters how clever I was in overcoming their brute incompetence – or their malice? No, but we need to know what it is we have. Otherwise, we cannot know what to do with it.'

'We know what we must do with it,' said Ksenia. Samuel pulled her to him.

'We've had that fight already, Ksenia. This is a discussion. So, Kirov. Here's my best guess. We now have the only working model of Version Thirteen. All this time – through the studying it on behalf of Ksenia and her mother – I've been focusing on the oil-drilling application. I suspect that all the claims made for this device are true – it will effectively increase the reclaimable world oil supply by a third or more.'

'Then there is no argument,' Ksenia interjected. 'We cannot destroy it.'

'Actually, Ksenia, I agree,' said Kirov. 'It's a good thing, and to preserve it is only right.'

'Perfect,' beamed Ksenia. 'And, father, please don't worry about Kolya. I can't wait to see my half-brother and sister. And I have money. So . . . as the Americans say, we're good to go. Right?' She looked at Samuel.

'Well, yes and no,' he said, rubbing his hands together against the cold. 'It's the right thing to do to keep it, I agree. But we're not thinking about the flip side of the coin.'

'You mean . . . a military application?' Kirov's brow was creased in concentration.

'I do. That was what saved us on the submarine. Why would the Black Widow go to such lengths to preserve and isolate the secret, to steal it from its inventor – and then want it destroyed? Suddenly, I saw the logic. And it confirmed my gut feeling that it was Medulev who killed Yavlinsky. He'd been trying to acquire it at an arms-dealing convention – I saw the photo in Yavlinsky's study, the poor sap. Yavlinsky deliberately incorporated a flaw in the blueprints, perhaps he thought it would protect him. Unfortunately it cost him his life.'

'And it would be right to assume that you have now corrected that flaw?' asked Kirov.

'My eidetic memory works best under extreme pressure. And I can't imagine a more extreme situation than the one we survived. But the whole retrieval process is exhausting. I have no guarantee I can repeat it. At least, not any time soon.'

'And did Anna know that?' Kirov asked quietly. Samuel shrugged away the unspoken question: did she knowingly put her daughter's life at risk, simply to get what was inside Samuel's head? Samuel glanced at Ksenia, she was staring into the middle distance. Had she even heard them?

She began to speak: 'So Medulev wanted it because . . .' Yes and no, then. Ksenia was working through the logic. 'Because the civil and military applications are incompatible in some way?'

'Exactly,' said Samuel. 'Version Thirteen's sonar aspect, the ultrasound that changes the behaviour of the supercavitational bubbles, is great for drilling, but disastrous for supercavitational weaponry.'

'So the bubble implodes and the torpedo or sub travelling in a supercav bubble will blow up around this thing?' asked Kirov.

'You mean it's an either or?' Ksenia linked her arm through Samuel's.

'I do. The piece of technology tucked up in your father's jacket is worth trillions to the world's oil industry. But it's kryptonite, the kiss of death, to supercavitional armaments. It destroys a multi-billion dollar market in conventional marine weaponry.'

Samuel looked towards the fishing port. Shapes could be seen loading the little boats. Such a simple life . . .

Kirov shrugged. 'I'm just a sailor, Spendlove. But, yes, the subs and the torpedoes are for sale, like everything else in Russia today. We're supposed to have been selling supercavitational arms to Iran since the 1970s.'

'It's what you might call an intense situation,' said Samuel.

Ksenia laughed. 'Nonsense! It's great news. We preserve it! We're agreed. Where's the problem?'

'The problem, daughter,' said Kirov, 'is that anything that fits into a shoe box and is worth a trillion dollars will have many, many dangerous people looking to acquire it.'

Kirov glanced up at the skies.

'Too true,' said Samuel. 'And this thing would probably be fiendishly difficult to disassemble and reverse-engineer. The lack of a proper set of designs makes this gizmo all the more valuable.'

'Gizmo?' Kirov watched a gaggle of men drift down a gangplank.

'This thing . . . With no proper plans and the inventor dead, if the arms-dealers find us and destroy Version Thirteen, that's it. Game over.'

Ksenia's hand flew to her mouth. 'My God! Are you saying . . . my mother's an arms dealer?'

'I didn't feel comfortable about taking money from her, even for Kolya.' Kirov shrugged. 'But this is appalling. Betraying our country for profit – murdering to protect that profit.'

'I don't think either of you should jump to that conclusion,' said Samuel. 'First of all, I'll bet your direct orders came not from the Black Widow, but Medulev. Am I correct, Kirov?'

'In truth, I don't know,' said Kirov. 'It was a man, one Anna knew. I'd have the occasional call with her, but the man would give me direct instructions. They were the only people – apart from you two – who ever called the number. I was a gullible fool.'

'You're hard on yourself, Kirov,' said Samuel. 'I think the Black Widow was in it for the money – but I'm not convinced you could call her an arms dealer. I have a theory, but I need your help to flush out the truth.'

Kirov watched the very last straggler leave the quayside. 'You saved the life of my daughter and my crew. You need to ask if I will help?'

'Well,' said Samuel. 'First, we're going to have to isolate a little something that I suspect is hidden in Version Thirteen. Could you take a look for me later? You studied engineering, correct?'

They'd decanted themselves onto the concrete quayside now, its creamy solidity just beginning to assert itself in the burgeoning light.

Kirov nodded. 'Of course. Anything else?'

'As a matter of fact, there is. I need you to commandeer a navy plane, and one or two little extras I'll brief you on. Our friends in Moscow have been hunting us down for too long. It's about time the hunted became the hunter.'

THE FAMILIAR RHYTHMS of the big bird kept him asleep for hours. Samuel awoke to the comforting drone of the Tupolev-69's engine. It was the same model of plane that had taken him out to Kamchatka. But the return leg was authentic military travel, and it was basic, borderline brutal. There was no heating in the plane apart from a couple of big, smelly old paraffin stoves that slid around alarmingly at any hint of turbulence. Samuel was warm enough beneath his coarse military-issue blanket, but the huge, empty interior of the Tu-69 was very, very cold.

Ksenia and her father, dressed in thick eider-stuffed dungarees, were up at the far end of the craft, chatting to the two pilots. Samuel reached for his own gear, dressed hurriedly, and walked up the ribbed wooden gangway to join them. The empty plane seemed vast, so much bigger than the civil version, with its rickety seats and curtain dividers. With just himself, Kirov, Ksenia and two pilots, the plane felt like a mobile bus garage.

He slipped his hands into a pair of mittens and flapped his arms against his body as he walked up to the cockpit, his brow raised in a gesture of enquiry.

'We're well into Moscow airspace, Spendlove,' said Kirov. 'You've been sleeping the sleep of the just.'

'Or the damned.' Samuel gave him a quick, not very convincing grin. He'd dreamt of the Moscow forest . . . *the muscle-bound man reaching out – and the push against his chest, into the abyss . . . Until he climbed out again, carrying Version Thirteen. Now he wanted that formula – and he knew that the only copy was in*

*Samuel's brain. Those huge hands reached out again – this time seeking Samuel's head . . . he was going to look inside, that brutish look in the commando's eyes said he would rip his head off his shoulders . . .*

'You've picked a good time,' said Ksenia, slipping her arm through his. 'We're just getting questions from Moscow Air Control.'

Samuel considered. This wasn't surprising. Kirov had basically mugged the quartermaster at the naval base in Petropavlovsk, and they'd hightailed it out of there before the arcane machinery of naval permissions had ground into gear. Kirov had a great deal of autonomy in Kamchatka, and that made certain things surprisingly easy. Acquiring the use of a plane was much more straightforward than procuring food for his family.

But, as Samuel expected, they were now closing in on the sharp end of things. Once you started heading for Moscow, all sorts of people paid serious attention.

A sharp burst of static from the radio grated on Samuel's ear. The pilot offered a staccato response, in Russian. This was obviously a tense exchange, and neither the pilot nor his interlocutor bothered with the international protocol of English. Kirov had his head bent towards the conversation. He shrugged.

'Looks like they're sending up an escort party. A few MiGs.'

'I suppose that was to be expected,' said Samuel. For all his best efforts, maybe the game was over, and the military authorities would arrest them. Still, there was a play or two to go. He looked back towards the rear of the craft. 'Is it ready?'

Ksenia nodded.

'Well, we'd better do it now, before they get here. I just hope we're in range.'

The Tu-69 was descending fast. Both pilots were now talking animatedly to traffic control. Samuel and Ksenia hurried down to the far end of the craft. From a rough, hessian sack, Samuel

332

withdrew a model plane. It was a beauty, a Messerschmitt 109 with a wingspan of perhaps a metre, and the most powerful petrol engine Kirov had been able to find. As Samuel had expected, there was a tiny micro-transmitter hidden in the device. Back at base, Kirov had teased it out with tweasers, and soldered it into the nose of the model plane.

They were approaching Moscow from the north, and as the bay door opened, Samuel could see the Ostankino complex. He took the model 109 ten metres back from the now fully open bay door – a brutal draft cut into them.

Samuel teased the tiny petrol engine into life, took the modeller's hand control and revved the engine as hard as it would go. The Messerschmitt trundled, then flew down the wooden gangway and out of the bay door into the blue afternoon sky. Samuel jammed the control down, hard to port, and the tiny Second World War mock-up began to head for Ostankino, give or take a couple of degrees.

They walked back up to join Kirov at the nose of the plane as the bat door closed.

'OK, Ksenia. Time to call mummy,' said Samuel. 'Whoa! What was that?'

He ducked instinctively as a dark flash swept past the nose of the Tu-69.

'Our welcoming committee,' said Kirov evenly. 'We're still landing at the naval air base at Vnukovo, but they've decided to hold our hands. Thoughtful of them.'

Two MiGs flanked the Tupolev at a distance of fifty metres either side. They could see into the cockpits of the fighters. The pilots' mirror visors would glance occasionally in their direction.

Ksenia made a face. She showed Samuel the screen of her phone.

'Reception's good, but nothing. Either she's not picking up, or she doesn't know we're coming.'

'I'm pretty sure your mother knows. In fact, I'll bet she's got something organised.'

Samuel looked at his watch. The Messerschmitt would be at Ostankino in a couple of minutes. Ksenia caught his train of thought and peered out of the northern cockpit window towards the distinctive tower.

'No need to squint,' said Samuel. 'The plane's invisible to the human eye now. And as for these,' – he gestured to the rows of monitors in the cockpit of the Tu-69 – 'that plane will have the radar signature of a crow.'

Ksenia was still scanning the northern horizon. 'So the only people who will know about it . . .'

'. . . are the ones tracking the transmitter, the one your father so ably found and so cleverly replanted.'

'And they would be?'

'Who, exactly? We'll see if we flush them out. But they'll be the ones who want to destroy Version Thirteen, who took out the inventor, and are looking to eradicate the design.'

Kirov joined them.

'Time to buckle up. We're coming in to land.'

The three of them sat together on a wooden bench seat as the pilots began their final approach. Kirov leaned across his daughter and beckoned Samuel closer. The engine noise was throatier than ever as the pilots throttled down.

'Tell me, Spendlove, I'm curious. I see the value of the diversionary tactic. But isn't sending the tracker off a way of letting the people who want Version Thirteen know that we know?'

Samuel instinctively glanced down at the box, tucked safely beneath Kirov's feet.

'I think they'd guess that, Kirov. It's meant to be a way of confusing them and making them show their hand. They'll be tracking this plane into Moscow, and seeing what they'll guess is Version Thirteen heading for Ostankino. Of course, we're in the territory of informed guesswork here . . .'

'So far, so good, Spendlove.' Kirov clapped him on the shoulder.

'The crew of the *Red Kite* haven't forgotten your guesswork. Nor have I.'

But Samuel was already in a reverie, eyes closed, head bent forward – *the Pushkin Café, Blandford and Medulev, erratic behaviour, Medulev almost flaunting his gun, his instrument of business, Medulev's tense conversation in Farsi, his abrupt disappearance and reappearance. The Iranian connection, the arms convention photo in Yavlinsky's study with lots of dark – maybe Iranian? – men . . . It had to be Medulev who'd killed Yavlinsky, Medulev who'd been dealing with Kirov, and Medulev who'd perhaps – very probably – been working for someone other than the Black Widow, someone who wanted Version Thirteen suppressed at all costs.*

*And if he recognised the signs, the arch, manipulative, ruthless behaviour, that person was his old rival, Khan . . .*

Samuel opened his eyes. The MiGs had gone, and now they were no more than a hundred metres above the ground. A collection of military police cars, fire engines and accident-recovery vehicles strobed red and blue up from the runway. They were parked at curious angles, like the spillage from a huge toy box, carelessly kicked over.

'OK, everyone,' called the pilot. 'Coming into land. Touchdown in ten seconds.'

Ksenia took Samuel's hand. She squeezed rhythmically, the nervous tic of the diffident flyer. But before Samuel felt her count reach five, he heard a curious thudding sound. At first he thought the undercarriage had made premature contact with the runway, but it wasn't that immediate – indistinct, but with the distant menace of a rolling thunderclap.

And then they were bounced up by a hard contact with the tarmac, swiftly followed by a curse and an apology from the pilot.

They began to taxi, and Samuel's thoughts turned to their reception committee. For once, the best tactic was plain honesty: it was time to tell the truth – or most of it – and see what happened.

As they stood at the head of the stairs, ready to disembark, Samuel's attention was focused on the motley gathering of official-looking cars, now joined by unmarked Hummers and limousines with tinted windows. Who was going to come forward and start the next phase of the dance?

And then – a wail from Ksenia. She grabbed his arm, and began to wilt. He put his other arm round her.

'Ksenia! What's wrong?'

She pointed vaguely northwards, where the sky was glowing orange.

Samuel knew what the problem was, and the meaning of the mystery thud on the plane, even before Ksenia spoke.

'Ostankino! It's on fire, Samuel! Someone's bombed my mother!'

# CHAPTER TWENTY-THREE

KSENIA SOBBED INCONSOLABLY into Samuel's shoulder for several minutes, Kirov's hand on her arm. Samuel thought briefly about offering some soothing words. Yes, it looked bad, but it was impossible to be sure that Ostankino had been bombed, merely because a ruthless band of arms-dealers were looking to protect their billions by eradicating the one thing that threatened it. But then he would be lying to her, and Ksenia deserved better than that. He said nothing.

It looked as though his plan had worked too well. Not for a second had he believed that anyone would dare attack ABTV and the Black Widow. She was too powerful; she offered too much protection to others, and she herself was just too big a target. Or so he'd thought.

Samuel looked over Ksenia's shoulder at Kirov, and grimaced. The glow of the Ostankino fire was increasing. Whoever had decided to destroy Version Thirteen wanted to do so very badly. How much power, how much confidence must they have to attack an oligarch?

He held Ksenia tight and surveyed the scattered fleet of vehicles. The natural leader of this pack would come forward and claim them soon enough.

And the leader's emissary seemed to be a liveried chauffeur in charcoal grey. He wore no corporate logo, making it impossible to tell just whose man the fellow was. He'd been hovering for a full five minutes before Samuel acknowledged him with a curt nod. Kirov was close by and signalled his agreement when the chauffeur bowed slightly and gestured for them to follow.

They walked slowly towards a large, shiny black Communist-era Zil. The chassis would be bullet- and bomb-proof, and the original Zil engine would have been replaced by something that actually worked, probably from America. Apart from the amusingly retro choice of marque, the car was otherwise standard issue for modern Moscow: enormous, sleek, black, mirror windows.

The chauffeur strode a few paces ahead, and waited for them to catch up before he opened the door. Samuel saw a dozen other cars, including military vehicles, begin to head off. If they'd ever had a job to do, it had been done.

Kirov and Ksenia preceded him into the interior, but he felt – or rather smelled – the presence of the occupant before he saw it. As he slipped onto the beige leather bench seat next to Kirov and Ksenia, he'd already detected the unmistakeable odour of a Sobranie cigarette. Sitting opposite them was the Black Widow – her black dress tighter than ever, the décolletage more perfect, the jewellery more sparkling, the eyes brighter, smile wider. Or so it seemed to Samuel.

Anna Barinova held out her hand.

'Ksenia.' Her daughter showed no inclination – or maybe ability – to speak.

The Black Widow nodded. 'Samuel, welcome. I see you have moved up in the world a little.'

'How so, Anna?'

'I've had a personal shopper for years. But a personal kidnapper? That's quite a mark of distinction. Every trophy wife in Moscow will want one as soon as the word gets out.'

'So you're not going to throw me to the wolves just yet?'

A nod, a hint of oxyacetylene in the glance. 'No. Not just yet.'

So maybe the kidnap ruse had really affected her. Maybe she felt a simple maternal love for Ksenia beneath all the self-regard, the driven posturing. It was difficult to believe she would orchestrate a torpedo attack on her own daughter, after all. And now the pursuit of the Version Thirteen tracking device had brought fire to Ostankino. Samuel could sense her watching him for a reaction. He bowed his head and kept his mouth shut. This was the Black Widow's meeting, and she could chair it. There'd be a plan, that much was certain. He'd judge the situation on the facts – *don't interfere with the data.*

The Black Widow turned and gave Kirov a look that could have been tender, or maybe just careful. She spoke slowly: 'Anatoly. *Skolko let? Skolko zim?*' How many summers? How many winters?

KSENIA LAUNCHED HERSELF at the Black Widow, threw her arms round her, and kissed her. A second later she flung herself back onto the bench seat.

'Mother! You're not dead! I . . . I could kill you!'

Ksenia's fury seemed to feed on her inability to deny the love she bore towards her mother.

'No, dear, I'm not dead. And I've been using every ounce if influence I have to keep you all alive, and out of jail.'

She looked again at Kirov.

'Yes, Anna. It's been a long time. Why didn't you tell me?' He gestured towards Ksenia.

The Black Widow opened a palm. 'Anatoly, you were always the navy's man, never truly mine. I fell in love with a glamorous sports star, before things went bad and he fell in love with vodka. But I loved you too. It would have been suicide to tell anyone who Ksenia's real father was. It would have been infanticide, more to the point. They would have thrown us out on the street. Secrets have a habit of coming out.'

'So you denied me the knowledge of *my daughter*, for your own convenience. You should have told me. Confided in me.' Samuel could see veins throb in Kirov's neck. He was more agitated than he'd ever seen him.

'True confidence is a delicate fruit, Anatoly. We share it, and it withers.' The Black Widow extinguished her cigarette and tapped on the partition dividing them from the chauffeur. The Zil began to glide forward. She leaned towards Kirov, and softened her voice: 'We are oceans apart, you and I, separated by time and tide. But we sailed so close, once. Please, Anatoly. I would have told you, of course. In time. You should save your passion for when it is useful. Your role as custodian of our secret asset requires constancy and diligence, not raw emotion.'

Kirov clutched his holdall to his chest, and subsided, still plainly furious.

'Anna, I have some questions for you,' said Samuel. The Zil was edging towards a major traffic artery.

'Yes? Where are we going? The Conservatory. Rostropovich is on the programme. Not my favourite, but I do have Stalin's old box. Samuel, Ksenia, Anatoly, I am hoping and expecting you will be my guests.'

Samuel said quietly: 'Destination's always relevant, but that wasn't first on the list. I'd be happy to come to the Conservatory eventually, even if it is Rostropovich. But won't I need to visit a lawyer first? The British Embassy seemed pretty anxious to find me when I was last in Moscow. Along with the police, and God knows what agencies of various governments.'

'I shouldn't worry about that, Samuel. The fact that we're all in this car, unchallenged by any authority, military, civil or a mixture of the two, is, as you lawyers say, de facto evidence that I have matters in hand. No?'

'But what about the explosion at Ostankino? Do you have *that* in hand too?'

The Black Widow tapped at a keypad set in the arm of her seat and brought up the volume on one of several television screens. A local news reporter was gabbling excitedly into camera. Behind him, a storage facility within the Ostankino compound blazed away, attended by three teams of fire-fighters.

'My people tell me it was just some kids playing with toy planes.' Her eyes flickered towards Samuel for a moment, then she continued: 'The military authorities overreacted, as they so often do. It's all rather annoying, and it really would have been quite inconvenient, but for the benefits of insurance.'

Samuel monitored her carefully, as she went on to explain how she sponsored the Conservatory, and had her own quarters there. They'd be fed, watered, given fresh clothes, and kept out of the media and legal circus. The Zil accelerated powerfully into a fast-moving stretch of motorway.

The Black Widow watched the pattern of the traffic, perhaps aware that Samuel was monitoring her every gesture. He sat back, and wondered at the Black Widow's control, her poise, her knowingness. She assured them of her protection, but this felt far from safe.

SAMUEL, KSENIA AND KIROV climbed the last set of stairs. Ahead of them was the entrance to Stalin's box.

Samuel breathed in deeply, wondering what was next. They had indeed been cosseted in ABTV's quarters at the Conservatory. The other two had eaten and slept, but Samuel just nibbled at some crackers and drowsed through the afternoon and early evening. The television and radio stations were full of the rocket-grenade attack on Ostankino. Or was it? The phrase 'rolling news' was well made. Supposition was what most of it amounted to. If unchallenged for more than a few minutes, supposition substituted for fact. Which was infuriating if you were interested in getting at the truth. Samuel knew that the tracker device in his Messerschmitt had incited a brutal overreaction from something or someone. There was uncertainty now as to the weapons involved. The surface-to-air S-300 or the Vympel R-77 air-to-air missile? And the object of the attack? The model Messerschmitt had morphed into a foreign military plane trespassing in sovereign Russian air space (competing theories had it as a US spy- or attack-drone). The consensus view agreed with the speculation that the intended victim was the Black Widow herself – a fine, upstanding Russian businesswoman unjustly victimised by the wicked American imperialists.

And she would be waiting at the top of this staircase, behind the thick burgundy velvet curtains now in front of them. Samuel reached up and pulled the drapes apart. The Black Widow was sitting in a tiny anteroom just outside her box. A bottle of champagne was chilling in an ice bucket; four flutes were set out.

'People's champagne,' she smiled. 'Russian, cheap, sweet. But my first taste of luxury as a girl. I still remember that first sip. I love it.' She waved a hand. 'Please, sit.'

The orchestra was tuning up in the auditorium. The sounds jangled in Samuel's ears; it was enervating, the musical equivalent of trying to make sense of flotsam on a beach – ugly and disordered.

The Black Widow raised her glass.

'Thank you for coming, and for trusting me, all.'

Samuel thought about interjecting for a moment. But no, let her think they were all her 'trusting' creatures.

'We have so much to say to each other. So much to discover, so many histories to relate. We will do this soon, in the safety of the environment I can create for us all – here, in Ostankino, around the world. But now, my family,' she looked from Ksenia, to Kirov, to Samuel, 'old, new, extended family – please, I beg your support.

'Follow me,' said the Black Widow. 'On the other side of this door, we enter a world where theatre is real. This is the drama play of power, of politics, of the face we show to the people. Rightly or wrongly, they have interpreted today's events as an attack on me. All eyes will be upon us. So, once on the other side of this curtain, whatever you do, show no weakness. The Russian people respect few things, but they do respect strength. If you are strong, you have the right to rule. This they acknowledge as *vlast*. We are in Stalin's box tonight. Let the *vlast* sit on your shoulders lightly, like a cloak.'

With that, Anna Barinova parted the curtains in front of her, and disappeared. Samuel, Ksenia and Kirov put down their champagne glasses and followed.

Stalin's box in the Conservatory was in the extreme right of the upper circle, the left as viewed from the stage. It offered an unparalleled opportunity to see and be seen. Since taking it over, the Black Widow had installed a gilded bust, twice life-size, of the great Georgian leader and patriot.

They took their seats and sat, straight-backed, waiting for the performance to begin. The VIP boxes and the stage were dressed with harpoons and nets, as the second half of the concert was a revival of an obscure 1950s composer's musical odyssey into the world of Soviet whaling. The bust, the symbols of industrial might and ruthlessness all made the message very clear: they were Stalin's successors, his direct descendants in the new society of pure money, pure power, pure savagery. A mere rocket attack was not going to make the Black Widow and her entourage hide.

The crowd couldn't see the thickset bodyguards, the earpieces, the mutterings into walkie-talkies, the covert circus that surrounded the billionairess, her daughter, ex-lover, Samuel – and their trillion-dollar piece of technology. The Black Widow had been careful not even to mention Version Thirteen directly since retrieving them from the airport. But she would know where it was, as a spider feels the vibrations of prey on its web.

The packed auditorium fell to a hush as they sat. All faces were turned towards them, enquiring, sympathising, but most of all searching for signs of weakness. The applause began somewhere at the back of the hall, but soon amplified to thunderous levels.

Samuel took his cue from the Black Widow. She stared forward at the stage. She did not move a muscle. She acknowledged nothing. The message was clear: the crowd's love and its hatred were the same to the Black Widow. She was where she was for that very reason. *Vlast*, while a creation of popular emotion, required its possessor to demonstrate total indifference to it.

They sat like statues through the minor storm of adulation. Eventually, the conductor, the maestro, appeared on stage. His own ovation was less enthusiastic than the Black Widow's, and he turned, sour-faced, to the massed, tail-coated ranks of his orchestra.

Forty-five minutes of tonal poem later, Samuel was fighting sleep. However, the music ended abruptly, and the interval came to his rescue. They retired to the leader's anteroom and a table stocked with canapés and more sickly-sweet sparkling wine.

Samuel munched down a couple of bits of cracker and caviar, then nodded at Kirov, who rummaged in his holdall and placed an aluminium device next to one of the trays.

'So, Anna,' said Samuel. 'Is this what you want?'

The Black Widow looked at it, an eyebrow raised.

'Version Thirteen? Thank you for bringing it.'

'You mean we had an option?'

'There are always options, Samuel. Choices made, according to our conscience.'

A couple of heavies took a step towards the table, but the Black Widow waved them away.

Of course, she was play-acting. That was one of the things she did. They'd just spent the past hour in the experimental theatre of *vlast*. But something told Samuel that her indifference was genuine.

'You don't care, Anna, do you?' said Samuel. He could see

where to go now. 'You got me to risk my life to acquire the blueprint for this. But you don't care about that, or even about the damned technology, do you?'

'Please, it's an exaggeration to say you risked your life to get the design. Your subsequent actions, perhaps they were risky.'

Samuel, Kirov and Ksenia were gathered round her. They'd played the Black Widow's game long enough.

'I'm not exaggerating, Anna,' said Samuel, very quietly. 'Anyone who comes into contact with this thing is in danger. Poor Yavlinsky, murdered. Blandford, disappeared. Those policemen, incinerated. To say nothing of the fact that we all nearly died a horrible death beneath the ocean.'

Ksenia reached for Samuel's hand. Their fingers intertwined. If the Black Widow noticed this minor intimacy, she showed no sign.

Samuel could feel the anger rising within him. Perhaps it was the shock of their so very narrow escape. On another occasion he might not have found the truth in time. Fear and rage flashed through him every time he thought of the possibility.

'Did you know about that, Anna? About the "*friendly fire*" – the near-accident that almost certainly wasn't accidental?'

He swallowed hard. He had to check the dark thing building within. He had to *think* – without thought there could be no clarity.

'You didn't want the technology at all, did you, Mother?' It was Ksenia's turn now. 'You just wanted people to think you had the secret, so you could play your game of market rollercoasters.'

'And you nearly deprived me of the love of my daughter,' said Kirov. He shook his head slowly, his gaze never leaving her. 'You nearly deprived me of knowing she existed. That's a kind of murder.'

'I'm sorry to be such a disappointment to you all. Really, I am,' said the Black Widow. She toyed with her glass.

'The thing is, Anna,' said Samuel, sitting back, 'you make a great play of dominance, but actually you have a submissive streak.'

'Is that so?' Anna murmured, 'Please – enlighten me.'

'Let's begin at the beginning. Why your intense activity around Kempis's death? You weren't interested in Version Thirteen, nor in Kempis, and certainly not in me. But someone else was – and it has to be Khan. If I interpret your actions as his, it's obvious. You might be one of the wealthiest people in the world, but you're Khan's creature. And that's a bad, bad thing to be.'

'Even if I were, how so?' She took a sip of wine. Samuel saw a small but definite tremor in her hand.

'Khan wants everything, and everyone, Anna. He wants to eat them up. Look how he's devouring you, making you turn the ones you love against you.'

Ksenia lent forward, incredulous. 'Who is he, this Khan?'

'Please, please.' The Black Widow was looking down tearfully. 'I owe him so much. I owe him everything. He made me what I am.'

The words hung in the air for a moment, pricked by violin pizzicato. The orchestra was tuning up for the second half.

Ksenia lifted her head: 'And what's that? What *are* you?'

'I am what I am, my child. I am a survivor. But you must understand, all of this, I did for you. Who else would protect you? Build your future?'

Suddenly, there was an arm around Samuel's throat. He was pinned to the chair and a big hand plucked Version Thirteen from the table. Then his captor, a bison in a shiny suit, released him. Samuel turned, rubbed his neck, and addressed the figure in the doorway – an amused spectator of events.

'Hello, Khan.'

'Hello, Samuel. Not even a little surprised?'

Khan smiled, a flash of brilliant white teeth. He was wearing a plain black T-shirt beneath a beige linen suit. He nodded at his heavies, stepped forward and stood beside the Black Widow's chair. Then he lowered an exquisitely manicured hand onto her shoulder – a calculated gesture of ownership. The Black Widow blinked, and looked down.

'It's been some time,' said Samuel. 'I have to say, Khan, I hoped never to see you again.'

'Why ever not? I thought we had an interesting relationship, wouldn't you say? But I'm forgetting my manners. First of all, thanks are due. You've done well to get this.'

'I'm really not interested in your views on anything, Khan.'

Khan tossed Version Thirteen up in the air, and caught it. 'How uncharacteristically rude of you. Ah well, modern business, I suppose. But there's something else you have, something that goes with this.'

He caressed the contours of Version Thirteen. 'I want the formula, dear boy.'

'There's no formula.'

'Yes there is. The one that's in your head.'

'I see.' Two heavies stepped close to Samuel. The bad dream about the commando was coming true. 'And these two oafs will beat it out of me?'

'No, no. Nothing so unsubtle.'

Khan's smile was undiminished. Samuel wondered if he had ever really known this slight, ageless, seemingly indestructible creature. Khan pointed at Ksenia, and nodded. One of the heavies wrapped a thick arm around her and placed a hairy hand over her mouth. The other stood menacingly over Samuel.

Khan took Ksenia's hand in his own and turned to Samuel: 'Brute force is much underestimated, I discover. A little physicality, applied to the right area, or the right person, can bring empires to their knees.'

Khan kissed the tip of Ksenia's forefinger with an exaggerated delicacy. 'Such grace, such beauty.'

He shot Samuel a smile. 'She has perfect cuticles, wouldn't you say? Sadly unlike our friend Yavlinsky.'

'You bastard! Don't you dare touch her!'

'Well, that depends, Samuel. It's all a question of co-operation. Give me what I want, and we'll all get along famously. If not, painful consequences may flow.'

Khan bit into Ksenia's fingertip. She emitted a little scream. Samuel and Kirov tried to get up, but the heavies, brandishing snub-nosed revolvers, pushed them back into their seats.

'Khan! What are you doing?' The Black Widow rose from her seat. 'Leave her be.'

Khan fixed her with a particularly brilliant smile. 'I don't think so, Anna. I'm afraid your daughter's getting kidnapped all over again – but this time for real.'

Khan parted the curtains separating them from public view.

'The second half is about to begin, and we must be saying our farewells. An extraordinary thing, Version Thirteen, isn't it? It can make or break the oil market. It can wreck a whole class of submarines and torpedoes. Everything you could want, all in one package. Version Thirteen is like your genius, Samuel – if I have it, that's OK. More than OK, it's perfect, in fact. But if anyone else has it . . . why it must be permanently destroyed. And therein lies my problem. I may have it physically, but the grand design with the flaws corrected – the secret in your head – that's what we must have. Mustn't we, Ksenia?

'So, Samuel, I'll be taking your new girlfriend with me for company, as I wait to hear from you. Don't take too long to send me a transcript – a perfect one.'

And with that, the heavies bundled Ksenia out of the door. Khan bowed slightly, turned on his heel and disappeared after them.

KIROV TURNED TO SAMUEL, then to the Black Widow: 'Who is this man?'

The Black Widow looked down at her lap.

'Khan will stop at nothing to get what he wants, Kirov,' said Samuel. 'He tortured and killed Yavlinsky. He orchestrated the torpedo attack on us, based on nothing more than a lucky guess – a hunch. Correct me if I'm wrong, Anna. And now he threatens Ksenia's life again and you just sit there and accept it?'

The Black Widow lifted her head. 'He was behind the torpedo attack?'

'I'm sure of it.'

'Very well,' said the Black Widow, standing up. 'Let's kill him.'

SAMUEL NEEDED no encouragement. Khan's callousness, his limitless sense of entitlement, had flicked some sort of switch inside him. He could feel the rage boiling up as he walked into Stalin's box. The corridor doorway from the VIP boxes was directly beneath them, and in a moment Khan would appear. He looked around at the security. Khan had left some of his cronies on the door of the box. He would have to choose his moment well.

As Khan's slight figure began to make its way towards the exit, Ksenia behind him, looking up, Samuel walked up to the industrial fishing display. He put his foot against the stucco plasterwork, and ripped out a harpoon. He weighed the weapon in his hand. It was surprisingly light, with good balance. Samuel was set to hurl it with all his might at Khan's retreating back, aiming to kill. But Ksenia was in the way. Perhaps Khan sensed his own vulnerability, and was using her as a shield. It was a very difficult shot, but he'd take it. He set his arm back and threw as hard as he could.

The screams of the crowd came too late to alert his target. If Samuel's aim had been true, he would have pierced Khan straight through; he would have been dead of blood loss and shock within seconds. But his fear of hitting Ksenia ruined it. He missed by yards, and the harpoon quivered, its head embedded in the pine-panelled floor like a giant arrow in a dartboard.

The crowd was in uproar, pointing, screaming up at Stalin's box. They created a circle of fear around Khan, the target. Khan's shock soon became a smile of pleasure when he saw the raw fury on Samuel's face.

A henchman held Ksenia pinioned, close to the exit, and Khan turned back and walked up to just beneath the box. Khan took out Version Thirteen, his trophy, and began tossing it up in the air.

Samuel knew that Khan's real victory was his own loss of control. Khan's heavies now had him by each arm, and he was powerless to do anything other than glare as Khan silently taunted him. He was tossing and catching, tossing and catching. Directly below them, almost close enough to touch. And he could do nothing.

Except – Samuel jerked one hand free, and pushed hard at the big gold bust of Stalin. It rocked, toppled, fell. And smashed into pieces, just next to Khan, who was smiling and tutting,

The same could not be said for the crowd. They were appalled at the desecration of the Stalin icon. And the horrified murmurs became angry shouts when someone recognised Samuel from his media pictures.

*Capitalist infiltrator! Foreign kidnapper! Rapist! Murderer! Thief!*

The crowd surged towards the box. Several angry young men were trying to climb up the wooden walls, and falling back. A couple were attempting to rip harpoons out of the stage decoration.

A red-haired man wearing a diamanté earring and a donkey jacket had managed to climb up into the next box. His companions below were giving each other leg-ups, in a frenzied attempt to join him. A harpoon thudded into the wall next to Samuel, and bounced back. It flipped down to the ground, pinning the long woollen shawl of a terrified *babushka* to the ground. She emitted a piercing shriek of fear. The mob saw this as Samuel's attack on a vulnerable old lady. A throaty, visceral roar went up.

*Kill him! Kill him! Kill him!*

A water bottle, then two beer bottles, whizzed past Samuel's head and smashed into the wall behind him. He was transfixed by the anger and malevolence of the masses. If they reached him, they would pull him apart. Car chases, murderous commandoes, torpedo attacks – now this. Another bottle hurtled past his ear. He ducked, waiting for the explosion of sound and glass.

But it never came. Samuel straightened, and looked over his shoulder. The Black Widow had caught the bottle like some elfin goddess. She held it like a trophy in a dainty, gloved hand. The other was held up high – a gesture of control amid all the pitiless chaos and the fury.

And yet it worked. The masses were stilled. Silence fell. Samuel could almost see the radial waves of power emanating from the Black Widow. This was *vlast* in all its dark glory.

'Fellow citizens,' she said. 'Things are not what they seem. This man' – she pointed at Samuel – 'is not our enemy. He is innocent.'

A small cry of dissent at the back of the auditorium. The Black Widow silenced it with a swift, deadly look.

'But this man . . .' She pointed down at Khan. 'This man is the terrorist who launched the cowardly attack on me and my employees at our Ostankino offices today.'

'Anna, I . . .' Khan wasn't smiling any more. The crowd was the Black Widow's creature, and was moving closer and closer to its prey. Samuel could see the small points of fear in Khan's eyes. He was a supplicant now, begging for mercy from Stalin's successor.

The Black Widow's forefinger moved down, pointing now at Khan – simultaneously a gesture of accusation and final damnation.

She spoke slowly and clearly: 'Let him pay the penalty.'

Samuel watched aghast at the unfolding fury below him. The crowd turned like an animal crazed with hunger as it scents its prey. Khan was swallowed up in a frenzy of flailing arms and legs. The red-haired man leapt off the balcony next door, and disappeared into a boiling sea of whirling fists and snapping heads. For a second, Khan's hand, holding Version Thirteen, was visible above the fray, but then it was dashed to the floor, and instantly trampled to pieces by dozens of scrabbling, frenzied boots.

Khan was going to be pulled apart. Samuel expected his head, or at least a limb, to be spat out of the teeming morass. But there was a fight, resistance of some sort. Khan's heavies were giving everything they'd got to get out. Protecting Khan, fighting for his life and their own, was the only way they had of escaping alive. Two big men were with Khan at the centre of the heaving mass.

And another was helping. Medulev clubbed his way from the back of the room towards Khan, using the butt of a revolver to create a path through the hordes. What a soldier he was, even now. Miraculously, Medulev fought his way to the tight knot of men surrounding Khan, and they began to battle their way out of the theatre.

Samuel looked for Ksenia, and froze. She was gone. Good news or bad? Had she been bustled into a car and driven away? Or was she free?

He didn't have long to wait. Ksenia appeared in the doorway, panting. 'Quickly, Samuel, let's go! Back stairs!'

# CHAPTER TWENTY-FOUR

THEY RAN HARD down the emergency stairs, through the orchestra's changing room, and out into a cold, cobbled side-street.

A boxy white Rolls-Royce waited for them nearby, thick grey smoke issuing softly from its exhaust. Kirov and the Black Widow ran to it, and climbed in. Samuel hesitated, his hand on Ksenia's arm.

'Quick! Get in!' called the Black Widow. 'What are you waiting for?'

'What am I waiting for, Anna? Another option. No disrespect to your hospitality – or your protection – but it's a bit too close to Khan for my liking.' Samuel looked around and down the street. He called loudly: 'Kirov!' And made a phone sign with his hand. Kirov nodded, smiled, and bade his farewell with a traditional naval salute: commander to assistant.

He grabbed Ksenia, and they ran in the opposite direction – towards a pale Zhiguli, which was parked a hundred metres away, its engine running.

THE DRIVER'S DOOR flew open, and they were greeted by Klinkov.

'Did you enjoy the concert?'

'Enjoy? Rostropovich . . .?' said Samuel. They jumped into the car and Klinkov hunched forward, peering myopically into the windscreen.

'Ha! Bourgeois claptrap. Even the horrible tone poems.'

He slammed the ancient Zhiguli forward with his customary, overconfident ferocity. His wife sat silently next to him in the passenger seat. The night was cold, clear and the city well lit. But as they hurtled along, it was difficult to feel safe.

'I saw you there, sitting in Stalin's crow's nest,' cackled Klinkov, swerving at the last minute to avoid a huge Toyota Landcruiser. 'The Romanovs, Stalin, the Black Widow. A terrible message, but we got it.'

Samuel thought they were going to run a red light, but they screeched to a halt just in time. The car's brakes made a horrible groaning noise.

'We've got something for you,' said Klinkov. He grunted and twisted round to engage Samuel and Ksenia in the back seat.

'What's that?' said Samuel. 'Don't tell me. It's a surprise.'

'Maybe more of a surprise than you think,' said Klinkov. A car behind hooted aggressively. Klinkov had been ignoring a green for a full two seconds – welcome to Moscow. He crashed into first gear, and they bounced onwards into the night.

SAMUEL AND KSENIA were slightly out of breath by the time they got to re-acquaint themselves with Yuri Gagarin and the spare room of the Klinkov household. The lift was not working again. The climb had been bracing for the young couple, exhausted after the events of the past few days. The Klinkovs followed a few floors behind.

Madame Klinkova insisted on producing tea and jam. Ksenia sipped delicately as Comrade Klinkov entered the room carrying a small parcel under his arm.

354

Samuel looked at it doubtfully. It had the same shape and dimensions as a Version Thirteen box.

Ksenia had noticed too: 'Is it . . . a working model? That would be a good thing.'

'That would probably be too much of a good thing,' said Samuel. He withdrew a package from his jacket, and placed it on the table next to the Klinkovs' teapot.

'Version Thirteen!' exclaimed Ksenia. 'But then, what did you give Khan?'

'A fake. Superficially, it wasn't a bad copy, given the short time Kirov had to get it done, but it's got nothing inside it – it's as useful as a shop-front dummy. I'm surprised Khan swallowed the bait so easily.'

Samuel watched Ksenia settle on the gadget, happy as a puppy with a new toy.

Klinkov returned from the kitchen, where he'd been thrashing about for a while.

'Here it is,' he said. 'This once belonged to Comrade Kempis. He and Yavlinsky used it quite a lot in the last few years. Kempis wanted you to have it once your adventure was complete.'

Klinkov looked at Ksenia, who was still clutching Version Thirteen to her bosom.

'It is complete, isn't it, Comrade Spendlove?'

Samuel glanced at the two old Communists, then Ksenia, a bright-eyed New Russian, and wondered what Kirov and the Black Widow would be making of their own evening. But the fact was undeniable: Version Thirteen was in Ksenia's hands, even if Samuel was thousands of miles, geographically and emotionally, from a safe place.

'I suppose so. A happy ending, of sorts.'

'And Kempis left you this note.' Klinkov produced a card, with the distinctively fragile hand, now essaying an ambitious mauve ink: 'To Samuel: "c4; c5"'

'Ah,' said Samuel. 'The English Opening.'

Samuel untied the string and opened up the parcel. A chess clock. Images jostled for attention in the back of his mind: long summer nights in Kempis's All Souls rooms, winter evenings in one of the snugs at the Eagle and Child on Saint Giles, or the back bar of the Turf – the two of them, talking of everything and nothing, hammering out moves and slamming down on the clock, passing the time-baton of chess. Your move, old man. Well, now it was Samuel's. Again.

There was an inscription on the clock, in Russian.

'This certainly didn't exist when Peter and I used it,' said Samuel.

'No, Comrade Yavlinsky added it,' said Klinkov. He picked up a pair of glasses and squinted from the effort of translation: 'To the genius of Viktor Korchnoi, whose will to win and appetite for combat was second to none.'

So for all his old-style Communist sympathies, Yavlinsky really was on the side of Korchnoi, the defector, not Botvinnik, the Soviet. He was a maverick, a free spirit, after all. Samuel picked up the clock and weighed it in his hand. It was a fine piece of equipment, a pleasant and thoughtful memento.

And then he got it.

Of course! The pattern, the Chinese-style dragon's tail swirls on the brass side-panels of the clock. He fumbled in his pocket and produced the brass key that had been delivered to his hotel room in the Ukraina. The key bore the same distinctive pattern. He turned the clock over and discovered a tiny lock at the base. The key fitted perfectly.

With trembling hands, Samuel removed the wooden back of the clock. Two tiny rolls of rice paper with fine, near-microscopic script on them fell onto the small table around which they were sitting.

'What is it, do you think?' asked Klinkov.

Samuel peered at the writing. It was difficult to make out, but the shapes were familiar.

*The capital Greek psi, underscored Roman Vs – unit vectors and a pristine k-vector symbol; the wave vector configured for three dimensions – this time with no amendments* ... $|\emptyset(t) \times V = K\, e{-}i2Mht\, |p0\rangle$

'The full specifications and system design for Version Thirteen. This time with no deliberate errors, I'll bet,' said Samuel.

Ksenia rushed up to him and hugged him: 'Such great news! We've done it – you've done it, Samuel!'

'Have I, really?' It didn't feel like success was supposed to. He put the first paper down, and turned his attention to the second. 'The Chinese Gambit,' he read.

'And what's that?' Ksenia had her arms round his shoulders and was peering at the fine script.

'I'm not sure. Mainly because everything apart from the heading is in a Chinese language I don't read. This may be Mandarin.'

'Do you think Kempis is setting you another task, Samuel?'

Samuel looked sideways at the note. He knew there was no such thing as the Chinese Gambit in chess. He just hoped that the message – and he knew he'd have to decode it, there was no gainsaying his curiosity – wasn't going to drag him into more trouble.

'No, Ksenia. He might be trying to, but the old goat's had all he's getting out of me. Time for a change of scene, a change of just about everything, don't you think?'

KSENIA HAD SEVEN missed calls, all from her mother, when she switched her mobile phone back on. Eventually, she called the Black Widow. A classic mother–daughter conversation of mutual indignation ensued. Why was Ksenia prepared to take the Black Widow's private jet to New York, but not accept her phone calls?

Ksenia said, yeah, thanks for the ride, but they were incredibly busy. She rang off.

Samuel and Ksenia were installed in the biggest suite in New York's Soho House, by 9th Avenue and 13th Street. Samuel looked at his watch. He had a couple of interesting meetings that afternoon. First was Miller, who had met them at Idlewild Airport – the 'real' one, used exclusively by the security services in upstate New York; not the commercial monster named after John F. Kennedy. Miller had come good for them, and ushered Dr and Mrs Jack Daniels through customs and immigration. Soon he'd have 'face-time' with Miller, followed by . . . Well, he couldn't be sure quite what.

Ksenia's mobile erupted, and she snatched at it greedily. Version Thirteen was a better mousetrap, and the world was paying court to Ksenia as the lead shareholder of Yavlinsky's company, Tortoiseshell. But this time, the call wasn't from a financier offering some incentive to be allowed in on the miracle technology. Samuel could hear Kirov on the line. Ksenia's happiness in arranging the visit to her extended family was evident in every word she uttered.

Samuel looked at her. She was adorable – smart, beautiful, idealistic, passionate. Where would they go together? Only time would tell. She was young and remarkably undamaged by the events they had been through together. Did he deserve her? Would he be able to give her the security and the love she needed?

'THERE YOU HAVE IT. An intercept.'

Miller tossed a data stick across the table. His only concession to the cult of trendiness in Soho House was to go tieless. The white shirt, the standard-issue black suit clinging to his thin frame, all remained unchanged. He sipped at a glass of water and called for some more coffee from a male waiter whose clothes were more-or-less exchangeable for Miller's. Except the waiter was wearing a tie.

Samuel began to reach for the data stick. But Miller reached out and stopped him.

'But you don't want to see it. Just take it from me, Blandford died bravely. Heroically, if you believe in that kind of stuff. The video captures his attempts to divert attention from you.'

'From me?'

Samuel glanced around; the fifth-floor clubhouse was filling up. His next appointment was booked in the private salon in the far corner in some twenty minutes.

'Yeah. Guess what: for a murder you didn't commit. Sound familiar? But this accusation never made the press. Remember the helicopter pilot?'

'Of course. I found it incredible that Blandford had killed the boy, but it had to be so. So you mean someone thought it was me?'

'His father – a Chechnyan warlord. He sent a professional assassin after you. I think you met him – in a forest on the north ribbon road outside Moscow?'

Samuel's head fell momentarily to his chest.

'I shouldn't take it too badly, Samuel. It was a dick move.' Samuel gave a curt nod. Miller's life was clearly blighted by other people's dick moves. It had to be tough to be so smart. 'That idiot had already targeted Blandford, mistaking him for you. We know what happened, and why.'

'Yes, but it's not pretty. Have you ever killed a man, Miller?'

'I'll take the Fifth on that. If I ever did kill anyone, and I'm not saying I have, you better believe the sucker deserved it.'

'Easy for you to say.'

'Oh, for Chrissakes.' Miller called over to a colleague sitting nearby. 'Paulie!'

A large, nicely put-together black man in a well-cut suit came over.

'This is agent Hollywood,' said Miller. 'He's just finished a tour of duty in Moscow – deep cover intelligence. Paulie, our friend Samuel here is concerned about the welfare of that muscle-bound punk, Vladimir. Can you give him some intel?'

'Happy to sir, happy to.' Hollywood offered Samuel a reassuring smile. 'The guy you encountered in the woods, Vladimir Absevnikov, was a professional Chechnyan hitman. We believe he was engaged to avenge the death of Shamil Khamzaev, and that he mistakenly targeted you. He certainly killed Blandford – killing the right man in the mistaken belief that he was you – the proof's on the data stick. When he realised he'd killed Blandford, he continued to pursue you. After your encounter with him in the forest in north Moscow, where Russian investigative agents Levitan and Aksyonov lost their lives, he emerged two days later, and hijacked a car driven by a young woman.'

'So he didn't die in the forest?'

'No, Mr Spendlove, he didn't. In fact, we're pretty certain he strangled the young woman whose car he hijacked, but then he passed out from loss of blood. He drove into an oncoming articulated delivery truck, which turned him into a pancake. The car exploded, there wasn't anything left of him.'

'So . . .' Samuel tried to take it all in.

'So he was a piece of shit, and you didn't kill him,' said Miller. His face cracked in a dry smile. 'Your soul's intact, Spendlove. Even if it took the death of an innocent bystander to save it. You live to sin again.'

WILLIAM BARTON HATED the meat-packing district. He liked New York well enough, but he loathed and detested this area. It was full of people who regarded themselves as 'cool'.

Still, he'd respected Spendlove's choice of venue and had hired a room at Soho House. Barton looked out of the window to the street below. There was a melange of construction workers, performance artists and stream-of-consciousness poets among shoppers flocking to the hip boutiques. And in between those extremes, there were delivery boys, retail workers, restaurant employees, lawyers, accountants, Europeans, South Americans, Africans, the world's people all going about their everyday business.

And New York didn't rank badly on nicotine consumption, either. It seemed that scores of people, mainly Hispanic immigrants, were enthusiastically smoking and talking on every street corner. Barton came away from the window and temptation, and sat down in the glass box he'd hired for the morning. He chewed a few times on a piece of lemon-grass-and-ginger nicotine gum, and spat it out in disgust.

He looked at his wristwatch. Not the Patek Philippe that Reiko had bought him for several thousand dollars last month, but the cheap, plastic digital thing he'd acquired in Shanghai seven years ago for the price of a beer. It still worked perfectly.

'Am I late?'

Samuel Spendlove let himself into the glass box.

Barton checked his wristwatch again. 'No. Perfect timing. I was early. The best of the many bad habits I have.' Barton's face yawed into a wide smile, and then reverted to the hangdog norm. With all the folds and wrinkles working at once, it was like watching a sea anemone close in on a piece of protein. He seemed genuinely pleased to see Samuel.

'Well, I understand you had a difficult decision to make, Samuel, but you did the right thing.'

'Well, faced with a choice of giving Yavlinsky's secrets to the Americans or the Iranians, it wasn't too difficult.'

Barton was staring at Samuel, who shifted in his seat.

'Normally, I hate people who walk around wearing their morality like some new fucking frock. But I have to say I like you, Spendlove. Your girlfriend is going to make billions and save the planet, while her mother takes most of the credit, and far too much of the cash for my liking. Business must run in the genes of that family. Still, it's good to have a stake, even a modest one, in a deal like this.'

Samuel could decode that one pretty easily: Barton was making another fortune from Version Thirteen. So be it. But this was his second private interview with this fantastically busy and important man in a matter of days. What did he want?

MEDULEV STRODE INTO Sports Universe, and cursed quietly at the new girl behind the desk in front of the VIP area.

He was just off the phone to Khan, who'd been arrested by the Moscow police. Anna wasn't returning his calls, and the self-styled Master of the Universe was screeching like some mountain cat caught in a trap.

Anyone could have seen that the money would assert itself in the end. Version Thirteen was simply too valuable as an oil-drilling technology. It could not be suppressed, not even by Khan and his powerful friends in Teheran, Geneva, Washington, Moscow and everywhere else. The money was impossible to fight – more dangerous, more powerful even than weapons of mass destruction. Especially now, given that they didn't work any more. Maybe it was best to let Khan rot. The past was the past, and Medulev had done more than plenty in saving Khan from the mob. Maybe it was time to make like Anna, and ignore him. She was no fool. In fact . . . If Medulev took over Khan's remaining, viable business operations . . . why, Anna might finally begin to pay him the attention he deserved. He be a made man, and a laid one too. At last . . .

'Sir? Sir?'

Medulev grunted. The empty-headed cow behind the desk was making him sign in. He thought about sacking her there and then. Didn't she know who he was? Obviously not. Well, she'd pay a price later. The girl was pointing at the guest book. Nice tits. He might do something with those.

Medulev picked up a pen, a sardonic sneer on his face, and signed himself in, one last time, for fun: S-P-E-N-D-L-O-V-E, the prick who'd been causing them all this trouble.

A few minutes later, Medulev was in his favourite chair in the command-and-control area. Admiral Borzov was back after a little while away – his favourite hooker had gone back to the States, apparently, and Borzov had been in mourning, of sorts. Well, he'd be in a pretty depressed state soon, when the deals with Teheran dried up. The message was getting through to the Iranians that supercavitation was over, a spent force.

Medulev chinked the ice in his Citron Absolut, and watched as Borzov, wearing a leather gimp mask and French maid's knickers and stockings, began crawling round on all fours. Medulev surveyed the screens, the plush furnishings, the pointless opulence, and wondered how long all this would last. Somehow it felt very temporary.

Still, he swung his feet up onto the desk and drained his glass. One of the screens offered the opportunity to witness a particularly vigorous beating. Fuck it, He'd enjoy it all while he could.

'THIS ISN'T A PROPOSITION, as such. It's not even an opportunity, Samuel. It's the only viable way forward.'

Barton chewed hard, and grimaced. He wasn't used to opposition. He glanced through the glass that separated them from the happy crowd of trendy liberals he despised, many of whom were probably employed by his media empire. He unwrapped two more sticks of the disgusting nicotine gum.

'But, Mr Barton, it *is* a proposition. And your propositions, however apparently innocent, always mean trouble. So no, thanks.'

Barton gave Samuel another analytical stare, the trademark look that Samuel knew could turn from benign approval to glacial enmity in a split second.

'You should hear me out. This is an opportunity to make a difference, perhaps an even bigger difference than recovering the formulae for the Version Thirteen technology did. Read this.'

Barton withdrew a letter from his breast pocket and tossed it over to Samuel. A quick scan revealed a note of effusive thanks to Barton from Senator Bob Zeffman, former Presidential candidate.

'. . . for all your moral support, and above all for facilitating the mechanism that has reduced global oil prices by two-thirds,' read Samuel, aloud.

'I'm a bit surprised that Zeffman was so happy, Mr Barton. Wasn't he a one-issue campaigner? I got the impression that the sudden drop in the oil price prompted his withdrawal from the race for the White House. Surely it would have been better for him if the price had remained high.'

'So there are plenty of things you don't get, after all, Samuel. Zeffman never wanted the actual reins of power. That's for the weak and the foolish, the easily manipulated.

'Zeffman achieved his aim. He shook up the presidential candidates and put the issue he really cared about at the top of the political agenda. With your help, he got the outcome he wanted – low inflation, political stability and a favourable business environment. You're a hero here, Samuel. So here's my proposal: I'd like you to come and meet some of the world's most influential people. It's an informal club, and the next gathering is here in the United States in a few months' time.

'It's not just me. The Bilderberg people want you there. They're keen to talk to you about the Black Widow.'

Barton's phone sprang to life. He grimaced at it.

'My wife. In the meantime, take a look at this.'

Barton pushed a laptop computer across the table to Samuel and then went to the corner of the room and spoke quietly, reverentially, into the phone. Samuel watched him neutrally, wondering how his wife could instil such fear. Strong women . . .

The laptop sprang into life. The volume was low, but it was just audible – and far preferable to listening to soft sounds of self-abasement from Barton.

The CNN logo swam towards him, then away, followed by a trailer for a World Edition Special Feature. Anna Barinova, female oligarch, eco-warrior and benefactress to the nation of Russia, had given CNN an exclusive. She was bringing new energy, new light, to the world. There was a picture of her, in a body-hugging black coat, bending to place flowers on a memorial, while making sure that the world got a good look at her miraculously cute ass. Samuel noted that the wreath was for Lieutenant Levitan and Sergeant Aksyonov, whose tragic deaths in combating evil (what type of evil wasn't specified) had inspired the Black Widow to establish a charitable foundation for the support of bereaved police families. Samuel noted the time, and moved on. So the Black Widow was not only a world-famous eco-warrior through association with Ksenia, she was also now a philanthropist. Whatever next? As such, she was untouchable. She could weave whatever web she desired.

He blinked, slowly. It was all fitting together . . .

*Just examine the facts.*

He'd been blinded by the trauma of Paris, and his fear and loathing of Khan. But the facts showed that Anna Barinova was the real winner – world-famous female oligarch, she'd made billions from Version Thirteen before she'd legally owned it. She'd sent the prototype to the one man in the world she had total control over – via a son whose medical care she paid for, and a daughter she didn't even let Kirov know about until he had to. She must have known the supercavitation arms market would collapse. Medulev had finished off Yavlinsky, but who owned the technology now – who were the legal, beneficial owners? Effectively, ABTV, the Black Widow – with Barton's empire part of the deal. Even the attack on the tracking device – which must have come as a surprise to the Black Widow – had worked to her benefit. Suddenly she was a martyr, a victim. And Khan was the villain. Her submissiveness, the idea that she was his creature was an act, just like so much else – she'd shown that when she threw him to the crowd. What was it she'd said to him? 'If the information is wrong or faulty, the markets find out just as surely as water flows downhill.' And if it's right and good, it will just as surely come out, too, no matter how hard the Khans, the arms-dealers pretended otherwise . . .

And Samuel's own role in all this? Why, he'd been doing things that other people found convenient, while not even working for them – Miller and the CIA, Barton, the unfortunate Blandford. And now Barton, and Miller and his bosses were all scared of the Black Widow, and quite rightly so. If Barton's little video show had any agenda – and everything Barton did had an agenda – it was to bind Samuel in to a wider purpose, a struggle in which the Black Widow was clearly a major opponent. But was this really his problem? His responsibility?

Barton slipped his phone into his jacket pocket, and settled again in the chair opposite Samuel.

'Well, come to the party and help keep the dangerous people in check. What about it?'

MEDULEV HAD HAD ENOUGH. His phone rang – *Unknown Number*. So probably Khan. He rejected the call, flicked a cursory glance at the bank of screens – a French investment banker was being attended to by three Mongol girls, and one was surely no more than twelve years old. Still, even if he'd given much of a fuck, it would have been pointless to ask for a birth certificate. This was just floating human trash, after all.

Outside, night had fallen, and the hawkers were in full cry. Of an evening, they would sell trinkets with an optical hook – little mirror-cased mobiles, laser torches and the like. The usual greasy-haired fellow from Uzbekistan was there, playing out a green laser on the slushy pavement beneath Medulev's feet. These guys never seemed to understand that he was a grown-up, and no, he wasn't going to buy a child's toy, no matter how drunk he got.

Tonight, though, the street-seller had gone too far. He flashed Medulev with a laser right in the damned eye. A bright red laser too, which was much more annoying than the green. A thunderclap. Red laser? *Red?*

A fleeting vision of Anna – supremely beautiful, etched in the darkest black, smiling.

Anna, in the Pushkin Café, raising a glass, returning his toast: '*za druzhbu*' – for friendship.

And then whiteness.

'I HAVE HIM, Godfather,' said the man on the building opposite. He'd already disassembled his rifle. A quick, final check with the night-sight, and he was heading down the fire escape stairs. The crowd round Medulev's corpse was looking about fearfully, and the sounds of the first police an ambulance sirens were making themselves heard.

'Is he dead?'

'Yes, Godfather. Spendlove is no more. Shamil's death is avenged.'

Ahmed grunted in satisfaction, and hung up.

'IT WILL BE a great insight into the way the world really works. Into the way people like our friend Anna Barinova operates. It's not about holding the reins, it's about telling the ones holding them what to do. What do you say?' asked Barton, chewing stolidly.

'Well, thanks, but no. I'm thinking of resigning and going back into . . . something. Something uncomplicated that's a more honest way of earning a living.'

Samuel smiled at Barton, who gave him another sea anemone impression.

'Think carefully before resigning, Samuel. It is rare to come across someone with your intellect, and I'm immensely grateful for all of your efforts. I really mean that.'

'My pleasure, Mr Barton.'

They shook hands, and Samuel headed for the lift. He'd accepted Kempis's challenge. He'd bought in to the bubble game, seen the bubble-market the world was obsessed by, using the light that Josef Papp had shed. Kempis had seen the danger presented by the Black Widow, and was exposing her, via Samuel, from beyond the grave. Except that the world was buying her story – even if just about everyone apart from arms dealers, seemed to be wining.

As the lift descended, Samuel pulled a piece of paper from his pocket: Kempis's next riddle. The Chinese Gambit, if he wanted to play that game. Did he? He didn't think he did. Or at least, not yet.

BARTON STOOD UP and gazed down wistfully at the happy smokers on the street corners. There was Spendlove, emerging with the Black Widow's daughter on his arm. Barton reached into his pocket and withdrew the invitation letter for the next Bilderberg Group meeting. As ever, there was no letterhead, no acknowledgement that the group actually existed. It was just like the dumb answering machine attached to the Dutch number. And, of course, the list of those attending was the most closely guarded secret of all.

A Mack truck had a flat tyre down in the street. The tiny hiatus in traffic flow prompted two-dozen New Yorkers to lean on their car horns. Barton took in the urban bustle and pulled thoughtfully at the flesh beneath his chin.

He wasn't the head of a global media empire for nothing. His sources told him that one of the people coming to the next

Bilderberg session was Anna Barinova, and she was dangerous – all the more so because he couldn't quantify quite how dangerous. There was no doubt that Barton needed Spendlove's help. He would just have to work out how to get it; how to turn that definitive 'no' into a 'yes'.

DOWN ON THE STREET, Samuel and Ksenia walked towards the Thai restaurant that Ksenia had booked. They had a date with sweet, spicy soups, fine noodles and subtle yellow curries, and then an engagement with their huge bed, which would have been freshly made by the time they returned.

Samuel stopped dead in the street, and took in Ksenia's lithe grace, her purpose, her simple, uncomplicated beauty. She walked on for a moment, then turned.

'What are you doing? No, don't tell me, Samuel – you're working on the final puzzle. That's me right?'

Samuel nodded.

'And specifically, whether you love me, and I love you. Correct?'

Samuel looked up. The nearby buildings looked like cardboard cut-outs against the clear blue sky. Pedestrians surged by. Taxis, horns blaring, bounced forward, stopped dead, bounced on again – the brutal tattoo of the New York cabbie. But to Samuel it all seemed silent, soundless. There were only himself and Ksenia standing in that street, staring at each other.

'You know how we can solve this final puzzle, Ksenia, you and I? How we can tell whether this is what we could call love?'

She stood there, smiling widely, waiting.

'We've just got . . . to observe the data.'

And he ran to her, swept her up in his arms, and kissed her. She threw her head back and laughed. In his arms, she felt almost weightless.

# SUBSCRIBERS

Unbound is a new kind of publishing house. Our books are funded directly by readers. This was a very popular idea during the late eighteenth and early nineteenth centuries. Now we have revived it for the internet age. It allows authors to write the books they really want to write and readers to support the writing they would most like to see published.

The names listed below are of readers who have pledged their support and made this book happen. If you'd like to join them, visit: www.unbound.co.uk.

Gordon Adgey
Ian Anderson
Annie Baker
Jamie Baker
Patrick Baker
Patrick Barclay
Brian Basham
Chris Beee
Dave Birch
Martin Bowen
Aleksander Bromek
Rhidian Brook
Orlanda Broom

Stephen Brown
George Burdon
Gareth Cadwallader
Jonathan Cameron
Ben Carter
Kathy Castro
Aditya Chathli
Pete Clark
John Clarke
Christopher
    Clement-Davies
Sylvia Coleman
Steve Collins

Denis Connery
John Cook
Luke Davis
Guy Dresser
Vanessa Dunsire
Andrew Ellis
Richard Evans
Bill Evetts
Mary Fagan
Shaun Fagan
Martin Fiennes
Jack Fishburn
Stephen Fitzpatrick

Isobel Frankish
Megan Frost
Mark Gamble
Rupert Gather
Chris Gayford
James Gibb
David Glover
Alison Graham
Dougie Graham
Bryan Gray
Mike Griffiths
Justin Hardy
Steven Hargreaves
Caitlin Harvey
Rupert Hill
Gary Jackson
Alexa Jago
Adam Kafka
Paul Kelly
Keith Kemp
Lee Kemp
Michael Kuhse
Ian Lacey
James Lascelles

Ron Lay
Jimmy Leach
Beth Lewis
Warwick Lobb
Charles Mcleod
Philomena Mcmanus
Charlie Mactaggart
Philippa Manasseh
Raymond Mansfield
Skender Memed
Pradeep Menon
James Moakes
Philip Moross
Tim Newton
Bridget O'Brien
John Stienfield
   Partouche
Matthew Patten
Peter Phillips
Justin Pollard
Andrew Price
Gordon Rae
Christopher Raggett
Jeanette Ramsden

Antonio Ribeiro
Richard Rivlin
John Rodgers
Padraic Ryan
Chris Salt
Mark Sandell
Christoph Sander
Marianne Scordel
Charles Scott
Susan Solovay
Christopher Steward
Donna Stewart
Glenn Stewart
Andrew Stuttaford
Brenda Taylor
David Taylor
Simon Tyler
Cynthia Valianti
   Corbett
Chris Webber
Neil Wynne
Nick Yeatman

## ACKNOWLEDGEMENTS

Huge, heartfelt thanks to the many Russianists who read the text; to all at Unbound, who are jolly good eggs – and John Mitchinson, who is inspirational. And above all, to my truly brilliant editor, Liz Garner.

# A NOTE ABOUT THE TYPEFACES

Times New Roman – now one of the world's most ubiquitous types – was created in the 1930s after Stanley Morison publicly criticised *The Times* for the poor quality and legibility of its printing. Morison, then the typographical consultant for the newspaper, was invited to design a new alternative; he poached Victor Lardent from the advertising department of the paper to draw the letter forms and together they created Times New Roman, about which Morison said, 'A type which is to have anything like a present, let alone a future, will neither be very "different" nor very "jolly".'

Headings are set in Univers, a clean, readable realist typeface designed by Adrian Frutiger in 1954. Born in 1928, Frutiger is attributed with influencing the direction of digital typography, particularly during the second half of the twentieth century. The ease with which the Univers typeface can be read from far off led to its use for the opening crawl of the *Star Wars* films; it was also the typeface used to label the keys of Apple keyboards from 1984 until 2007.